"*Red Sands* is a grand adventure in the classic sense, an odyssey unfolded by fine storytellers, sometimes funny, often poignant and always exciting. I look forward to reading more of Thompson's and Carter's work."

DAN PARKINSON
Starsong and *Jubilation Gap*

"A splendid magical desert adventure that belongs on a shelf with *Tales of the Arabian Nights.*"

DOUGLAS NILES
Darkwalker on Moonshae and *Black Wizards*

Other TSR™ Books

STARSONG
Dan Parkinson

ST. JOHN THE PURSUER: VAMPIRE IN MOSCOW
Richard Henrick

BIMBOS OF THE DEATH SUN
Sharyn McCrumb

RED SANDS

An Arabian Adventure

Paul B. Thompsom
and
Tonya R. Carter

Cover Art
Clyde Caldwell

TSR, Inc.

RED SANDS

This book is protected under the copyright laws of the United States of America. Any reproduction or other unauthorized use of the material or artwork contained herein is prohibited without the express written permission of TSR, Inc.

Distributed to the book trade in the United States by Random House, Inc. and in Canada by Random House of Canada, Ltd.

Distributed in the United Kingdom by TSR Ltd.

Distributed to the toy and hobby trade by regional distributors.

DRAGONLANCE is a registered trademark owned by TSR, Inc. FORGOTTEN REALMS is a trademark owned by TSR, Inc.

First Printing, December, 1988
Printed in the United States of America.
Library of Congress Catalog Card Number: 87-51448

9 8 7 6 5 4 3 2 1

ISBN: 0-88038-591-X
All characters in this book are fictitious. Any resemblance to actual persons, living or dead, is purely coincidental.

TSR, Inc.   TSR Ltd.
P.O. Box 756   120 Church End, Cherry Hinton
Lake Geneva, WI 53147   Cambridge CB1 3LB
U.S.A.   United Kingdom

To my cousin

Kenneth Dale Carter

1962 - 1986

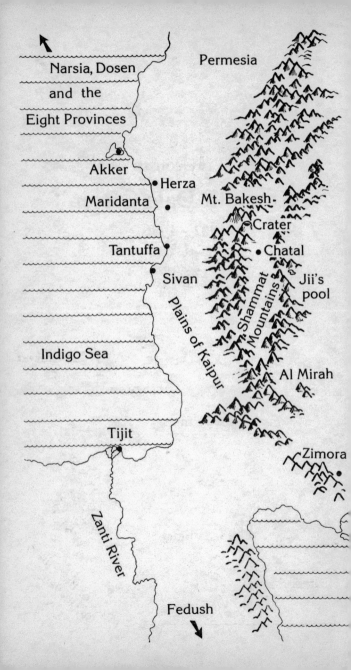

Nangol

Lost temple

Scorpion rock

Julli Oasis

Colossus

Omerabad

Fazir (Faziri Empire)

Rehajid

Royal Road

Talith

N

The Brazen Ring

Crimson Sea

Mtns. of the Pillars of Heaven

PART I:

THE CAPTIVES OF FAZIR

❖ 1 ❖

Jadira

The guard's heavy tread stopped outside the door. With a rustle and a clank, the wicket-gate slid back. A copper dipper rimmed with green scum appeared in the hole. It tilted, pouring water into the clay cup on the floor below. The dipper withdrew and a wheel-shaped loaf of bread dropped through. The wicket squeaked shut, and the footsteps moved on.

Jadira *sed* Ifrimiya crept slowly from the far corner of her cell to the door. She waited until the guard's movements could no longer be heard, then she gulped the scant cupful of water. The sickly metallic taste in no way diminished her enjoyment of it.

The bread she added to the small heap of loaves already stacked in the near corner. Jadira knew they were not enough to nourish her but would only tease her starved stomach and cause unremitting hunger pains. So she fasted. Her belly tightened, and after two days she no longer felt acutely hungry. There was no doubt in Jadira's mind that in time her strength would fail from lack of food. The loaves did serve a purpose. Her captor,

Sultan Julmet, by his grace, allowed his prisoners one serving of bread per day. By saving her rations, Jadira kept track of how long she had been imprisoned.

Five loaves lay in the corner.

Her people were desert dwellers, nomads, who obeyed no lord and asked for nothing more than a spring of sweet water and fertile flocks. Jadira was a *malam*, a married cousin in the elder clan of the Sudiin tribe. Thus, she was pure Sudiin, in both parents' lines.

In the days since the sultan's cavalry had taken her, along with most of her tribe, she had seen many of her kinsmen and friends end on the block—either the executioner's or the slavemaster's.

Faziri soldiers had first delivered her to Kemmet Serim, procurer of slaves for the sultan's household. Serim, his bloated face shining with olive oil and his breath sour with the smell of dates, took one look at Jadira and exclaimed, "By Dutu's beard, what have you brought me?"

The soldier who held Jadira's arms pinned replied, "A nomad wench from the Red Sands, Revered One. Newly caught by the Invincibles and offered for your consideration."

Serim closed one puffy eyelid and peered closely at Jadira. She was taller than him by two fingers. Sculpted by youth and molded by toil, she stood proudly before the slavemaster. The soldier had pulled down her headdress, exposing a sleek mass of long black hair. Jadira's eyes were twin signets of jet, set in a taut aquiline face. Serim, squinting at her, thought of falcons.

"Kitchen or seraglio; where, I wonder, would this one be better placed?" he said.

"She has arms like a wrestler," said the soldier.

"Yet her face is not uncomely," said Serim. "Remove

her robe, so that I may see the body beneath."

"I dare not release her, Revered One. She unhorsed two Invincibles during the attack on her camp, and this morning she blacked the eyes of Sergeant Zayin."

"Tshaw! She is cowed. Here, I will do it myself."

The sultan's procurer laid his unclean hands on Jadira *sed* Ifrimiya. Jadira promptly buried her unfettered foot in Kemmet Serim's soft and yielding belly.

The soldier knocked her down and planted an iron-nailed sandal on her neck. As her face was only a hand-span from the prostrate Serim's, Jadira spat at the revered one and said, "Do what you will with me, father of piglets! Put me in your kitchen, and I'll slay Faziris with cooking spits. Consign me to the harem, and I'll strangle the sultan with my silken veil as he takes his ease among his gilded wantons!"

"Treason! Blasphemy—!" Serim stammered, trying to rise. "Take her away!" Jadira tried to throw herself once more at Serim, but the burly soldier dragged her away, screaming in frustrated rage.

Thus did Jadira end in the sultan's dungeon. Her sentence: perpetual solitary confinement. Death was to be Jadira's only companion. She awaited it in her dark, dirty cell.

Her mind had not been idle in the darkness. She had examined every portion of the cell, often with only her fingertips as guides. The four walls, the floor, and the ceiling were all stone. The cell door was hardest *keshj* wood, strapped with black bands of cold forged iron. Jadira had no tools, little light, and less hope. She prayed to Mitaali, god of nomads, for succor.

Perhaps it was Mitaali who whispered in Jadira's ear: *How are the walls different?* How were they different?

The floor was smooth, but the walls were rough. The ceiling was one massive, seamless block. The rear and front walls were black-veined granite, set dry in sloping courses. The left and right walls were limestone and *set with mortar.*

Mortar?

"Thank you, Mitaali! The blessings of my family's name upon you!" Jadira said to the empty air.

She needed a tool. Her only implement, her water cup, was baked clay too soft for use in digging. Something harder was needed.

Above the door was a slit that admitted light from torches in the corridor. By this faint source, Jadira saw that the lintel over the door was smooth, yellow stone, quartzite. This was the hardest sort of stone used in building, yet the lintel was fractured in two places. The enormous weight of the upper floors of the palace was bearing down on it.

Jadira stood on her toes and strained to reach the lintel. Too high. She braced one foot on the door's middle strap and grasped the narrow light-slit with her left hand. The wall was so deep her arm did not reach all the way through. Still, Jadira stayed there, the strap rivet gouging her foot, as she picked at the broken lintel. After breaking four fingernails, she managed to pry loose a fragment of quartzite. It was as big as her palm and shaped like an arrowhead.

She decided to dig in the middle of the right wall. Her target was a roughly hewn cube of limestone, a block slightly wider than her shoulders. Jadira put the sharp end of the quartzite fragment in the finger-wide groove between blocks and began to scrape away the mortar.

It was tedious, painful work, and she quickly skinned the knuckles of both hands. By the time two more loaves had come through the door, she'd cut a socket as deep as her fingers could reach, all around the limestone block.

A new problem appeared. Jadira saw she would have to chip away the stone itself in order to get at the softer mortar deeper in the wall. She wrapped the quartzite in the trailing end of her headdress to deaden the sound of the chipping.

Peck, peck, peck. The block yielded in flakes and fragments. The hours passed. As Jadira's hands worked, her mind journeyed back in time to when she was free.

She had won the right to wear the black headband of the Sudiin when she roped and tamed a wild horse. What a fine animal he was—Khemay, "The Colors," was his name. He was black, so black he took on different colors at different times of day. In the chill desert morning, Khemay was dark blue, like the water in the deep wells of Julli Oasis. At sunset, he burned red like new copper.

Peck, peck, peck. Outside the walled city of Rehajid, Jadira knelt on a wool blanket and pounded rye and wheat into flour. Her brother, Mohar, and her husband, Ramil, argued over how much to demand per head for their yearling goats. Jadira tossed in her opinion as she dipped into the grain basket for more rye. Peck, peck, peck.

Clink.

The sound of metal on rock filtered through the thick wall and snatched Jadira from her reverie. She stopped chipping and held her breath. Had she been discovered? The cell door was silent and still.

There it was again. A bead of sweat rolled down the nomad woman's face. It was metal on stone all right. Jadira rapped her tool in reply. Her reward was a chorus of taps.

She chewed her lip as she pondered what this could mean. If there was a prisoner on the other side of the wall, then they could halve the time it would take to release the block. Of course, they would still be in the cells, but they might accomplish far more together than separately.

Jadira put an ear to the wall. The taps seemed to be in some sequence, but she didn't understand it. Finally she knocked until the other fell silent, then she started scraping at the mortar again. It was the only way she knew to convey what she wanted.

The next loaf of bread added to her pile made nine. The bottom-most were fuzzy with faintly luminous mold. Jadira was elbow-deep in the wall by then, and nearly delirious with despair. The wall seemed ten leagues thick. The tapping she heard was the malicious demon-king Dutu himself, leading her on with false hopes of success. Her fast had weakened her and she could no longer dig for hours at a time. The hard stone chip was wearing down to a blunt nub.

There were thirteen loaves on the floor when the quartzite arrowhead shattered. Jadira sank down on her knees and let the ruined bits of stone slip through her fingers. Tears filled her eyes. She wept bitterly, clenching her battered hands into fists. She cursed Mitaali and all the gods for their injustice, and when the last curse had left her lips, she slumped against the cold limestone block.

It shifted.

Oh you gods, torment me not! Jadira cried in her heart. She leaned her shoulder into the block. It moved a bit more.

From weeping, Jadira burst into laughter. She slid

away and turned around. Lying on her back, she planted both feet on the block and pushed. The stone crept forward, slipping grittily through powdered mortar. When Jadira's legs were nearly straight, she wriggled in closer and pushed anew.

It was all over in a rush. The block seemed to fly away from her feet, opening up a gaping hole. Jadira withdrew her legs and crouched by the opening. "Hello?" she called softly.

"Who is it?" answered a voice. The accent was not Faziri.

"A prisoner. Who are you?" she asked.

"I am a captive, also. I thought we would never get that stone out."

"Then you were helping me?"

"I've been digging at it for days and days."

Jadira smiled into the hole. "May I come through?" she said.

"Certainly! Come ahead!"

She had to lie prone in order to pass through the narrow tunnel. Just as she pulled her feet into the hole, a pair of hands grasped hers and drew her out. She stood up in her neighbor's cell.

An oil lamp burned in the gloom. By its light Jadira regarded her fellow prisoner. He was a young man from a northern clime, clad in close-fitting garments of heavy green cloth. White lace bloomed at his neck and wrists. He picked up the lamp, and she saw that his short hair was light, like river sand, and his eyes were sky-colored.

His mouth hung open. "By Tuus! A woman!" he exclaimed.

"You have not been in the sultan's keeping so long that you have forgotten women, I see," said Jadira.

"Your pardon, lady. I did not imagine my tireless companion beyond the wall to be a woman." He bowed at the waist. "I am Marix, third son of Count Fernald of Dosen."

"Jadira *sed* Ifrimiya, of the tribe Sudiin."

"You are Faziri?"

"Pah!" She spat at his feet. "The Sudiin are not slavish house-dwellers!"

Marix of Dosen was taken aback by her vehemence. "Your pardon," he said again. "You have the look—that is, the coloring—of such as we of the Eight Provinces call Faziri."

Jadira looked beyond the foreigner to the table where the lamp had been. The remains of a meal lay scattered about, together with an earthen jug. A bronze spoon, its handle worn to a stub, completed the scene. She licked her lips and stared.

Marix noticed her wide-eyed gaze and said, "It is poor fare, but you are welcome to it."

Jadira fell upon the table and devoured what was left of the meal. She stripped the squab's bones of every scrap of meat, then cracked the bones and sucked out the marrow. The old peach she ate, skin and all, down to the pit. The wine was very nearly vinegar, but to her barren throat it was nectar such as Mitaali never tasted.

"Is there more?" she asked after licking the plate shamelessly.

"Ah, no. I'm given only one meal a day. The scoundrels believe they can bend me to their will by starving me."

Jadira thought of the moldy bread in her own bare cell and laughed out loud. Marix said, "You find my plight amusing?"

"Not at all. I laugh for the joy of your company," she said. He bowed again and in a courtly fashion offered her his only chair.

"Why is one such as you languishing down here?" Jadira asked. "I should think a foreign noble's son would be an honored guest of His Magnificence."

"Alas, I am a pawn, not a guest."

"How so?"

"It is a long tale," said Marix.

"My ears hear only you," Jadira answered.

"It began when my father bade me go in the company of Sir Kannal Dustan from Dosen to the city of Tantuffa—"

"The seaport?"

"—yes, and there learn the trade of arms. I was to enter the service of Lord Hurgold of Tantuffa, but our party was ambushed by the sultan's men in the province of Maridanta. Sir Kannal died in the fight, and I was brought to Omerabad," said Marix.

"I see," said Jadira. "So now the sultan seeks to embarrass Lord Hurgold, and keeps you hostage until your noble father pays a ransom?"

Marix rubbed his hand on the top of the crudely made table. "There will be no ransom," he said.

"Why not? Surely a count can spare some gold, even for his third son."

Marix gave the nomad woman an intense look. Swiftly he knelt on one knee by her side and lowered his voice to a whisper.

"Are you a woman of honor?" he said quickly. "I must know. If you are a Faziri spy, leave now and trouble me no more!"

Jadira frowned. "If you think me a spy, then you can believe no answer I give you," she said. "But I am no spy." She pulled open her collar to reveal gaunt hollows in her neck, deeply shadowed in the lamplight. She held out her thin, scarred hands.

"I spent four days digging through that wall. I ate nothing, and the demon-king plagued me with dreams and deceptions, but I outlasted him. I am Sudiin of Sudiin; that is enough honor for anyone!" Her black eyes glittered in the half-light. "And as for being a Faziri tool, if we were not in this cursed hole, I would demonstrate my anger for such an insult!"

Marix pressed a hand over his heart. "Lady, forgive me. One hears that in the land of Fazir there is all manner of treachery, and what I know must not come to the attention of any minion of the sultan."

Jadira held her head high. "I've no way to convince you that I speak the truth. Speak or remain silent. I do not betray secrets."

"Do you know the Five Cities of the Indigo coast? No? Besides Tantuffa, they are Akker, Sivon, Maridanta, and Herza. These are the only sovereign cities on the east shore of the Inland Sea as yet free of Faziri control. But all is not well amongst them. Matters of trade and religion have brought them more than once to the brink of war.

"The sultan delights in their troubles. His emissaries do what they can to stir up the five against each other. Lord Hurgold, seeing the danger in division, proposed that a foreign prince resolve the cities' differences in an impartial hearing."

"What prince?" asked Jadira, somewhat adrift.

"In this case, my father's liege lord, Prince Lydon of Narsia. His Majesty sent one of his state seals with Sir Kannal, in token of his trust. The lords of the Five Cities are to meet in a conclave at Tantuffa on High Summer's

Day. If Prince Lydon's seal is not there, they will assume the prince declined to intervene. No treaty can be made."

"There follows war, and the only victor will be the sultan," said Jadira, seeing the truth at last. "What became of the prince's seal?"

Marix folded his hands and touched them to his lips. "Seeing our party outnumbered, Sir Kannal ordered me to save the seal. Drawing his great two-handed sword, he led the last of our brave men-at-arms into the very teeth of the Faziri lancers, where they perished to a man. With their cries ringing in my ears, I buried the box in a nearby olive grove."

"Could you find this grove again? The exact spot?"

"I am certain I could." The fellow sank back on his haunches. "Oh, this is idle talk! We are in the deepest prison in Omerabad. We shall die here!"

She ignored his despairing remarks. "Do the Faziri know of Prince Lydon's seal?" she asked.

"No. Only Sir Kannal knew, and he's dead."

"Good. They must have another use for you. Nothing good, I am sure." Jadira looked around the cell. Apart from its sparse furnishings, it was identical to hers. "I think I know how we may get out of here," she said.

Marix lifted his head. "How?"

"To get this much food in, the guard must enter your cell, yes?"

"He enters, once he sees I have retreated to the rear wall. You're not thinking of overcoming him, are you?"

"Why not?"

"He is uncommonly large, with some orcish blood, I think. He carries a cudgel of no mean weight," said Marix.

"Great trees will fall to a small axe," Jadira said thoughtfully. "Especially if they don't see the axe coming." So saying, she slipped to the floor beside him and told him of her plan.

❖ 2 ❖

Keys and Cages

Nungwun the guard halted at the cell door. He leaned his knotty club against the wall and shoved the wicket-gate back with one meaty hand. Bending down, he put an eye to the peephole and saw the pale foreigner by the far wall. Marix's hands were folded reverently and his eyes were closed.

"I bring food," said Nungwun. Marix remained in his prayerful pose. "You stay back or no eat," added the guard. Marix didn't move.

"Hmph. Crazy outlander." Nungwun closed the trap and released the latch. The heavy door swung inward. The guard hefted his cudgel in his right hand while trying to balance a trencher of food in his left.

"Is time to eat!" he bellowed. The fellow might have been a statue for all the response he gave.

Nungwun had to stoop his heavy frame to pass through the door. He set the meal on the table and approached Marix cautiously. Poking him with the narrow end of his club, he asked, "You sick?"

"Shh!" Marix hissed.

"What you do?"

"I'm praying."

"Why you pray?"

"I'm asking my patron deity for a favor."

"Huh! What favor you ask?"

"I'm begging Tuus, the sun god, to drop a large rock on your head," replied Marix.

"My head!" growled Nungwun. He stepped back involuntarily and looked up.

There was Jadira, feet and shoulders wedged between the ceiling corbels, her face contorted with effort. She clutched a tenth-talent block of limestone broken from the wall. When the guard raised his lumpy face, she released the missile. Nungwun toppled like a great tree.

"You see," said Jadira when she was on the floor again, "the gods do grant favors to mortals. Even when the mortal nearly spoils things by causing the target to step back."

Jadira rifled Nungwun's pockets while Marix stood watch at the door. The bulky guard had little on him they could use. One silver coin (with toothmarks), the cudgel, and a small notched iron rod were all he carried.

"Keep that," said Marix, indicating the rod.

"What is it?" asked Jadira.

"A key. The hall is empty. Let us be off!"

Marix bolted the door after Jadira joined him in the corridor. He pointed left and said, "I was brought that way and passed a guardroom as I came."

"So we'll go the other way," said Jadira, moving quickly to the right. They kept close to the wall. The massive blocks bulged outward from their centers like great stone pillars. A rime of soft gray mold filled every crack. Now and then a fat brown rat squealed softly and scurried away into a black hole in the floor.

The corridor curved to the right. They passed several cells, bolted and silent. The sickly smell of death was in the air. Without a word, Jadira reached back and took Marix's hand.

A new dark corridor opened up on Jadira's right. Hearing voices drift down the passage ahead of them she and Marix pressed themselves into the shadows. Marix took the cudgel from the nomad woman. She nodded briefly toward the oncoming voices, and he signed his understanding.

Two men, a Faziri soldier in mail and a leather-vested jailer, wielding a torch appeared in the tunnel. They were talking earnestly about dice when they spied Jadira standing proudly in their path.

"The sultan," she declared, "is the son of swine!"

The soldier snatched at the scimitar on his belt. He never drew it, for Marix burst from the shadows and bashed him across the neck. The Faziri's spiked helmet bounced and clattered on the paving. The torch-bearing jailer turned to flee, but in a flash, Jadira leaped on his back and bore him down. She cracked his shaven pate repeatedly on the stone floor until he stopped struggling.

More voices could be heard. As she quickly ran through the jailer's pockets, Marix retrieved the soldier's sword. He stuck it through his belt and said, "Get the torch."

They ran into the dark tunnel. A faint breeze washed their faces and flickered their torch as they walked down the passage. There had to be an outlet somewhere ahead.

They passed a series of niches in the walls. Jadira thrust the torch into each opening, looking for a way out. The niches held nothing but skeletons, some still clothed in rotting garments. All were chained to the wall. Spiders and other vermin crouched in their empty eye sockets, and the skull mouths hung open in unheard cries of silent agony.

"Tuus preserve us," Marix muttered as the parade of the dead continued.

Jadira steeled herself and turned to the next niche. This one was deeper than most. She stepped in—

A dim figure rose up with a clanking of chains. Marix and Jadira shrank back, torch and cudgel to the fore. From the umber depths of the alcove, a voice said, "Peace, my friends. I am a helpless prisoner."

Jadira pushed the torch closer. Chained to the wall was a portly man of middle age whose benign features and scalp lock identified him as a priest.

"May the warmth of Agma find you always," he said. "Can you release me?"

"I don't see how," said Jadira. "We have no tools."

"And no time," Marix insisted. "Let us be gone!"

"Don't leave me, I beg you! I am due to die on the morrow," said the priest.

"For what crime?" asked Jadira.

"For spreading the word of my god. I am Tamakh, reborn in the wisdom of Agma. The corrupt clergy of Omerabad imprisoned me, and they mean to take my life."

"This is hardly the time to discuss religion!" said Marix. "Guards may come at any moment!"

"Calm yourself. Even vultures take time to feed." Jadira examined Tamakh's fetters. "There are no rivets," she said. "How are they held together?"

"They're locked," Marix said. "Use the key."

Jadira was puzzled. She turned the iron rod over in her hands.

"How?"

"Oh, filth," said Marix in exasperation. "Let me." He took the rod, inserted it in a hole in a fetter, and turned. In short order, Tamakh was free.

"My soul is rekindled!" he said. "Thank you! Surely Agma will bless—"

"Can we go now?"

"Yes, yes," said Tamakh. "As you so wisely said, let us be gone."

Marix turned sharply on his heel, took two steps, and stopped. "Ah, which way should we go?"

"Into the wind," said Jadira. She led the way past Tamakh's niche.

The flow of air grew warmer and stronger. The floor began to slant upward. "I smell smoke!" Jadira said. That would mean they were near street level, where home fires were kindled.

They came to a set of steps. Wind flowed down the stairwell, tormenting Jadira's torch. Marix handed the cudgel to the priest and drew his scimitar. As one, the three took a deep breath and fairly ran up the steps. At the top Jadira stumbled. The flaming pine-knot flew from her hand—and fell, end over end, down a deep cylindrical shaft in the floor at their feet.

The men helped Jadira to her feet. Together they crept to the edge of the pit and peered down. Far below, the torch lay on the bottom, flickering feebly. The smell rising from the pit was horrible; not the odor of death, as in the corridor of skeletons, but more fetid and *alive*.

"What do you suppose is down there?" whispered Marix.

"I don't want to know," replied Jadira. She drew a fold of her headdress over her nose and mouth.

"The palace holds many secrets," Tamakh said. "In Omerabad there are many strange cults, many purveyors of dark magic. Any sort of monster could be housed in the lowest levels of the dungeon." He stepped back. "It was into one of these pits I was to be cast on the next dawning."

Jadira looked about. The pit filled the corridor from wall to wall, and beyond it was another solid expanse of stone. Truly a dead end. But where did the fresh air come from?

She tilted her head back and saw. Three paces above them, a domed cage of iron covered a skylight directly over the pit. Brief wisps of smoke blew through the bars.

"We must go up," she said.

"But how? We have no rope, no ladder, no scaling gear," protested Marix.

"Would you rather return to the dungeons?" Jadira unwound her headdress and coiled it around her arm. It was considered immodest for a Sudiin woman to uncover her head before strange men, but this was not the time for prudery. She studied her companions a moment, then said, "Your shirt, Marix; is it silk?"

"Of course."

"Take it off and tear it into strips."

"What!"

"Do as I say! We need rope." To Tamakh she said, "Holy One, you can spare us your sash, can you not?"

"Ha," Marix murmured. "There must be a good five paces of cloth there."

The headdress and the sash of the plump priest made an amply long rope. Jadira had Marix tie loops of silk from his shirt at intervals along the rope.

"How do we get the rope to the grill?" asked Tamakh.

Marix had an idea. He tied one end of the rope to the heavy club. Jadira kept hold of the other end as the fellow stood back and threw the cudgel with all his might.

The club struck the iron bars with a loud clang and fell back into the pit. Tamakh frowned.

"Less noise, I pray. It will alert the guards," he said.

Marix nodded and tried again. Another miss. Jadira reeled in the cudgel and gave it to him for another cast.

"Larsa the Hunter, guide my throw," he intoned, and heaved. The club passed between two bars and landed on the paving outside.

"Bravely done!" said Jadira. She carefully pulled on the cloth. The cudgel turned sideways and caught on the bars. Jadira smiled for the first time in many days. "Now we climb."

Tamakh cleared his throat. "I fear Agma did not intend me to climb threads like a spider." He patted his ample belly sadly.

"Don't worry, Holy One. We'll pull you out," Jadira said. Marix looked more than a little doubtful.

Jadira twined her hands in the silken loops. "Hold the end taut," she said. "I don't want to swing into the wall."

The priest and the young nobleman braced themselves at the top of the steps as Jadira began to climb. Her arms shivered with strain and her starved body cramped as she hauled herself hand-over-hand toward the roof.

The bars were far enough apart for her to pull herself through. She was on a causeway between buildings of the place complex. Finding no one in sight, Jadira collapsed and waited for her quivering muscles to calm themselves.

Putting her face between the bars, she whispered, "Marix!" He was shortly beside her. His green jacket snagged on the iron caging and tore, but he made it.

"That fat cleric will never get through," he said.

"Can we shift the grill?" A quick examination dispelled that idea. The iron dome was pinned to the paving in a dozen places.

"Hello?" called Tamakh hoarsely. "Why the delay?"

Jadira lay on the ground with her face over the pit. "Holy One, there is a problem."

"Soldiers?" he said.

"No, no, it's this cage. I fear it is too, ah, narrow to allow you to get out," she said.

"What is it made of?"

"Made of? Iron, I think. Too stout for bending, I fear."

"Haul me up," he said.

"But, Holy One—"

"It will be well. Haul me up."

Tamakh tied the cloth under his arms. Jadira and Marix planted their feet against the grill and began to pull.

"Oof! Religion is surely a weighty matter," Marix grunted.

"No—jests! Just—pull!" Jadira gasped in reply.

Soon Tamakh's shaven head bumped the bars. "Steady, my friends," he said, reaching his pudgy hands to the ironwork.

"Never—pull them—out," Marix puffed.

The priest spoke, but not to Marix. "*Agma*," he intoned. "*Agmas, copit neda! Copit desram Agman!*"

Marix glanced at Jadira, but she was concentrating on retaining her grip on the ropes, Marix's puzzlement turned to amazement as the iron bars slowly, so slowly, began to bend apart.

"*Copit neda*," insisted Tamakh. "*Agmas, suden copit desram!*"

Jadira's teeth were bared with the effort of holding the

priest's weight. Suddenly, she felt the cloth of the safety line jerk in her hands. The knot holding the sash to the headdress was beginning to slip. "Quickly!" she gasped. "Get him out!"

Marix, staring transfixed at the iron bars, shook his head as if to clear it and took hold of Tamakh's robe. Tamakh squeezed through the gap and rolled ponderously onto the walkway.

Marix reached out a tentative hand to touch the iron bars. They felt cold, solid, and as unyielding as ever. He snatched his hand back as Tamakh intoned his words of power again. The deformed grill slowly bent back to its original shape. The metal did not protest, but the entire process left their ears ringing.

"I didn't realize you were a magician," said Jadira, digging a finger in her tingling ear.

"I am not!" Tamakh replied with surprising verve. "I am not a vulgar sorcerer, confecting toad skins and bats' eyes. I am a servant of Agma, and the god sometimes grants me power to do his will. Iron is sacred to my god."

"Forgive me, Holy One," she said, touching her forehead respectfully. She untied her headdress from the priest's sash and rewound it around her head. As they walked to the edge of the causeway, Tamakh wound the sash around his ample waist.

"Say," said Marix. "If you can magic metal bars, how could the Faziris keep you fettered?"

"It is a matter of metal," Tamakh said. "Iron is sacred to Agma and obeys his will. My bonds were bronze and outside his influence. The very priests who called me heretic for believing in a false god were the ones who made certain my bonds were not of iron."

From the edge of the causeway, they could see the lower casements of the palace, and beyond, the city of

Omerabad proper. A million stars salted the heavens. A million lamps twinkled in the city's windows. Cook-smoke hung in a blue haze over the houses, mixed with temple incense and a mist formed by the cool night air. In the distance, there was a song of glass bells. They each inhaled deeply. Free!

But not safe. They were certain to be missed, Marix and Tamakh especially. The escape had only begun.

The Menagerie

The palace of Sultan Julmet was so vast, entire regiments of the Imperial Army could not have adequately patrolled its interior. Jadira and her companions gave thanks for that as they encountered no guards on the causeway.

The path ended at a squat tower sheathed in burnished brazen scales.

"Where to now?" said Marix.

"We must get to the outer palace wall and over," Jadira answered. She scanned the sky. "I wish I knew how much darkness we had left."

Tamakh cupped his hands around his eyes and looked up. He turned slowly on his flat sandals until he faced north. He pointed to a familiar constellation. "As I see the Chariot, it is not yet midnight," he said.

"Then we should have time."

They descended to the lower casement. From there to the street below was a drop of four paces, but the wall had such a pronounced slope it was no great feat for them to slide down. When Tamakh had bumped to the bottom (losing his footing and landing hard where he sat), they found themselves in a narrow cobbled lane between the palace and the inner wall. Jadira could smell that horses had passed by not long before.

Tamakh spotted some steps rising to the battlements on the wall. Up they went, crouching low in the shadows. Jadira reached the top first. She dropped prone and carefully peeked around the corner. Coming straight toward her were two soldiers armed with halberds and walking side by side. Starlight glinted on their breastplates, and their white cloaks hung limply from their armored shoulders.

Jadira put a finger to her lips and motioned for the others to move back. They slipped down to the street again and ducked under the stone risers. One Faziri tramped down the steps. At the bottom, he paused, leaning his halberd against the wall. After a quick look around, the soldier pulled a rattan-covered bottle from under his cloak. He uncorked it and drank deeply. The tang of cheap wine filled the air.

Jadira felt Marix tense. She knew what he was thinking—as the Faziri enjoyed his illicit drink, he might rush out and take the soldier by sword. She caught Marix's arm and held him. He looked at her questioningly. Jadira shook her head.

The soldier replaced his bottle and walked on. Tamakh let out a wheezing breath.

"Why didn't you let me drub him?" asked Marix.

"You might have been seen, or he might have withstood your first attack," Jadira said in hushed tones. "Besides, we can't leave a trail of fallen Faziri guards wherever we go."

"If the wall is closely patrolled, how will we get out?" The priest tugged thoughtfully on his scalp lock.

"There's the garden," he said.

"What garden?" asked Jadira.

"The Garden of Rare Beasts—the sultan's menagerie," Tamakh explained. "It lies in that direction." He pointed south. "It would not be guarded at night."

Jadira said, "Lead the way, Holy One."

They went on in silence. Once the warning clatter of hooves and wheels forced them under a scaffold erected for repair work on the palace casements. A two-horse team pulling a light carriage trotted by. Filmy curtains of gauze billowed behind it. A golden lion's head snarled from each corner of the curtained enclosure. Two fierce lancers rode behind the vehicle with weapons at the ready.

"Interesting," Tamakh said as the carriage turned out of sight. "Unless I'm mistaken, we've just witnessed the passage of a royal concubine."

"A what?" asked Marix.

"Never mind. Where is this garden you promised?" said Jadira.

Threescore paces farther along, they came to a low wall, plastered white and shining. Behind it grew a thick row of date palms, each twice a man's height. Tamakh rolled heavily over the obstacle. Marix vaulted the wall nimbly, and Jadira followed. They plunged into the trees.

They emerged onto a luxurious carpet of green grass. Rows of orange lilies, their blooms tightly furled for the night, rustled and swayed in the breeze. A path of crushed stone wended through the flower beds.

Tamakh moved surely through the garden, as if he'd been there a hundred times before. Chirping crickets fell mute as the escaping prisoners passed. Somewhere back in the green-black trees, a nightjar whirred its song. In response, a deep-throated growl reverberated down the starlit path.

"What was that?" said Marix, alarmed.

"Lion," replied Jadira.

"Griffin," Tamakh corrected. "The sultan collects only the rarest and most exotic of animals." Marix expressed a hope that the beast was securely caged.

The first of several oval pens appeared on their right. A large recumbent form lay at the rear of the enclosure, giving no hint of what strange creature it might be. Across from the first pen was a long rectangular cage, closed on the top. As Jadira passed in front, a large hairy arm shot through the bars and seized the trailing edge of her robe.

Jadira tripped and fell, turning to look up as she did. Two brown eyes the size of her fists glinted out of the gloom. She didn't scream, but kicked madly at the grasping hand. Marix leaped between the cage and the fallen woman. His scimitar curved upward, biting deeply into the thick, hairy arm. The hand let go, and the beast scurried to a back corner of its cage. It blubbered with almost human anguish.

"What in Dutu's name is it?" asked Jadira, on her feet once more.

"A giant ape, such as live wild in the south country," Tamakh said.

"Do they eat people?"

"Not as a rule."

"Listen to it weep," Marix said.

In spite of her fright, Jadira stepped nearer the cage. The ape flung itself at the bars again, its blunt, leathery fingers flexing for her.

"Cunning devil!" she said, flinching away. Marix raised the sword again, and the beast retreated hastily.

They hurried on. Cages and pens rushed by in a blur until they reached an intersection of four paths. Tamakh hesitated.

"Well?" said Jadira.

"I'm not certain which way is best," the priest murmured.

"Depends on where you wish to go," said a voice from behind them. The three whirled to face the speaker. The voice had come from a cage on a small platform, mounted shoulder-high on brick pillars.

Seeing nothing in the darkness, Marix asked, "Who's there?"

"One of the sultan's exhibits. Who might you be?"

"We might be the grand vizier, the sultana, and the hierophant of Baoud," said Jadira, "but in truth we're prisoners escaping from the palace dungeons."

"Not an easy thing to do," said the voice.

"Not if we stand here gabbing all night!" said Marix.

Tamakh stepped around the younger man and walked to the platform. "You speak quite well for a wild beast."

"And you speak well for an overfed cleric."

"Ai! It has a sharp tongue," said Jadira. "Beware, Holy One; it may have sharp teeth as well."

A shape stirred in the shadows of the cage. An arm, smooth as polished wood and dark as ebony, reached out to tweak Tamakh's bulbous nose. The priest smiled and took the black hand in his own.

"It's a woman," he said. "A black woman of Fedush."

"In a cage? That won't do," said Jadira. "Would you like to be free?"

"Of course she would," said Tamakh. "Give me the key." Marix stamped his foot impatiently.

Jadira handed Tamakh the rod. He circled the platform until he found the lock on the rear side. With some fumbling and grunting, he got it open.

The woman sprang from the platform to the path in front of Jadira. She stood so swiftly the nomad woman drew back in surprise.

"I am the daughter of Ondakoto and Isanfaela. Uramettu is my name," the black woman said. "I am indebted to you all for my freedom." She was very tall, two paces at least, and endowed with grace and obvious strength. Her constant, unblinking gaze appraised them each in turn.

Jadira made hasty introductions. "Can you lead us out?" she asked.

Uramettu adjusted her thin, thigh-length tunic, and promptly set off on the center path. Her long, loping stride soon had Tamakh panting far behind. Marix and Jadira had to jog just to keep pace.

"Do you know—where you are—going?" puffed Marix.

"The palace wall is guarded all around. The only way out is under," said Uramettu.

"Under?" questioned Jadira.

"The garden is watered by a pool. The pool is fed by a spring, and the overflow passes under the palace wall to the city cisterns."

Sure enough, when they rounded the next bend, a sheet of silver spread out across the entire end of the garden. The pool was bordered on two sides by high walls with soldiers marching in pairs along the top.

Uramettu crouched among the bulrushes and bade her new comrades stay low beside her.

"Slip into the water and make for the wall. Just left of the center is a culvert that leads under the wall to the Al-Makhi cistern."

"A problem," said Tamakh. "I cannot swim."

"Nor can I," said Jadira, eyeing the water uncertainly.

"Then you shall go on my back," Uramettu said to her. "And the priest may come with the yellow-haired one."

Tamakh nodded assent. Jadira looked behind once and then returned her gaze to the water. "I'm ready," she said.

Uramettu slid noiselessly into the pool. Jadira followed. She looped her arms around the black woman's neck. Uramettu pushed off from shore and swam powerfully toward the wall. A slight splash behind them told Jadira that Marix and Tamakh were also on their way.

The water was cold. Jadira snorted when it got in her nose. When Uramettu thrust ahead with extra vigor, a small wave hit Jadira in the face. She choked and sputtered so loudly Uramettu had no choice but to dive, lest the Faziri hear them. The black water closed over Jadira's head and for a second she thought Uramettu meant to drown her. But she held her breath, and a dozen heartbeats later they surfaced in front of the culvert.

The way was barred to keep in the large animals, but neither woman had any problem slipping through. In the tunnel, the water was only calf-deep and the culvert was short. They slogged to the other end and saw that the dark street beyond was empty.

Marix and Tamakh labored through the water to the culvert. Marix was complaining about the priest's weight, while Tamakh insisted the young noble had tried to shuck him off in mid-pool. Jadira, returning from the far end, stifled their bickering with a fierce glare and a finger pointing up; the sultan's soldiers were on the palace wall above them.

Marix crawled through the bars. Tamakh, going head first, got stuck halfway.

"Not again!" said Jadira in a harsh whisper.

"By Tuus, we ought to leave you there!" said Marix, pushing wet blond hair out of his eyes.

"Uncharitable wretch," Tamakh responded. He pushed mightily with his hands, trying to force his belly past the constricting bars.

"Can't you magic them?" said Jadira.

He wrapped his thick fingers around one bar and twisted. The dark green verdigris flaked off, revealing yellow metallic sheen beneath. "Bars are brass," wheezed Tamakh. "So's not to rust."

Jadira grabbed him under the arms and pulled. "I thought priests were supposed to lead lives of denial," she complained. Her grip slipped on the wet fabric of his clerical toga. She fell against Marix, who fell on Uramettu.

"The devotees of—ugh!—Agma follow the—oof!—god in all things."

Uramettu gently set Marix aside. "How so, Holy One?" she asked, taking firm hold of Tamakh.

"Agma is fire, and fire consumes all things."

"Oh, filth," said Marix.

"I can free you, my friend," said Uramettu. "But I can't promise in what condition. Shall I try?"

"I can't stay wedged in this drain forever," said Tamakh. "Haul away."

The black woman set her feet, and her shoulders knotted, the muscles in her arms coiling like live serpents. Tamakh let out a loud groan, then *pop!* he was free.

"Are you all right?" said Jadira.

"Largely," said Tamakh with unintended humor. "I feel like a cork newly pried from a wine bottle."

The water got shallower as the tunnel slanted up to street level. At the far end, which was open, a wide ditch ran a dozen paces into a city square. The ditch ended at a squat pillar with a conical cap. This was the filling hole for the Al-Makhi cistern. Tamakh warned them to keep clear of the hole. The suction there could easily pull them into the underground reservoir.

They waded along the ditch in single file. Bundles of torches burning atop the palace wall threw giant wavering shadows on the street beside them. A dog barked nearby; everyone froze. There was the sound of smashing pottery, and the barking stopped.

Midway to the cistern, Uramettu halted and climbed silently out. She helped Jadira and Tamakh over the side of the ditch. Marix, last in line, grew impatient. He put a hand and foot on the rim and began to climb out. The white brick edging was thick with slime, and his foot slipped. The others could only watch helplessly as Marix tumbled backward into the ditch.

The loud splash brought a helmeted face to the top of the wall. The Faziri flung a torch down, and by its light saw Jadira, Uramettu, and Tamakh.

"Who goes there?" he shouted. Jadira and Tamakh ran while Uramettu yanked Marix out of the ditch. The soldier changed his cry to "Alarm! Alarm! Sergeant of the Guard, come quickly!"

Metal-nailed sandals rang on the battlements as troops assembled on the wall. The Faziri who had given the alarm pointed at Marix's back as the latter pounded hard after the fleeter Uramettu.

A gong began to clang. The postern gate swung open, and a dozen imperial guards trotted forth, followed by a section of eight horsemen. The gong sounded remorselessly, calling the sultan's soldiers to action.

Uramettu flashed by Jadira. The nomad woman was astonished by Uramettu's speed and soundless tread.

Uramettu led them with uncanny insight through the narrow alleys and pitch-dark streets of Omerabad. Several times Jadira lost sight of the black woman as she stumbled along, half-dragging Tamakh. Marix, babbling in the native tongue of Dosen, ran up alongside and grabbed the priest's free arm.

"Where's Uramettu?" he gasped. In answer, the woman from Fedush reappeared, sweeping one long arm to her left. She turned and sprinted ahead down the twisting lane, springing with ease over raised cobbles, piles of rubbish, and other obstacles. Faziri horsemen clattered past the turn, but the last man in the section spotted the fleeing prisoners and called his fellows back.

Marix heard them coming. Letting go of Tamakh, he turned to face them. His hand went to the hilt of the stolen scimitar. No; he could not stop them that way. The horsemen would simply ride him down. What to do? He spied a pair of man-sized jars flanking the doorway of a large house. They held rainwater and street filth, gathered for pick-up by the imperial street sweepers. Marix dumped the jars out, sending a wave of sludge rushing down the street toward the Faziris. The first horse galloped into the muck and slipped. The horse recovered but the rider did not. The splendidly armored Faziri vaulted over his horse's head and landed on his white cloak in the filth. The trailing cavalry piled up in the street, and Marix ran on after his companions, grinning at the sound of neighing horses and cursing men.

His joy was short-lived. As he crossed an intersecting street, Marix saw a troop of foot soldiers trotting in formation toward him. The captain yelled a sharp command at the sight of Marix and gestured with his halberd.

"Marix! Come on!" Jadira's voice came from the rising street. He looked ahead and saw Jadira waving furiously. "Come on!"

He joined her and followed the breathless priest into an alley so narrow the houses closed together overhead. Uramettu moved like a phantom out of the darkness and said, "This way."

She led them past a row of vacant doorways. By the time Jadira and Tamakh arrived five steps later, a man had emerged from the last door. There was no time to dodge. Jadira, Tamakh, and the stranger collided and went down in a tangle.

"Get off! Let me up!" bawled the man in proper outrage. Jadira felt a hand go around her waist, feeling for a purse she wasn't carrying. Tamakh likewise felt fingers delve into the folds of his robe.

"Cutpurse!" said Jadira. "Pickpocket!"

"Shut up," the man growled in a much lower and stronger voice. Jadira caught a glimpse of metal, probably a knife blade. There was no point in getting stabbed for money she didn't have, so she closed her mouth and worked herself free of the man's grasp. Tamakh staggered to his feet and started running again. Marix had long since passed them.

Jadira got to her feet as the thief did. "I wouldn't go that way," she said, indicating the way they had come. The thief spat and ran, ignoring her warning. Jadira fled in the opposite direction, after her companions. A phalanx of imperial soldiers arrived at the foot of the alley just as Jadira reached the head. The thief frantically skidded to a stop only a few paces from the soldiers.

"There's one!" said one of the soldiers. "After him!"

The thief spun and took off like a hare. Jadira was fleet, but the thief breezed by her. "Told you so," she panted as he passed. He caught up to Marix and

Tamakh, too, and was soon matching stride with the much taller Uramettu.

The street forked. Uramettu went left, the thief right. "Go with the thief!" said Tamakh, reasoning that the man would know a good way to lose pursuers. The others followed him and Uramettu doubled back.

One soldier paused long enough to heave his halberd at the fleeing prisoners. It hit the paving ahead of Jadira, and she leaped high to clear the flailing shaft.

The cutpurse turned right again, entering a gap barely wide enough for a man to pass sideways. He glanced back once, scowled, uttered frightful profanities, and vanished.

The houses were so close on either side Jadira could smell the cook-fires and incense. The stench was so bad they could hardly draw breath. Half the soldiers started into the cramped passage, bumping and banging the clay walls with their armor and weapons. The rest of the troop double-timed around the block to seal off the other end.

Jadira stumbled into Marix. "Why have you stopped?"

"We've lost the cutpurse," said Tamakh.

"Is there a door?" Marix asked.

Jadira touched the wall. "There must be."

"Wait," said Uramettu. She put an ear to the wall facing her. "He's gone up. He's climbing the wall."

"Is the man a lizard?" said Marix. Uramettu ran her hands over the pale gray clay until she found what she was seeking. The thief had used this alley before; handholds had been chopped in the wall.

Without a word, Uramettu began to climb the wall. Tamakh went next. He discovered the alley was narrow, he could rest his weight against the rear wall as he climbed.

Marix mounted the wall. Jadira fretted as she waited her turn. She could hear the soldiers quite plainly. They had lost their torches while running, but they couldn't fail to catch her if she didn't start climbing soon.

Marix's suede boots vanished. Jadira dug her fingers into the ragged holes and started upward. She was scarcely three paces up when the Faziris met beneath her. She sighed silent thanks to Mitaali that they didn't think to look up.

The house at Jadira's back ended three stories off the ground. Several pairs of hands plucked her from the wall and pulled her onto the roof. Marix and Tamakh had her.

"Where are we?" she whispered.

"Ask the cutpurse," said Marix. Not far away, Uramettu was sitting on the prostrate thief.

"Let me up, you savage," he growled.

"Tut, tut, that's no way to speak to a lady," said Marix.

"What do you want of me?" asked the thief, fear creeping into his voice. "I took nothing from you. By the Thirty Gods, you had nothing to take!"

"There's little need for money in the dungeons of the sultan," said Tamakh.

The thief groaned. "Prisoners! I should have known, with half the imperial guard after you. Now, I am doomed!"

"We are not so fell as that," Marix said.

"I've been seen with you! The soldiers will be looking for me now, too. I'm ruined, ruined!" he moaned.

"Be still and listen to me," said Jadira. "We must be gone from Omerabad before the sun rises. If you can show us a safe way out, we'll take you with us and share everything we have with you."

"And what could you possibly have to share that I might value?"

"Freedom," said Uramettu.

The cutpurse groaned melodramatically. "Where will you go? Fazir is wide, and the eyes of the sultan see far."

"A good question," said Tamakh. "Where *can* we go?"

Marix and Jadira exchanged a private look. "Tantuffa was my original destination," Marix said. "Lord Hurgold would grant us sanctuary from the sultan's wrath."

"Tantuffa by the sea? That's a hundred leagues from here," objected Tamakh.

"What choice do we have?" Jadira said. "To the north lies cold Nangol, where the men wear skins and eat horseflesh. East, and we'd face the mountains upon which the vault of heaven rests. South are the slave dealers of the Crimson Sea—"

"Who I know well enough," said Uramettu. "West to Tantuffa seems the only route. At least from there I can buy passage on a ship bound for Fedush."

"You're all mad," said the thief. "As soon as day breaks on the road to Rehajid, the Invincibles will trample you into bloody dust!"

"Who are these Invincibles?" asked Marix.

"The sultan's own," Jadira said bitterly. "The same murderous devils who attacked my people and killed my family."

"So we won't follow the road," said Uramettu.

"Is there another way?" queried Tamakh.

Jadira entwined her battered fingers and considered. There *was* another way, a way hardly less deadly than the royal road.

"We can cross the Red Sands," she said.

"The desert?" exclaimed the astonished thief.

"Yes, through the desert to the Shammat Mountains, then over the plains of Kaipur to the sea and Tantuffa."

"It is certain death!" declared the thief. "Let me go. I want no part of this madness!"

Uramettu stood, and the thief sighed with relief. "Is that the only word you know?" she said scornfully.

"Have you a better scheme?"

"The city is large," the thief said. "I can hide from the sultan's men. They will—"

"—offer gold to every citizen of Omerabad," finished Jadira. "You would be betrayed in the first hour."

"I could throw myself on the mercy of the grand vizier."

"The same Lord Azrel who crops the ears of gossips and beheads short-changers in the market?" asked Tamakh. The thief covered his face with his hands.

"I won't deceive you," said Jadira. "The desert will be a hard trial; burning hot by day and cold as death by night. But it *can* be crossed, for I know it as Marix knows the forests of Dosen or Tamakh knows the precincts of his temple."

"And the Faziri will think thrice about pursuing us into the Red Sands," added Tamakh.

"But even if I survive, what will I do? Where will I go?" moaned the thief. "This is my home."

"You will be alive," said Uramettu. "With life, there is always hope." The thief continued to mutter about the dire fate that awaited them.

"Will you help us?" Jadira asked him. "Will you guide us out of the city?"

The cutpurse sat up, rubbing the small of his back. "If I must, I must." He hopped to his feet. "But I curse the ill-fated hour that brought us together."

Marix began a retort, but Tamakh's hand on his arm

stayed his tongue. "He is the only one who can lead us out of the city," Tamakh reminded him. "The hour that brought us together was not as ill-fated as he might think."

❖ 4 ❖

The Royal Road

Jadira awoke with a start.

She didn't remember falling asleep, or even lying down. The last thing she did recall was the thief Nabul agreeing to help them. There were alarums in the street below: the tramping of soldiers' feet, horses, shouts. After that, she knew nothing.

Jadira turned her head and discovered the comfortable pillow under her head was Marix's arm. The young man pushed pale hair back from his eyes and asked, "Are you well, lady?"

"What—what happened?"

"You swooned. Too much tumult and too little food have wrung you out."

She sat up abruptly. "How long have I been asleep?"

"Not long—perhaps one notch of the candle."

"Tamakh? Where's Tamakh?"

The priest set a hand on her shoulder from behind. Jadira flinched. Tamakh said, "Fire Star is setting. Dawn will break when it touches the horizon. Nabul will be back before then, and we must go."

"You mean you let that sniveling thief go?" asked Jadira.

"I was against it," claimed Marix.

"He convinced me of the truth of what he said," Tamakh said. "We could not hope to cross the Red Sands with only the clothes on our backs and no food or water." His round face relaxed, and he smiled. "Besides, Uramettu went with him."

"So they're off finding provisions?" asked Jadira. When the priest nodded, she groaned. "We'll never see them again, or if we do, it will be because he betrays us to the sultan's men."

"You must have faith," said Tamakh gently. "Our fate is bound with Nabul's by the god's annealing fire. He will return. What else can he do? The soldiers would likely slay him on sight."

The black dome of heaven warmed slowly to deep purple as the Fire Star declined to its rest. The air seemed to stir like a living thing with the coming of the sun. The purple sky gave way to rose red. Nabul returned.

Uramettu boosted the thief to the neighboring rooftop. She clambered lithely up and pulled a chain of bags up from the alley. Nabul produced a plank from a hiding place on the other roof and bridged the alley with it. He crossed, and Uramettu came over with the provisions.

"Four-and-thirty food shops in Omerabad, and all I could find was wheel bread and yogurt," said Nabul in disgust. "Six-and-twenty wineshops, and I couldn't even find a mug of wheat beer!"

"What is this?" asked Marix, sloshing a goatskin bag in small circles.

"Water. It'll go rancid in the heat, mark my words." Jadira rolled her eyes.

While Nabul unburdened himself from the rest of his

ill-gotten gains, Jadira helped herself to bread and
yogurt. From the folds of his robe, Nabul produced a
small copper pot, a mallet, a coil of coarse twine, cloth
for two *keffiya*, and a lump of soft white chalk. He
squatted on the tar-and-leaf roof and began to draw.

"The main gates of the city will be filled with armed
men," he said, scribing squares west and south. "Our
best chance lies at one of the posterns, here or here."
Nabul made two dots.

"Posterns will be guarded," Marix observed.

"Two men at most. No match for five desperate fugitives," said Jadira.

"Let us try the nearest one," Uramettu said. "An hour
hence and the sun will be well up."

Off they went. Nabul led them on a merry trail across
the housetops of Omerabad. Up a story, down a story,
leaping alleys and skirting courtyards. They trod the
roofs of the rich and the poor, the tapered peaks of
shrines, and the flat tops of shops. Finally Nabul
stopped.

"The city wall," he said. Ahead of them, the stone
curtain reared twelve paces high, well above the level of
the nearest houses.

The band descended a shaky iron trellis affixed to the
side of a tannery. Nabul scampered down easily, but the
others had trouble with the thorny creepers entwined in
the lattice. Together again on street level, they huddled
in the deep shadows opposite the postern gate. A single
Faziri, armed with a long spear and wooden buckler,
paced to and fro in front of the single portal.

"Who's the most innocent-looking among us?" asked
Jadira.

Without hesitation Nabul replied, "The priest."

"I agree," said Jadira. "Tamakh, you must divert the

guard so the rest of us can overcome him silently."

"How?" said Tamakh, looking uneasy.

"Lure him over here. We'll do the rest," Marix said, tapping his palm on the pommel of the sword.

"I cannot be the cause of bloodshed," Tamakh said.

"Do you have a better idea?" asked Marix.

"Almost certainly," said the priest and walked out of hiding. With great dignity, he stepped into the street. The first rays of the sun peeked over the wall, highlighting Tamakh in shafts of gold. Halfway to the gate, he halted.

Tamakh gestured to the empty air. "*Kobit*," he said sonorously. "*Namis kobit vobay . . .*"

The guard spied Tamakh. He ported his spear and strode toward the priest. As he drew nearer, his steps faltered.

"*Vobay namis, Agman!*" said Tamakh. Though he spoke at normal volume, the priest's words seemed to ring like the tolling of a great bell. Jadira felt a numbness take hold of her arms and legs. She saw Uramettu flexing her own ebon arms as if to preserve feeling in them. Nabul shivered violently, and Marix's face showed surprise.

"*Agmas, nam kobituri vobay moritu. Moritu!*" With this last, Tamakh's voice rose, and he flung out his right arm toward the soldier. Four paces from the portly priest, the soldier froze.

The spear rolled off his shoulder, and he remained rooted to the spot.

"By the Thirty Gods! What happened?" asked the thief.

Jadira nodded sagely. "Magic."

Tamakh rejoined them. "We can proceed. The guard will offer no trouble."

They passed on either side of the motionless soldier. Nabul waved his hand before the man's eyes. The guard never blinked. Tamakh reached out and gently, with his fingertips, closed the man's eyes.

"What did you do to him?" asked Marix.

"He is under a glamor, a paralyzing spell. He will hear and see nothing till the sun reaches its zenith."

"If I had such a talent, I would be the king of thieves!" Nabul said wistfully.

They hastened through the gate, though not before Marix relieved the Faziri of helmet, cloak, spear, and shield. Nabul took four coppers from the enchanted man's purse.

The road, white as a bolt of fine cloth, stretched out to the horizon. "The royal road to Rehajid," Jadira said. "Come; we can't be long on it."

The city fell away behind them. They marched briskly for half a league, but the ex-prisoners were in poor shape and tired quickly. Jadira and Tamakh rested on the sloping bank of the road. Nabul crouched nearby, muttering to himself. Marix, armed with a collection of Faziri weapons, stood on the road and watched the way back to Omerabad. While his back was turned, Uramettu padded off among knife-bladed grass.

There would be pursuit.

* * * * *

Azrel, emir of Bindra, vizier to His Magnificence Julmet III, was not a kindly man. The servants who awakened him from his nightly unsound sleep often got a beating for their trouble; of course, they received a worse lashing if they failed to waken him at the appointed hour. The physician who could not cure the emir's dyspepsia earned a flogging, and his tailor hobbled constantly from being kicked. Yet, Azrel was the sultan's eyes and ears, the harsh but effective power behind the Eternal Throne. By war and threat of war, Emir Azrel had enlarged his master's domain from the steppes of Nangol to the shores of the Crimson Sea. By subtlety and craft he enriched the Faziri Empire beyond the bounds of any previous vizier.

Now Azrel sat in the guardroom of the palace prison, boiling with unconcealed anger. Facing him was a tall, fork-bearded Faziri soldier in the scarlet cape and lion-etched armor of the Invincibles. The soldier's handsome yet immobile face reflected none of the emir's hostility.

"Captain Fu'ad, you are generally known as a reliable officer. Is this not so?" said Azrel.

"I do my best, Excellency," said Fu'ad. He wanted badly to scratch his nose, but dared not take such a liberty in front of the vizier.

"You must do more than your best, Captain. It is bad statecraft to send a coercive note to the count of Dosen when his son is no longer in our keeping. It is bad theocraft to promise the city priesthoods that we will suppress the heretical followers of Agma, then to allow one to escape. Am I making myself clear, Captain?"

"Perfectly so, Great Emir."

"Good. Good. I want no misunderstanding. It was my name on the note, Fu'ad; it was *I* who signed the priest Tamakh's death warrant. It is *I* who will have to explain to His Magnificence these blunders. Can you imagine how much the sultan—may he live forever!—likes to hear of blunders?" The vizier's voice had grown steadily in volume and was now a scream. "I want them back, Fu'ad! The prisoner Marix alive if possible, but back in my hands, do you hear?" The dead in their graves could have heard Emir Azrel.

"I will lead a troop myself," said Fu'ad. "They shall not escape."

"Take two troops. Anyone who helps them must die. I want all who are caught in their company put to the sword. There is to be no mercy in this matter, Captain. Mercy is the prerogative of the sultan—may he live forever—and I am not His Magnificence."

"My lance has never failed in his service."

"Good. Good. See that it doesn't."

There was a knock on the door. Azrel said, "Come." A foot soldier entered.

"Your command has been carried out, Excellency," said the Faziri.

"Show me," the emir replied.

The foot soldier held up his hands. In each he clutched by the hair a severed head. One was Nungwun, the guard who allowed the escape; the other was the warden-general of the prison. His crime was allowing Nungwun to allow the escape.

"Post them in the usual place," said Azrel. The soldier bowed and departed on his grisly errand.

"When do you leave, Captain?" asked Azrel.

"Before sunset, Excellency."

"They may get far by sunset, even on foot."

Fu'ad chose his words carefully. "I have dispatched riders from the Cobra Regiment to leave the city from all the gates to search for the criminals, Great Emir. When they are found, I shall ride forth with the Invincibles and catch the pestilent scum."

Azrel chewed fitfully on his graying mustache. "See that you do, Captain. It would distress many ladies in Omerabad to see your handsome head on a pole in Kefaaq Square," he said. "Such is the penalty for failure."

Fu'ad snapped to attention and bowed. "I will have them, Great Emir, or die trying."

Azrel smiled unpleasantly. "Is that not what I said?"

Fu'ad was glad to return to the sunny, dusty street outside the palace. The sultan's realm was home to scenes of great wealth and beauty—and heartless cruelty such as he had never known, even on the battlefield.

His second in command, Marad *gan* Rafikiya, held the reins of Fu'ad's horse across the neck of his own mount. He handed Fu'ad the reins as the captain put a foot in the stirrup and swung into the saddle.

"What is the word, my brother?" Marad asked.

Fu'ad answered, "We hunt them down. The yellow-haired one is to be brought back alive. The rest . . ." He drew a finger across his throat.

Marad straightened his back. The mail curtain around his helmet brim jingled musically. "The Phoenix Troop is ready," he said.

"Call out the Vulture Troop as well," said Fu'ad. "His Excellency Emir Azrel wants no effort spared in recapturing the prisoners."

Marad saluted and spurred his horse. He galloped up the crowded street, scattering a mob of traders and beggars, and upsetting a line of women who carried the morning's bread in flat baskets on their heads.

Fu'ad rode back to barracks of the Phoenix Troop. The men there were well into packing their gear for the chase. Fu'ad did not interrupt. His quarters consisted of a single room at the north end of the barracks, plainly furnished. Fu'ad drew the curtain across the door and unbuckled the strap of his heavy helmet. From under his armor, Fu'ad pulled a small golden disc on a chain. He turned the necklace until he'd inspected every link in the chain. The yellow patina revealed no signs of wear.

Fu'ad turned the amulet over in his hands. In low relief on the front was a profile of Sultan Julmęt. On the reverse was an inscription in archaic Faziri script: MAY HE LIVE FOREVER.

The amulet was one of the sultan's many eyes. Each man who took the oath as an officer in the army of His Magnificence was given an Eye of the Sultan to wear around his neck. Through it, the Faziri monarch could follow Fu'ad's actions. Though it did not show scenes like a magic mirror, it did send location images and feelings back to sensitive magicians at the court. They would know instantly of any triumph—or treachery. The penalty for removing the amulet was death. It was believed that the Eye of the Sultan was indeed capable of causing death, if removed. No one of Fu'ad's acquaintance had ever investigated this possibility.

Fu'ad packed a few items into his saddlebag. He went out to the barracks courtyard, where the Phoenix Troop was assembled. The Eye of the Sultan was hidden beneath Fu'ad's armor, close to his beating heart.

❖ 5 ❖

The Word of Agma

Noon found the companions sprawled beside the royal road. They had made fair progress, almost two leagues, and the easy path to Rehajid weakened their resolve to enter the desert.

They rested, in their own fashion. Tamakh knelt on a flat rock in meditation. He swayed slightly, back and forth, moving his lips in a silent litany. Not far away, Nabul was trying to fit himself with a *keffiya*. He put a piece of the white cloth he had stolen over his head, but the headband was too loose and the cloth slid, engulfing his face. Jadira stifled a laugh. The thief whipped off the hood and sawed at the headband with a wicked-looking dagger. He re-knotted the band and tried the arrangement again. This time only his eyes were lost.

Jadira scrambled up the embankment and saw Marix a few paces away, standing guard. With helmet, shield, and spear, the nobleman looked quite martial in the bright light of noon. She admired the straightness of his shoulders and the lift of his chin.

Marix spoiled the effect by turning toward her. The

heavy helmet was far too big for him. It squashed his ears outward in very comical fashion. She could not restrain a laugh.

"What's so amusing?" asked Marix. The spear slipped from his hand. Marix bent to get it, and the conical iron pot fell off his head. Jadira clapped a hand to her mouth to smother her laughter.

Marix replaced the helmet and came to her. "Am I such a buffoon?" he demanded.

"No worse than I would be in your country," Jadira replied generously, stifling more laughter.

Marix, disarmed by her response, looked quickly up the road. "No sign of pursuit. Indeed, no sign of anything."

"I don't like it," she said. "It would be better for us if the road were crowded. A fine, big caravan would mask us well from the Invincibles."

"What happened to Uramettu?" asked Marix. "Each time we stop she disappears."

"Perhaps she is foraging—" Jadira began. The drumming of hooves cut her off.

"Get out of sight," Marix said, pushing her to the bank beside the road. "Hurry!"

She skidded in the loose sand to the base of the slope. Nabul popped out from a desiccated *maqeet* bush. To his quizzical expression Jadira simply replied, "Hide!" She ran farther and grabbed the somnolent Tamakh by the shoulders. "Wake up, Holy One! The Invincibles are after us!"

"'Vincibles?" mumbled the priest. His eyes grew wide. "Agma preserve us!"

Marix threw himself down by Jadira and Tamakh. The rider was in sight now, a lone figure galloping hard from the direction of Omerabad. White plumes bobbed from the peak of his helmet. An aroused serpent was graven on his blackened breastplate.

"The Cobra Regiment!" hissed Nabul. "Nangoli swordsmen in the sultan's pay!"

"What shall we do?" asked Marix.

"Lie low and let him pass," said Tamakh.

"No. We must take him," said Jadira.

"But why?" the priest asked. "He does not threaten us. He doesn't even know we're here."

"We need a horse. And he'll have food and water."

"Right!" said Marix. Before anyone could argue further, the third son of Count Fernald stood and waved to the oncoming horseman. In cloak and helmet, Marix looked like a Faziri himself.

"He's coming. Are you ready?" Marix muttered from the corner of his mouth.

"Now you ask," said Jadira. Tamakh invoked his patron deity again.

The mercenary came on at a trot. Marix gripped the spear tightly, turning the hardwood shaft in his sweaty palms.

The horseman drew up short. He put up a hand and called, "*Kasah al'am!*" Was it a greeting or a challenge? The rider pushed back his brimmed helmet and repeated his hail.

"Oh, filth," muttered Marix. Then he shouted "*Yahh!*" and charged. The helmet fell from his head and his blond hair shone in the sunlight.

The Nangoli snatched his scimitar and spurred his mount forward. He caught the point of Marix's spear on his shield. It skidded off, and the young man crashed into the steed. Marix spun and fell just as the scimitar's tip swished by his ear.

Jadira uttered a Sudiin war cry and sprang to attack.

Nabul leaped to his feet and circled behind the mounted man.

The mercenary cut at Jadira, who had only Nungwun's cudgel to ward off the blade. Marix got up, all a-tangle in cloak and spearshaft, just in time to receive a blow on the head from the horseman's brazen shield. Down he went again.

The horse pranced as the fugitives surrounded the lone rider. Nabul had his dagger drawn, but he shrank back each time the mercenary rotated to face him. Jadira landed a good clout on the enemy's leg. He struck back with his sword, the flat of his blade catching the nomad woman on the neck.

Roused by the melee, Tamakh appeared in the road. The horse's tail swatted him in the face, and he tumbled backward on the sand.

"*Taqeet asah!*" said the mercenary in disgust. He grabbed the spear from where Marix had jabbed it in the ground. With the extra reach of this weapon, he could spit these annoying vagabonds without further ado. He singled out the dagger-wielder first, as he was the most seriously armed.

Suddenly, the horse began to buck and shake. It rolled its eyes and shook its head in stark terror. The rider kept his seat, but required both hands to do so. The spear fell to the ground.

A piercing howl arrested everyone in their tracks. The horse neighed and shivered. Jadira turned toward the sound, which came from the dunes on the other side of the road.

A dense black form hurtled through the air, striking the horseman and knocking him from the saddle. He landed heavily on his back with the black thing at his throat. The man screamed once, then lay still. The creature let go of him and retreated to the center of the road. Jadira caught the panicked horse and quickly soothed it.

On his knees, Marix pointed at the big creature coiled in the road. "A panther!" he said.

Jadira found the spear and pointed it at the black animal.

"Wait," said Tamakh. He was kneeling by the dead soldier, offering a hasty benediction. He peered intently at the panther. "Don't hurt her." The panther turned to the priest, and they locked eyes. Tamakh's face registered surprise and the animal's lips lifted in a snarl. Tamakh smiled.

"It's a killer!" said the terrified Marix. "Do you see what it did to that man?"

"She only did what the rest of you were trying to do," said Tamakh. Jadira heard bitterness in his words. "And she is one of us, after all," the priest added.

"What are you saying, Holy One?" asked Jadira.

"The panther is Uramettu."

"By the Thirty Gods!" Nabul made a sign to ward off evil influences.

"No wonder the sultan kept her in a cage," said Marix. "She is cursed!"

"Are you certain, Holy One?" asked Jadira.

"Agma lets me see through such enchantments. This animal is indeed our companion." He looked at each of them in turn. "She is a shape-shifter."

The sun had declined, almost touching the higher dunes. Its rays bathed the motionless panther in brazen color. The magnificent beast shuddered and twisted. Its hind legs straightened and lengthened with ominous pops and groans. The dense black fur thinned and disappeared into smooth dark skin.

"Cursed," mumbled Nabul, turning away.

Jadira watch in horrified fascination as the panther's head lengthened and flattened. Its long teeth and whiskers retreated. Just as she, too, would have looked away, Jadira's eyes found those of the panther. They *were* Uramettu's eyes. As the animal became a woman again, those warm brown eyes never left Jadira's face. They were the only part of the panther that did not change.

"I am grateful you did not spear me, friend Jadira," said Uramettu. She adjusted the spare scrap of linen that was her clothing and stood up.

"Be grateful to Tamakh. He recognized you, not I."

"My thanks, Holy One."

"Not bad for a fat cleric, eh?" said Tamakh with a wink.

"How is it you come by this power?" asked Marix.

"It is not unknown among my people," the woman from Fedush replied. "While I was in panther form, I was captured by Zimoran slavers. When they saw my true shape, they knew the sultan would pay well for such an addition to his menagerie."

Nabul stripped the dead man of everything he had. Armor, weapons, coins, and clothes he flung in a heap by the road. Tamakh handed the soldier's mantle to Uramettu.

Marix led the horse to her. "Since you defeated the enemy, by right of combat the horse is yours," he said.

"I don't think the poor fellow would appreciate me on his back." As it was, Uramettu's presence caused the horse to roll its eyes and quiver.

"Someone ought to ride," Marix declared.

"If the choice is mine, let the holy man ride," Uramettu said.

Tamakh's eyebrows rose. He pointed to himself and said, "You think me infirm?"

She shook her head. "I meant only to defer to your elder feet," she replied.

"My aged feet express their gratitude." The priest mounted clumsily. He unhooked the waterskin from the Nangoli's saddle and shook it. "Nearly full."

"We'll need every drop," Jadira reminded him. "We're leaving the road."

"But why?" asked Nabul.

"Consider what would have befallen us had we met a troop of horsemen instead of one. Why, the four of us ran about like headless geese before Uramettu vanquished him. What could we do against real cavalry? No, we must leave the road and use the desert to shield us from the sultan's soldiers."

"We'll die out there," Nabul predicted.

"If we do, I am sure we won't die with full pockets," said Marix, eyeing the thief.

They buried the mercenary by the road. Jadira began to distribute their meager possessions. She started to hand Nabul the spear but changed her mind and gave it to Uramettu.

"This is too much," Nabul grumbled.

Jadira handed Tamakh the cudgel.

Tamakh said, "As a cleric, it is not proper for me to bear an edged weapon. I would rather bear no weapon, but as we are not all reborn in the kindly warmth of Agma—"

Nabul cut him off. "Why is *she* deciding who'll carry what? She seems to be deciding everything."

"Jadira seems best suited to get us across the Red Sands, just as you were our best guide in the backstreets of Omerabad," put in Tamakh.

Uramettu agreed, saying, "I will follow her."

They all looked to Marix. He said, "Jadira is our best

chance to get safely across the desert. However—" he glanced at her—"it is only right that we all speak our minds."

"Are you satisfied to let me lead as long as we are on the Red Sands?" she asked Nabul, hands on hips. "Or do you profess to know the desert better than I?" Nabul made a terrible face, but he did not dispute the division of the meager spoils further.

Jadira kept the dead mercenary's sword, as Marix had one already. Nabul retained only his dagger. The five had two skins of water, a bag of wheelbread, and one medium-sized pot of sour yogurt. The provisions were hung from the saddle rings.

By the dying light of day, Jadira addressed her comrades: "Northward lies the great oasis of Julli. The oasis is at least ten leagues from here. There we will be able to find caravans, traders, and the supplies we need for the journey to Tantuffa. It will be hard going, as we cannot spare time to dally. When the Cobra rider fails to return, the sultan's men will scour the Rehajid road first. Unless the sultan wishes to challenge the Red Sands on equal terms with us, we will be safe once we leave Julli for the high desert. There we will be in Mitaali's hands.

"If the gods favor us, we should reach Julli early tomorrow."

* * * * *

Marix of Dosen had always believed deserts were infernos both day and night. He rapidly changed his mind on the Red Sands. By the time the Fire Star rose in the southwest, he was blue with cold. The Faziri cloak was a pretty piece of cloth, suitable for parades, but it held precious little warmth.

The others trudged on in silence, conversation crushed by the enormity of the desert around them. Jadira led the horse as Tamakh rode. At midnight, he dismounted and bade her ride in his place. She demurred until Marix pointed out that if she fainted again, he, for one, was not going to carry her across the desert. The rocking motion of the horse soothed Jadira's tired body, and she slept, as nomads often did, slumped over the horse's neck.

In sleep, Jadira left her companions. She journeyed through seasons past.

The vale of Al Mirah . . . a small cleft in the hills of Tabraq, flowing with sweet water and green with palms and shrubs. It was there, in the windy season of Jadira's thirteenth year, that she had met and been betrothed to her second cousin, Ramil gan Rustafiya. Ramil was renowned among the Sudiin for his patience. This was good, as his bride-to-be was equally well known for her fiery temper. The girl Jadira rode like one of the Demon King's own. She talked back to her elders and let her headdress slide down in disarray; her mother despaired of ever marrying her to anyone suitable. But after the steady Ramil dined twice in the tent of Ifrim, Jadira's father, the match was made.

Al Mirah. The couple clad in white, their heads uncovered, walked down into the sacred spring of Ishat. They annointed each other's head with cool water, said their vows, and they were married.

Ramil was a skillful herdsman. His goats waxed fatter than anyone's, and he tended them with devotion and care. Jadira fended less well. She chafed at the chores of domestic life. She wanted the freedom of her youth back. Soon her rides alone across the Red Sands were the scandal of the tribes. Neither Ifrim nor Ramil could convince Jadira she was behaving most immodestly.

Have babies, old Ifrim urged. They will slow her down. Ramil considered. And considered. And then—

In a pass through the lower Shammat Mountains, the red-cloaked Invincibles swept down on the Sudiin. The nomad men were slain where they stood. Women were herded into weeping knots, to be picked up by foot soldiers following the cavalry. Sudiin children saw their entire world trampled under the black hooves of the sultan's imperial horsemen.

Jadira fought. With tent poles and goat-goads, she fended off the laughing Invincibles until she was completely surrounded. The ring of lances closed on her. An officer with a golden lion on his helmet commanded her to cease her resistance.

"When goats ride horses and men give cheese!" she shouted, and flung the iron-tipped goad at the officer. It pricked his horse, and the beast immediately hurled the officer to the ground.

The Faziris stopped laughing. One dismounted and rolled his commander over. Dead. His neck was broken.

It would have been simpler had they slain her on the spot, but that they could not do. Captive women were by Faziri law the property of the sultan. The Faziris tied Jadira to a post. A dozen Sudiin men were dragged before her and, one by one, beheaded. Among them was Ramil, son of Rustaf. He said nothing before the sword blade fell. . . .

"Jadira? Are you well?" said Marix. She opened her eyes. The horse was plodding on, its hooves sinking in the soft sand.

"What—what is it?"

"Forgive me," he said, his face flushing. "You were sobbing. I thought—?" He finished the sentence with a shrug.

Jadira sat up and wiped her cheeks. "It is nothing. Whose turn is it to ride?"

"Couldn't we rest a while?" said Nabul. "My feet bleed!"

"Liar. You have better sandals than anyone else," Uramettu said. Nabul glared.

Tamakh drew himself up and exhaled loudly. "I would like to pause for a time, too. We have walked since sunset, and it is now near midnight. I think we have a sufficient lead over any pursuit."

Jadira put a leg over and slid off the horse. "One notch for rest. That's all we can spare," she said. Marix agreed and soon was stretched out on the sand, snoring.

Nabul lay down and turned his *keffiya* around to cover his face. The hood billowed and puffed like a frog's throat each time he let out a snore. Uramettu dropped on her belly. She scooped warm sand onto her back and legs, wiggling deeper and deeper until only her head showed.

Jadira unhooked the waterskin from the saddle. It was half-full, all the water they had left. She held the bag under the horse's nose. As a nomad (and a black-band Sudiin at that) she knew the horse was the key to their reaching Julli alive. Men will tolerate a certain lack of water, knowing some awaits them ahead. Horses will not. When thirsty enough, a horse will lie down and not get up. If that happened, they were doomed.

Tamakh moved away from the others, fluffed out his toga, and sat cross-legged on the sand. He was troubled. Though pleased at their successful escape from Omerabad, he was bothered by the thuggery they had been forced into. In his heart he was a peaceful man, and the doings of the past two days oppressed his spirit.

In times like this, he turned to his deity for help. As Tamakh leaned forward to chant his mantra, something hard jabbed his ribs. He searched in his robe and found the iron key that had opened his fetters and Uramettu's cage. He contemplated the key.

Iron was sacred to Agma. Other elder gods and spirits were venerated in gold and copper, silver or bronze. But out of the fire of the forge came iron, the hardest and strongest of metals. Agma sat on a throne of iron, deep in the flames of his ethereal plane.

Agma . . .

Tamakh felt his inner self rise out of his flesh. He saw the dunes fall away beneath his feet. The tiny black dots on the sand were his friends. A powerful voice filled his mind.

Tamakh.

"Yes, Great One?" he replied.

Do you know me?

"You are Agma, Master of Fire, Forger of Iron and Men."

I am He. I have come to warn you, Tamakh. Danger lives all around you. You must be wary.

"What will become of us, Great One?"

Peril lies ahead, devoted.

"Can we overcome it? Should we turn back from the Red Sands?"

Keep to your path, devoted, but know that death follows you. It rides hard to catch you.

"What form does death take, great Agma?"

I see two score and ten men. Their arms are long and sharp. Much blood falls from their hands, devoted.

"How shall we escape these men?"

You must use every bit of knowledge you have. You must rely on the strength of your companions, on your wits and their courage. Be not afraid to help the weak and the small, for they shall carry you over a great barrier.

"I-I do not understand, Great One. Who could be smaller and weaker than us?"

Rejoice for the fire that burns in the sky and beware the man who walks unseen.

"But—" Tamakh protested, but the cold and gloom resumed. He was shaking, and he returned to consciousness to find Jadira had him by the shoulders.

"Wake up, Tamakh!" she said. "It's time to move on."

"Uh? Yes, yes, very well."

Nabul finally got his wish and mounted the horse. Or tried to mount; he swung so vigorously over the pommel he kept going and landed head-first in the sand on the other side. Grinning widely, Uramettu pulled him out and set him gently in the saddle.

"There, my friend. Now hold on tightly," she said. Nabul managed a sickly smile and turned his head to spit out the sand he had swallowed.

"Which way?" said Marix.

"North by west," said Jadira.

"Under the second wheel of the Chariot," Tamakh said, pointing to the sky.

Walking again, Jadira fell into step beside the priest. She said, "You amaze me, Holy One. I would've thought you would be the first to fail out here, but you seem as fresh as a desert rose."

Tamakh glanced down at the iron key, still in his hand. Agma's vision had made the homely object sacred. He rubbed it fondly.

"We all have our secret strengths," he said.

The Faceless One

The brightening of dawn found the companions trudging up the slope of a particularly large dune. Uramettu was leading. She stopped suddenly, and Nabul, stumping along behind her, trod on her heels. "What're you doing?" he asked testily.

"Quiet!" Uramettu hissed. "I heard something."

They halted and stood poised to fight or flee. "I don't hear—" Nabul began, but Uramettu glowered down at him and he subsided. And then they all heard it. It was a full note, melodic and sustained, sighing aimlessly over the barren sands.

"What," asked Marix, "was that?"

Nabul shuddered. "I don't know and I don't want to know."

"Music, perhaps," Marix offered. "Like a great reed pipe."

"Do you suppose someone's out here playing music?" Nabul said sarcastically.

"It's not music," Jadira said to Marix, "it's a voice." With this cryptic statement, she led them up to the summit of the dune. There she held out her hands and said, "Behold The Faceless One."

The rim of the dune dropped away ten paces, then the sand flattened out. In the center of this depression stood a statue. It was a colossal piece of sculpture. The rectangular base reared four paces high, and more seemed buried in the earth. Seated on this sandstone pedestal was an enormous stone figure at least fifteen paces tall. The head bore a flaring headdress in red stone that draped over the broad, cracked shoulders. The torso was flat and masculine; a suggestion of strength still remained in the carved muscles. The legs and the hands resting on the knees were well-defined, but all the facial features had eroded away.

"What is it?" Marix asked. "Or rather, who?"

"It is The Faceless One," Jadira replied. "It has no other name."

The colossus's sightless visage stared at the eastern horizon. The ghostly voice boomed out from it again. Nabul and Marix clapped their hands over their ears. Uramettu and Tamakh winced at the powerful sound.

"Why does it moan so?" asked Uramettu.

Jadira shrugged. "No one knows. And we do not know who carved it, how such a thing was moved here, or why it was made."

Nabul flopped down on the crest of the dune. "How does it make that noise?" he whined. "Surely it will split my head!"

"There are many stories of why it sings. Each tribe has its own legend . . . some say he is a god who mourns his blindness. Some say he was a mortal still being punished for some ancient evil—but no one has any idea how it sings. The cry is most often heard just at sunrise, though some claim to have heard it at sunset. The Sudiin sage

Akhrim the Blind once heard it at noon."

"It makes me sad," said Uramettu. "Crying in the desert seems so lonely!"

The sun lifted clear of the horizon and its rays bathed the colossus in warm orange light. After a minute the sound came again, more muted than before. Marix felt the hair on the back of his neck stand up. He said, "A faceless thing of stone, and yet my heart is uneasy at its song."

In silence they watched the singing colossus for several long minutes. Finally Jadira broke the spell, saying, "Pity will not help it now. We should be off."

They skirted north of the colossus, and as they passed, four of the five glanced up at the towering figure.

Jadira did not. She kept her eyes on the western horizon, where the shadow of the colossus reached, seemingly to infinity. As the figure sang a final faint note, Jadira's face veiled briefly with pain. She had not told her own idea on why the colossus mourned. Akhrim the Blind had taught the Sudiin children that the statute was a likeness of the god Mitaali, father of all nomads.

It was only fitting, she thought, that the maker of the Sudiin should grieve when so many of his children were dead.

* * * * *

The sun rose higher, and a hot wind blew in from the south. The wind flung dust in their eyes and parched their throats even worse than before. They wrung the last drops from the waterskin before midday. Then the real fury of the Red Sands fell on them. The sun bore down, splitting their skins and pouring fire inside them. Though they had had only two sips of water in the morning, whole bucketsful ran off them as they trudged. As noon approached, the very air was transmuted into fire and Jadira called a halt. No one had any appetite (save Nabul), but Jadira convinced them all to eat something. Without food, they would go off their heads.

Marix opened the food bags. The bread had dried into tight curls as tough as sandal straps. He lifted the lid of the yogurt jar and gagged. The curdled milk was thick with weevils.

Nabul cursed. "I should have known!" he said. "Marut always did keep a filthy shop. See if I steal anything from that son of a dog again!"

"Weevils or no, we may have to eat this," Jadira said firmly. "Though a large oasis, Julli is small in the vastness of the desert, and we could walk past it unknowing."

Marix dropped the lid on the pot and swallowed audibly. "I'll starve first," he said.

"You may, my squeamish friend," said Tamakh.

Uramettu took the pot and dipped two fingers into the thick yogurt. Tiny black weevils crawled up her hand. She put her fingers in her mouth and swallowed, bugs and all. Nabul exclaimed in disgust.

"In my country, locusts and honey are considered a great delicacy. This 'yogurt' of yours is not as sweet, but it will sustain us on our journey," she said. Jadira swallowed, smiled ruefully, and reached for the pot.

"I can't watch," said Marix. He turned away and crouched in the small patch of shade cast by the horse. Nabul quickly joined him.

Tamakh stood. "You too, Holy One?" said Uramettu.

The priest mopped his streaming forehead. "Ah, well, hmm. The rigors of our passage would be better borne if I were of, umm, finer build." He bowed his head briefly and averted his eyes.

Jadira handed the jar to Uramettu. "Men are strange," she said. "They will rush to face a hundred swords, yet cringe at the thought of a few weevils."

"So I have found them in Fazir as they are in Fedush," the black woman replied.

"How long have you been in Fazir?" Jadira asked.

"I endured four new moons in the sultan's cage," Uramettu replied. "For that long I have been forced to transform myself and satisfy the whims of the sultan." She dug her hand deeper into the yogurt.

Resolving her apprehension, Jadira said, "I've been wondering—that is, I wanted to ask you—"

"About my ability."

"Yes, the changing. How is it you can become a panther? Were you cursed by an evil magician?"

"No, no, not at all. Understand, my sister, that on the savannah there are many powerful spirits: Ontoduma, the elephant spirit; Klikka, the monkey; and many others. Each clan has a totem spirit whom they appease and worship. My clan follows Ronta, the panther. We are famed as the best hunters in Fedush, and it is to Ronta we owe this skill.

"In some mortals, the bush spirits claim close kinship. When I reached womanhood, Ronta chose me. I went out from my village for one changing of the moon and lived as a panther. I returned and became chief huntress and wise-woman to my village sisters."

Jadira wiped her mouth with the back of her hand. "Then shape-shifting is a good thing?"

"It is a great honor," replied Uramettu.

"Can you do it at will?"

"Yes, but it is best if I do it fewer than four times per moon. It is easier to become a cat than to return to human form. The call of blood is powerful; the grip of Ronta so strong. Only once have I ever changed more than four times between moons."

This remark cried out for explanation. "When?" Jadira blurted.

"For the sultana," said Uramettu. "She . . . insisted."

"What happened?"

"I brought down a Zimoran bull and devoured it for the edification of Her Magnificence. The taste of blood was still with me, and I feared I would not be able to make the transformation to woman. My panther body lay in the cage for a day and a night as the change slowly took place. It was more painful than anything I'd ever borne before or since."

They ate in silence for a time. "What will you do once we get to Tantuffa?" Jadira asked.

"Find a way home. The slavers who sold me in the Brazen Ring never expect me to return, but when I do . . ." She opened her mouth wide and engulfed a large gob of yogurt.

"I wonder," Jadira said, taking the jar again, "if people can change to animals, do animals ever change into people?"

"Oh, yes," Uramettu said.

"I believe it, for I have seen jackals who walk and talk like men." She peered into the half-empty jar. "You know, this isn't so bad."

"Indeed. You and I will end by carrying our delicate male companions. Mark it, friend Jadira; it will come to pass."

The men looked up from where they sat and wondered what the two women could find to laugh at in this awful desert.

* * * * *

Captain Fu'ad clenched his teeth in futile anger. Two days out of Omerabad on the road to Rehajid, and this was the third major caravan the Invincibles had overtaken and stopped. The caravan master knew better than to protest, but his obvious evasiveness made Fu'ad's task all the harder. Already the troopers had found secreted bales of silk, jewels hidden in water gourds, and slaves not wearing owner's bracelets. All this to avoid the sultan's taxes, and in the current situation, Fu'ad could do nothing about it.

The caravan master approached, his tiny turban perched atop his broad face. "Is there anything else the excellent captain would care to see?" he said.

"I've seen quite enough," snapped Fu'ad.

"Then we may continue on, worthy sir?"

"When I give you leave!" The caravan master bowed deeply and rubbed his hands on his robe. He bowed and backed away, finally turning and shouting something harsh to his teamsters in his native dialect.

Marad rode to his commander. "There is no sign of the prisoners," he said. "No one in the party has seen them either, sir."

"Or no one *admits* seeing them," Fu'ad said in a low voice.

"Yes, sir."

Marad lingered, waiting for his captain's next order. Fu'ad surveyed the milling pack of horses, donkeys, camels, and men. "Where are they, my brother?" he said. "How could four people on foot have outdistanced us?"

"Perhaps they were disguised in one of the earlier caravans we searched," offered Marad.

"No, I cannot believe that. They are a distinctive band: a yellow-haired man, a nomad woman, a Fedushite woman, and a priest with a bare poll. No disguise in the world could shield them from me."

A donkey brayed and bucked when a heavy basket of trade goods was piled on its back. The driver clucked and whirred his tongue to calm the beast, to no effect. The wicker hamper fell to the ground and burst open, spilling beads and brass bangles on the road.

"Set these buffoons on their way," Fu'ad said. "We'll waste no more time with them."

"Very good, sir. What is our destination, if I may ask?" said Marad.

Fu'ad squinted into the setting sun. "We go on to Rehajid."

Two columns of Invincibles swung into their saddles in unison. Their peaked helmets blazed like torches and the dying wind billowed their cloaks. The caravan cleared the road to allow the lancers to pass. The Faziris looked ahead to the blood-hued horizon.

* * * * *

"I don't believe there is an oasis," Nabul said. His robes were undone and trailed forlornly behind him in the dirt.

"Oh, be still. All you do is complain," said Uramettu.

"How much farther do you think it is to Julli?" asked Marix.

"Two, three leagues," said Jadira.

"So far? I thought we'd come at least twenty from Omerabad."

"Omerabad," sighed Nabul. "Meat. Bread. *Wine*." Uramettu poked him with the butt end of her spear.

"The desert of the Red Sands misleads you," Jadira said. "One walks and walks and walks, and it seems you've surely reached the edge of the world. But I've kept count of our steps, and we've walked no more than seven leagues."

"At least the air is cooling," said Tamakh.

"It will get cooler still. By false dawn tomorrow, our breath will be mist."

Marix hitched the Faziri breastplate up from his narrow hips. "I've always wanted to see the edge of the world," he said. He picked up the pace, and the rest fell in line behind him.

They topped a long ridge of blown sand. The sun was sinking fast, and the west wind had awakened. Jadira loosened her headdress, then shook her hair and lifted it off her damp neck.

Marix looked into the setting sun. "Now I understand why these are called the Red Sands. The ground looks like it is made of new copper."

"Or blood," said Nabul glumly.

A notch past sunset, stars began to appear. Tamakh hailed his first glimpse of the Fire Star.

"There's Agma's Daughter," he said.

"In Dosen, we call that star the Wanderer, as it meanders across heaven in a yearly course," said Marix. "What do your people call it, Jadira?"

"Just 'Fire Star.' Our elders mark the seasons by it, and others, by methods kept secret, divine the future from its movements."

Nabul twisted his head to see the much-discussed star. As he did, he lost sight of his floppy robe. He tripped on the front hem and pitched forward. Rolling down the dune, he bowled over Tamakh. The two tumbled face-over-fundament past Marix, past Jadira, down the slope until they smacked bottom and came to rest in a spray of dust.

Marix jumped off the horse. Uramettu and Jadira skidded down the dune to help their fallen comrades. Nabul, as usual, had ended up underneath Tamakh. The portly cleric had his head buried in the sand like an ostrich. Nabul's feet gyrated wildly beneath him.

Uramettu lifted Tamakh off. He rubbed his eyes and spat sand while Uramettu tried to dust him off with his own scalp lock. Jadira dropped on her knees by the half-buried Nabul and dug. The thief popped out like a rat from a hot hole.

"Father of pig-eating dogs!" he cried. "I've had more than I can bear. Do you hear me, you Thirty Gods? More than I can bear!"

"Calm yourself, Master Thief. You've gained no lasting hurt," said Jadira.

"No lasting—! You may love breathing sand, you desert wench, but Nabul *gan* Zeliriya does not! I'm going back! Nothing the soldiers do to me could be as bad as this!"

"You can't go back to the city. You would be killed on sight."

"Maybe I wasn't identified. Have you ever considered that, clever woman? And even if I were captured, I'd explain what happened—"

"Of course you will. I hear the grand vizier is a very sympathetic fellow," Tamakh said.

Nabul smote the dirt with his fists. "It's not just! Why did the god of thieves steer you across my path? I never asked for much from life: a cup of wine, a bowl of dates, a fat merchant to pluck now and then. . . . What evil curse brought us together?"

"Who can know the minds of the gods?" said

Tamakh. "It remains for us mortals to accept our fate and live our lives within the patterns set for us. To contemplate otherwise is to court madness."

"The Holy One speaks wisely, though I would add that tyranny is not to be borne. The whole man is one who is free," said Jadira.

"Don't forget duty and honor," put in Marix.

Nabul scratched sand from his patchy beard. "You're all mad," he said. "Your mad beliefs will be the death of us all."

Jadira offered the thief her hand. Nabul glared at it. "Take it," she said. "Take it and go on with us to Julli. Once there, if you can find a caravan to Rehajid or Zimora, then part in peace."

His mouth was too dry to spit. The practical Nabul grasped her hand.

* * * * *

As Jadira promised, night in the deep desert grew colder with each passing hour. As stars thickened to a dense canopy overhead, Tamakh took a reading of their position. He lay flat on his back, aligning his feet to the north star. That way he was able to tell which way was north-by-west.

Jadira rested her head on her knees. She drew the trailing part of her robe close around her legs and shivered. Next thing she knew, Marix sat down beside her, draping his Faziri cloak around her shoulders.

"No," she said. "You need this yourself."

Through blue lips he bluffed, "I am used to chill. In Dosen we have snow for six turnings of the moon each year." He shivered and feigned a chuckle to cover it.

"What is snow?"

"Snow is, uh, very cold rain. So cold it is white and solid."

"You sport with me. Water is not solid."

Marix put a hand on his heart. "By my ancestors, I swear I speak the truth."

A sharp breeze whisked the cloak from Jadira's shoulders. He replaced it, letting his arm linger across her back. While Tamakh explained the desert sky to Uramettu and Nabul stamped his feet to keep them warm, Jadira leaned her head on Marix's shoulder and drifted off to sleep.

The thief roused her a short time later. "The priest says we should go."

Marix yawned. "Is there any water?" he asked.

"Not a single drop. And the horse is making odd sounds."

The horse was standing with its knees together. Dry grunts puffed out its open mouth. Jadira lifted the beast's head and pried its teeth apart.

"This is not good; the tongue is swollen. If we don't find water soon, the horse will die," she said.

Marix cajoled everyone into line again. In spite of the hardship, he was in good spirits. Now that the imminent dangers of the city were behind him, he had begun to enjoy this new adventure.

He hummed a marching song, punctuating the beat by striking the ground smartly with the heels of his boots. His pace proved too much for Tamakh, who dropped back with Nabul.

Marix marched in place four beats and fell in beside Jadira. She smiled at his martial air.

"What is that song?" she said.

"This? 'The Company of Bren.' It's about a free company of men-at-arms who worked in the Eight Provinces in the time of King Barrus II."

"I didn't realize you were a soldier."

"Oh, aye. All noblemen's sons learn arms," he replied. "My eldest brother, who will be count one day, is a battle captain to Prince Lydon, and my middle brother is a knight."

"And what have you been trained for?"

"I was to be a man-at-arms, had I reached Lord Hurgold as planned."

Jadira lowered her voice. "When we find Prince Lydon's seal, Lord Hurgold will make you a knight."

His face shone. "Do you think so? I—"

"AAIII!" The thief was shouting. Where the fine, dry sand had given way to crumbling shale, the ailing horse had stumbled in the loose rock and was down.

"Get him up," Uramettu was saying. "Once down, they quickly die!"

Nabul tugged on the bridle. "Stand, you wretched animal! Don't you dare die!"

Tamakh came over. His ragged sandals had been cut to shreds by the rocks. "Will it be all right?" It was then Jadira noticed how drawn his formerly sleek face had grown.

The horse kicked feebly. Uramettu said to Tamakh, "Can you do something?"

"I have no knowledge of horses," he said sadly, shaking his head.

It was soon over. The poor beast gave its last gasp and was still. The five stood around it, saying nothing for a long time.

"This is the fate that faces us all," Nabul pronounced.

"When we get to Julli—"

The thief howled and grabbed for Jadira's throat. She clawed at his face and hands, and Marix wrenched

Nabul's arms back.

"We'll never get to the oasis!" Nabul cried. "It doesn't exist! We're going to wander around out here until the sun bakes us into hard red bricks! How will you lead a band of bricks, O wise desert-dweller?"

Jadira bent over slowly and scooped up a handful of pebbles, which she flung at Nabul. "Rocks, you alley-rat! Do you know what that means? Where there are rocks in the desert, there is water. Julli is near, I tell you!" she exclaimed.

"We could have walked past it in the dark and never known it!"

Uramettu put a strong hand on Jadira's arm and said, "He's right. He may be an uncouth scoundrel, but he is right. Now that the horse is dead, do we have any chance at all to reach this oasis?"

Before Jadira could answer, the eastern horizon flashed red. "False dawn," the nomad woman said. "Only one notch of darkness left. I will make you all a bargain: I will scout ahead for signs of Julli. If I am not back by sunrise . . ." She finished the offer with a shrug. "Let everyone thereafter fend for himself."

Jadira knelt to unhook the empty waterskins from the dead horse's saddle.

"I'm coming with you," Marix said.

"No." She stood and looped the handles of the waterskins around her own neck. Looking into his concerned, pale eyes, she smiled and said, "I'll be back."

She started off in the presumed direction. Uramettu came after her. "I will go with you. I can smell water a league away."

Jadira shook her head. "I must do this alone." Softly she added, "You must keep them together, Uramettu. Men have no heads for journeying."

"As you wish, my sister. Ronta go with you and guide your steps."

The rocks made the way treacherous. Twice Jadira slipped on the uneven surface and scored her hands and knees on sharp stones. At the top of a low hill, she turned and looked back. Tamakh's white robe stood out in the blue-black night. She waved. Jadira could not see if anyone returned the gesture.

She walked northwest, always keeping the star Qalax dead in front of her. Tamakh had assured her this would keep her on a straight course.

The hillocks flattened, but the soil remained stony. By the time Jadira had walked half a notch, the eastern sky was lightening. She hurried her aching legs on. But fear and need tangled her normally quick limbs, and she fell heavily on her face.

Jadira knew she had failed. They were lost, lost in the vast Red Sands, and they would die. Her vaunted Sudiin heritage had not helped them a bit. And the worst thing was that that whining, city-soft thief would be right.

She unclenched her burning eyelids and caught a single cold tear on her fingertips. One drop of water. One lone salty drop.

She stared at the tear . . . and saw *moss on the stones*.

Jadira picked up a rock that was spotted with gray-green moss and pressed it to her heart as if it were finest gold. Moss meant water! Somewhere near, there was water!

Her long shadow reached out four paces ahead of her as she stood. The last breaths of night wind brought her a scent she knew well.

"Water," she said aloud. "Water and camels." She hurried on, racing with her giant shadow. She ran, feet lifting off the stony ground with the ease of one reborn.

The jingle of brass on camel harnesses, the bawl of contrary animals rose out of the ground. Jadira ran right to the edge of a sharp drop-off. From there, the copper-colored desert turned green—green as far as her parched eyes could see.

The disc of the sun lifted from its purple bed of sleep and shone brightly on Julli Oasis and Jadira *sed* Ifrimiya.

❖ 7 ❖

Julli

The fugitives sat on a rise at the edge of the oasis and looked over their destination. "Any sign of Faziri soldiers?" asked Marix.

"No obvious ones." Tamakh shaded his eyes and looked around. "I had no idea the place was so large. One, two, three wells, and a lake? It looks like a town with caravans and tents—and *so many* people! I imagined a muddy pool and a stand of palms."

"Oh, no. Julli is famous for its water and abundant fodder," said Jadira. "In olden times, it was the custom of each caravan to plant a tree or bush here when they arrived. After a century, the practice had to stop; there wasn't enough land to support so many plants."

"What does 'Julli' mean in your language?" asked Uramettu.

Jadira swept her arm around the ridge. "Do you see how the entire oasis is sited in this sunken area? 'Julli' means 'navel'."

"Enough prattle," said Nabul. "I'm going down there!" For once there was no dissension.

Being ragged, dirty, and on foot, they gathered a few curious stares, but no one challenged them. The crowds were thickest around the wells, so they went straight to the bean-shaped lake. Camels and horses looked on stolidly as, one by one, the fugitives threw themselves into the water.

"Have you ever tasted anything so wonderful?" exulted Marix. Jadira laughed and ducked him. He came up spouting and returned the favor. Tamakh waded in knee-deep and sat down. His toga floated out across the surface, making him look like a dirty white water lily.

Uramettu went in only shin-deep. She splashed her arms and face, then returned to the shore to watch the others sport. Marix and Jadira joined her after thoroughly soaking themselves and feeling their parched skin begin to breathe again.

"Where's Nabul?" Marix said, shaking himself like a foxhound.

"Filling his belly, no doubt, or searching for someone to rob," Jadira said. She pulled her sodden, cloth-wrapped hair over her shoulder and began wringing the water out of it.

"I saw him near the camels wearing the black harness fringe," Uramettu noted.

"Zimoran traders," Jadira said. "Most likely bound for Rehajid. Nabul must be trying to talk his way into the caravan."

"Good luck and good riddance," said Marix fervently.

A concerted cry of "*Hai-ai-ai!*" rang across the oasis. A band of men on horseback, wearing red and white burnooses, galloped past the lake. Jadira chewed her lip as she watched them ride up to one of the wells.

"Do you know them?" said Marix.

"Fellow nomads," she said. "The Aqir tribe. I know

their chief."

"Would he help us?"

Jadira hastily arranged her headdress and pulled the damp trailing end of her robe between her legs and tucked it into the sash around her waist. "Stay here," she said to her friends.

The Aqir riders were clustered around the Well of Hearts. There, another group of nomads, coarsely bearded men with metal gorgets around their throats, waited for their turn at the water. These were the Bershak. They were not known to be friends of the Sudiin.

Jadira slipped between the Aqir ponies until she reached the stone-walled well. A squat, one-eyed man, his face tanned to the color and texture of old leather, stood on the wall drinking from an elaborate silver cup.

"Hail, Yali Mit'ai!" said Jadira eagerly.

The cup swung down, and a single yellowed eye fixed on her. Keen intelligence showed behind that ancient orb.

"Who are you, woman, and why do you accost me like a bead-seller?" said Yali Mit'ai sternly.

"Forgive me, Yali." She touched her forehead in the gesture of respect. "I am Jadira, daughter of Ifrim, Sudiin of Sudiin."

The Yali of Aqir jumped down from the wall. He was half a body shorter than Jadira, and a whole body wider. It was said that Mit'ai had some dwarvish blood.

"Sudiin, eh?" he said. "When I was at Topoktoroci, I saw none of the Sudiin. Since then, I have heard that the sultan's men had killed or enslaved them all."

"It is true, Yali. May flies infest his nostrils! For all I know, I am the only Sudiin on the desert now."

Mit'ai held out the cup. Jadira took it and drank. There was more than water in it; strong-sweet wine flowed down her throat and splashed warmly into her empty stomach.

"A tribeless woman," said Mit'ai. "A Sudiin without Sudiin. Is this the kindness of the gods, that they allow the pig-eating sultan to sweep an entire tribe off the Red Sands?"

She gave him back his cup. "I cannot say, Yali. The gods were kind enough to grant me escape from the sultan's own dungeon. I am here with four others, all fugitives from Faziri tyranny."

"You escaped from Omerabad? This tale I must hear. You will come to my circle tonight, Jadira *sed* Ifrimiya."

She touched her forehead in agreement. "With my companions?"

"Yes, bring them all. Such a band of worthies should be feasted for their deeds," said the chieftain.

"Thank you, Yali. Mitaali bless your generosity."

Mit'ai waddled to his mount. The short-legged pony had extra long stirrups to allow the little chief to gain his saddle unaided. Swinging up, Yali Mit'ai tossed his silver cup to one of his many sons.

"One notch after sunset, you will come," he said. He reined about and led the shouting Aqir away.

Jadira started back to the lake. The Bershak men who had waited for the Aqir to drink followed her with their eyes.

* * * * *

Captain Fu'ad led two troops of Invincibles through the gates of Rehajid. They had been ten days on the road, having stopped and searched with minute care every caravan and donkey train they met. Dust was thick on Fu'ad's tongue, and his failure to find the escaped prisoners was heavy on his mind.

The sultan's governor, Satrap Mobani, received the imperial cavalry surrounded by his entire retinue. A quartet of pipers, followed by two Fedushite drummers, played a military tune as the roadworn troopers filed into the city square. Mobani strolled with sedate majesty under a canopy of cloth of gold, borne at each corner by a thick-armed slave. The governor was as tall as Fu'ad but enormously fat. His dark eyes shone like amber through the smoothness of his round face. A beatific smile curved his fleshy lips. Mobani's robes were of the purest white satin, and a brilliant blue sash stretched itself taut around his prodigious girth. He bowed to the captain, causing the ends of his sash to drop into the dust.

"Greetings, Esteemed Warrior!" he declaimed. "Rehajid is honored by your most awesome presence."

"Thank you, Excellency. It is good to be off the road. Will you see to the care of my men and horses?" requested Fu'ad.

"At once, Flower of Fazir." The satrap clapped his flabby hands, and a gang of attendants trotted out to take the horsemen's bridles.

Fu'ad dismounted and pulled off his mail gauntlets. A slave girl appeared, bearing a golden bowl of rosewater. Fu'ad dipped his hands in the sweet-smelling liquid and rinsed away the dirt of many leagues. He held them, dripping, wondering where a towel might be.

"Use my robe, lord," murmured the slave girl. Fu'ad shrugged and dried his hands on the loose cloth of the girl's sleeve. He enjoyed the glimpse he had of her well-shaped brown shoulder.

"If the Valiant Captain will follow me?" Mobani said with a sweep of his arm.

"Marad? Marad!" Fu'ad called. His lieutenant ran to

his side.

"Yes, sir?"

"See to the quartering of the men. I'll be with the satrap."

"Very good, sir."

Mobani sank into a large litter, thickly gilded and elaborately curtained. Six bearers grunted, lifting the fat official to their broad shoulders. A second, less-decorated chair awaited Fu'ad. Unbuckling his sword, he placed the sheathed blade across his lap. The bearers carried his litter alongside the satrap so that the two men might converse along the way.

"I received a dispatch from our revered Emir Azrel, Noble Horseman, concerning the miserable scum who dared escape from the dungeon of the sultan—may he live forever! No one of their description has entered Rehajid in the past changing of the moon," Mobani said. He opened the lid of a small compartment in the arm of the litter. Delicately, so as not to damage his long pearled nails, the satrap picked a shelled nut from the compartment.

"*Quabba* nut?" he said, offering Fu'ad the first one.

"No, thank you." Fu'ad smote his knee with one hard fist. "Dutu take them! They can't have vanished like the moon-thief of legend."

"Perhaps, Pillar of Manhood, the wretched villains never came in this direction? After all, my reputation as a vigorous enforcer of the sultan's law—may he live forever!—is widely and justly feared."

"I begin to believe it is so. But where else could they have gone? The signs are clear that they left the city by the Rehajid road, yet past ten leagues there was no trace of them. They might have taken to wing for all we found."

"Could they have left the road?" asked Mobani.

"To go where?"

"Where the road is not, Peerless Fighter."

Fu'ad leaned closer to the satrap. The litter-bearers staggered with the off-center burden and nearly collided with Mobani's conveyance. "You're not suggesting, Excellency," he said with a slight sneer, "that the fools went into the desert?"

"Halt, you louts!" Mobani said sharply. They had arrived at the residence of the imperial governor. The bearers first lowered the satrap, then the captain to the ground. A row of petty officials and palace functionaries stood waiting for their master. They bowed repeatedly, their gold turbans and gauzy coats flashing in the sun.

"Away, away," said Mobani, making a brushing gesture, and they scampered back up the wide staircase into the palace.

The satrap led Fu'ad up the staircase and through the outer hall, past the court where he dispensed the sultan's justice, to an airy, columned suite of rooms on the north side of the building. It was cool there. Fu'ad noticed, smiling, that large striped awnings wafted back and forth, stirring the air. Somewhere, whole gangs of slaves were engaged turning cranks or pulling ropes to power the satrap's artificial breeze.

"Wah, I am done in!" Mobani exclaimed breathlessly. He fell heavily on a vast mound of pillows and lay limply for a moment, staring at the ceiling. "Such exertions I make! But it is all part of duty, is it not, Lord of Battle?"

Fu'ad grunted a vague affirmative and cast about for a decent chair. The satrap apparently didn't believe in sitting when he could recline. Finally, Fu'ad sat cross-legged on the mirror-finished marble floor.

"I have been considering your remarkable notion,

Excellency," he said thoughtfully. "I suppose the miscreants could have left the road before reaching Rehajid."

"Then your task is done, Terror of the World, for the squealing gutter rats are dead. None but scorpions and witless nomads can survive in the Red Sands."

"One of the prisoners was a nomad woman, one of the Sudiin."

"Ah, the Sudiin! That tribe inhabits the desert as fish inhabit the sea," said Mobani. He sighed, sending small tremors through his abundant jowls. "Then they may yet live. Assuming the maggot-infested beggars still breathe, how may I, a humble servant of His Magnificence, aid you in your righteous quest?"

"I shall need to draw supplies from the imperial stores," Fu'ad said. "Food, water, fresh horses."

"All I have is yours, Gracious Swordsman." Mobani loosened his straining collar. He reached back into the ocean of cushions and produced a large water pipe, formed to resemble a hooded cobra. "A pipe?" he said, offering one of the jeweled mouthpieces to Fu'ad.

"No. It clouds the mind."

Mobani winked one porcine eye and shouted for fire. A small servant boy came running with a brazier.

Fu'ad pressed his knuckles to his chin as he thought. His nostrils filled with the aroma of roses. He remembered the slave girl with the smooth brown shoulders. No, no, he chided himself; duty, Captain. Duty first.

The satrap was blabbering at him again. "Excuse my impudent interruption of your contemplative moment," Mobani said, "but would the Vigorous Lancer care to remain in this, my lowly residence, for the night? We shall spare no effort for your comfort."

Fu'ad surveyed the satrap's gaudy raiment, his multitude of rings, and his sparkling palace and wondered what Mobani would consider opulent. "No, Excellency. Your offer is very kind, but I always barrack with my men."

"I understand; the comradeship of arms, the brotherhood of warriors, is sacred to a man like you. Ah, would that the sultan—may he live forever!—appoint me to the army. By his mercy, I envy you!"

Fu'ad tried to imagine mounds of satrap stuffed into a lancer's coat of mail, but could not. He rose and said, "I will take my leave of you now, Excellency. The only other service I would ask of you is to send a rider back to Omerabad with a complete account of our conversation. You may also communicate my intentions to the Emir Azrel."

The vizier's name brought fear to Mobani's face. "What *are* your intentions, First Among Invincibles?"

"I shall enter the desert," said Fu'ad simply.

* * * * *

A bonfire burned in the midst of the Aqir camp. The penalties were severe for bringing the touch of flame to the grass and soil of Julli; the Aqir's bonfire burned in a bronze dish, three paces wide. It had ten bronze legs to support it, each one molded to resemble the foot of some desert animal. The dish was so big and so prized by the Aqir that one camel was devoted to carrying it and nothing else.

Jadira and her companions—except Nabul, who was elsewhere—sat on Yali Mit'ai's favored side. They ate from the chief's own pot, and passed the communal wine cup. Jadira noticed that the wine was much stronger than it had been at the well. Less water was being used to dilute the spirits. Mit'ai was being generous.

The Aqir's guests told their stories. First Jadira, then Tamakh, then Marix. Without hesitation (or perhaps loosened by Mit'ai's good cup), Marix described his personal quest to recover the seal of Prince Lydon. The others heard his story for the first time. The words poured out before Jadira could caution Marix.

"And if you find this seal, what then?" said Yali Mit'ai.

"Why, then I'll go to Tantuffa-fa and deliver it to Lord Hurg-Hurgold," said Marix.

"What will come of it? Will you be rewarded? Will this outlander lord fill your pockets with gold?"

"Gold?" said Marix contemptuously. "A gemmulman does not do a deed o' honor for gold!" He belched. "'Tis my duty to fullafill my charge to Sir— Sir—what his name was. And so doing I also get to shpit in the eye of the Sultan o' Fazir!"

The Aqir rumbled with approval. Yali signed for quiet. "May all your foreign gods go with you. The sea is a long and dangerous journey from here," he said.

Tamakh leaned close to Jadira. "I don't remember hearing about this seal."

"There was no time for telling," she whispered.

The Yali then turned to Uramettu. "Many times have I met men of your race in the cities of the Brazen Ring, but never have I met a Fedushite this far north."

"It was not by choice that I find myself here, Honored Chief. I was netted in the forest of my country and sold by Brazen Ring slavers. They, in turn, sold me to the sultan's Procurer of Entertainments. I languished in captivity for half a year before my desert sister and her companions freed me," said Uramettu.

The Yali ordered his chest of treasure brought out. Four Aqiri, their naked swords flashing red in the firelight, carried a large cedarwood box before the chief. The hasp was closed with a white wax seal, Mit'ai's personal insignia. Mit'ai kept the signet on a thong around his neck. He broke the seal and let the lid fall back with a bang.

Mit'ai liked jewels; that was obvious. Scattered through the treasure were gods' tears (diamonds), cat's eye rubies, amethysts, peridots, sapphires, opals, and pearls . . . floating crystal islands in a sea of gold coins. Mit'ai swirled his hand into the gorgeous hoard and came up with a fistful of treasure. He poured this in a heap in front of Jadira.

"Oil, says the poet, smoothes the axle, but gold smoothes the road," he said.

"Yali, you are too generous!" Jadira said.

"Your uncle Hemmet once saved me from a pair of cobras, when I was but a boy. Mit'ai remembers, and repays his debt to the last of the Sudiin." He clapped his hands. "The tales are done! Let there be merriment!" A frightful squealing of pipes arose, and the dancing began.

Jadira bundled the treasure into her robe, and, with her three companions, moved away from the firepan to examine their windfall. Yali Mit'ai did not have a large hand, but he had managed to grasp three Faziri gold piastres, a square Zimoran silver crown, a rough amethyst, and most remarkably, a Tantuffan mark made of electrum.

"We can buy many supplies with this," Jadira said. "Perhaps even a camel."

Uramettu looked around uncertainly. "It does not feel right," she said. "So many people coming and going. The thief is out there, too. We should keep close watch tonight."

"Absholutely," agreed Marix, swaying slightly on his feet.

"I think I'd best walk his lordship around and sober him up," Jadira said.

"I will do it," offered Tamakh.

"No, stay with Uramettu and guard the gold. We'll be back when Marix can walk a rope on the sand."

Truth was, Jadira was feeling a little lightheaded herself. She looped Marix's arm in hers and walked briskly away. Once out of their friends' sight, she stopped. She spun Marix around to face her.

"You are such a young fool!" she hissed.

"Wha'? Why d'you say that?"

"Telling everyone in earshot about the seal! Don't you know that half these people will end up in Rehajid or Omerabad before the moon turns again? What do you think they'll talk about once they're there? Of the prisoners who foiled the sultan's designs, *and the seal they sought to recover!*"

Marix blinked. "By my ancestors," he said faintly.

"Your ancestors indeed! The sultan has a thousand ears in every bazaar. If word reaches them in time, we may find the entire imperial army waiting for us in Kaipur," Jadira said hotly.

Marix leaned one arm against a palm tree. He buried his face in his sleeve. Soon Jadira heard sobbing.

"Ah, now then," she said, embarrassed. "You needn't take it so hard. At your age, you can't be used to wine."

"I am undone!" he said with genuine anguish. "I have betrayed my trust!" Marix grabbed the hilt of his sword. "I ought—"

There was a crash, and a mighty metallic clang from the Aqir camp. The music faded with a discordant shriek, and Jadira saw a knot of men struggling near the fire.

"Come on," she said, and Marix quickly forgot his despair.

They ran to the firepan and found Nabul, the thief, firmly in the hands of a half-dozen nomads. The bronze dish had been upset, and a pile of glowing coals sizzled on the green turf of Julli.

"Hang the swine! Hang him!" some Aqir were shouting.

"Fire-spiller!" cried others.

"What happened?" Jadira asked.

The Yali Mit'ai appeared between two tall nomad women. "What is this disturbance?" he roared.

"Noble Yali, this pig-Faziri has overturned the firepan," said one Aqiri holding Nabul. Other Aqiri were busy snuffing the flames and trying to replace the coals in the prized bronze dish.

"I know this man," Jadira said. "He is the cutpurse we spoke of. He helped us escape from Omerabad."

"This one?" said Mit'ai. He walked up to Nabul. The Aqiri forced the thief to his knees, so that the chief might look him in the eye. "Faziri," said Mit'ai, "the law of Julli decrees that fire-spilling is the worst crime a man can commit here. The penalty is death by hanging."

"No!" Nabul protested.

"Be silent!" Mit'ai commanded.

"It was an accident! I tripped—!" Nabul exclaimed, fear in his voice.

"Don't whine, man!" Mit'ai nodded to his men. They dragged Nabul away.

"What will happen now?" said Marix, wide-eyed.

"For now he will be held in the pigeon pens," said the

Yali. "On the morrow, he will hang from the Julli posts."
He referred to the stone pillars, very ancient, that stood
in a circle at the heart of the oasis.

Another question formed on Marix's lips, but Jadira
put a hand over his mouth and steered him away. She
kept his mouth covered until they rejoined Tamakh and
Uramettu. The priest was snoring softly. The woman had
her back against a tree, her hands nestled between her
knees. She was the panther in repose, alert, watchful.

"There was a disturbance," she said.

"Yes. Nabul managed to overturn the Aqiri's firepan," said Jadira. Marix said "Umma-mm-mm" and she
dropped her hand from his mouth.

"We can't let them hang Nabul for tripping!" he
said.

"Hang?" said Uramettu.

"It is a difficult matter," said Jadira. "Nabul did give
us aid, but it would be very bad to offend the Yali Mit'ai
after his generosity to us." She dropped down beside the
sleeping priest. "And Nabul *did* overturn the dish and
spill fire on Julli."

"An accident," insisted Marix. "For once he did not
act from malice."

Jadira chewed her lower lip. "I know."

Tamakh caught a snore in his nose and snorted loudly.
Jadira looked down at him and after a few seconds her
expression softened. "Wake up, Holy One," she said.

Tamakh sniffed and yawned, opening his eyes. "It's a
very dark morning."

"It's still night. We need your help."

"What help?"

"Magic," Jadira said.

"What magic?"

"Nabul is in danger. Can you work your magic so that

he doesn't hang?"

"Eyah! Do you think I am King Tozra, that I can clap my hands and my will is done? What small things I can do are all part of my holy orders." He paused. "Who's hanging the thief, and why?" Jadira explained in a few words. "You surprise me, Jadira; you also, Marix. I would have thought you would be glad to see Nabul on the end of a rope."

Jadira looked surprised herself. "He vexes me very much, but I do not wish his death."

"Nor do I," said Marix. "No man should die merely for clumsiness—not after a life of worse sorts of wickedness."

"What exactly are the 'small things' you can do?" asked Jadira.

"The working of iron, the making of fire, summoning certain primitive spirits subservient to the will of Agma—"

"Is that all?"

The pudgy cleric drew himself up and replied, "I told you: I am *not* a vulgar sorcerer."

"Well, I hope it will be enough. Come with me; you too, Uramettu," Jadira said.

"Where are we going?" asked the Fedush woman, rising.

"To find an ironmonger."

8

Scorpion Rock

Morning, and Julli was alive with men and animals forming into caravans, ready to depart for points east and south. A team of camels, a cow, and three yearlings trotted by the sleeping companions. A Nuzi tribesman chased after them, calling maledictions. His whip cracked in vain.

Marix rubbed the sleep of just two notches from his eyes. They had worked long past midnight at the pillars, setting the stage for Jadira's plan. Even Tamakh chuckled over it when they were done. Now, from a copse twenty paces away, the companions awaited the Aqir and the doomed prisoner.

They were not long coming. Poor miserable Nabul, a pole thrust under his arms and his elbows pinioned together behind his back, stumbled ahead of Yali Mit'ai's squat little pony. He was gagged to prevent him cursing his executioners with evil fates.

"Hold!" cried Mit'ai. The mounted Aqiri milled to a stop. Two of them dismounted and grabbed Nabul's pole. They hustled the thief forward to the stone columns.

There were sixteen pillars. Some had fallen in the dim past, others had cracked, leaving only stumps standing. The columns were deeply grooved with spiral lines, which ran up the pillars to the flat, drum-shaped capitals. Hard wooden beams usually remained in the sockets between the capitals, but this morning, there were none.

The Yali squinted into the bright blue sky. "What sort of foolery is this?" he said. "We can't hang the dog without a cross-beam!"

A furious discussion broke out among the Aqiri over what to do. As it grew in intensity, Nabul was all but forgotten. He made a few tentative steps for freedom, but was easily caught and dragged back.

"Have they stewed long enough?" said Marix, grinning.

"Not yet," said Jadira. "A while longer, then we'll oblige them."

The Aqiri were hotly debating alternate methods of dispatching Nabul. Some wanted him dragged by horses. Some opted for beheading. One stickler for legal detail said they should build a human pyramid and hang Nabul from the top.

The companions walked from the copse toward the shouting mob. The horsemen parted for them, and they reached the Yali. Mit'ai was standing in his saddle, shouting for all he was worth.

"Be silent! BE SILENT!" he roared.

"Yali," said Jadira calmly.

"BE—! Oh, it's you. What do you want?"

"We noticed your predicament, Yali, and we've come to help." The imprisoned Nabul snapped around and gaped in disbelief.

Yali looked down at Jadira from his perch. "What do you propose?"

"Since you have no wooden beam to hang the rascal from, perhaps you could use a metal rod," she said.

"Metal? Where?"

"That one, yonder." She pointed across the circle of columns to the most distant pillar. A black rod protruded from the top. Uramettu had climbed the pillar and placed it there herself.

"Well, now, that was very sharp-eyed of you, my child." Mit'ai's smile quickly hardened. "Why do you aid us? I thought this Faziri was your friend."

"Friend? This man is no one's friend. He was useful when we needed him, O Yali , but the law of Julli is my law. The Faziri spilled fire on Julli, and he must pay for his crime," she said. Nabul chewed his gag in terror.

"All right. What are you waiting for?" Mit'ai snapped at his men. Nabul was lifted by a half-dozen worthies and carried to the rod-bearing pillar. A seventh man trailed close behind, a thick coil of rope around his slender torso.

The seventh nomad climbed the pillar, using only his fingers and toes in the shallow-cut hieroglyphs. At the top, he unhooked the rope from his waist and threw it over the rod. He looped the noose around his arms and gave a sharp cry of *Hai!* Aqiri on the ground lowered him fast, and he landed on his bare feet, grinning.

"Begin," ordered Mit'ai.

"Wait!" said Jadira. "This man"—she pointed to Tamakh—"is a priest. May he say some words of comfort to the condemned?"

The Yali scratched his beard. "I suppose, if he is quick. We must start for Zimora before mid-morn."

Jadira patted Tamakh on the back. The priest went to

the trussed-up thief and uttered a blessing. He bent close to Nabul's ear and whispered a few words, then stood back with his arms upraised. Tamakh incanted:

> Agmas copit neda!
> Copitur desram Agman,
> Copit neda!
> Agmas!
> Suden copitur desram!

Tamakh intoned the archaic words with expressive gestures of his upraised hands. Jadira tensed, wondering if the Aqir could sense the vibrations of magic in the ether. She felt it—a palpable pressure inside her head as the priest recited the formula.

Mit'ai listened to two repetitions of the incantation. Whether by heritage or by sheer impatience, he gave no sign of feeling anything unusual. He signaled his men to haul away on the rope. Nabul danced up on his toes as the rope grew taut. The Aqiri pulled hard, but the thief never left the ground. A whole circle of rope piled at the nomads' feet. The Yali shouted for them to cease. Nabul sank gratefully down on his heels.

Mit'ai looked up. The metal bar had bent under the weight in an extraordinary way. Both ends were straight and solid, but the center—where the rope was—had sagged in a limp bow, like soft bread dough. Even as the Yali looked, the center of the bar blew floppily in the breeze.

"Bajid!" he said. The slender nomad who first climbed the pillar reappeared from the crowd. "Fetch me that rod!" Mit'ai ordered. "Someone is playing us for fools!"

In a trice Bajid was back with the rod. He handed the wrist-thick metal bar to his chief. The Yali tried to bend it. The rod was solid. He braced it against his knee and grunted with effort. The metal did not change shape.

"What is this witchery?" he demanded. He gave the rod to Bajid. "What would you call this cursed thing?"

"It seems a rod of common iron," said the nomad. Jadira hid her smile behind her headdress. The Yali turned to her.

"What do you know of this?" he said.

"I, Great Chief? I am but an ignorant woman."

Tamakh cleared his throat. "If I may speak, O Yali?"

"Speak then."

"I think, Great Chief, that my god has interceded in the case of this thief."

"God? What god cares for the welfare of a sniveling Faziri pickpocket?"

"Ah, Agma does. Being a new sect, we value each and every convert," said Tamakh.

The Yali looked suspiciously from Nabul to Jadira. He stamped his foot on the iron rod and winced from the impact. Gradually a look of puzzlement replaced his frown of anger.

"He has power, this god of yours." Mit'ai scratched his ear with a blunt thumb. "Would this god Agma care to acquire some new followers?" he said almost humbly.

Tamakh spread his arms and smiled. "All are welcome."

* * * * *

"I still say you could have given me some warning," Nabul said. He was perched on a short-legged donkey. Every few steps the animal took, his toes dug in the sand.

"There wasn't time," said Uramettu. "We couldn't free you by force or negotiation, so all that remained was guile."

"Deception by magic," Jadira said vaguely. Tamakh tapped his new donkey with a switch and came alongside her.

"You are troubled," he said.

"I feel I have used the Yali ill," she replied.

"In what way? Surely we owed Nabul this favor, after he guided us out of Omerabad. And perhaps the just path of Agma will benefit the entire Aqir tribe."

Marix urged his beast forward. "It was a princely jest!" he chortled. "Imagine hoodwinking that crafty old chieftain out of his victim, and converting the nomads to the worship of Agma as well! And the look on Nabul's face when he thought we had abandoned him . . ."

"Most humorous! I'll bet you used to oil the tips of beggars' crutches," Nabul called from behind.

"Are you complaining, thief?" said Jadira over her shoulder.

"Me? Complain? What an idea!" Nabul's comrades laughed as one as they rode northwest from Julli toward the distant mountains.

* * * * *

They had bought donkeys from a trader at the oasis with the coins Mit'ai had given them. They purchased five, though Uramettu said no beast of burden would tolerate her on its back. She continued to walk, and the fifth animal was loaded with their provisions.

A day's journey north, the desert elevation rose. The wind picked up and blew steadily from the west. As Tamakh reckoned their location, they had only to travel due west to strike the southern range of the Shammat. Jadira estimated they had seventy leagues to go.

Two days out of Julli, the companions were resting in the lee of a dune when Uramettu rose from her usual crouch and began pacing the sand.

"What is it?" said Marix.

"I sense something. A presence—someone lurking nearby," she said.

Nabul drew his dagger. "The Aqiri!" he said. "They found out you tricked them!"

Uramettu adjusted the sash of her new burnoose. "I shall see just who it is," she said. Marix held out the spear to her. Uramettu shook her head.

"I won't need that," she said, and she loped off around the base of the dune.

"What do you suppose she meant?" asked Marix. His question was punctuated by the high, wavering wail of a prowling panther. The four exchanged worried looks and sat down in a close group, backs together.

The day stood still. Blown sand drifted around Tamakh's motionless feet. He scratched at the short stubble beginning to poke through the soft skin of his face. Nabul rubbed the blade of his dagger absently against a sandal strap. Marix hummed a Dosen tune. Jadira felt his shoulder on hers.

The donkeys brayed unhappily and churned around the stakes that held their reins to the ground. Then a dark form flowed over the rim of the dune, and the companions stood up.

The panther slunk toward them. She held something in her mouth, but Jadira was distracted by the smear of bright blood on Uramettu's flank. The stump of an arrow protruded from her leg.

"Uramettu!" she said, starting forward. Tamakh hooked her arm.

"Careful. Wounded, she may not react kindly to us,"

he said. "Let me approach her."

He pushed back the hood of his burnoose and walked slowly toward the injured animal. He spoke in low, soothing tones. Despite that, Uramettu bared fearsome fangs before Tamakh got within an arm's length of her.

"Beware, Holy One!" Marix said.

Tamakh knelt and put his face down to the sand. Uramettu's nose twitched. The priest inched forward, keeping his face averted. When the sunburned skin of his shaven head was just a finger's breadth away, Uramettu uttered a throaty rumble.

"It's all right," said Tamakh soothingly.

Tamakh gently removed the wad of cloth from Uramettu's mouth. It was a nomad's headdress, nut-colored with a black border. Spots of red flecked the underside.

"What do you make of this?" said Tamakh, tossing the headdress back to Jadira.

"Bershak," she said. "There were several at Julli."

"I'm going to remove the arrow," said the priest.

"She'll kill you if you hurt her!" Nabul exclaimed.

Tamakh stroked the cat's dense black fur. "I think she trusts me," he said. "Bring me wine. I want it—"

"This is no time for drinking," chided Marix.

"—to dress her wound," Tamakh finished.

"I don't think we have any wine," said Jadira.

"Yes, we do. Ask Nabul."

Nabul tried to look innocent but failed. He went to his donkey and came back with a bulging kidskin bag. "How did you know, holy man? More magic?"

"I knew you wouldn't leave Julli without the comfort of spirits," Tamakh said. He quietly backed away from the panther to his friends to get the wine. Tearing a wide strip from the bottom of his clerical toga, he edged back toward the panther.

"Dear friend," he said calmly, "be at peace and it will soon be over." Uramettu laid her head on the sand and closed her eyes. Her loud panting quieted.

Tamakh examined the wound. "It missed the bone," he announced. "It should heal cleanly enough." He soaked the bandage in dark red wine and dabbed at the drying blood. Uramettu never flinched until he took hold of the arrow and, with one quick jerk, removed it. Then she raised her head and howled, a heart-chilling cry. Tamakh swiftly wrapped the injury and splashed more wine on the bandage.

Uramettu began to quiver. Her arms and legs elongated. The thick, powerful body flattened into a slim torso. A keening screech erupted from Uramettu's throat as the bones of her skull spread apart. The heavy black coat of fur metamorphosed into ebon skin. Tamakh drew a blanket around Uramettu's canted, feminine shoulders.

"My sister," she said weakly. Jadira came to her. "My sister, a band of men on horseback is trailing us."

"Bershak. The headdress tells all," said Jadira.

"I seized one to identify, but his comrade put an arrow in me. I bit off the shaft and ran, away from our camp."

"You're very brave," said Marix.

"Why would these nomads be tracking us?" asked Tamakh. He fixed on Nabul. "Did you rob any of them?"

"How would I know?" said the thief, shrugging. "They all look alike to me."

"Bershak were present at the Well of Hearts. They must have heard Marix's story about our escape and the seal of Prince Lydon," Jadira said.

"So?" questioned Tamakh.

"So, the Bershak see an opportunity to make an easy

fortune. They capture us, sell us to the Faziris, and go off rich men."

"Base cowards," Marix said. "We will deal with them!" Out came his scimitar.

"Hold your blade," said Jadira. "The Bershak are many, and they are armed with bows."

"How many did you see?" Tamakh asked Uramettu.

The Fedushite licked her lips and said, "Two less than a score, short the one I felled."

"Too many to fight. How far off were they?"

"Less than a quarter-league."

Jadira said, "I see their plot. They seek to shadow us until we lead them to the hidden seal, then they will sweep over us like locusts. Now, unless they know Uramettu is a shape-shifter, they won't relate the attack of a wild panther to us."

"Which means?" said Nabul.

"Which means we're safe enough for a time."

"I don't like it," Marix said darkly. "Brigands dogging our heels."

Uramettu raised herself gingerly to her feet. "I say we steal up on them as they sleep and slay them."

"They'll have watchmen," Jadira reminded her. "The Bershak are masters of man-hunting, sharp-eyed and keen-eared."

"I say we take them," Marix insisted.

"It is they who will take us!" Nabul replied.

"Be still, will you? The brigands will hear your declarations in their own camp," said Tamakh. "Consider this: if we feign ignorance, the Bershak may not close with us till we reach the Kaipur plain."

His wise counsel won out, and it was agreed that they would go on as before. Marix and Jadira supported Uramettu back to the donkeys. They put her on the back of the steadiest beast. It rolled its eyes and pawed the ground, but gradually settled down as Uramettu stroked its neck and spoke gentle words in its ear.

* * * * *

The dry wind, steady as breath, uncovered all sorts of strange rock formations. Three days and two nights out of Julli, the companions camped at the base of a sculpted pile of red sandstone. The low, angular table formation swept up to a high, sharp point. Nabul and Tamakh pegged the donkeys to the rocks and joined the others on the lee side of the rock.

"That filthy wind cuts like a knife," said Marix.

"I could do with a fire," complained Nabul.

"I have a flint, but no kindling," said Jadira. Uramettu shivered beside her. She was feverish from her wound.

Tamakh rose without a word and went to the donkeys. He unstrapped a nearly empty pannier from the pack animal and dumped the remaining victuals into the next basket.

"This should burn nicely," he said. The dry wicker hamper would indeed blaze well.

Jadira felt in her sash for her flint. It wasn't there. She ran desperate fingers around her back, trying to find the precious firestone.

"My flint is lost!"

"Oh, filth!" exclaimed Marix.

"Worry not," said Tamakh. "Fire is the sacrament of my god." He set the pannier upside down against a flat section of rock wall. He held his hands, palms up, a hair's breadth from the wicker. Eyes clenched tightly shut, Tamakh moved his lips in silent concentration. After what seemed like a long time, wisps of smoke rose from the hamper. The priest slowly closed his trembling hands into fists. . . .

Crack! A flash of heat struck their faces when the pannier burst into flames. Tamakh snatched his hands away and toppled over, breathing hard. When his friends hauled him to his feet, they noticed that his robe was soaked with sweat.

"An exhausting task," he said with a sigh.

The fire crackled in the lively air. Nabul whittled strips off a haunch of dried mutton and seared these in the flames. Fat sizzled out of the meat and made the fire blaze higher.

Marix wrinkled his nose. "What is that smell?" he said.

"It's the mutton," said the thief.

Jadira made a face. "No, I smell it, too. *Ai!* It's awful!"

"I don't smell—"

The rock behind the fire cracked, sending a shower of gritty fragments over them. Everyone scrambled away, dropping whatever they were holding.

"It's getting worse!" said Marix, pinching his nose. The odor was truly sickening—an overwhelming stench of carrion.

The rock wall collapsed, burying the fire and many of their possessions. By the glow of the last scattered embers, they saw that a hole had opened in the stone wall. And within the hole, a circlet of red jewels glowed. A loud rasping issued from the hole.

"By the unholy—! Find a weapon! Find one now!" said Marix.

A claw the size of a lute pushed out of the dark aperture. It opened and closed with a metallic click. A second claw appeared, translucent red like the first. With a flurry of many legs, an articulated body covered in glistening red armor scuttled into sight.

"Scorpion! A giant scorpion!" cried Jadira.

The monster sallied out, aroused by the fire built on its nest. Its deadly tail flexed upward, a stinger as long as a man's arm oozed black poison from the tip.

The tail lashed out at the nearest target, Marix. He slashed at it with his sword, but the armored hide of the monster was too tough. Jadira, though dazed with horror, leaped in and cut at the thing's right claw. The tail plunged at her. Marix shoved her aside, and the stinger met only air.

The last bits of flame winked out, and the battle went on in darkness. Uramettu jabbed from a kneeling position with her spear; Tamakh's cudgel thumped one of the monster's red stalk-eyes. Faced with such determined resistance, the scorpion sidled around and backed away.

"It's going for the donkeys! Stop it! Kill it!"

Marix duelled with the stinger every step back to the tethered donkeys. While engaged with the monster's tail, he failed to keep track of its claws. One clamped hard on his leg. Marix screamed and fell. The tail thrust down—

—and was knocked aside by Jadira's scimitar. Tamakh pounded on the hinge of the claw, but it refused to open. Uramettu, strongest of them all, hobbled forward and thrust the spear point into the thing's palps. A gust of rancid air gushed from the monster. The claw opened, and the scorpion swung around, the spear still buried in its face.

"Nabul! Don't let it get away!" Jadira cried.

"Get away? Get away?" the thief yelled back as the battered monster scuttled toward him. He gauged the distance and let fly his dagger. The point skipped off the armored thorax and the dagger fell harmlessly aside. That was enough for Nabul. He ran. "Get away!"

The others followed behind the scorpion, hounding it with screams and blows. The stinger seemed to have a mind of its own, and it twice swished past Marix, missing by the closest of margins.

The donkeys were in paroxysms of fear. Though blinkered, they were driven mad by the sound and smell of the scorpion. The pegs came loose under their frantic prancing, and all five ran off into the night, traces jingling. Most of the group's supplies were still lashed to the back of the pack donkey. Nabul went scrambling after them.

Its easy prey gone, the scorpion rotated quickly on its jointed legs to face its foes. A fast exchange of claw-snaps and sword-cuts followed.

"How do we kill it?" Marix gasped.

Jadira parried the notched claw and ducked an overhead sweep of the tail. "I don't know!" she said desperately. "It has no throat to cut, no head to strike off!"

Clack! The monster's right claw caught Jadira's blade. She twisted the hilt to free the sword, and the blade snapped in two halfway along its length. As she stared in shock at the sword stump, the stinger bore in like a battering ram. It struck Jadira full in the chest and smashed her to the ground.

"No! No!" Marix dropped his scimitar and threw his arms around the tail. He wrestled against it, trying to withdraw it from Jadira by force. In that moment, Uramettu stepped over the engaged claw and grasped the shaft of her embedded spear. She put all her weight and strength into it. The leaf-shaped head crushed through the monster's mouth. As it gave, Uramettu twisted the shaft right and left, tearing the scorpion's soft guts to pulp. When she finished, the spear was half-buried in the stinking carcass.

Suddenly all was quiet. The monster's tail slowly relaxed and uncoiled. Marix let go and it rolled aside. Uramettu stood on her good leg, coated from neck to knees with reeking brown blood.

Tamakh took Jadira's head in his lap. Her eyes were open, but she could not speak. Uramettu asked calmly, "Is she dead?"

Tamakh put a hand to her throat. "No, but she is paralyzed."

"There must be something we can do!" Marix said.

"If the wound is deep . . ." Tamakh did not finish the statement. He didn't have to.

Uramettu knelt and began untying Jadira's sash. "Find the spot," she said. "Find it, and suck out the poison."

Jadira had worn a blanket roll across one shoulder. The stinger had gone through the thick layers of wool, but the blanket had probably saved her from instant death. By the time Uramettu uncovered Jadira's skin, she was still alive, so, obviously, the stinger had only pricked the nomad woman. Yet because of the poison within it, the wound could still prove fatal.

By the indistinct light of the stars, Uramettu found the wound, just above Jadira's navel. "A knife," she said. "Get a knife. Get a stone, a shard, *anything* sharp. Now!"

Marix found his broken scimitar. Uramettu used the snapped edge to make two deep cuts over the site of the sting. Blood oozed slowly from the cuts. Uramettu bent over, but Tamakh stopped her.

"You are wounded yourself," he said. "The poison

could kill you."

"I'll do it," said Marix. He quickly ducked in front of Uramettu and pressed his lips to the wound. He sucked, drawing in his cheeks.

"Pah!" He spat on the sand and sucked again. "Gah!" And again.

Jadira's eyes closed. Her breath caught, then settled into a shallow rhythm.

"Enough," said Uramettu, after Marix's fourth try. He coughed and turned away. Poison burned in his mouth. He crawled off a short way and was sick.

"If I were in a civilized country like Fedush, I would put a poltice of *gopi* paste on the wound," Uramettu said. "Here we will have to trust the gods to heal her."

The tinkle of brass announced the return of Nabul. He was leading three of the donkeys.

"I caught some of the scurvy beasts," he said. He halted when he saw the panorama of the dead scorpion, bloody Uramettu, and prostrate Jadira. "By the Thirty Gods! Is she all right?"

"She was stung. The strike was not a deep one, but with a scorpion of that size death is an unhappy possibility," Tamakh said. "Did you get the pack donkey?"

"No, I lost that one."

"Have we any food at all?" Uramettu asked.

"Just what each animal was carrying. The water was well divided, but the bread, dates, and cheese were lost."

Marix staggered into view. "Have you been drinking?" asked Nabul.

"Fool, he sucked the poison from Jadira's body," said Uramettu.

Nabul looked from one to another and back again. He went to Marix, who was tottering on his heels. The thief grasped the nobleman about the waist and brought him to where the others sat. The four companions stayed there the rest of the night, keeping very close and holding Jadira between them.

9

The Eye of God

Heaven to the nomads is a place of cool air and rain. There the righteous have honey and cheese to eat, and clean, sweet water flows out of the ground at a command. Jadira could taste the water. It kissed her dry lips and moistened her arid tongue.

She opened her eyes and saw a dark shape above her. "Mitaali?" she murmured.

"Alas, my godhood is still a long time off."

"Who? Marix?" The dark shape laughed gently. "I can't see you," she said.

"It is not a wonder. Until recently, the venom had you deaf, dumb, and blind."

Jadira moved her arms experimentally. Inhaling deeply, she felt a sharp stab in her stomach. She touched the hurt and through her robe felt the cut Uramettu had made.

"Never mind," said Marix, pushing her hand away. Something cold touched her cheek, and water flowed into her lips again. "How is that?"

"Divine," she said.

A second blur joined the first. "She is awake. How do you feel, my sister?"

"Sore. As if I fought twenty of the sultan's soldiers." She put out a hand. Uramettu closed her long fingers over it. "How long have I been unfeeling?" Jadira asked.

"A day and a night," said Marix. He was a bit clearer now.

"And the scorpion?"

"Dead. Uramettu gutted it like a trout."

"I thought I was dead, too."

"So you would have been had Uramettu not known what to do for you."

The black woman responded, "My brother Marix hides his own light. It was he who risked his own life to draw the vile poison from your body."

"Thank you both, my friends." Jadira looked into Marix's blue eyes. She felt his cool hand on her brow and slipped into a gray haze again. The shadows that were her friends merged into the darkness.

When next she knew, the world was blue sky and hot wind pouring over her. She seemed to be swaying in some steady rhythm, side to side. She sat up. The others had rigged a carrier out of blankets and slung it between two donkeys. Jadira grasped the stiff gray hair on the donkey's back and turned her head as far as her aching body would permit.

They were in the high desert. Unlike the lower Red Sands, between Omerabad and Julli, the high desert was completely flat. No dunes of fine, blown sand. No gullies in which to hide from the incessant east wind or the heavy lash of the sun. Her companions strode with leaden deliberation across the hard-packed earth. Uramettu limped. The cleric led the third donkey. Nabul and

Marix walked some paces ahead, their burnooses billowing out to the left in perfect sympathy.

"Hello," Jadira called. "Why doesn't someone else ride for a while?"

The others stopped and came back to surround her. "You're awake!" "You're awake!" "You're speaking!" they exclaimed together.

"Stop the donkeys, will you? I want to stand." Tamakh caught the right animal's bridle. Jadira slid off the blanket and let her feet touch the Red Sands again. A twinge ran through her, but she straightened and smiled.

"As right as new," she said. "Where are we?"

"About six leagues north of the scorpion rock," said Tamakh. "Another day's journey north, and we'll turn west for the mountains."

"Why are there only three donkeys?"

"They ran from the scorpion, but Nabul was quick enough to retake these three," said Marix.

"And the supplies?"

"Two-thirds were lost," said Nabul flatly.

Jadira moved around the donkeys' tails and stood alongside the left one. "What are you doing?" Marix asked.

"I will walk. There's no sense burdening the poor beasts any more than necessary."

"Are you strong enough?"

She pressed her palm to her wound and inhaled. "I am." The others regarded her skeptically. "Any sign of the Bershak?" Jadira asked Uramettu.

"Nothing direct. Our delay at the rock confused them, but finding the fly-infested carcass of the scorpion answered their questions, I'm sure."

They resumed the march. From time to time,

Jadira spied Marix watching her with concern. His attention pleased her for reasons she didn't fully understand.

There was more life visible in the high desert. Wisps of brown wiregrass grew out of the bricklike soil. Flies buzzed, and high above, black vultures wheeled through the cloudless sky. Nabul spotted a cobra once in time for them to give it wide berth. Two injuries were enough.

After reading the stars, Tamakh decided it was time to head west. They walked for two days with the sun rising at their backs and setting in their faces. On the morning of the third day, the incessant wind vanished.

"Wait," Jadira said sharply. "Wait for the wind." It did not resume.

"What does it mean?" asked Marix.

"A severe change, I fear. We must wait to see from what direction the wind returns. If from the north, there will be thunder, lightning, and rain such as mortals seldom see. If from the south, the dust of the low desert will rise to fill the air."

"What about the east?" said Nabul.

She shuddered. "Pestilence. Fever, boils, and death." There were no more questions.

Just before noon, the air stirred. It swirled around from all points, finally settling into a pulsing flow from the south. Hot and dry as a furnace, it made the travelers' ears hum and their skins crack.

"We must find some shelter," Jadira shouted above the rising whistle of the wind.

"Jadira's right," said Tamakh. "We'll wither like dried apples out here if we don't find cover."

"Where?" cried Nabul, gesturing toward the flat land. "Shall we burrow into the earth?" He kicked the baked dirt. "Iron mattocks could not penetrate this!" he declared.

They stumbled on. The press of wind forced them north, in order to keep the blast at their backs. Two notches past midday, Jadira felt a tug on her robe. She turned and saw Uramettu pointing into the wind.

A line of moving figures dotted the horizon. Uramettu's lips formed the word "Bershak!" but the rushing air stole the sound. It was clear what was driving the nomads into the open; several leagues behind them was a wall of brown reaching hundreds of paces up into the sky. Sandstorm. The boiling mass of airborne sand was rapidly overtaking the galloping Bershak. Jadira grabbed Nabul, who warned Marix and Tamakh.

"What can we do?" shouted the thief. The wind had risen from a shriek to a roar.

"There must be a place—somewhere—out of the wind!" called Marix.

Jadira shook her head. "I can't think of any, and we can't outrun a sandstorm!"

Tamakh put a hand in his toga and found the iron key. He shouted a prayer to Agma for help. As he did, they saw the rearmost riders in the Bershak band engulfed by the wall of sand. They disappeared.

"It's coming very fast!" Uramettu said. The little thief was plucked from his feet and blown ten paces like a rootless bush. Marix chased after him and caught the hem of his sleeve. He dragged Nabul back.

All at once, Tamakh flung his hand up and held the key over his head. Jadira blinked. She saw a bright orange halo form around the old key.

"*Agma! Namat zan!*" Tamakh cried. Down came the key to eye level. Holding it stiffly ahead of him, Tamakh began to walk.

"Where's he going?" Marix wanted to know.

"I don't know, but I think his god is helping us again!" Jadira replied.

They trailed after the priest, the four clinging tightly together and leading the donkeys. The priest marched with quick steps north by west. Nabul glanced over his shoulder. There was no sign of the Bershak, and the wall of sand blown by the storm was only half a league behind them.

Tamakh stopped moving forward, though his feet churned in place. The arm that held the key swung in a wide arc as if seeking a new direction. The orange aura dimmed until the key pointed north by northeast, then it flared brilliantly. Tamakh took off running as fast as his thick legs could carry him.

Suddenly, looming out of the amber haze, were stone columns and a tumbled-down wall. Some of the columns were so broad that Jadira and Uramettu would have been unable to join hands around them. They rose nine paces and their tops were lost in the flying sand. Their sides were polished smooth as glass. Tamakh dashed straight through the broken colonnade and vanished into the maze of ruined walls.

Marix tied the donkeys to a wall that offered shelter from the storm. The companions then set off along the covered corridor in search of Tamakh. The air thickened. Particles of dust and sand sang through gaps in the stones. Here, protected from the fury of the elements, the columns were fluted with deep grooves.

"Tamakh! Tamakh!" Jadira cried. All she got was a mouth full of dirt.

"Holy One! Where are you?" shouted Uramettu. She turned about. Taking Jadira by the shoulder, she said in the nomad woman's ear, "I've lost Marix and Nabul!"

"Where?"

"Somewhere since that last turn!"

"We'll have to go back."

They retraced their steps to an intersection of four walled corridors. The air was completely brown now, and visibility was less than arm's length. Jadira and Uramettu held hands as they moved through the murk. Neither saw the pit Jadira stepped into. All they knew was that the next second, Jadira was dangling in space at the end of Uramettu's strong arm.

Two hands spanned Jadira's waist, mindful of her injury. "It's all right," said Tamakh. "The drop is less than two paces." He dropped her gently to the ground.

Uramettu jumped into the hole after Jadira. Everyone was there.

"I thought we'd lost you for good," exclaimed Marix, hurrying to Jadira's side.

"We believed the same of you," she replied. "What is this place, Tamakh?"

"In the distant past, this was a temple," said the priest. "Come; let us withdraw into the tunnel out of reach of the storm."

They felt their way about ten paces down a dark, stone-lined passage. The howl of the storm diminished. The choking dust was thinner, but the heat was still stifling.

"I can't see a thing," Nabul complained.

Something rattled on the wall. Uramettu, who could see quite well in the dark, said, "There are torch holders on the walls. If we had a flame, we could light them."

"Tamakh, can you make a fire?" asked Jadira.

Though depleted by his exertions in locating the temple, Tamakh managed to make a spark after several minutes of concentration. A small, smoky flame began in the ancient holder. Tamakh examined the device. It was bronze, and the cup held a black, tarry substance that burned with little heat.

They found more torches and lit them from the first. The tunnel gradually came into view as a long, straight passage with a rounded roof. The walls were made of gigantic blocks of native sandstone, notched at the corners and fitted without mortar.

"How old is this place, do you think?" wondered Marix.

"Oh, twenty centuries," Tamakh mused.

"Twenty!" Nabul exclaimed.

"Maybe twenty-five. No one since the time of Tarka the Vile has lived this deep in the desert." He touched the worn wall. "There are stories, legends. . . . It is said that two thousand years ago the Red Sands were green and bountiful."

"I've heard that," said Jadira. "It was a beautiful, lush country until the gods fought over who would have dominion over the land and its people."

"And fire fell down from heaven and burned the Red Sands," finished Tamakh.

Air snapped at their torches. They closed together in a common impulse. Nabul said in a low voice, "How long do you think we'll have to stay here?"

"As long as the storm lasts," said Tamakh.

Jadira straightened her shoulders and squinted at the holy man. "How did you find this place?"

The priest smiled in a satisfied way. "I called upon Agma to shelter us from the storm. The key was my beacon. Through it, Agma drew me to this place." He put a hand out to touch the sandstone wall. "This is—or was—a sacred place."

"Well, I'm for exploring," said Marix. "Let's see what we can find."

"Not I," answered Nabul. "All you'll find here will be spiders, snakes, or worse."

"Worse?"

"Ghosts," said Tamakh, with a wink to the women. "Of course, in ancient days temples were the center of entire districts, and all manner of treasure was stored within them by the priesthoods."

Nabul's face twitched. "Treasure?"

"Oh, very likely."

"Then let us be off, young fellow! Let it never be said that Nabul *gan* Zeliriya was afraid of the dark."

Nabul took the lead down the passage. The floor had a very gradual slope, taking them deeper into the ground. The air grew cooler, and signs of moisture appeared on the floors and walls. The corridor ended at a doorway, whose top was narrower than the bottom. Slabs of broken stone clogged the doorway.

"Someone battered this down," offered Marix.

Beyond the doorway, the passage widened into a room some eight paces by ten. On the other side of the room, a very narrow opening showed, while on their right a more spacious corridor beckoned.

"Which way?" asked Jadira.

Tamakh wandered over to the far wall. His torch picked out a lattice of stone cells sunk into the wall. He thrust the light into one and recoiled quickly.

"What do you see?" hissed Nabul eagerly.

"Corpses. Very old, very dead men." He checked the next niche. A shrunken, eyeless face stared back at him.

"Nothing but mummies," he said. "Probably these were acolytes of the temple twenty centuries ago."

"Leave them," Marix said. He went to the wider passage. "Oh! Come look!"

The hall illuminated by his torch was decorated with blue and yellow tiles, as fresh and bright as when they were first installed. The hall continued beyond the reach of his light.

"Follow me!"

Marix dipped into the passage. Nabul was hard on his heels. Uramettu was about to follow when a low, scraping sound at the side of the corridor made her pause.

A thin arm, encased in dry, leathery skin, emerged from a black cell and groped blindly in the air. Mutely, Uramettu made Jadira and Tamakh look. A second pair of desiccated arms appeared.

"Temple guardians!" Tamakh said. "We've intruded on a sacred place! Run!"

They did, even as six mummified acolytes dragged themselves out of the dusty darkness and stood on legs of dry bone and rags. As the companions pounded up the passage, they called for Marix and Nabul to beware. The pair did not answer.

The harsh scraping of dead men's feet spurred them on. They came to a vertical fork in the tunnel: one ramp leading up beside another leading down. Uramettu, her huntress sense in control, naturally took the ascending path. As soon as she passed through the upper doorway, a massive block of stone slammed down, sealing the entrance. Jadira and Tamakh skidded into the obstruction.

"Back! Go back!" Jadira shrilled.

The mummies—six loathsome collections of animated skin and bones—were advancing toward them up the foot of the ramp. Their clawlike hands reached out for the desecrators.

"Tamakh! Can you magic them?" said Jadira.

"What magic? I am a priest, not—"

She shoved him off the ramp. He fell heavily to the lower path they had rejected and rolled down the incline. Jadira jumped after the priest just as the mummies' talons raked through her headdress.

The descending ramp bent right into a steep sand-choked stairwell. Tamakh was ascending on his hands and knees when Jadira caught up and dragged him forward by the neck of his toga.

Two of the mummies tumbled off the rising ramp and disintegrated into a jumble of bones. These twitched and jittered for a moment, then were still. The other four plodded around the corner. They tramped blindly through the debris of their fellows and started up the steps.

"Do you have the cudgel?" said Jadira. "Oof! How can you be so heavy after so many days in the desert?"

"Large bones," grunted Tamakh. "And the cudgel is on my donkey's back."

The steps rose to a dizzy height, becoming steeper as they went. Suddenly, the stairway was blocked by a stone wall. Jadira pounded on the unfeeling stone in vain. The mummies were twenty steps behind.

"Listen, Holy One," she whispered. "When I give the word, I want you to jump feet first at those dusty devils. The two of us ought to be able to crush them."

"No. No. We'll fall all the way down the steps. We'll be killed!" Twelve steps. The smell of ancient death wafted up from the mummies.

"Killed? By Dutu, I don't think those fellows are

coming up to kiss us!" Eight steps.

"Try the stone again!" Tamakh leaned his shoulder into the plug at the top of the stairs. Grimacing at the ache in her belly, Jadira wedged in beside him. They dug in their toes and pushed for their lives. Four steps. The shriveled hands flexed, ready to tighten on their throats.

The block suddenly split into two at its center, the two sections swinging wide apart. A deluge of storm-driven sand smashed into Jadira and Tamakh. They stumbled forward until they were outside again. Tamakh turned back to the stairwell, but Jadira yanked him aside. The mummies blundered into the storm. Whatever senses they possessed were as confused as any mortal's by the roaring, spinning mass of sand. They formed a semicircle and spread out, seeking the violators of their sanctuary.

Tamakh and Jadira ducked back into the temple through the opening they had discovered. The mummies turned after them. Jadira pulled one pivoting slab of stone inward. Tamakh grabbed the other, and the doors boomed shut before the mummies could get inside. They beat their spindly limbs on the rock, scratched with their sharp-clawed hands. The storm sandblasted them away as they pounded, eating their centuries-old flesh to finer and finer dust. The sound of their scraping grew fainter and fainter, and finally ceased.

"Praise Agma!" said Tamakh, shaking sand out of his clothes. "I thought the fiends had us."

"The fiends may have us yet," said Jadira. "What happened to Marix, Uramettu, and Nabul? And where in Dutu's infernal realm are we?"

The priest had no answer. "The best thing to do is retrace our steps," he said. Wearily, he began to descend.

* * * * *

Uramettu futilely gripped the block that had closed the passage behind her. Her long, powerful arms and legs hardened as she strained, but to no avail. She gave up. Retrieving her torch, she faced the passage ahead. The walls were painted white and covered with peculiar hieroglyphs, which meant nothing to her. After a few dozen paces, the floor slanted sharply down. The ceiling continued level, creating a great vertical hollow. Uramettu's footsteps, light as they were, echoed and reechoed in the vast still chamber.

* * * * *

"I can't find any door!" Marix said. He and Nabul had gone through a small square hole off the main passage and now stood in a large circular room. Their point of entry was now a mystery, as the panel had closed silently and without trace.

"It *must* be here somewhere!" Nabul cried in frustration. He waved his torch in a wide swath. The walls glittered and sparkled like the desert sky at night. "By the Thirty!" he said, rushing to the wall. "Jewels! Thousands of them!"

Marix looked. Mighty figures of mortals and gods were sculpted in low relief in the stone. Their eyes, necklaces, and bracelets were inlaid with real gems. By the time Marix reached the wall, Nabul already had his dagger out and was digging at the gems.

"Look at that ruby! Large as a pigeon's egg!" He poked the jewel into his burnoose. "Here's another— and it's *bigger!*"

"Oh, leave them, will you? We've got to find a way

out of here," Marix said. He felt in all the cracks and joints along the wall. Nothing moved or gave to his touch. Nabul skipped from figure to figure, muttering with glee at each new prize. When some particularly fine stone was out of his reach, he cursed fearfully and smote the wall with the butt of his dagger.

Marix circumnavigated the room, checking all the walls without success. "We're trapped, you fool. Much good those jewels will do you. There's no way out."

"Nonsense. We came in, we can go out," said Nabul. Marix slapped an ox-blood garnet from the thief's hand.

"We're trapped, I tell you! And all you can do is pilfer shiny rocks!"

Nabul's nostrils flared. He threw the dagger down and lunged for Marix. The two men, fueled by long pent-up frustrations, rolled across the sandy floor, clutching at each other's throats.

"Lying Faziri thief!" gargled Marix.

"Stupid pig-eating foreigner!" Nabul retorted.

They rolled right to the feet of the largest figure in the room. Nabul, pinned on his back, glanced up and saw a sight that made the fight and everything fade to insignificance. He threw Marix off.

"Strike me blind! Look at that!" he said.

Even Marix was impressed. There, five paces off the floor, set in the eye of a godlike image was the largest sapphire either of them had ever seen—had ever imagined. From one faceted edge to the other, it was easily the size of a dinner plate.

"I want it. I must have it!" Nabul said. He leaped, trying to dig the tip of his dagger into the rim of the sapphire's setting. He fell far short.

"Help me?" he begged Marix.

"Well, I—"

"We'll share. Half the value is yours if you let me stand on your shoulders and pry it out."

Marix agreed. He leaned forward, and the smaller man clambered up his back. With some wavering and grunting, Marix managed to straighten. Nabul clung to the wall with his fingertips as the jewel came within reach. At the neck of the god's image, Nabul planted a foot on each of Marix's shoulders. He ignored the topaz and lapis lazuli set in the god's necklace. The tip of his dagger probed the soft sandstone around the eye, searching for a loose spot.

And then, with the mildest ping, the sapphire popped free and fell. Nabul gave a strangled cry, sure the gem would shatter when it hit. Instead, the sapphire hit the fine sand in the center of the room.

Suddenly the sand began to shiver as a deep vibration moved the chamber. The god's eye started to sink into the sand.

"*Ai!* Catch it, Marix!"

The nobleman had other problems. The floor was shifting under his feet. He staggered away from the wall with Nabul still poised on his shoulders. He finally tripped on his torch and collapsed. Nabul went flying. He landed in the sand headfirst, a hand's length from the sinking sapphire.

"Ha, now I've got you!" he cried. The stone continued to sink. So did Nabul. "Marix! Help! The floor is sinking!" Marix scrambled on his hands and knees to the thief.

"Not the floor," said Marix. "The sand is draining from the room like an hourglass!"

"Dutu take the sand! What about us?"

"We'll go, too. Better hold your breath."

"I don't want to hold—" The sand reached Nabul's lips, and he shut them just in time. Hot, choking grit slid over his mouth. Marix dimly felt himself bumping into solid stone before he and Nabul slipped into oblivion.

10

Kaurous

A great rumbling filled the corridors. The ancient temple complex shook from end to end.

Uramettu, hurrying toward the sound, came to an intersection. Clouds of dust billowed out of the tunnel on the left. She turned that way and found a vertical shaft with a torrent of sand roaring down it. In a few seconds, the air cleared. The Fedushite woman lay on her stomach and lowered her torch into the pit. Through the swirling dust she could see that the main shaft had smaller vents in its vertical sides. Although the sand had ceased falling from the main shaft, it was still draining away through the side vents.

Uramettu took a chance. Where so much sand could flow a person could go. She slid feet first into the pit.

* * * * *

The rumbling was also heard by Tamakh and Jadira, elsewhere in the temple.

"Whatever it was, it's stopped," said Jadira.

"Whatever it was, I'll wager the thief had something to do with it," Tamakh added. "The man has a gift for finding trouble."

"Don't we all? So, Holy One, what shall we do?"

"Go toward the disturbance. There we will find our companions." There was firm certainty in the priest's voice.

He moved to go, and Jadira followed. "More magic, Tamakh? Or has Agma shown you where they are?"

"No, just my common sense."

At the vertical split in the ramps, they found the door that had closed behind Uramettu was now open. Tamakh balked at going through it. "Suppose it shuts again and we can't get out?"

"Do we have a choice?" asked Jadira. They didn't. The block stayed up after they had passed.

Tamakh noticed the hieroglyphs. "Um," he said. "The dead tongue of the Hankarans. So they were the builders of this place."

"Can you read it?"

"A little. It's very difficult." The cleric put a finger to the wall and followed the vertical columns of picture writing. "Here is a royal name, Met-wah, and a priestly one, Kest-no-ray. This long bit I can't fathom; something about gifts or chattels of the god of the sky . . . Here's another name—Kaurous."

"King or priest?"

"Neither, as far as I can tell. The name's not Hankaran anyway. This says, 'All vigilance is to be given to the keeping of Kaurous'."

"What does that mean?"

"Perhaps an enemy of the Hankarans, or some precious thing—it doesn't matter now. We have to find our friends."

Jadira agreed. As they moved on, she wondered what perils her lost friends were facing at that moment.

* * * * *

"Don't move."

Nabul was lying on his stomach. The avalanche of sand had deposited him and Marix in a large underground room. Marix was nearby, on his back. He had his arms and legs spread wide. "Don't move a muscle," the nobleman said.

Nabul's entire body tensed. "Why?" His voice was hoarse.

"I think we've fallen from one deathtrap into another."

Nabul turned his head. Immediately his whole body began to bob like a cork in the sea. "What in Dutu's name!"

"We're lying on a pool of liquid," said Marix. "Enough sand fell to cover the surface, but if we move too much, we'll sink."

Just then a hissing flood of sand poured from a large, vertical opening in a nearby wall. The cascade spread out over the rim of the pool, leaving Nabul's and Marix's hearts quaking in fear. But when the dust settled, out stepped Uramettu, upright and unhurt.

"Help!" Nabul said. "Help us, Uramettu!"

"Keep clear!" warned Marix. "We are adrift."

Uramettu dipped a finger in the pool. The liquid was thick and black and clung to her skin. She rubbed it off. "What manner of water is this?" she said in disgust.

"Bitumen," replied Marix. "It wells up out of the ground in some places. The people who built this grotto must have valued it and built this pool to collect it. If we go under, we'll never escape."

"We can't lie here forever!" Nabul cried. "Even now, my limbs ache to bend."

"Patience, wily one. Let me study the situation." Uramettu hopped lightly onto the retaining wall around the pool. The basin was twenty paces wide, and the two men had fallen almost in the center. Sand lay scattered over much of the surface of the bitumen, and it was impossible to tell by looking how deep the well was.

Uramettu went back to where she had fallen into the chamber. She scooped up a double handful of sand and threw it on the tar.

Marix couldn't see her. "What are you doing?"

"Building a bridge," she said, throwing on more handfuls of sand.

* * * * *

Jadira and Tamakh located the chamber of jewels. They stood on each side of a wide chasm, formed when two of the floor slabs had fallen to make a funnel for the emptying sand.

"They were here," said Tamakh.

"How can you tell?" Jadira asked.

The cleric waved at the reliefs. "I see the handiwork of our friend Nabul." Ugly gouge marks disfigured the images of the gods. From the freshness of the marks, Jadira knew that the work was recent.

"Do you think they went down there?" she said, pointing into the chute.

Tamakh shrugged. "Is there any other way out?" He studied the wall inscriptions. "Here's something: 'To the vault of Kaurous'." Between the striding legs of the great god figure was the outline of a door. By consulting the glyphs on either side, Tamakh was able to trick the door open. The smell of brimstone wafted out, making Jadira cough and cover her nose.

"It *smells* like Dutu's realm!" she exclaimed.

"Perhaps it is."

"You encourage me, Holy One." The nomad woman bowed and gestured grandly with one arm. "After you."

Beyond the door, they found a narrow stairway cut into the rock, the steps daubed in an alternating pattern of red and white, a curiously gay color scheme for such a grim place. The air grew thicker as they descended. Tamakh's torch shrank to a dim orange feather of flame.

"I feel giddy," said Jadira after a few minutes. "These vapors have lightened my head!"

"There is magic afoot here," Tamakh replied in a loud whisper. "Very old and very strong."

They reached bottom after more than two hundred steps. The exit at the foot of the steps was blocked by a fine curtain of sheer cloth, still pliant after twenty centuries. Tamakh thrust through the veil.

They found themselves in the greatest room yet, a vast vault the size of a city square. Four stone columns were giant lamps, with something burning at their tops. By the light the columns provided, it was easy to see the central feature of the vault: a black sphere as wide as ten men, resting on a low, cup-shaped base carved from black marble. The base was incised with Hankaran hieroglyphs inlaid with gold.

"What is this place?" said Jadira in awe.

"A tomb. The resting place for the one named Kaurous," replied Tamakh. "Not royalty or of the priestly order; perhaps a sorcerer." He bent way back to take in the enormity of the black sphere. "A very powerful sorcerer."

Jadira noticed that the floor was deeply grooved and worn around the base. Many feet had walked around the stone for untold years to wear such ruts. She went to the bottom of one of the fire pillars. A sticky black residue had trickled down the side. It smelled strongly of sulfur.

"That's how they kept the fires burning untended all these centuries," said Tamakh. "The flames must be fed by some reservoir of pitch."

The rim of the vault was a gallery of doors, some to stairwells, others to corridors and antechambers of various depths. Jadira went to each opening and shouted, "*Hai, hai!* Marix! Uramettu! Nabul! Can you hear me?" She tried more than a dozen doors before a faint voice replied.

"Here, here, down here!"

"Tamakh, I found them!" The priest ran, puffing, to her, and they plunged into a passage that was cluttered with pottery shards, fragments of desiccated wood, and scrolls of stiff cloth that disintegrated at the slightest touch.

The passage finally opened into a room containing a pit of tar. Uramettu was still piling sand on the surface of the tar, trying to firm it enough to rescue Marix and Nabul.

A chorus of happy shouts erupted when the separated companions caught sight of each other. Uramettu quickly apprised Jadira and Tamakh of the situation.

"We passed a hall full of rubbish we could use," Jadira suggested. She and Tamakh returned to the passage and gathered armfuls of trash. Wood and clay stiffened the layer of sand. Finally, Uramettu, moving on her hands and knees like some giant insect, went out onto the surface of the treacherous pool.

"My friend," she said to Marix, "I am going to toss you the end of my sash. Hold to it tightly, and I will pull you to safety."

The Fedushite backed up, and Marix slid on his back to the rim. He rolled over the wall and threw his arms around Jadira. He broke the ardent embrace and, looking embarrassed, clapped Tamakh on the shoulder.

"You look hale, holy man," he said. "Now, let's get Nabul."

The thief was in a more difficult position. He didn't dare lift his arms to grasp Uramettu's sash, and she couldn't cast a loop over his head. "You're going to have to move some," she advised. "Try to turn over."

Nabul slowly lifted his right shoulder and turned. He was on his side before his left arm pushed through the sand into the tar.

"Yah, ha! Help!" he cried. "It has me, it has me!"

"Take the end and hold on!" Uramettu urged. Nabul, trying to keep from panicking, grasped the sash and wrapped it around his free arm. The black syrup was already to his chest.

"Don't thrash about—you'll only sink faster," Marix called from the edge. Uramettu braced her knees wide apart on two shards and pulled. Nabul rose a bit from the mire, then sank back as Uramettu ceased pulling; her own position was becoming precarious.

"The grip is too strong," she said. "I need help!"

Jadira climbed over the wall onto the bridge of rubbish. The surface gave under her feet and hands. She crept forward as fast as she could. Marix followed.

"Take hold of Uramettu's feet," he said. "I'll hold

your feet, and Tamakh can seize mine."

This they did. "Now pull!" said Uramettu.

Nabul, half under the tar, was praying to the entire Faziri pantheon for a merciful death. Suddenly the grip of the bitumen eased, and he slid up onto a raft of old lathing. He wept and thanked his companions for his deliverance.

When everyone was safe on solid stone again, all the torches in the room dimmed in unison.

"I don't think we're alone," whispered Tamakh.

"You mean the one in the tomb?" said Jadira. "Surely he is dead."

"Death is not always the end. I want to return to the vault and read the inscription."

Nabul rubbed the sticky black gum from his arm and neck. His robe clinked as he rubbed. Dipping a hand in, he came out with a fistful of jewels. Well! He hadn't lost all his loot.

In the vault, the fire pillars had dimmed to fitful glimmers. Tamakh had to feel with his fingers to make out the exact shape of some of the gold-filled hieroglyphs.

"I don't understand," he said.

"Can you not read it?" Jadira asked.

"Yes, but the meaning evades me. It says: 'Any man may set him free.' Is that a request or a warning?"

"This is a sepulcher?" said Nabul breathlessly. He had forgotten his near brush with death when confronted with the mighty black sphere.

"So it seems," said Marix.

"Think of it! Think of the treasure that must lay buried within so magnificent a tomb!"

"Let it stay buried," said Tamakh sharply. "There is power at work here, even after two thousand years.

Such power should remain entombed."

"Rot! The dead are dead. They have no use for gold."

"The dead in this place are not idle," Jadira said. She told them how mummies had chased her and the priest.

"There are no mummies *here*." The thief stepped up to the sphere and touched his fingers lightly to its surface. It was cold and smooth.

"What's it made of?" asked Marix. The thief took out his dagger to scratch the flawless material. With a loud click, his blade stuck to the sphere.

"Lodestone!" said Uramettu. Nabul tugged at his dagger. It slid across the surface but would not come free.

"Leave it, man!" Tamakh said. Nabul planted his foot on the magnetic stone and dragged at the hilt of his weapon.

"Don't—" Jadira began.

The giant globe, balanced on the narrow base, shifted under the thief's pressure. The dagger hilt popped free, but the blade remained. Nabul put both hands on the pommel and yanked with all his might.

The tip came away, and Nabul fell back. The black sphere shifted ponderously off its base. It crashed down the three wide, shallow steps and rolled into one of the flaming pillars. The tower of small fitted stones collapsed. Thick streams of bitumen spewed out of the shattered column, drenching the sphere. The giant black globe stuck fast and stopped.

Nabul leaped up and ran to the rim of the hole revealed by the movement of the sphere. He stared into the pit, hoping to see the first gleam of a wonderful hoard. One by one the others joined him. Instead of the glitter of gold and jewels, however, the pit was filled with a glowing pink mist that appeared to be welling up toward them.

"Now what?" Marix said. The level of the fog rose rapidly, overspilling the rim. Its color deepened to red. It flowed over Uramettu's bare feet, and she hopped aside.

"It's cold!" she said. "So cold it feels hot."

They all stepped back. In the center of the mist, a spindle-shaped mass coalesced. It began to pulse and rotate. Faster and faster, it built into a whirling column of blood-colored smoke. Lightning cracked from the head of the spinning mass, scoring burned furrows into the walls. The whirlwind sucked the air inward, whipping at the companions' hair and clothing. Jadira lost her footing. Marix caught and held her. The wind shrieked around them in a deafening cacophony. Just as it seemed they would all be sucked into the icy, hot cloud, the cyclone solidified into a giant muscled figure, ten paces high. Only the waist-up portion of the giant resembled solid flesh; below that it was still mist.

"I, KAUROUS, LIVE AGAIN!" boomed the behemoth.

"Mercy! Mercy!" Nabul cried.

A bald head as wide as a wagon swiveled down. Green tusks as long as a man protruded from the apparition's mouth, and his earlobes hung down to his shoulders. Kaurous was red all over, even his barrel-sized eyes.

"WHO HAS FREED ME FROM THE PIT?" he roared. Nabul cringed and said nothing. The others were transfixed with wonder. "WHO FREED ME?"

"We did, Mighty One," said Tamakh at last.

"HOW LONG HAS IT BEEN SINCE I LAST SAW THE SUN?"

"We think—I would say, almost two thousand years."

"TWO THOUSAND? IT SEEMED MUCH LONGER."

"Pardon me, sir, but what are you?" asked Marix.

"HAS THE WORLD SO SOON FORGOTTEN THE GREAT KAUROUS, PRINCE OF THE EFREETI?"

Tamakh seized Marix's arm and dragged him close. "Beware, my friend! The efreeti are dangerous, untrustworthy creatures of great power. Pass that on." Marix whispered to Jadira, who spoke in Uramettu's ear, who mumbled a warning to Nabul.

"FOR FREEING ME, LITTLE ONES, I SHALL GRANT YOU TWO WISHES."

"Only two? I thought three was the customary number," said Marix. Kaurous exhaled fire from his nostrils.

"HAD YOU COME A THOUSAND YEARS AGO, I MIGHT HAVE GRANTED THREE. A THOUSAND YEARS HENCE, YOU WOULD GET BUT ONE."

Tamakh nudged Marix and said humbly, "Thank you, Mighty One. We are deeply grateful."

"AS YOU SHOULD BE. WELL, MAKE HASTE WITH YOUR PUNY REQUESTS. MY SUBJECTS AWAIT ME."

Nabul sat up. "I want—" Uramettu clapped a hand over his mouth.

"This calls for discretion," said Jadira. "My people have a saying: 'Ask an efreet for a knife, and you'll get it point first'."

"Why not wish for more wishes?" suggested Marix.

"No! Mortals do not bandy words with demigods! He would slay us all in the blink of an eye," interjected Tamakh.

"What do we need most?" asked Uramettu.

"The seal of Lydon," said Marix.

"No," Jadira answered. "The seal is safe enough hidden where it is. If we had it with us now, we would risk losing it before we reached Tantuffa."

"What then?" asked Marix.

"I AM WAITING, INSECTS."

"What are the two most essential requirements for a dangerous journey?"

"Food," said Tamakh.

"Money," offered Nabul.

"Weapons," said Marix. Jadira nodded.

"Yes, food and weapons. That's what we'll ask for." She turned to the towering efreet and missed Nabul's disgusted grimace.

Tamakh caught Jadira's elbow. "Be careful how you ask," he said. "The efreeti love to trick mortals."

"O Great Kaurous," she began. "We five travel across the Red Sands to the sea. We ask two things to make our journey easier."

"DO YOU DESIRE A FLYING CONVEYANCE?"

Jadira looked startled. "I hadn't thought of that."

Tamakh shook his head frantically. "No, no, keep it simple."

"Of course. O Kaurous: provide us with a provision bag that is easily carried, yet can never be emptied of food."

"IT IS DONE."

A pannier of red leather appeared at Jadira's feet. Marix picked it up and looked inside. "Bread, dates, olives, and honey," he said.

"Dump it out," advised Tamakh. Marix poured the food on the floor. The bag refilled instantly.

"All right. Next, we want a weapon that slays at a distance and never misses—"

"Sized for a mortal," inserted Tamakh.

"—and which is sized for a mortal," Jadira added.

A bow of dark wood, inlaid with ivory and silver, materialized in Marix's hands. A quiver of black-fletched arrows appeared on his hip.

"THIS EFREET BOW WILL NEVER FAIL TO HIT AND WILL ALWAYS SLAY. NOW MY DEBT TO YOU IS DISCHARGED. I SHALL QUIT THIS CURSED PLACE."

"Prince of Efreeti, may I humbly beg one last indulgence from you?" asked Tamakh.

The enormous creature scratched his chin. His nails were like sabers, but then his hide was thicker than an elephant's. "WHAT INDULGENCE?" said Kaurous.

The priest remembered Agma's warning and wanted to further it. "With your power to see far beyond the horizon, can you tell us if we are being pursued?"

Kaurous inflated his massive crimson chest. "I SEE TWO SCORE AND TEN LITTLE BEETLES WITH BLOOD ON THEIR HANDS. THEY FOLLOW IN YOUR TRACKS LIKE GREEDY HOUNDS ON THE SCENT. WHERE EARTH AND SKY JOIN TOGETHER THEY HAVE REAPED A HARVEST."

"Why don't these powerful beings ever speak plainly?" complained Marix.

"Shhh!" hissed Jadira.

"Is there anything else you can tell us, O Great Kaurous?" Tamakh asked.

"HEAR THIS WISDOM, INSECTS: NEVER TRUST A CRUEL CAMEL SELLER OR A BAKER OF THIN

LOAVES, FOR ONE ABUSES HIS BEASTS AND THE OTHER ABUSES HIS YEASTS."

"Now he's telling us bad jokes," Marix muttered.

"Well, he hasn't heard any good ones in two thousand years," said Nabul.

"FAREWELL!"

The efreet ignited into a whirlwind of flame again and rose out of his pit. The whirlwind touched the peaked ceiling and bored through, melting solid rock as if it were soft cheese. Sparks and drops of liquid rock rained down, and the five took hasty shelter in an antechamber off the main vault.

Gradually the fierce red glow faded. In its place came a soft, steady light, shining down the wide shaft bored by Kaurous. Jadira stepped out into the cone of white light.

"The sun!" she said. "The storm is over!"

11

The Hand of the Sultan

Captain Fu'ad poured a gourd full of water over his hot, dusty head. The coolness of the liquid trickling behind his ears refreshed him far more than drinking it would have.

The Invincibles had crossed the desert from Rehajid to Julli oasis—a journey half again as long as the route the fugitives had taken. Nine horses perished from the heat, and two lancers went off their heads. Now at Julli, Fu'ad encountered a stone wall. None of the nomads or caravaners would say anything about Marix and company.

Marad returned to his commander empty-handed. "No one will speak, my brother," he said. "The nomads regard the Sudiin woman as a sister, and neither gold nor threats will loosen their tongues."

"Then perhaps we should carry out our threats," said Fu'ad.

"I would not advise it, sir. These are proud people, and a harsh act against one will turn them all against us."

Fu'ad scowled. He wiped the slim blade of his scimitar

with a clean cloth and returned it to its scabbard. "Are the men reprovisioned?" he said.

"The horses have been watered, and the Phoenix Troop is refilling its food and water bags."

"Very well. Hurry them along. The scum have an eight-day lead that we must overcome."

Fu'ad strapped on his sword belt and adjusted the drape of his surcoat. When all was in place, he set out on foot to cross the oasis from end to end. It could be that some clue to the destination of the fugitives was waiting to be discovered.

He found a tent set up among the pillars. A mixed line of people—nomads, Faziris, Zimorans, and others—waited to enter. Fu'ad accosted the rearmost man.

"Hail, fellow. What is in the tent that generates such a long line?"

"Have you not heard? This was the scene of a divine manifestation, not half a moonturn ago. A fire god of the East, Agma, saved a man from hanging."

Mention of the heretical sect brought Fu'ad's attention to sharp focus. "Agma, you say? I thought the sultan—may he live forever—had forbidden worship of that deity."

The stranger looked Fu'ad up and down. "Your pardon, Captain. Speaking for myself, I deplore superstition, but Julli lacks the diversions of a real town. I was curious to see the relic left behind by the, ah, false god."

"Relic, you say? I shall see about this."

Fu'ad cut to the head of the line. Two Aqiri guarded the flap of the tent. When they saw Fu'ad, they crossed their arms in a gesture of peace and let him enter unopposed.

A wooden trestle stood in the center of the small tent.

On it burned a brass brazier. In front of this votive fire
lay the iron bar from which the Yali Mit'ai had tried to
hang Nabul. The deep bend was still in it. An Aqiri
cleverman told Fu'ad how the rod came to be bent.
Fu'ad listened keenly.

"Who were the companions of this thief?" he finally
asked. "Did you see them?"

"Oh, as closely as I see Your Mightiness. There was the
holy man of stout figure. It was he who blessed us and
promised—"

"And who else?" Fu'ad said sharply.

The Aqiri blinked and recalled to whom he spoke. "A
foreign man with pale skin and hair. A very tall black
woman who walked like a prowling cat. And a nomad
woman. She was *malam.*"

"Was this woman of the Sudiin?"

"Ai, yes; she was Sudiin of Sudiin."

"And where did these people go after the 'miracle'?"

"Who can say, my lord? Off to do the god's business."

Fu'ad grabbed the Aqiri by the throat and thrust the
point of his dagger into the tight skin of the man's neck.
A single drop of blood oozed out. The Aqiri gasped and
went pale.

"Now harken to me, nomad; I want to know where
the four who saved this thief went, and exactly how long
ago, or I'll push this little blade into your throat up to
the hilt." The dagger was a handspan long.

"S-s-sir! They returned to the Red Sands! N-north by
west, they went. I swear!"

Fu'ad wiggled the tip of the dagger. "And how long
ago?"

"S-six days, Merciful One. Six days!"

The dagger went back to its sheath. "For your most
helpful cooperation, I will not trample this false shrine

into the oasis grass; I have not the time to waste. But you, my unworthy friend, had best not be here when I return," Fu'ad said.

He strode outside. The line of hopefuls wanting to see Agma's sacred relic had vanished. Word of Fu'ad's identity had spread fast.

Marad trotted up. "My captain! The men are ready to depart."

"Very good, my brother. We leave at once."

"To go where, sir?"

"Back into the desert. North by west."

* * * * *

The Invincibles loped across the high desert in two long lines. There was no need for outriders or pickets; visibility was to the horizon. Fu'ad could feel the sweat saturating the quilted tunic under his armor. Dampness spread down his chest and back until he squelched with each forward swing in the saddle.

Miserable place for a fighting man, the Red Sands. Too hot for armor, too hot for hard riding. The desert had an insatiable appetite for horses, too. So many fine animals died of heat and thirst. Fu'ad would have given up at Julli and ridden home, but the Eye of the Sultan would transmit his lack of resolve to the sorcerers in the pay of Emir Azrel, back in Omerabad. Professional disgrace was not the only penalty Fu'ad could suffer.

He scanned the far horizon. These wretched prisoners had cost him much sweat, much effort. They would pay for their troublesomeness. They would pay dearly.

"*Aiyah!*" A shout from the right column. Fu'ad reined up.

"Who goes there?" he shouted. The air scalded his

tongue and throat.

"Trooper Kedir, sir! I see men! On foot, sir!"

Marad rode to his captain. "It might be a mirage. I've seen odd things myself in the heat of the day."

"Kedir is a steady man," Fu'ad replied. "Let's see what the Red Sands have done to his eyes."

Fu'ad ordered the troopers to halt while he and Marad cantered to Kedir's position. The trooper was staring into the glare of the late sun.

"There they are, sir. I count eight in all."

"Eight? Doesn't sound like our quarry," Marad said.

Fu'ad looked and, sure enough, eight dark figures stumbled across the hard red soil toward them. The leading figure, spying the lancers sitting high on their horses, raised a cry.

"Have the column deploy. I want to net these wanderers," said Fu'ad calmly.

Marad put the signal trumpet to his lips and sounded two short blasts. The forty-two surviving Invincibles formed a circle and enveloped the men on foot. The strangers did not seem concerned; indeed, they rushed to meet the nearest horsemen.

One dirty, bearded fellow limped up to Fu'ad where he and Marad had remained by Kedir. The newcomer and his companions wore metal gorgets around their throats and black-banded, nut-colored headdresses.

"Hail, valiant soldiers!" he said in a hoarse voice. "The blessing of Mitaali upon you! We are saved!"

"You are found, at any rate," said Fu'ad dryly. "Who are you?"

"Zuram *gan* Dalifiya, most gratefully at your service, lord."

"You are a nomad?"

"Of the tribe Bershak, yes."

"What are you doing in this part of the desert, on foot and in such obvious distress? I thought you people could live indefinitely on the Red Sands."

Zuram folded his hands and bowed. "The illustrious captain sees much. In truth, we were a party of eighteen out hunting when we were caught in a terrible sandstorm. Ten of my brothers and all of our mounts died, and we, we were at hope's end until you found us."

"Hunting? What could you possibly be hunting in this wasteland?" asked Marad.

"The wiliest game of all, lord—men."

Fu'ad and Marad exchanged guarded looks. Fu'ad unhooked a waterskin from his saddle. It fell to the ground. He said, "There, son of Dalif, drink. Drink and tell us who you were hunting."

The Bershak filled his cheeks to bursting and swallowed. "May you dwell forever in Paradise, noble captain! In eternal joy and—"

"Yes, yes, get on with it."

"As the captain desires. Some days ago, my brothers and I were in the oasis of Julli seeking employment with a caravan as guides. Many wanderers of the Red Sands were there, too: the Nuzi, the Draka, the Aqir—"

"Stay to the point!"

"Yes, sir. We could not find work, as so many were already there. So we lingered at the wells, hoping to hear some news to our advantage. We did. A youth from a distant land drank too much wine and told the Yali of the Aqir of a royal ornament they sought to recover."

Fu'ad's heart beat faster. He clenched a mailed fist around his horse's reins and asked, "What sort of ornament did he speak of, and where could it be found?"

"It was the seal of a prince from across the sea, as I recall." Zuram took another long swig of water. "It was

buried by an outlander knight far in the west. The foreign boy and his companions intend to dig up this seal
and take it to— What was the place? Some vulgar western name. Tuba? Tooga? A city called thus."

"He said perhaps 'Tantuffa'."

"That's it!" the nomad exclaimed.

Fu'ad smiled and excused Zuram. He drew Marad
aside for a hasty conference. "Our luck has changed, my
brother!" he said excitedly. "This dirty nomad has given
me the means to a satrapy!"

"How so?" asked Marad.

"The one described must be Marix of Dosen. The seal
can only belong to the Dosens' overlord, the prince of
Lydon. Do you not see? We took the nobleman from an
armed party of westerners. Their leader, a knight, was
killed, and the reason for their presence in Kaipur was
never revealed. The sultan—may he live forever—did
not want the young nobleman put to the torture, lest his
ransom value decline. His Magnificence believed that a
few days in the dungeon would loosen his tongue.
Before he weakened, however, he, the nomad woman,
and the heretic priest escaped."

"His Magnificence would truly reward you if you
seized this prince's seal," Marad observed.

"Exactly! I shall lay the trophy at the sultan's feet, and
thereafter claim the bounty of his good will."

"What of the Bershak?"

Fu'ad snapped out the first few fingerwidths of his
sword. "I have orders from the vizier that anyone assisting the fugitives is to die," he said.

"They were not assisting; the Bershak were tracking
the criminals, even as we were."

The captain clasped Marad's forearm in the soldiers'
brotherly grip. "If these nomads are not silenced, they

will tell all and sundry at Julli of their predicament. Every cutthroat and freebooter in the wasteland will be after our quarry, and they will make our task immeasurably more difficult," said Fu'ad. He relaxed and sat back, smiling. "Besides, I pledged my life to their recapture, and I will not share the glory with anyone."

"Not even your brothers-in-arms?" asked Marad quietly.

A tense silence built between the two men. Finally Fu'ad turned his horse to the waiting Zuram. The Bershak gave the captain back his waterskin. Fu'ad thanked him, then said to Marad, "Sound the call."

"What call, sir?"

"You know the one. Do it."

Marad hesitated only a second. He put the trumpet to his lips and blew three notes, paused, and blew them again.

"What is that?" asked the puzzled Zuram.

"'No quarter'," replied Fu'ad. And none was given.

* * * * *

"You know, I think I'm beginning to bear the desert well," Marix said. They had left the ruined temple and were now heading due west. The peaks of the Shammat Mountains could be seen far away, dim blue shadows shimmering in the reflected heat.

"You are nearly brown enough to be a nomad," Jadira replied, studying his tanned face, "but your hair and eyes are still too light."

"And he walks too fast," said Nabul.

"How would you know?" Uramettu chided. "You ride more than you walk." It was true. Nabul could usually be found on one donkey's back or another.

"Never mind," said Jadira. "We're all doing well. It's no wonder, though, what with an everlasting supply of food."

"Ugh," said Nabul. "The same food, day after day. . . ."

"The grumbler is right," said Uramettu. "If I eat another olive, I'll sprout leaves!"

"And if I eat any more honey, I'll grow bee's wings!" Marix added.

"I warned you about gifts from an efreet," said Tamakh. "To them it is a great jest to rook a mortal."

"Speaking of wings and gifts, why would you not let me ask Kaurous for a flying cart or chariot?" Jadira said.

"Too much room for treachery," said the priest. He paused to flick a pebble from his sandal. "A magical conveyance might have flown us to Tantuffa in a few notches, only to dash us to death from a great height. You can't be too cautious with efreeti."

Marix ran a finger down the unstrung bow they had gotten from Kaurous. "You don't suppose this thing kills the archer, do you?"

"That's an idea. Kaurous did say it would never miss and always slay. . . ."

"Filth!" Marix had insisted on being group bowman. Now he wasn't so blindly enthusiastic. "Uramettu, you have long arms; you would draw the bow so much deeper than I. Would you like to have it?"

She laughed, a warm, throaty chuckle that made Jadira smile. "Ah, my friend, you flatter me! My weapon lies in here"—she pressed a hand to her chest—"and I need no other."

"Nabul?"

"Not me. I don't want to wind up with my own arrow in my back." Marix sighed. The others laughed good-naturedly at him.

The day ended, and the moon rose full and golden. By this time, the land was dotted with gnarled *pirca* trees and fluffy dry *samsat* grass. Uramettu and Tamakh each gathered an armload of kindling and laid a fire. Tamakh called upon Agma. His spark caught so quickly a wild puff of flame gushed from the tinder pile and singed the tip of his nose. Nabul hurt himself laughing while Jadira dabbed olive oil on the priest's blistered nose.

"Don't be so ardent next time!" Nabul said through his tears. "I though you were going to kiss the flames!"

When it was fully dark, Uramettu got up from the circle and went silently out into the darkness. Marix started to call to her, but Tamakh stopped him.

"She's feeling the call to hunt," he explained. "It's harder on her than the rest of us to eat bread and fruit all the time."

"What can she hope to find out there?" said Marix.

"There is game in the high desert," said Jadira. "Hares, snakes, hopper-mice, sandspikers."

"Sandspikers?"

"A small, flightless bird," Tamakh put in.

"Rabbit would be good just now," said Nabul wistfully.

"In her present form I don't think she'd be inclined to share," observed Tamakh.

The priest and the thief fell asleep before the moon set. Marix and Jadira sat close together and watched the moon creep ever so slowly to its rest.

"Waning from full," said Marix. "Our time is half gone."

"We are more than halfway to the coast. We will make it," she said.

"I was thinking about that. Finding the seal—and

what comes after."

"What does?"

He shifted. "My life will resume in Lord Hurgold's army. Tamakh will serve his god. Uramettu will seek passage to Fedush, and Nabul—well, there's always work for a thief. But what will you do, Jadira?"

"I hadn't really considered. As a tribeless woman, I have no standing with other nomads. Yali Mit'ai esteems me, but he could not adopt me without provoking dissension in the tribe. There remains a hard course . . ." Marix prompted her. "I could make myself a bonded wife to a clan leader."

"You do not sound enthusiastic."

She said, "I am not. I would become the slave of my husband."

"I see you as many things, but never a slave."

"Yet I must have a place, a livelihood. Never will I sell myself in the streets of a city. I would shave my head and hide among the Promised of Jihai first."

He took her hand. "Could you bear to stay in Tantuffa?" said Marix.

"With you?"

"With me."

"You think unbalanced things, my friend." He leaned closer, but Jadira eased away. "I sense your feeling for me is due to our situation and not to true bonding of the heart. As the wise chief said, 'Even vinegar is good wine on the Red Sands'."

"You doubt me? I admire you greatly. You are a strong woman, far stronger than the airy girls of my homeland—"

"Stop. Say nothing more, please. Think, dear Marix; think and think again. I am widow, nomad, a tribeless woman. You are the son of a western lord. Our worlds were never meant to follow in the same track. The gods have thrown us together for a purpose only they know. When all is resolved and the world is balanced once more, you will see the gulf between us is wider than all the desert."

Marix slowly released his hold on her hand. "I wish I thought you would be wrong," he said.

Her throat felt tight. "So do I."

❖ 12 ❖

The Reflection

The land changed. Contours returned; hills and hollows appeared in the flat desert. The limits of the companions' vision became the rising gray-blue curtain of the Shammat Mountains, and with each passing notch the mountains reared higher.

Dew drenched them at night. Green plants were common, and crossing a gully Uramettu often flushed coveys of doves or a wild pig. Marix ached to shoot some game, but he was still afraid of the efreet bow. Uramettu eyed the fleeing animals but kept her human form. Her expedition some nights before had been largely fruitless—a few stringy rodents.

They camped in a green hollow fringed by tall cedars. Marix was in raptures over seeing real trees again. He cut an armful of boughs and brought them back to camp.

"What are you going to do with those?" said Nabul.

"Sleep on them. The smell is wonderful!" The city-born thief scratched his head at the strange ways of foreigners.

Marix offered some boughs to Jadira. She smiled in a

distant way and let him arrange them in a rough rectangle on the ground. Tamakh approached with the provision bag. "Anyone hungry?" he said.

"Not for bread, dates, olives, and honey," said Nabul.

"What else is there?"

"Meat. Fresh rabbit, or pigeon pie."

"And where, pray, can you get those delicacies?" asked Tamakh.

"She can get them," replied the thief, pointing to Uramettu.

All eyes focused on her. "Could you?" said Jadira.

"It is not usual for me to take more than I can eat alone," she said, "and it is often difficult to make two kills."

"So the question remains: could you hunt for us?" said Marix. "Would you bring us back fresh meat?"

"What does my sister say?"

"Any change from our forced diet would be a delight," said Jadira.

"It seems we have a culinary emergency," said Uramettu. She stretched her sleek arms and yawned. "If you will excuse me . . ."

She loped off up the hill and disappeared among the trees. Nabul rubbed his hands together and said, "All we need now is a stew pot."

"Don't you ever think of anything but your stomach?" said Marix scornfully.

"Sometimes he thinks of money," Jadira offered. Nabul stuck his prominent nose in the air and assumed an air of dignified disdain. Once he was behind Marix, he snatched off the nobleman's Faziri helmet.

"This will make an excellent pot," he declared. Jadira laughed.

"No!" exclaimed Marix. "That's my helmet!"

"Not anymore!" Marix tried to grab the iron pot back, but the nimble thief skipped out of reach. As he started to rise to his feet, Jadira put out a hand and stopped Marix.

"Be at ease," she said. "We will clean the helmet after we use it."

His angry expression faded at her touch. "Oh, all right. But I get first serving!"

"Agreed." She cast about for the water skins. "I'd better find some water, or we'll be eating dry soup for dinner."

Jadira found two of the bags. Tamakh was using the third for a pillow. He lay on a short camel-hair blanket under a flowering *tanis* bush. A limp green leaf shaded his eyes. Jadira regarded Tamakh fondly. She couldn't disturb so restful a sleep. Two skinsful of water would do for now.

She followed the slope of the hill upward, her sandals slipping in the loose mix of broken stone and dirt. From there, Jadira could see the double line of Uramettu's tracks converging with her own.

The fragrant cedars loomed ahead, dark and sighing softly in the breeze. They grew so closely Jadira had to squeeze between them. Sticky aromatic resin got on her hands and stuck to her clothing. Beside her, the bare footprints changed to four-clawed spoors.

Beyond the trees was the pinnacle of this range of hills. From there Jadira could see in all directions. She knew there would be water in one of the draws, probably the one with the most foliage. To the southwest she spied a vale where the trees were taller and thicker than anywhere else. That should be it.

It was past midday, and the shadows were growing longer as she walked. The hills were silent, save for the infrequent call of a mourning dove. So much of the tension of the past days had dropped away when they reached the fresh air of the mountains. Jadira could almost hear the swelling sea, could nearly see the walls and towers of far Tantuffa.

They had come through much, this motley band; Tamakh was hale, Nabul's outlook improved daily, and Marix . . . Marix. What about him? He was a brave fellow, resolute and strong. How could she tell him how she felt? Could she allow herself to love one who was not of the Red Sands?

There was water in the draw all right. Jadira could smell it as she rounded the falling buttress of rock. Hear it, too; the flowing stream rang in the stillness like hidden temple chimes. The very air of the glen seemed cleaner. It was almost crystalline in its clarity.

The stream bubbled out of a layer of pink-veined granite. It cascaded down to a wide, shallow pool bordered with ferns and moss-painted stones. The banks on each side were covered with hundreds of tiny flowers, each consisting of four fat, snowy petals surrounding a golden head. Jadira sank into the deep bed of flowers. Nowhere, not even the vale of Al Mirah, could compare to the simple, affecting beauty of this spot.

She leaned over the water. Her thin face, tanned by the sun and tautened by the wind, smiled back at her. Jadira let down her headdress and opened the neck of her robe. She dipped a hand into the pool. The water was cold. She put her head back and let droplets run through her hair. Closing her eyes, she poured another handful into the hollow of her neck.

Yes. Beautiful.

The words came unbidden to her mind. Jadira opened her eyes. No one was near.

"Uramettu? Is that you?" Her voice sounded flat in the perfect air. Unnerved, Jadira dropped the first waterskin in the pool and forced the neck under. Bubbles gushed out.

Beautiful one. Speak to me.

"Who—who is it?"

Look into the pool.

Jadira bent over. Her reflection was there. Her lips said, *Look, beautiful one.*

Jadira had not spoken.

Stay here. Rest. I, your reflection, will go in your place.

"What do you want . . . must go . . ." She was tired, so tired. How good it would be to lie down in the ferns and sleep. No worries. No dangers. No difficult choices of life, death, and love.

Sleep. I will go to your companions. They shall know me as they know you and I shall love them as you do.

Jadira reclined in the green fronds. Two hands took out the filled waterskins and carried them away.

* * * * *

"On guard!"

The blunt tip of the Faziri scimitar wavered. Parry—cut! Hilt high to the shoulder. Slash right, loop cut left. Back to guard and hold. Overhand whirl and cut—

"Be careful, will you? You're going to hurt somebody with that thing," said Nabul. Marix turned on one heel and brought the blade down with both hands a whisker's length from a sprig of cedar he'd thrust in the ground. With one deft movement, Marix shaved all the greenery from one side of the sprig.

"You were saying?"

"You're bold with a bush. How would you do against a real man with a real sword?"

Marix slipped the scimitar back into its scabbard. "Time will tell," he said. "Unless you care to practice with me now." Nabul clucked and spat.

Jadira came down the hill, stepping cautiously over the shifting ground. She balanced a skin of water under each arm. Marix went to help her. He took one skin and offered a hand to guide her down.

"Thank you," she said warmly. She leaned heavily on his arm. Her headdress was down around her shoulders and her robe was parted past the base of her neck. A blush of pale skin showed there.

"I found a marvelous spring," she said. "The water is so clear and cold!"

"Let me have some," Nabul said.

She dropped a skin at the thief's feet. The spout popped open and a cold jet sloshed on Nabul's legs. "*Ai*, what's this? My anointing?" But Jadira's eyes were on Marix.

"Bring a cup. I'll pour you a libation," she offered. The young nobleman looked at her curiously, but went to the donkey pannier and got one of the tin cups they'd acquired at Julli. Marix blew grit from the cup and handed it to Jadira. She squeezed the waterskin firmly, directing the narrow stream into the cup.

She held it out to him. "Drink." Marix tried to take the cup, but Jadira maintained her hold. "Drink," she said.

His blue eyes followed her brown ones intently as the cup came to his lips. Marix's hand closed over Jadira's. Something tangible passed between them, something silent and powerful. Cold water trickled down Marix's throat. When the cup was empty, she lowered it. The gap between them narrowed. Jadira leaned closer, her hand to Marix's cheek.

"Is there water?" said Tamakh, popping up from his blanket. His voice shattered the stillness. Nabul, who had witnessed the sharing of water, shook his head like a drunkard.

"All those days in the desert and *now* I'm going off my head!" he said. Jadira turned away from Marix and refilled the cup. Tamakh scratched his belly.

"What a restful place this is," the cleric said. "You know, this would be a fine place for a sanctuary to Agma."

"Wouldn't that disturb the spirits who already dwell here?" said Jadira.

"What spirits?"

"Surely you must know, Holy One, that wherever sun, earth, and water exist to give life to plants and animals, there also will be spirits."

"Well, yes, that's basic theology," said the priest. "I was wondering why you choose to put it that way—'disturb the spirits who already dwell here'?"

She laughed lightly. "How else would I put it?"

Marix rubbed his eyes and inhaled deeply, like a man awakening from a long sleep. "I wouldn't drink the water, Tamakh," he said. "Its kick is stronger than Narsian wine!"

Tamakh sniffed his cup. He dipped a little finger in and licked the drop off. "Hmm, mineral water," he remarked, "but I detect no soporific quality." He tilted his head back and drained the cup. "Ahh!" Marix and Nabul watched the priest for signs of giddiness. When he merely sat back down and took another long drink, they gave up.

Jadira settled herself close to Marix. Whatever else the

water did, it certainly had warmed the nomad woman. Tamakh studied her for a moment. There was something in the air, almost like the presence of the confined efreet.

He pulled a long ravelin from the hem of his toga and knotted it. "Who will play?" he asked. The others looked at him, puzzled. Tamakh worked the loop of thread between his hands, then presented the results to his friends. "Cat's cradle," he said.

Nabul grinned. "I am the best cradle player on Naaki Street." He and the priest were soon apparently engrossed in back and forth manipulations of the string.

"Is your mind clear now?" Jadira said to Marix in a private tone.

"It is. Jadira, I—" He struggled for an easy phrase. He could find none better than "I love you, Jadira."

"It pleases me to hear you say that."

"Does it? But I thought you said it could never be."

"Is a mortal heart a thing of stone? If we measure our lives by the happiness we experience, why should we settle for less than a full cup?"

He stared. "You sound like a court poet."

"Forgive me. I do not mean to cloud the air with words."

"They were beautiful words." He bent to kiss her, but she put a finger to his lips.

"Not here," she said, slanting her gaze at Tamakh. "Let us walk a ways."

Nabul presented the Prophet's Coffin to Tamakh. "Aha!" he said. "Make something of that!" While the priest pondered the web of string, Nabul watched Marix and Jadira stroll off together.

"The journey has finally brought them out," he said.

"Eh? What?"

"Our friends have discovered each other at last," said

the thief. He gestured with his shoulder. "There, see?"

Tamakh looked. His eyebrows bunched together as he frowned. "Odd," he said.

"To a priest perhaps, but not so odd to less spiritual folk." Nabul wiggled his bound hands. "Come on, Holy One, don't stall. Play or admit defeat."

Tamakh hooked his little fingers on two strands, pulled them apart and stuck his remaining fingers underneath the side of the 'coffin'. He lifted the arrangement off Nabul's hands and tightened the string.

"Success!" he said, but the string slipped off his thumbs and went slack. Nabul laughed triumphantly. Tamakh didn't notice. He was once more watching the swaying boughs of cedar where Marix and Jadira had gone. He returned the string to Nabul and stood up. "I believe a walk in the woods might do me good," he said thoughtfully. The thief cozened him to try his hand again, but Tamakh started off for the trees.

* * * * *

"The priest is right," Marix said as they walked hand in hand. "This is a tranquil place."

"I have always loved it."

"Oh? Have you been here before?"

"No, I meant I've loved it since we arrived." The sun flashed down behind the highest peaks of the Shammat. Violet shadows sprang up to claim the glens and hollows.

"I could stay here forever," said Marix, taking in the view.

"Truly? Would you?" asked Jadira.

"You know we cannot. Scarcely eighteen days remain before the conclave in Tantuffa, and we must get the prince's seal to him by then."

"Would it be so terrible if you gave up this mission?"

He dropped her hand. "I don't understand you. I made a pledge, on the honor of my family, to fulfill Sir Kannal's dying request. Why would you ask me to fail in my duty?"

She touched his cheek, tracing the line of his jaw with her fingers. "There are reasons, beautiful one, reasons I will tell you if you truly want to know." He caught her stroking hand and pressed it to his lips.

"I will listen."

Jadira embraced him. She lifted her head, and began to whisper in Marix's ear.

"*Stop!*"

They broke apart like guilty children. Tamakh was standing beneath the trees, a burning branch in his hand. Nabul peeked curiously over his shoulder.

"Tamakh?" Marix said. "What's wrong?"

"Beware, my boy, for all is not as it seems!" warned the priest.

"Go away, holy man. This does not concern you!" Jadira said angrily.

"Speak plainly," said Marix. "What do you warn me of?"

He stabbed a blunt finger at Jadira. "Her."

"You go too far, Tamakh."

"Look at her, Marix. When has our Jadira behaved in so immodest a fashion? Hair down, robe open, and walking like some veiled city wanton?"

Marix's face contorted with confusion. The romantic haze cleared and he stepped away from Jadira. "You *have* been behaving differently since we last talked."

"Do you doubt me now that I show that I love you? Forget what the spiteful priest says! He thinks only of his crude god of fire. If I am different, it is because your love has transformed me," said Jadira.

"Pretty words! Who do they come from? Our Jadira would never beg a man for anything, not even love," Tamakh snapped.

"Then who is she?" asked Nabul.

"Jadira possessed, I'd wager. By whom or by what I can't say. But there is a way to find out." The priest started forward. Jadira retreated, putting Marix between her and the advancing Tamakh.

"Marix, don't let him hurt me!" she cried.

Marix turned and gripped her by the arms. "Tamakh would never hurt you," he said. An agony of indecision was in his voice. "Why are you afraid? Could what he says be true?"

"No, never!"

"Then stand your ground and face him."

Tamakh held up the dungeon key. "As fire consumes the impermanent things of this world, so may the will of Agma consume the spell on this woman." He touched the knobbed end to Jadira's forehead. "Let it be done. *Copus deram fessit!*"

Tamakh expected Jadira to revert to her normal self, perhaps fainting if the shock were too great. She did neither. Her dark eyes swirled and faded to green slits. Her nut-brown skin turned to jade, and her black hair became a sheaf of glistening watercress. The cloaked aura of ethereal power burst forth, and the men cringed before its impact.

"By the Thirty!" gasped Nabul. He spun to flee, tripped on a tree root, and sprawled in the dirt.

"My ancestors," Marix gasped. "What have I consorted with?"

The creature picked up the key from where Tamakh

had dropped it. Tamakh tried to hold his ground, but the green apparition forced him back with its powerful presence.

"You have dispelled the semblance of the woman Jadira," she said. (For all her alienness, the creature was still female.) "Are you happy, priest?"

"Who are you?" asked Tamakh carefully. The merest contact with the creature's eyes was painful to him.

"I am the guardian spirit of the spring. You may call me Jii." Tamakh's face showed recognition. "You know me, holy man?" Jii asked.

"I know what you are." He looked at Marix. "Spirits were bound to the mortal world in the days when the gods warred over this land. For siding with the rebellious forces of Dutu, the guardians must spend eternity fixed to one place. They cannot leave, on pain of instant dissolution."

Marix found his tongue. "Where is Jadira?" he demanded. "What have you done with her?"

Jii's sharp features softened when she looked at Marix. "Do you love her, beautiful one? I sensed it from far away. I came to your Jadira, and drew her to my pool. There she remains, adrift in timeless sleep."

Out came the scimitar with a scrape of steel. Tamakh stayed Marix's arm. "Don't be a fool!" he said. "She could kill you with a nod."

"Put up your blade, beautiful one. While I may have used the form of another, I do truly love you."

"Love? You're not even human!"

"Is that a barrier to the heat of the heart? The beasts of the field love, as do the gods on high. Is Jii less than a beast or more than a god?"

"You've known me only a few hours," Marix said. "How can you love me?"

"For ninety and nine seasons have I dwelled alone, unseen and unloved. My spring is hidden so deeply that few come here. So cold has my heart become, at times I felt I might fade from this plane. Then I sensed the living warmth of the one called Jadira. In her mind I found her love for you." Tears of brilliant green appeared in Jii's eyes. "My heart beats again to feel this. Stay with me, beautiful one, and I will teach you the secrets of the water, woods, and mountain. I will shelter you and feed you, and make you the happiest of mortal men."

Marix turned helplessly to Tamakh. "What can I do? I don't wish to hurt this creature, but I don't love her. I want Jadira back, hale and safe."

"I agree," said Tamakh. To Jii, he said, "Guardian, you ask for what cannot be yours. Please, if you care for Marix, let him go."

"You ask for my life. If I go on alone, my torment will be endless."

Tamakh nodded solemnly. "We understand, but if Marix fails to complete his mission, thousands of men, women, and children will die, and thousands more will have to endure the rule of a grievous tyrant."

"The lives of your distant mortals are like stars; if a thousand fall from the sky, are the heavens lessened?"

Tamakh gave up. He took Marix aside and whispered, "You're the only one who can influence her. She must renounce you, else she'll never let us go."

Marix studied Jii's tear-streaked face. In a loud voice, he said to Tamakh, "Leave us, Holy One. Take Nabul and go back to camp." Tamakh helped the surprisingly speechless thief to his feet and ushered him away. When the priest and the thief were gone, Marix said sternly, "Take me to Jadira."

Jii wiped her smooth cheeks. She said, "What do you

wish of her?"

"I need to see her."

Jii did not fear to grant his wish. She gave her hand to Marix. He took it uncertainly. Her hard green flesh was cold, and she smelled of damp and dew. Marix would not meet her eyes, so Jii gripped his hand tightly and led him away.

They came to the stream. In the ferns by the pool, Jadira lay, lost in slumber.

"Waken her," said Marix.

"That I will not do."

"You must!"

"Will you stay with me?"

"Would you coerce me into love?" he said desperately. "How could you ever believe any sweet words or caresses I might give you, knowing I am kept against my will?"

"You will grow to love me."

"Never!" he snarled, knotting his hands into fists. "Never!" he cried again, drawing his sword. "Yield Jadira and my freedom, or I will slay you where you stand!"

Jii waved a hand. The hardened Omerabad steel blade shattered like cheap glass. Marix threw the useless hilt into the pool. He fell to his knees by the sleeping Jadira and gathered her into his arms.

"Stubborn, willful woman," he said, weeping. "Now you'll never get to visit my country, never share my house. . . . If I had been more a man and less a fool, I might have won you. Now it's too late." Laying his cheek next to hers, Marix held Jadira's limp body to him. Jii stared impassively down at them. The spirit inhaled sharply. A ripple of subtle force passed from her to Jadira. Marix felt it.

Jadira stirred. She coughed and opened her eyes. "I never said you were a fool," she said thickly.

"You can hear me!"

"Of course I can, you silly foreigner. . . . Where am I?"

"Where you must be," said Jii, now standing calf-deep in the pool. "I see that you two are destined for each other. I will not hold you, beautiful one."

Jadira started when she saw who spoke. "Who in Dutu's name is that?"

"The keeper of this place," said Marix.

They got to their feet, never losing sight of Jii. Marix half-expected some trick, but the guardian let them go without hindrance.

Jadira and Marix hurried away from the pool. Halfway up the hill, they heard Jii's light footfall behind them. Not daring to look back, they hurried on. Jii followed them, knowing it meant her destruction. When the bond between Jii and the spring to which she was bound was severed by distance, Jadira and Marix heard a high, wavering cry: the final lament of a lonely, dying spirit. The mournful sound dispersed among the dark evergreens and ultimate silence replaced it.

* * * * *

Tamakh and Nabul were amazed when they walked into camp unharmed. Marix gruffly brushed off their anxious questions. He went to the fire and sat with his back to them. Nabul moved to join him, but Jadira warned him off.

She slipped in beside him. Marix told her in short, tired words the story of Jii. When he was done, she put an arm across his shoulders and held him.

"Is all that true?" she asked.

"Every word."

"You risked the wrath of a spirit for me?" He nodded a silent affirmative. "Then you were twice wrong."

"Oh? How so?"

"You are a man, and no fool."

A dark shape cut through the bushes, looming in the swaying shadows. Jadira and Marix looked up fearfully. A pair of dead rabbits hit the ground, and Uramettu stepped into the circle of firelight.

"Greetings, my sister and friend. I bring you meat," she said. When neither moved, she added, "Do I have to skin them as well?"

Nabul darted in. "No, indeed! That's one chore I'll enjoy!" He whetted his dagger on a smooth stone and set to work.

"Well," Uramettu said cheerfully, lowering herself to a stone seat. "What did you do today?"

Nabul opened his mouth, but Jadira forestalled him. "What we always do," she said, easing her hand into Marix's. "Survive."

PART II:

SHAMMAT

❖ **13** ❖

Pass by Night

As the mountains rose higher, the weather cooled by day and night. The loose robes the companions had found indispensable in the Red Sands now were too light. Marix, experienced in cold climes, showed them how to convert their clothing to the new conditions. He tied lengths of cord or thong about their wrists and waists, drawing their robes close to their bodies. With that, and scarves wound around their legs, they were warm.

Signs of humanity began to appear again: a mountain deer, dropped by a heavy crossbow quarrel, lay skinned and quartered of its best meat on a ledge below the trail. Uramettu sniffed the carcass and said it had been killed less than four days before. She fetched back the quarrel.

"I don't like this," said Marix, turning the short arrow over in his hands. "Steel heads and goose fletching are the work of soldiers. No mountain artisan made this bolt."

"Could it be Faziri?" asked Tamakh.

"Could be, but I doubt it. The Shammat is free territory. There's nothing here the Faziris could want."

"We're here," said Jadira.

Nabul took the quarrel. "Western, I'd say. Bowmen from the Brazen Ring cities use leather fletching."

Other signs appeared. They found tracks of boot-shod feet, wide horseshoes, and two-wheel carts. A party of equipped men had been through this pass not long before.

Nabul was nervous. He scanned the high ground for lurking archers. He expected at any moment to see a two-span hardwood quarrel sprout from one of their backs. Fear is more contagious than the deadliest plague. The companions took to wearing their weapons, something they had not done since leaving Julli.

They camped on an easily defensible pinnacle that night. Marix watched the empty sky and worried. It was the time of the new moon. He had only fourteen days to find his liege lord's seal and get it to Tantuffa.

Uramettu, too, watched the sky. After passing supper in silence, she fretted and paced around the fire. Jadira tried to speak to her, but the Fedushite snatched up her spear, and stalked off into the night.

"What troubles her?" Jadira wondered aloud.

"Her time of change," Tamakh said. "I imagine every time the moon renews our friend is tormented by the forces at work inside her. In effect, her conversion from a mortal woman to a werepanther begins again with each new moon."

"Is there anything we can do?"

"Stay quiet and distant. That is best."

The quiet soon put them all to sleep. The fire sank into a bed of coals and went out.

Rock clattered on rock, snapping Marix to wakefulness. He reached for his sword—the one Jii had

destroyed. Filth! All he had was the efreet bow, and it
wasn't strung. In any case, he was afraid to use it.

He fumbled at the neck of his robe. The bowstring
was looped around his neck. Before he could get it, a
hand closed over his mouth from behind. He yelled into
the phantom palm. Nabul hissed in his ear: "Be still,
you silly foreigner!"

The hand came off. "Filth to you!" Marix growled.
"What are you playing at?"

"I heard something moving out there."

"So did I."

"Are you armed?"

"I have the bow."

Nabul's grimace was visible even without moonlight
or fire. "You go first," he said.

Marix stood and grabbed the bow. It was heavily
recurved, and the force required to bend it for restring-
ing made him grunt. Nabul poked him in the back.
"Not so loud!" he whispered.

Marix gripped the bow and nocked an arrow. The
string was so taut he wondered if he could draw it back to
his nose. He looked at the unmoving humps that were
Tamakh and Jadira. Swallowing hard, he started toward
where the scraping sound came from.

The pinnacle was only a few paces wide. Marix went
right down the center of the path. He didn't want to
stumble off the mountain—at least not before he shot
himself with the efreet's gift. Nabul followed him, moving in Marix's footsteps so skillfully no one would have
known that two men had passed this way.

Something darted out of the rocks below. Marix
straightened his arm. Fear giving him strength, he drew
the arrow back to his ear. Even more astonishing, the
head of the arrow glowed blood-red.

A tall shape appeared on Marix's right. He swung and loosed the shaft. Even as his fingers let go, Marix realized that the shape was Uramettu.

"No!" he shouted. Uramettu froze, right in the arrow's path. The glowing missile flashed toward her. She ducked. The arrow rose, soaring well over her head to vanish in the rocks beyond. Marix closed his eyes and waited for it to circle around and strike him.

A hoarse, guttural cry rang out from the slope. Jadira and Tamakh sat up, roused by the cry. Uramettu turned and sprinted toward the sound. There was another noise, a rattle of metal on stone. Nabul darted past, his drawn dagger upraised like the scorpion's stinger.

Jadira found Marix standing with the efreet bow hanging limply from his hand. "What is it?" she said.

"I shot someone," he replied, astonishment in his voice.

"Who?"

"I don't know."

She grabbed his arm. "Come, let us see."

When they arrived, Nabul and Uramettu were standing over a body. The black woman put a toe under the corpse and rolled it over. Nabul recoiled. "That's not a man!" he said. Jadira bent to see.

It was not a man, but some sort of man-beast. The creature had a long, wolfish face covered with fur, yellow fangs, and high, pointed ears. It wore a heavy jerkin of leather, studded with circular plates. Woolen leggings covered its lower limbs. A short, thick-bladed sword was still sheathed in a shoulder scabbard. Just out of reach, as though flung there by its dying spasm, lay a steel sprung crossbow.

Nabul knelt and patted the beast-man's pockets. "What an ugly wretch," he said. He found a worn ring in the creature's belt pouch. "Smells bad, too."

Tamakh reached them, carrying a glowing brand. Its light showed them the efreet arrow buried deep in the creature's heart. It had punched through the jerkin as though the leather were soft butter.

"So that's it," said Tamakh. "Gnoles."

"Gnoles?" said Jadira.

"A squalid race, given to mercenary war and brigandage. Judging by this one's outfit and the previous signs we found, I'd say a band of gnoles was active in the mountains."

"How did it get here?" asked Marix.

"It was following me," said Uramettu. "I came across a trio of them down the valley. One had a wolf on a leash. They'd butchered a cow and were carrying haunches on their shoulders when the wolf smelled me. They gave chase, but I lost them all save this one."

"At least we know Kaurous's bow works," said Jadira.

"I don't know that," Marix said. "It—I—aimed at Uramettu by mistake, but the arrow flew wild and hit this gnole-thing, which I hadn't even seen."

"Interesting. The efreet promised us that the weapon would never miss and always slay. But did it hit the gnole because it was an enemy? Or because you *aimed* at Uramettu? Or—"

"Must we bandy fine points of magic in the night over a stinking corpse?" grumbled Nabul. "It's so vile I can't bring myself to take anything save this ring."

"Ah, a principled fellow," Marix said under his breath.

Uramettu picked the gnole up by the front of its vest and hurled it down the mountainside. She picked up the crossbow. The stock had smashed when the gnole dropped it. She threw it after its owner.

"We'll have to be more watchful," said Tamakh. "Gnoles are vicious, but they're not unreasoning brutes. They're cunning, strong, and see as well as wolves by night. Some of us will have to stay awake and stand guard."

"I will," said Marix, "if someone will lend me an honest sword. Magic bows are not for me."

Jadira gave him the scimitar she carried. "I'll stay up with you," she said. "I've slept enough for one night."

With Uramettu's spear in hand, Jadira sat back to back with Marix on the path. Silent wariness surrounded them, and they remained alert till daybreak, when a heavy fog formed on the mountainside and enveloped them in damp and clinging mist.

* * * * *

Tamakh had fits of sneezing as they descended to the narrow valley between the two ranges of the Shammat. Nabul claimed they were caused by too many olives and dates. Marix diagnosed the sneezing as an ague brought on by the radical change in temperature. The poor priest wheezed and sneezed, his nose and cheeks getting redder and redder.

The trail bottomed out on a gravel road, well-worn but untended for a long time. The hungry donkeys cropped the grass that grew among the pebbles. Jadira said to let them graze; it might be a while before the animals got fresh, free provender again.

A definite tang laced the gray fog. Uramettu put her nose in the wind and said, "Smoke. Wood fire."

"Cooking?" asked Nabul hopefully.

She wrinkled her nose. "I think not. It's a dry fire."

The smoke smell came from the south, so they drove

in the donkeys and headed that way. A stone's throw short of a league, they came in sight of thatched roofs and stone animal pens. It was a village of some twenty houses. An obelisk erected in the square in the time of Sultan Wa'drillah identified the place as Chatal.

No man nor beast stirred in the single street of Chatal. The companions entered cautiously, holding their weapons and taking care not to give any alarm. The goat and sheep pens were empty. The shuttered windows of the houses showed no signs of life. Jadira, who was leading, stopped in the middle of the road and pointed at the chimney of one house. "There's the fire."

They knocked on the door of the house. Smoke wafted lazily in the damp air, sometimes dipping into the street. Tamakh sneezed. When they heard a stirring in the house, Marix and Nabul pushed open the door and went in. The others followed.

Inside they found half a dozen villagers barely alive. Three men slept like the dead, never noticing the sudden intrusion. A woman leaning against the chimney tended the weak fire. She was feeding it from a mound of filthy rags. Two children clung to her legs. Their faces, like all those in the house, were pinched with hunger.

"Greetings. We mean you no harm," said Marix. He dug an elbow in Nabul's ribs and the thief echoed his sentiments. The woman regarded them listlessly and did not reply.

"What's the matter with them?" Marix said. "Tamakh, are they bewitched?"

The priest sniffled and leaned over one of the sleeping men. He raised one of the man's eyelids. The fellow moaned and rolled over.

"Not bewitched, starved," said Tamakh. "For some time, too, I'd say."

"Eighteen days," murmured the woman by the fire.

"What?" Jadira sat on the hearth beside her. "You haven't eaten in eighteen days?"

The woman nodded. Her head sagged, and Jadira had to hold her chin up to hear her faint words. "That's when the horde of Ubrith Zelka came."

"The gnoles?"

Nod. "An army of beast-men, discharged by some northern warlord," the woman said. She swallowed dryly. "They killed our hetman and ran off all our stock. What food we had was stolen. Since then we've lived only on roots and gleanings from our gardens."

Jadira waved to Uramettu, who was carrying the food bag. She handed it to Jadira. "Find a pot," the nomad woman said. "We'll boil a pudding for these poor people."

Nabul rolled out a formidable iron kettle. Marix dipped water from the rain barrel and half-filled the pot. Into this Jadira dumped dates, honey, and torn-up bits of wheel bread. Uramettu hung the weighty pot on its hook over the fire.

"Where's some proper firewood?" Jadira asked the woman. The latter gestured feebly to a bin behind the chimney.

"Why were you burning these rags?" said Marix once the flames were stoked with good hardwood.

"My husband's clothes," was the answer. "He was hetman."

The woman's name was Murjess. The sleeping men were her brothers; the boy and girl her son and niece. Murjess had to be hand-fed the sweet pudding. She quickly gained strength, though, and soon was helping feed the children.

There was a scratching at the door. Tamakh opened it.

Outside were scores of gaunt, gray people of both sexes
and all ages. Most held wooden bowls or clay plates.
Their hunger-sharpened senses had smelled cooking,
and the smoking chimney told them who was doing it.

"Food . . . food . . ." they pleaded, pressing in toward
the priest.

"What shall I do?" said Tamakh.

Marix tossed him the provision bag. "Hand it out," he
said. "After all, it can never be emptied." Jadira was
waving frantically for his attention.

"Don't say that!" she warned, too late. The people of
Chatal heard. With fevered looks, they lunged for the
efreet's magic bag. Tamakh held onto the strap as a
dozen scrawny arms wrestled with him for possession of
the bag. Sticks appeared, and blows thumped on shuttered windows. One set flew open, and more starving
villagers began to climb in.

"They'll outflank us," Marix said. Out of habit, he
reached for the scimitar he wore on his belt.

"There's enough for all! Enough, I tell you!" Tamakh
cried.

"They're too hungry to reason," Uramettu said. A
pair of young men slipped in the window. She laid one
out with a rap of her spear shaft. "They don't care if they
kill us, as long as they get the bag!"

"Then give it to them!" said Jadira. Murjess was crying, and the children started in, too. Marix parried staff
blows, but didn't cut with his blade.

"We can't fight these poor wretches," he said, giving
ground. They were all backed up to the hearth. Someone
threw a plate. It hit Tamakh squarely in the forehead. He
toppled sideways, releasing the bag and bowling over
Jadira and Nabul. A low, hoarse cheer filled the throats
of the villagers, but a fight began for sole ownership of

the food bag. Hoes and staffs cracked on arms and heads.

"Stop! Oof, get off, Tamakh—stop it, I say! The bag can feed you all!" cried Jadira.

Blood flowed in the crowd. The bag was torn from hand to hand, slowly making its way to the door. Once it was outside, the starving mob pulled the leather container to pieces. Olives and dates spilled out. Loaves whirled through the air. Honey spattered in golden droplets to the dirt. The Chatalites scurried and grasped for every morsel, right down to the spilled honey.

When it dawned on them that the bag had been destroyed, a new sound filled their mouths: low, gargling fury, driven by the merest taste of food.

"Time to go," said Nabul.

"I agree," said Uramettu. She swept her spear point in a wide arc, keeping the snarling mob at bay.

They pushed Tamakh to his feet. Jadira picked up a lost herding staff. She couched it like a lance and murmured, "If we don't depart, these beggars may decide to eat us."

"Here. Over here," said Murjess. She held open a low back door. "Follow the steps up the hillside. There's a cave at the top. It will take you through the mountain."

"Thank you," said Marix. He slipped off the bow with new confidence and led the way. Jadira waited till last.

"Good-bye," she said. "I wish we could have been more help."

"They cut their own throats," said Murjess of her neighbors. "Go, and may the gods bless you for your kindness."

Jadira ducked through the door and was outside. Nabul called, "This way! Here, here!" He was many paces up a steep incline, standing on bare rock. She spied a series of steps cut into the face of the mountain and started after him.

The Chatal mob tore Murjess's house apart looking for more food. They even broke down the chimney. All this accomplished was to set fire to the house. The flames from the burning thatch were a sad beacon to the companions as they climbed to the cave and safety.

❖ 14 ❖

Wings

Just after passing the peak of the ridge, Marix paused and waited for his friends to catch up. They straggled up the crude steps panting for breath. Jadira was the last, and she sank down beside Marix. "They're not pursuing," she said gratefully.

"They haven't the strength," he replied.

"Neither—have we," gasped Nabul.

"There's a more serious problem," Tamakh said. "What do we do for food now, with the bag gone and the mountains picked clean by this band of gnoles?"

"Uramettu can—" Nabul began.

"—do little or nothing," the Fedushite finished for him. "These beast-men are like no creatures I have ever encountered. They have wolf-sense and can track me on a moonless night. It would be folly indeed to hunt where they are near."

Jadira looked back over her shoulder. "Is that it then? Are we to end like those villagers down there, starving savages?"

"Not if I can help it!" Marix declared. "By my ancestors, we came through the cauldron of the desert; we can come through the mountains, too! There are but a few days left before High Summer's Day. We—I—must get to Tantuffa before then."

"Well, we can't forage on our backsides," Tamakh said. Using Nabul's shoulder for support, he wobbled to his feet. "Shall we?"

They crossed the spine of the hill and skidded down the slope to a winding goatpath on the west face. Marix set a strong pace for them. Uramettu had no trouble keeping up, but the others faltered, and Marix had to slow his stride. By sundown, they had traveled some fifteen leagues from Chatal, a remarkable distance for foot-sore and hungry marchers.

There was some discussion about where they should camp. Nabul and Tamakh wanted an easily defensible position, like the pinnacle they'd had the night before. Marix and Uramettu pointed out how easy it would be for a potential enemy to blockade and besiege them in such constricted space.

"Better to camp in the open, where there's room to maneuver," said Marix.

Jadira had the deciding voice. She listened, looked over the terrain, and said, "Let us stay in the open. It will be safer."

"Hardly impartial," muttered Nabul, glancing from Marix to Jadira.

They found a circular space twenty paces wide where coarse wool on the rocks and shrub branches indicated that sheep had been driven. Tamakh sneezed a bit, but they settled down in the center of the clearing. No fire was lit for fear of arousing the marauding gnoles.

Jadira lay awake, looking at the cloud-capped sky. Here and there a star peeked through as winds in the upper air hurried the soft black clouds along. She was nearly asleep when a voice said, "Piastre for your thoughts."

It was Marix. "You pay a high price for dreams," she whispered in reply.

"Since I have nothing, I can offer much. What were you thinking?"

"Flying. Isn't that foolish? I was lying here gazing at the sky and thinking about flying."

He slipped an arm under her head, and they nestled together. Marix said, "Do you prefer a winged horse, or a magic chariot?"

"Actually, I was wishing I had wings of my own. Great wide white things, feathered with stiff quills, ai-ha!" She waved an arm through the air with a sweep of imaginary feathers.

"Go t'sleep," rumbled Nabul.

"Sorry," returned Jadira.

"And where would you fly to, my desert falcon?" Marix asked softly.

"The ends of the earth," she said. Jadira turned suddenly and looked Marix in the eye. "But first, to Tantuffa."

"Of course." Marix touched his lips to hers. He snapped his head back. "What was that?" he hissed.

"Too brief a kiss."

"No, listen!"

She strained to hear what had so startled him. Nothing. Nothing. Then—a rustle, a flap. Jadira thought it was cloth snapping in the wind. Only there was no wind.

They sat up. Uramettu was already on one knee, ready to spring. The flapping multiplied until it was all around them. But they could see nothing.

What is it?" howled Nabul.

"Birds?" suggested Tamakh. He ducked his head involuntarily each time the rustling increased in tempo.

"At night?" said the thief.

"Bats, then." Tamakh gave up and threw himself on his face. By this time, Marix had their only sword out and was on his feet in the middle of the clearing.

"All right, whatever you are! Face us or flee like the vermin you are!" he exclaimed. A dark, leathery form hurtled into view, aimed right at him. He swiped at it, missed cleanly, and spun around. Another thing zoomed past his head. The scimitar sliced the air futilely.

Uramettu watched with her keener eyes. In a strike too quick to see, she thrust her spear into the air. But before she could pull it back, it was whisked from her hands. Marix's sword was plucked away also, and Jadira's staff.

"Together! Come together, back to back!" Uramettu urged. They converged on Marix and huddled closely. The aerial harassment ceased, and the flapping sounds faded.

"Now what?" asked Jadira.

"What" was light footsteps, coming toward them. From the deep shadow of the peak came a small figure, walking on two feet. It hopped from one foot to the other. Plainly it was not used to walking.

The thing drew near enough to see: it was small, only twelve palms high, and colored light gray. Its face was dominated by two enormous eyes, and it had long, pointed nose and ears, and a V-shaped mouth. The torso was thin and muscular, and for good reason. Attached to the creature's back were a pair of folded, skin-covered wings.

"*Ukat dey rom pucoa*," the creature said in a sharp, staccato voice. "*Missay rapa.*"

"Does anyone understand it?" asked Jadira.

"It's a Kaipurian dialect," said Tamakh. "But I can't make out the meaning."

"I have the bow," Marix said tautly. "Shall I put a shaft through its gizzard?"

"No! There could be a hundred of them out there. Let's see what it wants," said Tamakh.

"Not to mention the fact that the shaft could as easily end up in one our gizzards," Nabul pointed out.

"*Pucoa dey! Roma misk rapa. Rapa!*"

"It doesn't sound happy," Nabul said.

Jadira stepped out of the huddle and held out her empty hands. "We mean you no harm."

"I'd rather hear *it* say that," said Nabul. Uramettu laid a hand across the talkative thief's mouth.

Jadira pointed to herself. "Jadira. Jah-deer-ah."

The creature thumped its hairless chest with one winged hand and said, "Elperath."

"Elperath," Jadira repeated, pointing at it. She pulled Marix out of the group. "Marix. Mah-ricks. Marix, man. Jadira, woman. Man. Woman."

"Marix, Jadira. *Pucoa.*" The creature called Elperath unfurled its wings. The span was truly impressive. It uttered a high, wavering call, and the flapping began again. Soon dozens of similar creatures settled onto the ground. They were different colors—brown, black, gray, even a few white. When the whole congregation was assembled on the ground, Elperath folded its wings and said, "Pip'strelli. Pip'strelli. Elperath *ukat* pip'strelli."

"I see," Tamakh said. "My friends, we are the *pucoa,* and our winged hosts are the pip'strelli." When he pronounced the word, the mass of creatures began to pipe and make whirring sounds in their throats. A single pip'strelli, smaller than Elperath and colored a rich red-brown, sidled forward to the speaker's side.

"I, Elperex am. I friend am. Speak to you, speak to me," it said.

"Aha, a translator." Tamakh bowed from the waist and assumed his most clerical expression. "On behalf of my friends, let me say that we come in peace."

"Peace men have sharp stick," said Elperex.

Uramettu removed her hand from Nabul's mouth. She said, "We thought we were being attacked. We have heard there are dangerous creatures in these mountains."

"*Sha.* Yes. *Rapa* come, catch 'strelli and hurt. Many *rapa* in mountain these days."

The conversation went on, with each of the companions introducing themselves and providing parts of the narrative of their adventures. Elperex chattered to the other 'strelli in a mixture of Kaipurian and clicks, whistles, and squeaks no human tongue could emulate.

"*Pucoa* know many things. 'Strelli, not so many. You come, eat good, sleep good, and help 'strelli. *Sha?*"

Jadira looked at the others. "What do you say?"

"I'd like to eat good and sleep good," said Nabul.

"No doubt, but can we help these creatures? What is it they want?" said Uramettu.

"And will they interfere with us if we don't go with them?" wondered Marix.

"We face a difficult enough task without them," Tamakh observed. "If the 'strelli can feed us and shelter us, the least we can do is aid them in their troubles."

So they agreed, with reservations. Jadira went forward and shook the clawed hands of Elperath and Elperex.

"Are you the chief?" she said to the former. Elperex translated.

"Do you not see?" said Elperex. "Elperath make child."

"Oh, she's female?"

"I give child to Elperath."

So they were more than clansmen; they were mates. Jadira noticed all the 'strelli paired off to fly. The females were more strongly built than the males. Carrying babies while flying required generous muscles.

The 'strelli lifted into the air with a rush of wing-made wind. Elperex flapped lazily in front of the humans, and guided them up the trail to the dwelling place of the winged creatures.

* * * * *

The 'strelli village was remarkable. Beyond the serrated ridge that the companions had followed for several days lay a vast volcanic crater, leagues across. The floor of the crater was covered with rock cinders and hardened flows of black lava. Sprouting from the crater bottom were hundreds of tall flues, hollow towers of rock from which fountains of fire had once spewed. The largest of these flues were the homes of the 'strelli. The creatures had carved openings in the sides, smoothed the interiors, and installed platforms inside. Some of the flues towered up to fifty paces high and housed more than a hundred 'strelli.

Elperex got tired of flying so slowly. Uramettu offered to carry him. He settled in her long arms, and she bore him without strain.

"How large is this crater, Elperex?" Tamakh asked.

"Many flaps across. Many, many flaps."

The priest smiled. "How many towers are there?"

"Many, many."

As they moved through the village, they encountered strange smells—'strelli cooking and housekeeping. Nabul noticed small lights glimmering from the interior of some of the towers. He asked Elperex what those were.

"*Tuk-diol.*" He stood, bracing himself against Ura-mettu's shoulder. "Wait. I show," he said. He took off and flew to the nearest flue. He disappeared into a round opening and emerged a short time later with a glowing object in his mouth. He swooped down, flapped hard to soften his landing, and presented the light to Nabul.

It was a living beetle, as big as a hen's egg. Its fat abdomen was distended and glowing a soft yellow.

"*Tuk-diol,*" said Elperex. "Him we feed *diol*, growing in dark places. When it get dark, him glow."

Nabul handed the bloated insect back to the 'strelli. He wiped his hands on his robe, front and back, many times.

"Do you suppose our friends eat bugs, too?" wonder-ed Tamakh. Marix laughed, but Nabul was not amused.

The 'strelli were nocturnal—that accounted for their large eyes and busy habits in the dark. The whole village was astir when the humans walked in. Elperath had flown ahead and told of their coming. 'Strelli of all colors and sizes perched in doorholes or clung to the rough sides of the volcanic chimneys to get a glimpse of the visi-tors. The companions walked on until Elperath fluttered down before them.

"*Noi docay sum kala; noi docayo missay rapa,*" she said. Jadira caught the reference to the *rapa*, the gnoles.

"The Speaker, my childkeeper, wish to tell of the great bad done to the pip'strelli by the *rapa*," Elperex said. His mate went on, and the male 'strelli translated: "Much catchings and hurts of the 'strelli by the *rapa*. *Rapa* throw sharp sticks in the air and tear wings, or go through body so make to fall the 'strelli. Here is our childmaker Eldannek with such stick."

A male 'strelli was carried in, wrapped in a fine mesh net. They laid him on the crusty soil and unfolded the net. A crossbow bolt stuck out of the poor creature's side.

"You can make this better?" said Elperex.

Tamakh and Uramettu consulted over the wound. They didn't know 'strelli anatomy, but the wound was deep. Uramettu remarked on the amazing fact that the creature still survived. Tamakh said a quiet benediction over Eldannek. To Elperex he said, "Alas, my friend, the wound is mortal."

"Nothing can you do?"

"Nothing that will change the outcome."

Elperex's head sagged and a shiny tear squeezed out of the corner of one eye. Uramettu patted the translator's head. "Is this one your friend?" she said.

"My brood-mate."

The 'strelli gently bore the dying Eldannek away on foot. Jadira said, "These bloody gnoles are fit comrades of the sultan! I'd like to strike a good blow at them!"

"Do you speak with truth?" asked Elperex. Tears, looking like watery pearls, beaded around his nose.

"I always try to speak with truth," she said. Nabul was desperately pinching her arm. Jadira gave him a swift side kick, and he desisted.

"*Rapa* are not far off. They are camped below the Joj Xarar."

Tamakh recognized a bit of Kaipurian. "*Joj* means 'sacred'. Sacred what?"

Elperath chattered at Elperex a moment. The male 'strelli flexed his wing out and tapped the tip on the nearest flue. "Xarar. From the Joj Xarar comes the sacred fire of the pip'strelli. Now evil *rapa* have come, flame goes out. The dark close in on all the pip'strelli."

"The gods invest natural wonders with great power,"

the priest explained. "Without that power, the 'strelli are easy prey."

"For all bad thing. Now many, many bad thing."

Tamakh looked way up at the tops of the flue-houses. 'Strelli fluttered among them like leaves in a mountain gale. "You are wise, my winged friend. Here indeed are many, many bad things."

Sacred Chimneys

The village quieted just before dawn. The humans, having been awake most of the night, settled down as the 'strelli crawled into their high homes and drew dark curtains over their doors. Because the murky clouds threatened rain, Jadira and Nabul stretched a rope between the bases of two towers and made a tent out of their blankets. There they rested until almost midday.

Awaking thirsty, Jadira decided to look for water. She wandered among the forest of rock flues, winding in and out of the jagged lava crusts at their bases. An admirable defense, these formations. One would have to fly to get to the door of a 'strelli house.

She turned a corner and stumbled onto a garden. The heavy volcanic soil had been lightened with sand and loam, and lush plants grew in the midst of the desolation. Blossoms perfumed the air, and fruit hung heavy on several types of plants Jadira did not recognize. She sniffed a large, bright globe of fruit. It smelled sharp and tangy. She twisted it off a woody stem.

Before biting the fruit, she had a thought: poison? All

of the food they'd had last night had been excellent, though most was strange to her. She hadn't seen any fruit like this. With a philosophical shrug, she bit through the tough skin and was rewarded with a gush of sweet, tart juice. Sucking greedily, Jadira soon reduced the fruit to a handful of rind and pulp. She picked another, and drained it dry, too.

She filled her robe with the bright orange fruit and carried them back to her friends. Rousing Marix, she shoved one in his hand and told him to bite it. He opened one sleepy eye and peered at the fruit.

"What's this?" he asked.

"'Strelli food. Eat it, it's good."

He tried to bite it, but his teeth slid off the thick skin. He tried it twice more and couldn't get a firm bite. Jadira watched with amusement as he next tried to split the fruit with his thumbs. The skin resisted, resisted—then gave, sending a squirt of juice into Marix's face.

"Oh, you think that's funny, eh?" he said. Jadira tried to stifle her laughter but failed.

"What's all the row?" said Nabul. He didn't bother to sit up.

"Food," Marix whispered.

The thief was on his knees in the wink of an eye. "Food?" Jadira gave him one of the orange globes. The smell of ripe fruit and the smacking of lips woke Tamakh and Uramettu. Soon they all gorged, and their hands and faces were sticky with spilled juice. Nabul lay back and belched.

"This won't do," said Tamakh. "Surely these creatures have water somewhere. I must wash!"

"Come along, Holy One; we'll search for some," said Uramettu. She asked Jadira for directions to the garden and received them. "There will be water nearby," Uramettu said. "Our winged friends are not the sort to haul heavy buckets."

The priest and the Fedushite woman set off on the prescribed path and reached the garden without incident. As Tamakh examined strange plants and sniffed exotic flowers, Uramettu stood upwind of their perfume and opened wide her senses.

"Tamakh," she said sharply. The priest had his nose buried in a silken blossom. "Holy One!" she said, louder.

He cocked an eyebrow but did not remove his face from the flower. "Hmm?"

"Beast-men. I can smell them."

He was all attention now. "Near or far?"

"I am not sure. The smell is strong . . . but I hear no movement. Many beast-men, far away." Uramettu turned her head slowly. "That way," she said, pointing north.

"I would have a look at them," said Tamakh.

"What! Why?"

"I have a personal enmity for gnoles—Agma forgive my hard heart! It was a band of mercenary gnoles that sacked the temple sanctuary of Murhai when I was an acolyte. My spiritual master, the pious and wise Agopa Gulh, was slain."

"And you want revenge?" Uramettu asked.

"No, not revenge. Agma teaches tolerance, even to grievous hurts. But I would see if this is the same band that destroyed Murhai some twenty years ago."

"How could it be? Surely there is more than one mercenary company in the border regions of the Faziri Empire?"

Tamakh didn't answer her query. He was already padding through the cinders in the indicated direction. Black, glassy grit clung to his sandals and begrimed the hem of his toga. Uramettu sighed and shouldered her spear.

It began to rain. The drops did not so much fall as drift through the air, clinging to every dry object they touched. Tamakh's clothes quickly became sodden. He loosened the toga and slipped his arm out of it, letting it drape over his back like a mantle. Uramettu stared at him as he stood in his light linen smock.

"Something?" he said.

"All this time we've traveled, I've never seen your arms or legs," she said. Tamakh's limbs were pale compared to his sunburned hands and face.

"Well, here they are," he said, smiling. Water collected in the creases on his forehead and trickled down his face. Uramettu blotted a drop from the end of his nose with her thumb, and they both laughed.

Good humor was forgotten as they proceeded, however, for the misty rain slowly turned the volcanic soil into black glue. Every few steps Tamakh had to stop and use his hand to pull his sandals from the sucking grip of the cinders. Finally, he gave up and went barefoot, like his companion.

Uramettu caught his arm. "You hear?" she said in the faintest voice. Tamakh put a hand to his ear. Ahead in the drizzle were definite clinks and rattles, the sound of tools and weapons. Uramettu signed for him to keep quiet and crept forward.

An extremely broad volcanic flue blocked their path. Narrower ones on each side effectively made their course a cul-de-sac. Tamakh started to double back, but Uramettu signed for him to stand still. She slipped into the narrow gap and pressed herself against the larger tower.

Beyond was the most open space they had seen since coming to the crater. From wall to wall, the clearing was one hundred paces wide. The sides sloped up in perfect symmetry, creating a sort of natural amphitheater. Near the far north end of the bowl stood two of the tallest flues Uramettu had yet seen. No doorholes were bored in them; instead, plumes of smoke rose from their tops, mixing with the mist and dispersing. The clearing was alive with gnoles.

Uramettu quickly retreated. She guided Tamakh to the other slot and bade him see for himself.

The gnole camp followed the curve of the walls, and Tamakh counted ninety-two tents. Each tent could hold as many as ten gnoles, so nearly a thousand beast-men were camped around them. He could see cook- and forge-fires and hear the strike of hammers on steel. The gnoles were not languishing in the crater. They were arming for new depredations.

He saw no horses. That was not surprising, as gnoles and horses didn't mix well. A crude rock-walled pen on the west side held a number of cattle (stolen, no doubt), and a sizable herd of sheep milled inside a stick-and-board enclosure. Huge gray wolves strained on leather leashes in the sentries' hands.

A familiar shape hobbled into view. It was a 'strelli, and its broad wings had been cruelly pinioned to prevent it flying away. The crippled creature towed a small cart loaded with hay, and it stopped at the cattle pen to distribute the fodder. A gnole strolled by and poked the 'strelli with the butt of its javelin. The 'strelli lost its footing and fell backward in the mud. The gnole laughed and went on.

Tamakh and Uramettu met at the back of the broad flue. "What do you think?" said the priest.

"An army is needed. Those are hard, violent soldiers." He looked her in the eye. "I want to help the 'strelli."

Uramettu looked straight back. "So do I."

*****

"A thousand!"

Nabul almost choked on his fifth fig. Marix rubbed his jaw, and Jadira gripped her knees until her brown knuckles went white.

"How can we deal with a thousand warriors? We're not demigods!" Nabul continued. Elperex sat quietly on his narrow haunches, listening to the humans debate.

"I don't propose to charge down on the camp and put them to the sword," said Tamakh. "If we could somehow frighten them away—"

"And restore the Sacred Chimney fire," said Elperex. His Faziri was rapidly improving; the 'strelli were very imitative speakers. Elperath was beginning to use Faziri as well.

"On the day the *rapa* came, a great wind bore down the crater and snuffed the flame. Truly, the Ones on High have cursed us," Elperex added mournfully.

Tamakh patted the 'strelli's leathery shoulder. "Never fear, my friend. What has been done can be undone."

"This is madness!" Nabul said. "Why must we always put our heads on the block? We've escaped from Omerabad, crossed the Red Sands, saved an efreet, fought mummies, a scorpion, and a love-sick spirit. What more do you want?"

"What would you have us do, Nabul? Turn our backs on the 'strelli and go our merry way?" said Jadira.

"Yes."

A heavy silence surrounded them. Nabul broke it by saying, "Is anyone with me?"

Marix stirred. "Time is fleeting. The High Day is coming. . . ."

"Are you siding with him?" asked Jadira indignantly.

"No, but I—we—can't afford to tarry here too long."

"I'm not going to tarry at all," said Nabul. "My belly and pack are full, and I'm going on now. Will anyone go with me?"

Marix felt every eye on him. "Not I," he said.

"You're all mad," the thief said. He stood and hitched his bundle higher on his shoulder. "If you stay and fight these gnoles, you'll all find nameless graves." He walked away.

Tamakh started to call out to him, but Jadira stopped him. "Let him go," she said. "He's earned his independence. If he wants to leave, it's better to let him go; if he stayed, he'd hate us for keeping him."

Elperex said, "The rest, you will help?"

"We will help," said Jadira. She folded her arms. "What's our first step?"

"Reconnoiter the enemy position," said Marix.

"We did that," said Uramettu. They had heard her and Tamakh's description of the gnoles' camp.

"That's not enough," Marix said. "We have to know where their commander is, where their weapons are stored, how many there are—we need a complete plan of the camp."

"The 'strelli could fly over and spot for us," said Jadira.

"This we dare not," Elperex said. "The *rapa* have stick-throwers—pardon, I mean crossbowmen—on the heights above the camp. We cannot fly high enough to avoid their nets and crossbows. They kill many, many pip'strelli."

"Then we'll go to the heights ourselves," said Uramettu. "Tonight."

The four humans and the 'strelli huddled together and made their plans. So absorbed were they, they had no time to think of the departed Nabul.

❖ **16** ❖

Hard Duty

The jingle of spurs echoed in the valley. A long double line of horsemen rode slowly along the rutted trail. Horses' and men's heads hung low, for they were near exhaustion. How different now were the proud Phoenix and Vulture troops than when they first departed Omerabad!

From fifty, their number had shrunk to thirty-seven. Six of those walked on foot, as their mounts had perished in the high desert. All were wrung-out and saddle-sore, but not one Invincible thought of turning back. The sultan's methods of dealing with failure were known to all, most especially to Captain Fu'ad.

His gleaming helmet bounced loosely from a saddle ring. The chin strap it hung by was stained and rotting. Fu'ad had cut a crude hood from his cloak and wore that on his head. Dust and sweat had dulled his mail from silver to gray. Only his lance tip still shone, so diligently did he polish it.

He signaled to Marad, who rode up to him. "What is

it, my brother?" asked Marad.

"How are the men holding up?" Fu'ad said.

"As Invincibles should," said Marad. "Though more than one has wondered if we can ever find the criminals' trail again."

"We know their destination is Tantuffa," said Fu'ad. "They should have reached the mountains four days ahead of us. If we keep moving and traverse the central valley from Mount Qaatab north, we're bound to pick up their trail."

Marad surveyed the peaks on either side. "So many passes. They could have gone through any one of a hundred."

"It matters little where they crossed. On foot, they cannot open the distance between us unless we falter." Fu'ad remounted. "Column! Forward!" he shouted. The Invincibles kicked their tired horses and moved on.

Marad paced his commander. "There should be villages in the valley we can provision from," said Fu'ad. "Do you have the map?" Marad tugged a vellum scroll from under his surcoat and gave it to the captain. Fu'ad looped the reins around his forearm and unrolled the scroll.

A staggered row of green dots followed the contour of the valley map. Each dot bore numbers and a name in Faziri characters. The numbers referred to a column of writing along the right margin, which told the reader what resources could be found in each village.

"The best place in this region is here"—Fu'ad stabbed the map with his little finger—"the village of Chatal. According to the survey of Sultan Wa'drillah, they have three wells, orchards, cattle, and goats."

"The survey is old. Do you suppose the information is

still accurate?" said Marad.

"Life changes very little in these isolated hamlets. When you and I are dust, my brother, I expect the folk of Chatal will still be tending their orchards, cattle, and goats."

Fu'ad studied the landmarks. "Eight leagues; perhaps nine. Pass the word to the men: I want to make Chatal by sundown. Tell them, fresh food for dinner."

Marad saluted with a smile. "By your order, sir!" As Fu'ad's command filtered down the line of horsemen, the tempo of pursuit increased notably.

The day faded, and the valley constricted to a winding chasm. Fu'ad's soldier-sense played on his nerves. He didn't like being at the bottom of a close ravine. No telling who or what might be at the top, ready to strike down at his confined troopers. . . .

A rider he'd sent ahead came galloping back. "Sir! Sir!" the Faziri called. "Smoke, sir! From the village!"

"Smoke? Why shouldn't there be smoke from a village, you fool?" Fu'ad snapped.

"No, sir, not hearth-smoke. It looks as if houses have been burned."

"Marad! Marad!" His lieutenant cantered up from the rear of the column. "Marad, there may be something amiss in Chatal. I want you to keep half the men here. I will take the rest into the village. If I need you, I'll have the trumpeter sound."

Marad saluted. "By your order, sir."

Fifteen Faziris from the Vulture Troop formed a block three men wide and five deep behind Fu'ad. "Boot your lances!" he cried. Fifteen ashwood and steel lances clanked into stirrup cups.

"Troop, forward; at the trot!"

The Invincibles clattered down the trail. After negotiating a tight turn, Fu'ad saw a heavy smudge of smoke rising from the hillside. In the fast-declining light, small fires flickered in the ruins of the village of Chatal.

"Deploy by threes, column right!" The lancers spread out in the more open ground below the village. "Present—lances!" Sixteen deadly points swung down in unison. Fu'ad waited. Nothing stirred in Chatal. "Forward, walk!"

A mongrel dog appeared, yelping at the horses. Its ribs showed plainly through its patchy brown hair. So maddened was it by hunger and fear, it tried to bite a trooper's horse. The Faziri put the poor beast out of its misery.

"Troop, halt." Fu'ad looked around. Chatal had been sacked, and not a living thing was in sight. "Form a circle, and keep your eyes open," he said. He handed his lance to a trooper and dismounted. Fu'ad went to the smoldering ruins of a hut. He kicked over a charred post and pulled a brand from the fire. Holding this light, he proceeded up the street.

"Hello! Hello!" he called. The only response was the crackling of flames. He came to a low stone wall stained with blood. Fu'ad was about to return to his men when he heard a groan. He circled the wall and found a man on the other side, propped in a sitting position. A grievous wound showed through his torn tunic.

"What happened here?" said Fu'ad. The man spoke a few broken words in his native Kaipurian. Fu'ad did not understand him. He recognized the man's wound, though. He'd been thrust through by a broadsword.

"Vulture Troop, to me!" he shouted. The Faziris trotted to the sound of their captain's voice. Fu'ad asked,

"Do any of you speak Kaipurian?"

"I do, my captain," said a trooper. Fu'ad knew him as Yalil.

"See if you can make out what he's saying." Yalil dismounted and bent to the dying Chatalite. The villager's lips moved briefly, then his body went slack. Yalil stood.

"Very strange, sir," he said.

"Well, out with it, man!"

"He said the beast-men came back. They were very angry because one of their number disappeared near the village. When the locals professed to know nothing about it, the leader of the beast-men went wild and destroyed the place. Sir."

"Beast-men? What sort of nonsense is that?" said Fu'ad.

"I do not know, sir."

In that instant, Trooper Yalil ceased to know anything, for a steel-tipped crossbow quarrel struck him hard in the chest. Yalil threw up his hands and fell, dead before he hit the ground.

"Ambush!" cried Fu'ad. "Dismount! Take cover!"

Quarrels hailed on them from the mountainside above Chatal. Fu'ad leaped over the wall and threw himself down. They were in a bad position. The burning huts highlighted them for the hidden archers but just deepened the shadows in which the enemy hid.

"Anyone hurt? Speak out!" he said. Each man called out his name. Only Yalil was hit. Fu'ad watched the horses anxiously. If the bowmen decided to shoot them, they'd be marooned on foot at the enemy's mercy. Oddly enough, no quarrel was aimed at the tempting targets.

"Trumpeter, can you hear me?"

"Yes, my captain."

"When I tell you, I want you to blow the call for 'Rally.' Is that clear?"

"By your order, sir."

Fu'ad slipped off his helmet so that the gleam wouldn't attract the enemy's eye. He peered over the top of the wall. The mountain was a dark blur on which he could see nothing.

"Men," he said, "when I order, we'll stand and draw swords. I want you to spread out and work your way to the mountain. Anyone or anything you meet is to die." He replaced his helmet. "Invincibles! Stand—up!" A line of mailed men rose up behind the wall. "Swords out!" Curved scimitars whisked out of scabbards and glittered in the firelight.

A brace of quarrels flickered at them and missed. The Faziris spread out and began climbing the slope toward the hidden bowmen. Fu'ad lifted his heavy mail skirt and slogged up the hill.

Something moved in the shadows ahead. He shouted, "*Wah-lai-lai!*" and ran at the figure. The crossbow thumped, and a bolt shot past his head. Up went the scimitar, and down. The enemy brought his bow up to parry the blow. Fu'ad altered his angle and cut under the bow. He felt his blade strike home, and the archer dropped his weapon with a deep grunt. Fu'ad advanced and slashed twice across the foe.

The sounds of swordplay reached him. He cried, "Rally, Invincibles! Rally to me!" The trumpeter put the horn to his mouth and blew.

Marad heard the call he'd been straining to hear. "Column of twos, forward! At the gallop, charge!"

Marad's men thundered through the ravine, followed by those on foot. The Faziris set up a wailing war cry, the feared cry Fu'ad had uttered when he spotted his attacker. But by the time Marad reached Chatal, the fight was over. Fu'ad's men had killed three bowmen, and dragged their bodies to the village street.

Marad's horse skidded to a halt before the captain. "We are here, my brother!" he said. Fu'ad wiped his smoke- and sweat-stained face and gave Marad his hand.

"You arrived with dispatch, but the enemy has already fled," he said. "Look here."

Marad got down and examined the slain bowmen. "These are not men!" he said with revulsion.

"'Beast-men.' That's what a dying villager called them," said Fu'ad. "I've heard tales of such creatures who dwell west of Nangol. They hire out to ambitious warlords as soldiers."

"What are they doing in the Shammat?" Marad wondered.

"No good, you can wager on it." Fu'ad ordered his troopers to disperse in pairs and search for other villagers or prowling gnoles. When he and Marad were alone, he said, "We must consider what this means to our quest."

"How so, my brother?"

"If the wretches who dishonored the vizier and the sultan—may he live forever—have encountered these beast-men, then they may well be dead. I do not believe that myself; any band clever enough to escape the dungeons of Omerabad is not likely to succumb to wandering mercenaries.

"So the nub is this: not only do we have to struggle against Nature and the wits of our criminals, now we have to beware of armed marauders in the hills."

"As if our task was not severe enough," said Marad.

"Be of good cheer, my brother. Are we not Invincibles? Is there another company like us in the world? Our trouble is multiplied, true, but our duty is still the same. And we shall persevere."

"It is a hard thing, duty."

Fu'ad regarded his dwindling force. "Hard and costly," he said.

17

On the Black Bowl's Rim

With the coming of night, the 'strelli took to the air to hunt, to work, to play. A steady thrum hung over the village of chimneys as thousands of wings fanned the air. The companions stood assembled in the square formed by the four tallest flues. With them were Elperex and Elperath, plus a dozen 'strelli warriors of both sexes. The fighters had no armor, but wore wicked metal spurs on each ankle. The scythe-blades could easily separate a man's head from his shoulders.

"Are you sure this is necessary?" Marix said. Jadira was smearing an ointment of soot, grease, and water on his face. Her own was already blacked.

"The gnoles see ten times better in the dark than humans," she said. "Isn't that right, Tamakh?"

"Oh, at least ten times."

"And we don't want that pale face of yours giving us away, do we?" She dabbed an extra-thick glob on the end of his nose and smiled. Her teeth stood out like pearls against her soot-daubed face.

"I feel like a painted savage," he complained.

"On the contrary, friend Marix," said Uramettu. "For the first time, you resemble a true gentleman." Tamakh burst out laughing.

The 'strelli had painted themselves, too, though not to conceal. Their task was to distract the gnoles so that the humans could get into position at the crater lip and spy on the camp. So their slender, hairless bodies were marked with streaks of glowing *diol*. Elperex showed Tamakh where *diol* grew, in the damp blowholes in the once liquid lava. *Diol* were long and stringy mushrooms, and the spores yielded the glowing paste.

When Marix was fully painted on face and hands, he reached for his Faziri helmet. Uramettu told him to leave it behind.

"But why?"

"Tonight we move fast and quietly. Armor adds weight and makes noise."

Marix dropped the helmet in the cinders. "Cuirass, too?" he asked. Uramettu nodded. Jadira helped him unbuckle the metal breastplate. "Strangest thing I ever heard of," he said to no one in particular. "Going into battle without shield, helm, or armor, face black as a kettle, and on foot, no less."

"I pray we're not going into battle," said Jadira. "We're four against a thousand."

Elperex hooked one of his wing-fingers on Jadira's sleeve and said, "The time to go is now."

Elperath gave a piping command to her followers, and the armed 'strelli took off. From the ground, the humans could see the glowing strips blinking in and out of sight as the 'strellis' wings flapped deeply, screening their torsos. They set off in single file with Uramettu leading. She decided not to assume panther shape for the reconnaissance, as the gnoles' guard-wolves would detect her strong cat-scent.

The airborne 'strelli led them to a crack in the crater wall. Rock and dirt from the surface had filtered in, making a rugged ramp out of the crater. They emerged after a short climb and luxuriated in the cool, dry wind blowing across the mountain.

The walk to the gnoles' end of the crater was fraught with tension. Elperex had told them the gnoles patrolled aggressively, and more than once the companions had to lie low and let the marauders pass. Beast-men swaggered by, talking loudly in their own tongue. They chewed charred mutton joints and passed jugs of strong liquor back and forth, but were still too vigilant for the humans to ignore.

Elperex alighted noiselessly behind Marix and tapped him on the shoulder. Marix started so violently the last pair of gnoles paused and looked back. The quick-witted 'strelli made a very high, keening sound, and two of the *diol*-streaked warriors swooped down on the gnoles. There was a muffled thud, a scraping sound, and the ghostly fliers zoomed back into the sky. The gnoles lay on the ground, one face up, the other face down. Neither moved.

Uramettu darted out. She dragged the bodies off the path and rejoined her comrades.

"Dead as doorposts," she reported.

"That was very good!" Marix said to Elperex. "If your people can fight like that, why haven't you driven the gnoles out?"

"Stupid *rapa*, they not wear iron like most. Also, *rapa* awake all the time, and in bright day pip'strelli cannot see to fly," he said.

"Stalemate," said Jadira.

The crater widened as they neared the place of the

Sacred Chimneys. The wind was off the east, and a vile odor blew over them. Tamakh said, "The vapor coming from the sacred flues seems not only flammable but mephitic."

"What did he say?" asked Marix, pinching his nose.

"It stinks," said Tamakh.

"That it does!"

"Quiet," said Uramettu. She dropped on all fours and crept to the rim of the bowl. The camp below was lit by several large bonfires. Groups of gnoles were standing around the fires, singing and chanting in unison. The song was a monotonous succession of three notes, over and over.

"I've heard better singing in a dogfight," quipped Marix.

"They're not just crooning for amusement," said Tamakh, on his belly beside Marix. "They're building their power."

"How so, Holy One?" asked Jadira.

"It's a standard magical practice. They chant slogans together, things such as 'We are great', 'We are strong', 'Death to the Enemy', and so forth. This excites the mind, and they become convinced what they say is true. And it *is* true."

"What would they be building power for, do you reckon?" Marix said.

"War. Plunder. Death."

From behind the largest bonfire strode a veritable giant among gnoles. He was taller than Uramettu by a head and as wide as the portly priest—only this gnole was not fat. On his head he wore a cylindrical helmet of Narsian design, and golden spikes radiated from the crown like solar rays.

"That must be their leader," said Tamakh.

The gnole general was naked to the waist. The firelight bathed his massive torso in crimson as he walked with deliberate tread around the circle. Fists on hips, he glared fiercely at his singing horde. His presence inspired his warriors to louder, harsher cries as he passed.

Elperath and two 'strelli glided in behind the watching humans. "See, see!" the 'strelli chief whispered. "Ubrith Zelka!"

General Zelka stopped his march around the fire. He threw his hands up, and the gnole army fell silent. Ubrith Zelka addressed his troops in a vast, booming voice that echoed in the ragged crater.

Elperath tugged on Marix's foot. "You come," she hissed. "See Joj Xarar."

They moved on. Halfway around the bowl, they found the body of another gnole guard. Nearby, a 'strelli warrior also lay dead, impaled on the gnole's javelin. "Brave Eltonath," said Elperath. "She did not give a death cry. She did not reveal us to the *rapa*."

The rear of the crater was where the tops of the chimneys were closest to the wall. The wind was clearing the gas away, so the companions and the 'strelli settled into a cleft in the crater rim and observed the Joj Xarar.

The surfaces of the flues were a good deal smoother than the ones the 'strelli lived in. Elperex explained that generations of his people had polished the hard volcanic rock to its present state.

"It will be very difficult to climb," said the priest.

"Why climb at all?" said Jadira. "Since the 'strelli can fly, why don't they take a torch aloft and relight the sacred fire themselves?"

Elperath and her mate had a brief consultation. Elperex said, "Know, walking friends, that the vapors which rise from the Joj Xarar are deathly. Know, too, that the *rapa* keep watch, and net or shoot any pip'strelli they see."

"Filth," commented Marix.

Jadira lifted her head and studied the angles between the chimneys and the rim of the crater. "Could we, do you think, shoot a line across to the top of the spout, climb over, and relight the flame?"

"Agma preserve me! Do I look like a monkey?" said Tamakh.

"And the gas—remember, to breathe too much is fatal," said Uramettu.

"All right. I bow to your greater wisdom. So how do we ignite the Sacred Chimneys?"

Marix tapped a finger to his lips. "Climb," he said. "From the base to the top."

"How?" asked Jadira. "There are no hand or foot holds."

"There is a way." He turned his back on the scene and drew his knees up to his chest. "In my country, we have many trees. Some, like the oak, grow to heights as great as these chimneys, yet the woodmen of Dosen climb them and top out the trees before felling them."

"Trees have branches," Uramettu observed. "The flues do not."

"The tall oaks of Dosen have no lower limbs," said Marix. "Not for ten, fifteen, or even twenty paces up. The woodmen climb the trunks by means of spikes on the sides of their shoes, and wide leather straps that encircle the trunk."

The others couldn't see what he meant. He stood and demonstrated. Facing the group, he leaned back. "See, the leather strap acts as a brace against the climber's back and the tree trunk." He put out his hands, gripping an imaginary strap that ran around his waist.

"Clever," said Uramettu, "but the method raises another serious problem. In order to climb, we must be able to reach the base." She looked past Marix and Jadira at the gnoles below. Ubrith Zelka had stopped haranguing the horde. They began chanting again. The gnoles banged javelin shafts on their shields, creating an unholy racket.

"The dark one speaks true," said Elperath. "To reach the foot of the Joj Xarar could cost many lives."

"Many, many lives," added Elperex.

"Then we'll have to find a more stealthy approach," said Jadira. The sound of leather scraping rock reached them. A gnole guard, standing on an outcropping some paces away, had stumbled. "Let us retire to a safer spot," Jadira continued in a whisper. Everyone agreed. The 'strelli flew away, and the companions slipped, one by one, out of the cleft and made their way back to the village by the way they had come.

* * * * *

The Invincibles withdrew from Chatal and camped across the valley. Fu'ad posted men on the heights to guard against sniping bowmen, then settled his troopers into a snug canyon.

"Cold camp," he ordered. No fires were to be lit to reveal their presence to the gnoles. The Faziris grumbled a bit, but they knew their captain's aim was sound. So, like the well-trained men they were, they unsaddled their horses, groomed them, and dined on raisins, bread, and pressed figs.

Fu'ad curried his horse with long, straight strokes, working out the dust and grime of a hundred leagues. It was a distracting task; one of the few in a cavalryman's life that made him forget his imperative duty.

A trooper on foot came clattering down the rocky slope to where Fu'ad stood. His helmet was askew and his sword had worked around his waist to where it threatened to trip him.

"Sir!" said the trooper. "Corporal Rustafa reports that someone is moving in the village."

"Just one?" said Fu'ad.

"Yes, my captain."

"And adjust your belt before you fall on your face."

"Yes, my captain."

A short time later, Marad and his party rode out to Chatal once more. Fu'ad knew that there was a chance the situation might be an ambush, but he had to know more about the locale, the people, the gnoles, and where his elusive human quarry might have gone. There was no one he trusted more to get this information than Marad.

Fu'ad's horse was munching on the native mountain scrub when Marad returned. A limp form was draped over his saddle horn. The intruder wore the robes of a nomad, but his sandals were those of a city dweller.

"Is he dead?" Fu'ad asked.

"Indeed not, my brother. Our old rabbit here produced a rather nasty dagger, so I had to clout him with my lance shaft. He was very peaceable after that," Marad said with a grin.

"No doubt, no doubt." Fu'ad pulled off the man's headdress. He grabbed a handful of dark hair and yanked the unconscious man's head back. "I don't know him," he said.

The man groaned. "*Ai*, my head . . ."

"He speaks Faziri!" said Marad.

"Why not?" said Fu'ad. "He is Faziri." He shoved the man backward off Marad's horse. The fellow sprawled on the ground. Fu'ad walked around and drew his scimitar. As the man sat up rubbing his temple, Fu'ad put the keen edge of the sword under the man's left ear.

"Now, you scum, you're going to tell me what you're doing in these cursed mountains, yes?" he said.

"Oh! Gracious c-captain! I have only just escaped, and was searching for water before I began the long journey home," the man said.

"Who are you?"

"Nabul *gan* Zeliriya, your unworthy servant, great one!"

Fu'ad lifted his blade slightly, forcing Nabul to raise his head. Their eyes met. "You are Faziri," said the captain.

"I am, lord. From Omerabad."

"And you were with a band of prisoners who escaped from lawful imprisonment in the dungeons of the sultan—may he live forever."

"I-I was."

The scimitar cut ever so slightly into Nabul's earlobe. "Then answer every question I ask you, and I'll promise you a quick death, you pig."

"Don't kill me! I'll tell you everything, I swear!"

Fu'ad sheathed his sword. "Where are the others?"

"I do not know, lord."

Fu'ad put his right foot to Nabul's chest and pushed the thief over on his back. Keeping the foot lightly on the thief's chest, Fu'ad said, "Shall I tell you the fate the Emir Azrel has decreed for all those who have aided the vile criminals in evading justice? I can strap you to a horse and have you back in his hands before the moon is whole again! Is that what you want?" Nabul babbled it was not. "Then tell me the truth!"

"I am, lord, I am! They are on the move, great captain. I can show you where I last saw them."

"How long ago was that?" Fu'ad put weight on his leg.

"Yesterday! Yesterday!"

Fu'ad relented. "Marad, have this swine chained. At first light he's to lead us to where his friends are."

The unhappy Nabul was dragged to a nearby boulder. His arms were stretched around the rock and heavy manacles locked on his wrists. A trooper was detailed to watch him through the night. As for Fu'ad, he retired to his bedroll and slept more soundly than he had in weeks.

18

Nabul's Prize

For most of the next morning, the 'strelli were busy gathering lengths and bits of rope, twine, and cord from their homes. From this mass of cordage, Jadira and Uramettu wove two wide, flat straps. These would be used to climb the Joj Xarar.

Tamakh made slow-matches. He had realized that in order to light the escaping gas and survive, some sort of fuse would be needed. In his days as a young acolyte, Tamakh had learned many secrets of fire. While his comrades wove, he twisted strips of cloth and lint together and dipped them in a hot solution of wood ash and saltpeter. Once ignited, the slow-match would burn steadily and could not be extinguished by wind or rain. Only cutting the cord would stop the smoldering.

The plan called for Marix and Jadira each to climb a flue. At the top, they would fling one end of the slow-matches, weighted by stones, into the holes, and then climb back down. Tamakh would then light the other end of the fuses, and they would have plenty of time to flee before the sacred flames re-ignited.

"And what is my part in this?" Uramettu asked.

"You're to protect Tamakh from any passing gnoles," said Jadira.

"I don't see how lighting these sacred chimneys will rid the 'strelli of the gnoles. What possible difference can it make?" said Marix.

Tamakh explained. "There are thousands of 'strelli in other portions of the crater. All of them originated in the bowl where the Joj Xarar once burned. To them, it is a sacred sanctuary, the cradle of their race. When the flames go out, they lose the will to resist the invaders. If we can re-ignite the flames, the 'strelli will gather together and put an end to the gnoles."

"Do you really think so?" said Jadira quietly.

"Absolutely. I've learned that the Joj Xarar are symbols of 'strelli unity. When the unity is restored, they will purge the invaders from their land." Tamakh looked grimly at the coil of match at his feet. "In an odd way, I feel sorry for Ubrith Zelka and his beast-men. Can you imagine the fury of thousands of 'strelli descending from on high?"

"Would that my people had a symbol around which they could unite," said Jadira. "Then we might throw off the odious yoke of the sultan."

"Symbols are not always towers of stone," Marix said. "Sometimes they are flesh and blood." Their eyes met for a moment. A curious look from Jadira found no response from Marix.

Elperex approached on foot, waddling from side to side on his small, fragile feet. "Hail, comrades!" he said. "Heralds have gone out to the other crater folk, telling them of the great deed to come. They will watch the sky, walking-friend Tamakh. They will watch, and when the Joj Xarar gives its flames to the air again, the pip'strelli will take to the sky."

"Very good. Now, do your own warriors know the plan?" said Marix.

"I have repeated it to them thrice."

"Good. When the sun disappears behind the crater rim, we will set out for the sacred flues."

Some hours passed with very little talk. Tamakh went off by himself to commune with his god. Jadira inspected every thread in the harnesses and ropes while Marix sat nearby, his back to a 'strelli tower, whetting the blade of their only sword. Stone and metal made simple music as he drew them against each other.

"Do you know what I wish?" he said, lifting the stone from the curved tip and bringing it to the hilt again.

"What do you wish?" said Jadira.

"I wish the thief were here. He was a coward and a complainer, but he had his uses."

"Such as?"

"He could climb like a tree-rat. If he were here, he could go up the other chimney instead of you."

She bristled. "Do you think I can't climb?"

"No, no. I'm just worried about you. I wouldn't want anything to go wrong."

"I'll tell you something, Marix of Dosen. I've been fighting all my life. I fought for my place in the tribe, fought for the right to ride a good horse, and fought not to be a chattel of my husband. I don't want to die; even less do I want to fall into the hands of Zelka's gnoles. So I will fight with my whole heart tonight, and you'd do better to worry about how *you* will do."

He said nothing but stared at her intently until she was unnerved. Jadira said, "What are you staring at?"

"Someone very remarkable," he replied.

* * * * *

Nabul walked ahead of Fu'ad's horse, chains clinking in the clear mountain air. His wrists were fastened in front and a long length of chain led back to the captain's saddle. The ground was rugged and rising, and Nabul had to lean far forward to keep his balance.

"How much farther?" called Fu'ad.

"Another two notches at this pace, my lord. It would go faster if I were not shackled so," said Nabul.

"Ho, ho! I dare say you would go much faster if not chained! On this mountainous terrain, a man on foot could easily escape one mounted, and I have no bowmen to bring you down."

Nabul plodded on. He cursed himself inwardly for his folly. Why had he left the others? They were silly, overly noble types, true, but they looked out for each other, and nothing really bad had happened to him . . . even taking on an army of savage beast-men didn't compare too badly with his present situation.

A sharp tug on the chain brought Nabul up short. He became aware of Fu'ad shouting at him.

"Are you deaf, imbecile? Can't you hear me calling?" Fu'ad was saying. Nabul squinted into the late morning sun.

"Yes, great captain? What is your pleasure?" he asked.

"Stand still and be silent!"

Simple enough. Nabul gathered in a few paces of chain and sat down on the ground.

One of the flanking riders was galloping hard to Fu'ad. The Faziri was bent low over his horse's neck, and his lance was stuck out high behind his back. When he reached his captain, the trooper straightened in the saddle.

"My captain!" he said. "A band of foot soldiers, twenty or more, are marching on a lower trail east of us."

"Are you hit?" asked Fu'ad.

The Faziri plucked the quarrel from his sleeve. "A wound for a tailor, not a physician, sir."

"Good. Rejoin your troop. Trumpeter!" A young Faziri with a square-cut beard sidled forward to Fu'ad. "Sound the recall. I mean to have these footmen."

"What about me, lord?" said Nabul.

The trumpeter blared a strident song. Fu'ad dismounted, holding the end of chain. He took a U-shaped spike from a saddlebag and went to the nearest boulder. With four blows of his boot heel, he drove the spike through the first link into the boulder. Fu'ad tugged experimentally on the chain, was satisfied Nabul was pinned, and went back to his horse.

"My advice to you is to lie low and pray you go unnoticed," Fu'ad said. "I will come back for you after the skirmish." Nabul ached to tell the captain what he could do with his advice. But he was right; Nabul would be easy prey for the marauding gnoles. The thief dragged the chain out of sight and crouched behind the boulder.

"May the Thirty Gods smile on you, generous captain," he said with phony heartiness. Fu'ad spat, wheeled about, and dug in his spurs.

Nabul immediately began working on the spike. The finger-thick staple was deep in the cleft, and no matter how hard he pulled or twisted, it wouldn't budge. Curses on the mother that bore you! he thought of Fu'ad. Nabul would need a tool or more force to free the spike.

Force. Like the power of a racing horse. An idea grew

in Nabul's quick brain.

Fu'ad's thirty-six men disposed themselves in close column, four men wide and nine deep. His men without horses were riding double with those whose mounts had survived. The overburdened horses would never be of use in a straight cavalry fight, but against infantry they would be quite effective.

Back down the trail there was a shallow draw connecting the upper trail to the lower. Fu'ad's Invincibles mustered in the draw and waited for signs of the enemy. The men and horses stood as still as a bas-relief.

Heavy feet crunched on the gravel path. A double line of gnoles appeared, marching in broken step. Dark, hairy muzzles protruded from under the wide brims of their iron hats. Each gnole carried a large, steel-sprung crossbow over one shoulder and a studded mace on his belt loop. They did not look up as they went past Fu'ad's position. The Invincibles waited. They would hit the end of the column, trapping the gnoles away from their base.

The last pair of beast-men slogged by. Fu'ad hand-signaled "Forward, slowly." When the first rank of horsemen had turned onto the lower road, Fu'ad lowered his lance and cried, "Invincibles, charge! *Wah-lai-lai!*"

The rearmost gnoles whirled when they heard the captain's cry. They had no time to cock their bows or grab their maces before the lancers struck them down. The rest of the gnoles scattered and climbed the steep hillside where Fu'ad's horses could not follow. They struggled to get their crossbows loaded.

Fu'ad saw the enemy was retreating out of range of his lancers. Rather than sit on the road and be picked off by quarrels, he ordered his men to dismount and close with their swords.

"I want prisoners! Get me prisoners!" he ordered.

The Faziris closed on the outnumbered gnoles. The latter were disadvantaged by their weapons, for the bows could not be fired fast enough to keep the Invincibles away. Nor were their clumsy maces as effective as the Faziri swords. The gnoles were tremendously strong, much stronger than an equivalent number of men, but when three-quarters of them had been slain, a cry for mercy went up.

"Round them up," said Fu'ad. Marad and eight troopers shoved the five remaining gnoles down to the road. They were forced to their knees. Their wrists were secured with rough strips of rawhide.

"Now," said Fu'ad, striding before the prisoners. "Who among you speaks Faziri? Anyone?" The gnoles said nothing, but panted loudly, their black tongues lolling over their prominent teeth.

"I don't think they can speak," Marad said. His face was streaked with blood from a cut on his forehead where a gnole had hit him a glancing blow with a mace. "Faw! They smell awful!"

"Their smell is no matter to me. I want information, and I believe at least one of them understands me." He stopped walking. He pushed the first gnole's head forward with a fingertip. Then, with one powerful swing of his scimitar, he struck the beast-man's head from his shoulders.

The other gnoles shrank back from their dead comrade. They made hoarse, choking sounds. One or two whined.

"As I thought," said Fu'ad, wiping his blade on the dead gnole's tunic. "For all their ferocity, these creatures are afraid of death."

"Not afraid," rumbled one gnole.

Fu'ad brightened. "Ah, it's found its tongue. What did you say, animal?"

"We not afraid of death. We sorrow for our dead sergeant."

"Is that what it was? The goddess of chance has favored me. In choosing the first available neck, I also found your leader, eh? So, beast-man, tell me who you are and what you're doing here."

The speaking gnole looked at his fellow prisoners. He grunted a few syllables and the others replied in kind.

"They say, no hurt to speak. I Mukduth, soldier of the host of Ubrith Zelka. Zelka great general. Fight many, win many. He came to mountain to recover strength after long march."

"And where did this Ubrith Zelka march from?"

"Nomgorod city."

"That's in Permesia!" Mukduth nodded his broad head. "You mean, you marched five hundred leagues from Permesia just to find these mountains?"

"Great General Zelka have—how you say?—falling out. Him fall out with lord, High Boyar in Nomgorod. Take Gray Wolf Company away to south, find new lord to serve."

Fu'ad digested this. There was one point he still didn't understand. "Why have you stayed in this range so long?" he asked. "What keeps you here? The Kaipurian plain is far richer in plunder than these remote mountain villages."

Mukduth cast his black eyes down and licked his dry lips. "Great general's orders. We stay."

Fu'ad raised the gnole's muzzle with the flat of his blade. "Why don't I believe you? I think there's something you're not telling, Mukduth."

"Tell much."

It took the deaths of three comrades before Mukduth spoke again. "I tell!" he said. "I tell! Great general wants treasure. Much treasure!"

"What treasure?" said Fu'ad calmly.

"In mountains live little men with wings. Flying men collect anything that shine—gold coin, jewel, glass. Keep in big pile in village. No guard, no soldier. Great general wants to find treasure. With treasure he raise big army, take Nomgorod away from High Boyar. *Skriick.*" The last was Mukduth's imitation of a throat being cut.

Fu'ad took Marad aside. "What do you think of that pretty tale?"

"A pretty tale indeed. Flying men. Treasure! But the beast believes it, I'm certain," said Marad.

"Now that we know what the beast-men are after, we should be able to keep clear of them."

Marad tilted his head toward Mukduth. "What do we do with that one?"

Fu'ad shrugged. "Serve him the same as the others."

The gnole wasn't terribly bright, but his ears were keen. He knew he was about to die, and he wasn't going to sit still for that. Especially since Fu'ad was no longer standing over him with a drawn sword.

Marad turned and came toward Mukduth. He planned to administer a quick strike with his dagger. He never got the chance. Mukduth sprang to his feet and butted the lieutenant in the belly. Marad went down with a great outrush of breath.

"Stop!" shouted Fu'ad. He aimed a high overhand slash at the fleeing gnole. His blade bit deeply into the studded leather on Mukduth's shoulder, but the burly gnole kept running. "Troopers! Ride him down!" said Fu'ad.

Two troopers who had been idling in the road snapped to attention and spurred after Mukduth. He bellowed a challenge so loudly one Faziri's horse shied. The other came on, and at the last moment, the gnole ducked under the lance tip by hurling himself in front of the horse. Hooves clipped Mukduth's legs as he rolled in the dust. The tough gnole wasn't done yet. He got to his feet and limped to the edge of the road. As another pair of lancers bore down, he jumped. Down he slid on the seat of his pants. The rocks and gnarled roots clawed at him. Mukduth slid fifteen paces and halted only when he hit bottom in the narrow ravine. He was up and going again by the time Fu'ad got to the edge of the road.

"Shall we go after him, my captain?" asked a trooper.

"No, you would never get a horse down there, much less a man in mail. He's gone."

Marad came up, rubbing his stomach. "Hard-headed savage! I think he cracked my rib!" He saw Mukduth's broad back disappearing among the scrub cedars. "He'll warn his general about us," he said.

"If he lives. He must have torn something in that fall, and his hands are still tied. There are many wild beasts in the mountains." He turned his back. "Troopers, assemble!"

They rode back to the place where Nabul had been left. A score of paces from the boulder, a loud voice sounded: "Stop where you are!"

"Who goes there?" countered Fu'ad.

"Nabul, son of Zelir, you carrion bird!"

"It's that worthless thief." Fu'ad eased his horse forward a few steps.

"I've had enough of your cruelty, captain of swine! Here's where it ends!"

"Keep wagging your tongue, vermin, and I'll have it out," Fu'ad shouted.

"Come and try! You're very bold with unarmed nomads, women, and children. How many helpless people have you butchered, noble captain? A hundred? A thousand? How many enemies of the sultan have you murdered as they slept?"

"*Aiyah!* I'll have your head for polo!" Fu'ad roared. He couched his lance and dug in his spurs. He could see Nabul's feet projecting from behind the boulder. He would split the foul-tongued rascal from end to end!

Fu'ad shifted his lance over his horse's head and prepared to skewer Nabul as he galloped past. As he reached the boulder, a line of stout chain sprang from the road. The feet were sandals stuffed with grass. Nabul was on the *other* side of the road, holding the chain taut as a barrier—

Horse and rider slammed into the chain. Both fell, and the impact tore the spike free. With a yelp of triumph, Nabul ran forward and leaped on the fallen captain. He pinned Fu'ad's arms with his legs and wrapped a loop of chain around his neck.

The other Invincibles rushed forward when they saw their leader fall. Nabul found himself fenced in by a forest of lance points, each wielded by a grim Faziri.

"Keep off, or I'll wring his neck!" Nabul said. His voice cracked with emotion.

"Release him or die like a dog!" Marad snapped. Nabul tightened the chain a fraction, and Fu'ad, who had been stunned by the fall, coughed his way back to consciousness.

"*You,*" he sputtered.

"Yes, my fine captain. Now I'm in the saddle, and

you are my captive."

"Marad, slay this vagabond!"

A lance tip wavered before Nabul's face. The thief said, "Even if you spit me, I'll still have enough strength left to snap his neck!"

"What do you say, my brother?" asked Marad.

"Hold your hand." To Nabul, Fu'ad said, "What are you scheming for, thief? Your life? You may have that, too."

"Yes, I would have it, as long as it took to draw one breath after releasing you. Then I'd be paled like a gamecock, eh? Well, not Nabul!" He looked at the encircling troopers. "Who has the keys to these manacles?"

"I," said Marad after a long moment's hesitation.

"Unlock them." Marad did. Nabul yanked the dagger from his belt. "Move away," he said. "All of you move away! Ride away, around the bend. I don't want to see anyone!"

"You'll kill our captain," Marad objected.

"Him?" said Nabul, tapping the flat of the dagger to Fu'ad's bearded cheek. "I shall protect him as I would a babe. Now go!"

"Sir?"

"It's all right, Marad. He won't hurt me. He knows what will happen to him if he does."

Marad led the Invincibles away. Nabul got up slowly, the forked tip of Marad's dagger pressed against Fu'ad's neck. "Rise," he said, "but have a care to go slowly. My hand is none too steady."

Fu'ad got to his feet. "Put the manacles on your own wrists," said Nabul. Glaring, Fu'ad complied. Nabul backed away. He wrapped several turns of chain around the captain's chest, binding his arms tightly.

"Now we walk, noble horseman."

"To where?" asked Fu'ad.

"Some place less frequented by your fellow Invincibles."

"Then what?"

"Then we shall talk, good captain. I have a bargain to offer you."

19

Hand in Glove

The city thief and the cavalry captain walked the better part of a league before Nabul called a halt. He kept looking back over his shoulder for signs of the Invincibles. He saw none. That was the disturbing aspect, for he knew they'd follow.

"Nervous?" asked Fu'ad casually.

"Don't be witty," said Nabul. He scanned the open vista along the top of the ridge. "This seems like a good place."

"For what?"

"Just shut your mouth and open your ears, *noble* captain. My bargain is this: your life for the lives of myself and my companions."

"The proportion of worth is right, but I'm afraid duty won't permit me to make such a trade. You see, my men and I are charged by the vizier himself to bring back the foreign boy alive, and the rest dead. So you might as well kill me now, as it is the Emir Azrel you must bargain with, not me."

"Are you made of stone, man? You're a hundred

leagues from Omerabad and the vizier. Ride back and tell him we all died in the desert. You found our picked bones in the sand." Fu'ad shook his head. Frustrated, Nabul struck the captain across the face.

"By the Thirty! Save me from men of honor! You're as mad as they are!" he said. "Am I doomed to be the only reasonable man in the world?"

He grabbed a handful of links and hauled Fu'ad forward again. "What now?" asked the captain.

"I'm going to introduce you to my friends. You'll like them; they're mad, too."

* * * * *

High noon, and the 'strelli rested. Tamakh and Uramettu did likewise, he flat on his back under the canvas, she curled up beside him. Whenever a snore threatened to break free from his throat, Uramettu's foot came back and thumped the priest. Her eyes remained closed.

Marix and Jadira were practicing their climb. They chose a pair of flues in sight of each other and worked on the technique. The task proved safer than Jadira had feared, for the rough surface of the flues held the wide straps fast, and didn't allow them to slip. On the other hand, that same roughness made moving the straps up or down difficult. Each pull left tufts of fiber sticking to the abrasive rock.

From the top of the ten-pace chimney, Jadira could see far and wide. The black crater walls, so omnipresent on the ground, receded to a simple border on the horizon. She shaded her eyes from the sun and breathed deeply. She hadn't realized how much she missed the open spaces of the Red Sands until she'd reached the top of this flue and looked about.

Bubbles of gas had risen through the liquid lava eons ago, creating fantastic blowholes and tunnels. The crater wall above the level of accumulated ash was a honeycomb of these holes, and from her high perch, Jadira could see thousands of openings around them. The sun slanted in. As she followed the perimeter of the crater, a flash in one tunnel caught her eye. She looked back. It flashed again.

"Marix," she called. "Over there: do you see something shiny?"

He pushed his Faziri helmet lower on his face. "Yes. There's something in that cave."

"What could it be?" she asked. He leaned back against the strap and shrugged. "Let's find out."

"We ought to get some rest. There's a long night ahead of us," said Marix.

"It will only take a blink of a dove's eye. Where's your curiosity?"

"All right—race you to the bottom."

He won. Jadira got her strap twisted trying to slide it over the widening girth of the flue. By the time she stepped on solid ground again, Marix was waiting for her. He squatted in the gritty soil, a smug look on his face.

"You're a prize hound, aren't you?" she said.

"Ah, merely skilled."

"On your feet, O Skilled One. We've a hike to make."

They wended their way through the sleeping village. Twice, they saw a 'strelli deep in the grasp of the god of dreams, fall out an open door of its chimney house. So light were the 'strelli, they could fall a score of paces and not be hurt. Often they did not even wake up. Just a soft *plop* in the cinders, and they slept on.

Jadira and Marix cleared the cluster of flues. A band of

open ground perhaps one hundred paces wide separated the 'strelli village from the crater wall. Out of the shade of the chimneys, the cinders underfoot had grown hot in the sun. They walked gingerly to where the curved crater wall met the hot cinders.

"It's like glass," said Marix, running a hand over the fluted wall. "We'll never be able to climb it."

"The hole I saw looked close to the ground," said Jadira. "This way, I think."

They peeked into a number of openings without success. Most of the holes were as clean as a Zimoran gutter, which is very clean indeed. The holes joined the galleries of other hollows, rising through the solid rock to the outside of the crater. Wind whistled mournfully through them.

One hole, larger than normal, did not whistle. Jadira could just barely reach it. She felt the edge of something cool. "Give me a boost," she said. Marix cupped his hands and stooped over. Jadira stepped into his hands, grabbed the rim of the hole, and hauled herself up.

She bent double into the opening and landed facedown in a heap of gold. "Strike me blind!" she said, her voice echoing oddly in the tunnel. The floor of the blowhole, as far back as she could see, was laden with coins, chains, baubles, and bricks of gold. There was silver, too, blackened by age, and jewels lay scattered about like hen feed. And more: glass beads, shiny tin cups, brass and bronze ornaments of every size and description; panes and chips of lapis lazuli, jade, opal and agate. No wonder the tunnel glowed with its own light!

Jadira gave her hand to Marix. He rolled ungracefully into the tunnel and sat up. "By Tuus!" he gasped.

"Have you ever seen the like?" said Jadira.

"Not even in the arsenal of Prince Lydon," he said.

"There's no order, no discrimination," she said. "Why do you suppose the 'strelli put it here?"

"Who says they did?"

"Who else could easily get into this little space without a ladder? They must have been collecting this hoard for years and years."

"I have seen no use for money among them."

"Nor have I. Hmm . . . you know, crows and eagles gather bright stones for their nests. Could it be that our winged friends collect pretties for their own sake?"

"They have a king's ransom here; nay, an emperor's!"

Jadira drew her brows together and frowned. "Or a sultan's undoing," she mused.

Marix scooped a double handful of gold and jewels. "With but a small portion of this treasure, we could live like dukes for the rest of our lives," he said.

"'We'?"

"Of course 'we'. You and I, Jadira, and not a fig would we care for the world's disdain."

"And Tamakh? Uramettu?"

"There's plenty for all."

"And the 'strelli?"

Marix's fevered expression faded. "You're right," he said. "We can't just take it from them. And yet, if they don't appreciate the worth of it—"

Jadira said, "I won't cheat them."

"No, never, but if we ask for payment for the services we're about to perform?"

"Which we would do for nothing. Really, Marix, you begin to sound like Nabul."

He dropped a shower of gold into the pile from which it had come. "I am ashamed," he said quietly. "I, a son of a noble house of Dosen, swooning over money like a tradesman."

"Never mind," she said, patting his arm. "Gold has turned higher heads than yours."

They dropped down from the hole and started back for the village. Twice Marix looked back regretfully. Such a temptation for a young, landless man! Jadira linked her arm in his and drew him along.

Tamakh and Uramettu were awake when they returned. Marix described in breathless detail the accumulation of riches in the 'strelli's cave.

"Interesting," said Tamakh.

"Nice," said Uramettu. She crossed her legs and stretched her arms until the joints cracked.

"Well, hang me if I understand you!" said Marix. "Is worldly wealth of no interest to either of you?"

"In truth, my young friend, I am very interested in this treasure find of yours. It may explain why the warband of Ubrith Zelka has stayed so long in these barren mountains, and why he squanders so many soldiers on wide-ranging patrols."

"You think he seeks the treasure?" asked Jadira.

"Just so. His other depredations are merely foraging forays."

"Strange that Elperex didn't mention the treasure to us," said Uramettu.

"I'm sure they know the greed gold inspires in men," said Tamakh. "That's why they made their request of us in terms of compassion and honor."

"Honor doesn't fill the belly," Jadira said.

"Now *you* sound like Nabul," said Marix.

* * * * *

With night, the 'strelli roused, but this night they did so in eerie silence. No trilling swarms filled the sky. No swish of wings threatened to drown out ordinary speaking. The ground around their house-flues was crowded with walking 'strelli, hopping about on ungainly feet.

Elperath and her consort joined the companions. "Tonight the light returns to our sky," she said. Most of the shrill accent was gone from her Faziri. "All the pip-'strelli in the crater have heard what is to happen this night. They wait, and watch the horizon, for the new dawn to break their darkness."

Elperex said, "My heart boils! I cannot wait to begin!"

"Patience, my winged friend," said Jadira. "It begins all too soon."

A warrior 'strelli wheeled overhead, jabbering a high-pitched warning. Elperath whistled a quick reply. Her mate translated: "Two walkers come down the crater. One wears iron like the *rapa!*"

Jadira shot a look at Uramettu. The Fedushite woman hefted her spear and loped off with the 'strelli warrior flying ahead of her.

A few anxious moments later, Uramettu's voice rang out: "Hail, good friends! The thief has returned with a prize!"

"Nabul!?" exclaimed Marix.

In a few moments, the thief strolled into view with Fu'ad walking before him.

"I thought we'd never see you again," Marix said.

"It's a pleasure to see you, too, foreigner."

Fu'ad shuffled forward and stopped. "What in Dutu's name is this?" said Jadira.

"An Invincible that I caught in the mountains. A captain, no less," said Nabul. He puffed out his scrawny chest proudly.

"Invincibles? Here?" said Tamakh. "You there, Captain; what are you doing so far from home?"

Fu'ad stared at each of them in succession but didn't answer.

"He and his men were searching for us," said the thief. He kicked Fu'ad in the rump. "Isn't that right?"

Jadira walked slowly toward the Faziri soldier. When they were face to face, she peered into Fu'ad's eyes. Then, like a cobra striking, she spat in his face.

"Murderer! Filthy, bloody killer! You are the one! You!" Her fingers went for his throat, but Marix restrained her. "Let me go! Don't you understand, this is the jackal who attacked the Sudiin! This is the man who killed and enslaved my people!"

"No, no!" said Marix. He wrestled her away from Fu'ad. "This one is only the instrument of a larger body. The *sultan* ordered the destruction of your tribe. This man only carried out the orders."

"Only carried out?" she sneered. Marix finally got her turned around in his arms. Nose to nose, she tried to free her wrists from his grasp. Her angry tears flecked his face. "Stop it," he said. "Behave like the strong woman you are."

"I want vengeance," she said haltingly. "Vengeance for all the Sudiin."

"Then take it on the one who deserves it: the sultan."

Fu'ad laughed. "What fanciful rot you speak," he said. "Do you suppose a band of ragged criminals can harm His Magnificence?"

Nabul snatched at the chains, sending Fu'ad to his knees. "We can harm *you* right enough, so hold your tongue."

"My death isn't important."

"We don't have time for this now," said Uramettu. "It is nearly time to go."

"This is true," said Tamakh. "Put the Faziri aside, and

we'll deal with him later."

"Elperex? Elperex!" Jadira called. The little 'strelli alighted by her side.

"So there are flying men," said Fu'ad. He wondered: and treasure, too?

"You call, walking friend?" said Elperex.

"This man"—she waved contemptuously at Fu'ad—"is an enemy. Can you spare some of your people to watch over him while we go light the sacred fires?"

"It shall be as you wish, Jadira." Elperex ululated to his comrades. A pair of robust warriors armed with ankle scythes landed. Elperex explained the situation to them. The 'strelli folded their wings and took up positions on either side of the kneeling captain.

Jadira addressed him. "You speak Nomadic?" she said in that language.

"I do."

The others looked on curiously. Jadira went on. "Then hear me, Faziri. Pawn or king, you will pay for your crimes."

"If you return. You go to meet the beast-men, do you not?" She nodded curtly. "Then you are going to die."

"I have been counted dead many times before."

"No doubt. You are a clever and resourceful wench, I grant, but the odds are running out on you. The beast-men will have your heads, all of them."

She took a half-step toward him but paused, mastering her fury. "Wait for our return, Faziri butcher. For we shall come back, with heads or without, and then I shall settle you!"

They gathered up their arms and equipment. Jadira hastily outlined their plan to Nabul. Marix strung the efreet bow and offered it to the thief. "Will you stay on the ground and aid Uramettu?" he said.

"Me? Stay on the ground? I'm the best second-story thief in Omerabad! I'll climb, you stay on the ground."

"Then switch tasks with me," said Jadira. "I can draw the bow, and you are a better climber than me."

They agreed. The final dispensations were made, and the reunited companions set out for the Joj Xarar under the waiting, hopeful eyes of thousands of 'strelli.

20

The Fire on High

The air was still when the companions reached the rim of the crater. Clouds crept slowly over the moon's face, dimming and brightening the night at irregular intervals. Once they'd gathered at the top, Elperex and half a dozen 'strelli swooped in, dropping heavy coils of rope. Tamakh waved wordless thanks as the winged forms climbed into the murky air again.

The gnoles' camp drums thumped in the distance. Like galley slaves, the beast-men worked at a steadier pace when cadenced by drums. As they drew nearer the site, the companions could see the glow of bonfires illuminating the bowl.

A gnole on guard appeared out of the dark. He spied Marix in the lead and brought his javelin to 'attend.' He growled a challenge. Marix drew his sword, as Jadira, Nabul, and Uramettu fanned out behind him. When the guard saw he was outnumbered, he reached for the steer's horn on his belt to sound the alarm.

"Get him!" hissed Marix. They charged. Uramettu threw her spear. The long pike was not meant for throwing, but from her powerful arm it flew straight and true. The horn never reached the gnole's mouth; he collapsed with two spans of spear-shaft protruding from his back.

Marix picked up the guard's javelin and offered it to Tamakh.

"I cannot," said the priest.

"It has no edge."

"The rules of my order—"

"This is no time for slavish adherence to rules! Take the filthy thing!"

"Be quiet!" Jadira snapped. "The Holy One is right. The javelin is not for him."

"Oh, filth!" With his scimitar, Marix struck the iron head off the javelin. "Now it's a bludgeon. Will that do?" Tamakh accepted the wooden pole without further demur.

They moved on. Jadira touched Marix's hand and said in a tone only for him, "Be easy, my love. Save your fury for the gnoles." Marix grasped her hand and squeezed it affirmatively.

Nabul put his smudged face to a notch in the rocks. Below, the gnole camp was a-boil with movement. A phalanx of halberdiers were drawn up at the mouth of the bowl, facing out. Companies of crossbowmen were jogging up behind them, taking their places on either side of the phalanx. The mighty figure of Ubrith Zelka could be seen by the largest of three bonfires, roaring and waving for his troops to get in position.

"Wonder what all the row is for," whispered Jadira.

"I guess the Invincibles' prisoner made his way home," said Nabul. He related what he knew of Mukduth's escape from Fu'ad.

"The gnoles know a party of Faziri lancers is nearby," said Tamakh. "That will be to our advantage."

"How?" asked Nabul. "They are alerted."

"Yes, but they are expecting a cavalry charge through the bowl, not a strike from above. Why, three-quarters of Zelka's force must be massed to meet the cavalry."

Marix said, "That's astute tactics for a cleric."

Tamakh touched his forehead. "Abstention from worldly ways does not mean giving up one's wits."

"Just so. What are we waiting for?"

A terrible sight greeted them as they reached the cliff opposite the Joj Xarar. The gnoles had massacred four 'strelli captives and left the bodies there. The crude sign attached to one of the stakes said that this was retribution for the deaths of the guards on the night of their last visit.

"Does anyone have doubts about going on?" asked Jadira quietly. Visions of her slain husband Ramil surged out of her memory. She silently vowed that one of the five remaining efreet arrows would end its flight buried in Fu'ad's heart.

Marix was tying off the first shank of rope. "You first, Uramettu," he said. The black woman coiled rope around her forearms and backed to the edge of the crater. She had cut the sleeves from her robe and shortened the hem above her knees to give herself maximum mobility. After experimental tugs to make sure the rope was well anchored, Uramettu stepped backward over the edge. She lowered herself smoothly and steadily, with a hand-under-hand grip on the rope. Thirty paces down, her naked toes touched the powdery cinders. She freed her arms and ran to the base of the southern flue. She crouched low and peered around the broad side.

There were gnoles as close as ten paces. One was obviously a cook; he stirred a big kettle with a paddle. Beside him, a trestle table was laden with stolen beef and mutton waiting to be smoked.

Jadira skittered down the rope next. She slipped too fast near the ground and let go before her hands were burned. As a result, she hit bottom rather painfully. She got up quickly and unslung the efreet bow. In the broad shadow of the north flue, she nocked an arrow and waited. Pulse pounded in her fingertips where she gripped the bow.

Tamakh could not climb down; his arms were not strong enough to support his weight. Nabul and Marix tied a rope under his arms and lowered him. The priest alighted gently on his toes, without so much as a single rude bump. Marix and the thief came down together, burdened with their climbing straps and the slow-matches.

The next step was delicate. They had to get the wide straps around the flues. The web of rope and fibers was carefully blackened with soot, but they were too floppy to go around without an extra pair of hands to carry them.

Uramettu took the free end of Nabul's strap. She went on all fours and crept like a shadow around the base of the flue. Her poise and silence were eerie. She seemed, in that instance, more panther than woman.

Jadira prepared to bring Marix's gear around. Her throat was dry, drier than it had ever been in the Red Sands. She watched the gnole cook tasting the night's soup. Making an unsatisfied face, he turned his back to her and reached for a small keg of salt. Jadira darted around the sacred chimney so fast she scraped her right ankle against the base. The black tower may have looked smooth, but it was, in fact, highly abrasive. After she thrust the end of the strap in Marix's hand, Jadira noticed her leg was bleeding. Tamakh wrapped a strip of cloth around the wound.

"Can you stand on it?" he asked.

"Yes, but it burns!"

Tamakh tied the slow-matches to the climbers' left wrists. Recovery ropes dangled from their waists. When all was prepared, Nabul looked to Marix. The count of Dosen's son and the street thief of Omerabad exchanged hand gestures of good luck.

"Tuus and Larsa serve me," Marix muttered.

"May the Thirty smile on the son of Zelir," intoned Nabul.

They climbed. Nabul, not having had a chance to practice with the straps, lagged behind Marix at first. He soon got the knack of it and scraped along. The technique was simple but demanding; first, you pushed yourself up as far as you dared with your feet. Then, you pulled the strap up from behind your thighs to the middle of your back. The hardest part, working the widest portion of the strap level with the rest, took more than half the time and effort of every pace gained.

Bits of fiber and tufts of rope rained down. Tamakh, standing with Jadira, said, "The bands are wearing too fast on the rock."

Jadira touched the bandage on her ankle. Blood was seeping through the single layer of linen. "The surface is like sandpaper," she said. "Pray it does not cut through the straps before the job is done!"

The stone towers narrowed as they got taller, requiring the men to brace their legs at wider and sharper angles. Halfway to the top, Marix lost tension on his strap and fell against the flue. He slid some way before the strap caught and held him. His slow-match got caught between Marix and the flue. It broke. The longer part fluttered to the ground.

Jadira bit her lip in frustration. She didn't dare call out to him. Tamakh made a hushed plea to his god.

Marix raised his arm and waved. He got his feet properly aligned and started up again. Nabul, who had not seen his comrade fall, was nearly to the top.

"Marix has lost his match," said Tamakh, picking up the fallen strand.

"What can he do?" asked Jadira. "Come down?"

The priest mopped his brow with his scalp lock. "No, he mustn't. Too much chance of being seen or heard." More bits of strap drifted down. "The bands may not hold as it is."

Something plopped into the volcanic ash at Tamakh's feet. Jadira picked it up. It was a note from Marix, scribbled in soot on a strip of match. It read: T CLIMB, LIGHT FIRE."

"Agma bless me!"

"He's right, you know," she said to the priest gently.

"Oh, why can't you carry the broken slow-match to him? That would work."

She laid a hand on his shoulder. "The match would be too short." She held out the portion that had fallen. "See?"

Uramettu padded over from her flue. "What's this delay?" she said. Jadira explained Marix's predicament. Uramettu pondered the problem.

"The only way we can continue is for Tamakh to go up. Only he can make fire with his magic. It has to be done," she said.

"What of Nabul's match? What about that?" Tamakh asked a bit desperately.

"You can light it first, then have Marix haul you up," suggested Uramettu.

Jadira shook her head. "I doubt Marix can haul our

Holy One up alone."

In the end, it was decided that Uramettu's solution was the only viable one. Tamakh and she skulked over to the other flue, where Nabul hung patiently below the top vent. The priest closed the end of the slow-match in his hands and muttered the words of power. Wisps of smoke curled around his fingers. Sweat stood out on his face.

"Hurry, Holy One," said Uramettu.

Tamakh flung his hands apart. A ribbon of flame arced between them, and faded with a crackle. The ragged twist of cloth flickered for a second, then settled into a steady smolder.

"Now, go! Marix and Jadira await!"

Jadira had hastily sent a note up the recovery rope to Marix, letting him know the new plan. He dropped the rope and braced himself for his coming burden.

Tamakh was trembling. "Be of stout heart," said Jadira.

"I wish I were less stout," he replied. He blotted his damp lip on his sleeve. "Invoking to flame is much harder than creating sparks. I hope I have enough power left to ignite Marix's match."

"I have faith in you, my friend." She tied the rope securely under his arms. Two short tugs, and the rope strained to hoist the fat cleric aloft.

"Fare you well," Jadira whispered. Tamakh made the sign of Agma in the air and looked up.

He rose a couple of paces, stopped, and sank slowly toward the ground again. Marix was barely strong enough to lift him. Jadira glanced at Nabul's flue. The thief was descending even as the match burned its way to the top. They passed each other less than halfway up.

Nabul touched down with a light thump. Uramettu

told him, "Go and see if you can help get Tamakh up the tower."

He wrapped the rope rapidly around his elbow. "What will you do?"

"It is time for me to check our escape route."

Nabul skipped across the lighted gap between the towers. He was fast and noiseless, but not enough to avoid detection by a guard's wolf. The gaunt gray beast growled deep down in its throat. It stiffened against its chain, and the gnole tending the wolf ceased walking his post. He unhooked the chain from his wide leather belt.

The wolf did not rush into the unknown beyond the firelight. Instead, it crept toward the flues, its broad feet coming down in the dry cinders so softly they scarcely left a mark.

"Dutu strike him!" hissed Nabul. Jadira looked to see what alarmed him. The wolf was barely eight paces away.

She glanced up quickly to see how Marix and Tamakh were faring. The priest was a third of the way up. Marix was using his backstrap as a pulley, having looped his recovery rope over it before Tamakh was tied on. The rope slipped, and the priest plummeted half the height he'd gained before Marix caught the runaway line. Tamakh bobbed and swayed, then slammed into the flue. His breath rushed out.

The wolf stopped. The shaggy gray head lifted, eyes focused on Tamakh's swaying figure. A long, piercing howl formed deep in the animal's throat—a howl it never uttered, for out of the dark sprang a powerful black form. Uramettu, in panther guise, reached the wolf in a single bound. Her fangs sank deep in the dusty fur of the wolf's throat. The howl was stifled, but the tenacious animal wasn't finished. Wolf and panther rolled over and over in the cinders—gray, black, gray, black—

farther and farther from the shelter of the sacred flues.

Jadira was distracted from Tamakh's plight by the fierce battle between Uramettu and the wolf. She gazed in horror as blood began to flow, for she couldn't tell whose it was. Then the fight caught the eyes of the gnoles. The guard who'd released the wolf shifted his javelin to throw it. The cook looked up from his kettle.

Jadira straightened her bow arm. She hooked the finger tab on the taunt sinew. For a brief moment, she feared she'd not be able to draw, but the nock came smoothly back to her chin. Jadira aimed at the guard, who was hesitating to cast for fear of hitting his own animal. She let fly.

The efreet arrow sped straight at the guard—to the last possible moment. Then it swerved left like a drunken raven and struck the cook in the chest. The stout gnole stared at the shaft that appeared in him as if by magic. He closed his eyes and toppled against his pot, upsetting the soup. A wave of boiling broth overtook the guard. He yelped and spun aside, dropping his javelin. By then the wolf was lying limply on its back, its life wrung out by Uramettu.

Jadira turned from this mayhem to see that Tamakh was nearly at the end of the shortened slow-match. He reached out for the twist of grimy cloth. Swaying, he missed. Again—the match fluttered just beyond his fingertips.

Higher, Marix! Please get him higher! Jadira prayed.

"The other match is near the top," said Nabul, pointing. A distant firefly glimmered against the stone bulk of the flue. Only seconds remained.

The scalded guard cried for assistance. Jadira set another arrow in place. She had only four left. A group of gnoles, led by a very large specimen wearing a brass gorget, hurried up. The injured guard pointed to the dead wolf, the dead cook, and the overturned kettle. The gnole officer barked commands, and his band quickly rolled the cook over and righted the pot. One gnole called sharply to his leader. The officer strode over. They showed him the stump of the efreet arrow. That was all it took.

Horns blared all over the camp of the beast-men. Those who were not assembled to face the supposed cavalry attack streamed to the point of alarm.

At that moment, the first flue exploded.

A brilliant gush of flame erupted from one tower of the Joj Xarar, igniting all the gas that lingered in the still air over the crater. Tongues of blue fire swirled around the tower, and the detonation made the ground tremble. A blast of boiling air lashed at the companions huddled around the second flue. Nabul cried out.

"What is it?" said Jadira.

"My eyes—I was looking at the flue—I can't see!"

She tore his clutching hands away and examined his eyes. His eyelids were already puffing. Soon, his eyes would be swollen shut.

"Listen," she said. "The flash burned your eyelids. I'm sure it didn't hurt your eyes." She grimaced at her lie; she was not at all sure. "Once the swelling goes down, you'll be all right again."

"I'm blind! Blind! What good is a blind thief?"

Jadira cast about wildly. Uramettu was nowhere in sight. Marix was slapping the sparks of flame that had started on his strap. Tamakh finally snagged the slow-match and had it pressed between his hands.

"Be still, Nabul. Everything will be well," she urged. Jadira ripped a strip of cloth from his sleeve and tied it around his head to protect his eyes. She guided him back to the crater wall and sat him down. "I'll be near," she promised. "Stay here."

The majority of the gnoles had thrown themselves on the ground when the first flue ignited. The beast-men were cruel and savage fighters, but they were also superstitious. The damping of the sacred flames they took as a good omen; the return was an obvious sign of the gods' wrath.

Through the milling chaos came Ubrith Zelka. The general berated and kicked his troops to their feet. Jadira didn't need an interpreter to know what Zelka's words meant. She watched as every gnole rose slowly to his feet and stood, head low, accepting the general's abuse.

Tamakh was descending. Hitting the cinders, his knees folded. He pitched on his face and lay on the ground, unmoving. Jadira turned him over.

"Holy One! Are you well?" she asked.

"I live," he said feebly. His face and arms were scratched raw from rubbing against the abrasive chimney.

Marix came slipping and sliding down. His clothes were smoking, and the hair on the left side of his head was singed. "Whew!" he said. "What a blast! Now I know what a tallow candle feels like!"

"Are you hurt?" Jadira asked anxiously.

"Nay, nay, not so much as a broken bone." His expression gladdened when he recognized her concern. "And you, my love?"

"Close to screaming, but my skin is unpierced. If we could find Uramettu, we could be gone."

Marix regarded the burning flue. The rear of the bowl was now in high light. "The 'strelli should be on the wing even now."

"We can't wait for them. We must flee!"

They managed to get Tamakh on his feet. At the crater wall, Nabul was crawling on his knees, feeling for the escape ropes. He found one and stood up. "Hurry!" he said. "The second flue will burn soon!"

"Where's Uramettu?" exclaimed Jadira. "We can't leave without her!"

"Here." Uramettu was woman once more. She said, "I had to deal with some of Zelka's gnoles." As Uramettu stepped into the ruddy glare of the Joj Xarar, Jadira saw that her abbreviated dress was soaked in blood. Uramettu followed Jadira's eyes and looked down at herself. "Calm yourself," she said. "This is not mine."

The gnole general had succeeded in massing a fairly stable band of soldiers in the open ground between the cooking fires. Wielding a formidable knout, he whipped his troops into a rough square, bellowing the whole time in a voice like thunder. The gnoles locked their rectangular shields together with their javelins poking out. At Zelka's command, the spiny formation lurched forward.

"Now is the time to depart," said Marix. He leaped and caught the knotted rope overhead. Uramettu went up the next rope.

"Go on, Nabul," said Jadira. "You can climb, can't you?"

Hearing the general's roar and the clatter of the approaching beast-men, Nabul needed no further urging. He shinnied up the rope so quickly he passed Marix, who had had a considerable headstart.

"Come, Holy One. Let me tie this one to you," said Jadira.

He waved a hand. "No, child. Leave me. I am too weak. Even should you manage to hoist me to the crater rim, I would never be able to run from our pursuers."

"Nonsense! You'll get your second wind by then."

Tamakh closed his eyes. "I am foredone. Save yourself."

From overhead, Marix called, "Jadira! Tamakh! For Tuus' sake, climb!"

"Tamakh won't go," she shouted back. The phalanx of gnoles had passed the spot where the wolf had died. Jadira could see their sweat-stained jerkins and yellow teeth. The points of their weapons dipped and wavered with each cadenced step as they advanced.

"Hear me, priest," she said fiercely. "You've no right to give up your life! We all need you! We can't go on without your wisdom and guidance. You're condemning us all by lying here, *so get on your feet!*

Thus urged, Tamakh managed to rise. Jadira tied the rope under his arms and shouted, "All of you up there! Pull! As hard as you can!"

Marix, Uramettu, and Nabul braced their feet and heaved, and Tamakh shot off the ground. Jadira grabbed the nearest free rope and started up herself. Her arms ached, but she thought of the beast-men below and kept climbing.

The block of gnoles halted between the Joj Xarar. The front rank of spearmen knelt, revealing crossbowmen in the second rank. At Zelka's command, the bowmen took aim on the only two targets they had: Tamakh and Jadira.

"*Kassu!*"

A hornets' swarm of quarrels riddled the air. They ricocheted off the wall around Jadira, the square iron heads striking sparks. There was a pause as the bowmen reloaded. "*Kassu!*" the gnole general cried again. Something stung Jadira's leg. Dampness spread down her right calf. *Mitaali, I'm hit,* she thought.

The second flue took fire with a blast not much less

than the first. Jadira banged into the wall, spun, was sucked outward by the torrent of heated air, and dashed against the rocks again. The impact numbed her, but she clung fervently to the rope.

The gnoles were scattered like chaff. Only Ubrith Zelka himself stood unbowed. The Joj Xarar lit up the crater bowl like day, and from where he stood, the general could see Marix, Uramettu, and Nabul on the rim. He called to his colonel of skirmishers. The colonel ran, tripping over the cringing soldiers on the ground, to his commander's side.

Marix clutched a handful of Tamakh's toga and hauled the heavy priest to safety. "I'll wager you're glad to be here!" he said. Tamakh did not reply. Neither did he move. Uramettu turned him over. A dark, wet stain spread over his right side.

"He's hit," was all she said.

Marix hauled furiously on Jadira's rope. The top of her headdress appeared at the rim. He almost wept with relief. She put out a hand. He grasped her wrist and helped her up. She fell into his arms.

"You're safe. You're safe," he said, holding her close. Even as he spoke the words, he saw the skirmishers forming on the plain around them. At least a hundred gnoles, fast-moving and lightly armed, had surrounded the companions on three sides. The fourth side was the sheer drop back into the crater. The beast-men held off at a hundred paces, awaiting their general's word to close for the kill.

21

Winged Victory

Jadira was almost paralyzed. Her leg wound was only a cut, made by a flying rock chip. It was the gnoles who terrified her. There seemed to be no escape this time.

"His wound is not mortal," Uramettu said of Tamakh. "The arrow passed through the flesh without striking anything vital. A leaner man would be dead."

"It hardly seems to matter," said Jadira.

"What? What is it?" said Nabul, trying desperately to peer through his swollen eyelids.

"We are surrounded. The beast-men are coming for us."

Marix struck a defiant pose. "Then we shall entertain them to the last! Do you have the bow?"

"What good is it?" Jadira said. "Three arrows against a hundred spears?" Marix lifted her sagging head until their eyes met.

"This from a Sudiin of Sudiin? Are you afraid to die?" he asked.

"I'd rather live, you and I together."

Uramettu finished bandaging Tamakh's wound. "We

must fight," she said. "Fight until the enemy strikes us down."

They disposed themselves in a semicircle around Tamakh. Uramettu gave Nabul the javelin shaft Tamakh had carried. "Don't worry about seeing them," she advised. "When you hear them close in, lay about in front of you with this stick."

A single voice rang from the ranks of the gnoles. At a command, the ranks of javelins fell into place. There was a roll of drums, and the line began to move.

"Where are the 'strelli?" Jadira wondered. Though the sky was well lit by the flaming Joj Xarar, not even a bat fluttered over the crater.

"Oh you gods, who number thirty, accept this unworthy one into the realm of paradise. You gods, whose names are Rau, Taalbah, Subaith . . ."

While Nabul prayed, Jadira waited, tapping the shaft of her third arrow against the grip of the bow. She glanced at Marix. Sooty and singed, he still embodied a jaunty air of martial ardor. The scimitar hung casually from his right hand as his left was planted firmly on his hip. On the other side, Uramettu leaned on her spear. Her wide, liquid-brown eyes followed the progress of the gnoles with calm detachment.

Fifty paces. Death was halfway to them. Jadira checked for the 'strelli again. The sky was clear. She cursed the flying folk as worthless allies. She wrapped a finger around the tapping arrow shaft to still it.

". . . Kabrax, Raleg, Mortum, Shimdawi . . ." Nabul's litany went on.

"Do you know what the worst of this is?" Jadira said quietly. The gnole sergeants calling cadence could now be seen, head and shoulders taller than the rank and file.

"What?" said Marix.

"We'll never have children."

His expression of astonishment was so complete she asked what he had expected her to say. "That you would regret not being able to kill that Faziri captain," he said.

"There is that, also."

Twenty paces. She could see the hack marks on the gnoles' lacquered shields. At ten paces, the right and left blocks halted. The center came on. Jadira drew a bead on the tallest, loudest gnole. He must certainly be an officer. The gnole's helmeted head wavered over the point of the arrow. Why try so hard to aim? she thought. It will strike home somewhere.

She relaxed. The fear, the feeling of impending loss slipped away. She was with her friends and the man she loved. It was a good time, a good place to die.

The gnoles stopped. The officer at the rear of the phalanx was looking back over his shoulder. He bellowed something Jadira didn't understand. The gnoles unlocked their shields and began to turn around.

"By Tuus! Would you look at that!" said Marix.

"I wish I could!" moaned Nabul. "What's happening?"

"They're turning away!"

"But why?" Uramettu said. The gnoles on their left were turning too. And then, four bright notes from a trumpet split the air. A body of horsemen appeared on the flat beyond the crater rim. Pennants whipped from their lance tips.

"Faziris! The Invincibles are here!" said Jadira.

Marad and the troopers had ridden hard to find their lost captain. From a plateau a quarter league away, the Faziris saw the Joj Xarar burst into life. By their flames, Marad saw the drama on the crater rim unfold—five brave humans besieged by twenty times their number of outraged gnoles. He did not hesitate. He gave the order to charge.

The lancers slammed into the beast-men at full gallop. The lightly equipped skirmishers were no match for heavy horsemen. They fell under the mailed onslaught of the Invincibles even though they strongly outnumbered the Faziris. The whole right flank company broke and ran as the Faziri trumpeter blew 'Free Chase' while standing triumphantly in his stirrups.

Marix ran forward and engaged the nearest gnole. The skirmisher parried the sword with his javelin and banged with his shield until Marix lost his footing. The gnole raised his javelin for the kill, but Uramettu swept his legs out from under him with her spear shaft. Marix jumped up and finished the job.

Jadira moved forward a few steps. Nabul was shouting over the din of battle even though he still could not see a thing. The gnoles' front burst asunder, and mounted men four abreast tore through. While the troopers harried the remaining gnoles, Marad rode up to Uramettu and Marix. "I am Marad *gan* Rafikiya, of the Invincible Cavalry of His Magnificence the Sultan—may he live forever!"

"Marix, third son of Count Fernald of Dosen."

"Uramettu, daughter of Ondakoto and Isanfaela."

The Faziri nodded curtly. "Is Captain Fu'ad with you?" he said.

"No, but we know where he is," said Marix.

"You will take me to him." A thrown javelin struck quivering at the feet of Marad's horse. The animal shied, but the lieutenant reined him in sharply. "You will return our captain to us unharmed, or I shall ride away and leave you to your fate."

Jadira appeared, leading Nabul. She heard Marad's

threat. She said, "If we are killed, you will never find him."

"I will not haggle with you, nomad. Give me my captain!"

"You have no choice. We have one wounded and one blinded. Take us out of here and we'll give you your precious captain," she said.

Marad scowled. "Very well. But afterward—"

"Afterward is meaningless if we're killed," she said pointedly. Marad called in some of his men. After putting the unconscious Tamakh in the hands of a burly horseman, each of the companions mounted a Faziri horse behind an Invincible. The trumpeter sounded recall, and the troopers assembled. The flat was littered with fallen gnoles. Marad's band was intact.

"Where to?" he said to Jadira, who was holding him about the waist.

"Down into the crater," she replied. "To the village of the 'strelli."

"Company, follow me," he said. The lancers formed into a column and spurred away from the scene of the fight.

"There's a natural ramp leading into the bowl," said Jadira, "about five hundred paces ahead on the left."

They found the ramp. Marad led his men down. Halfway round the spiraling path, they ran head-on into a mass of gnoles. Quarrels flicked from crossbows. Faziri saddles were emptied.

"Come about!" cried Marad. "Go back the other way!"

The horsemen galloped up the ramp. At the top, they met some of the skirmishers, who were trying to find Ubrith Zelka's main force. Marad and his men trampled them and kept going.

"Now what?" he asked.

"Ride!" Jadira said.

More and more gnoles popped up from hiding places. Quarrels, arrows, javelins, and throwing axes rained on the Faziris. More troopers fell. Marix found himself alone on his horse. He crouched low over the animal's neck and dug in his heels.

The flat ground dwindled to an expanse of broken rock and boulders. Gnoles with halberds were picking their way over the broken ground toward the trapped horsemen. One ugly specimen clambered onto a boulder as high as Marad's horse. He swung his halberd in a wide arc. Marad fended him off with his lance. Jadira fumbled for the efreet bow.

Suddenly, the halberdier dropped his weapon and pitched forward. Deep red cuts showed on his back. Other gnoles were similarly cut down around them.

"Is this magic?" asked Marad.

"No! The 'strelli have come at last!"

A small gray form settled on a rock. Wings spread wide, ankle blades bright with gnole blood, Elperex whistled a shrill song of victory.

"We have come, walking friends!" he piped. "Even as I speak, the pip'strelli scour the crater below clean of the foul *rapa*."

"What took you so long?" demanded Jadira.

"It was the decision of my mate Elperath that we should not strike until all the tribes had gathered," said Elperex. "But rejoice, walking friends! The night of deliverance is here!"

It was true. In ever-increasing swarms, the arriving 'strelli picked off the gnoles. Isolated and unorganized, the beast-men on the crater rim were easy prey. In the bowl, it was another matter. Many 'strelli flew for the last

time that night, for Ubrith Zelka and his best troops
fought on and on.

* * * * *

When the first glow of dawn came to the mountains,
the sounds of combat had ceased. The silence was not
merely a token of death, but also of exhaustion and victory.

Jadira awoke in Marix's arms. All around them the
surviving Faziri troopers dozed like dead men beneath
their horses. They'd gotten no more than a notch of
sleep.

She shook Marix awake. Marad stirred nearby. Uramettu stretched her long legs and poked Nabul. The
thief unwound the wrapping from his eyes. The swelling
was much less now, and he could see.

"How's Tamakh?" asked Jadira. Her voice was a dry
rasp. Uramettu gently patted the injured priest's face.
His eyes opened.

"Have you joined me in the next world?" he asked
Uramettu.

"We've not left this one yet, Holy One."

She helped him sit up. He groaned from pain but
managed to stay upright. When he recognized the trap-
pings of the Faziri soldiers, his face displayed a flash of
panic. Then Uramettu explained what had happened
after he was wounded.

"How ironic. Those who want our death saved our
lives," he said.

"We shall see," Marix replied. "For here we are still in
the midst of them."

Marad rose and buckled on his sword belt. "You are
indeed, young lord. And now, if you please, take us to

Captain Fu'ad." His tone was not as polite as his words.

Slowly the weary troopers shook off the burden of slumber and remounted their equally exhausted horses. Jadira and her companions had to walk. She led them to the ramp so hotly contested the night before.

The ground was thick with the fallen. Here and there among the gnoles was an Invincible, felled by a quarrel or axe. Marad's men rode single file down the ramp, with the companions just ahead.

The 'strelli slept where they had alighted. Reefs of them, their leathery wings furled about them like cloaks, covered the rocky walls of the crater.

The procession descended to the crater floor. In the midst of the dead, 'strelli and gnoles alike, lay Ubrith Zelka. His wounds were grievous, but it was obvious that no single being had struck the mighty general down. Just as an ant can bring down an oak, so had a hundred 'strelli finally broken the strength of Zelka. His reign of terror was done.

Jadira turned north for Elperath's village. Along the way, they found many signs of flight. Carts and wagons overturned and smashed. Livestock running free. Arms and booty from half the lands north of the Shammat were scattered on the trail of the fleeing gnoles.

Something moved in the morning shadows ahead. Marix drew his sword. Jadira stayed his hand; the moving figure was Elperex.

He was walking. Slowly, painfully, but walking. His wing-arms were closed around a heavy bundle of some kind. Jadira caught up with him and tapped him on the back.

Elperex turned. His face was etched with sorrow. "My walking friends," he said, "the night was ours."

"What is it, Elperex? What's wrong?"

He unfolded his wings to reveal the lifeless form of Elperath. "My mated one is gone," he said. "She sought out the leader of the *rapa* and smote him time and again. He caught her and, with his bare hands, broke her back."

Jadira signaled to Marix and Uramettu. "May we help you, Elperex?" she said. She knew it was terribly difficult for 'strelli to walk any distance. He said nothing, but conveyed Elperath gently into Marix's open arms. The chief's body was remarkably light.

"I thank you," said Elperex. He spread his wings as wide as they would go. "My wings and eyes for the life of my mated one back!" he cried. His hopeless wish echoed down the crater walls unanswered.

The village of flues loomed above them. Jadira called a halt.

"Wait here," she said to Marad. "I'll get the captain."

He dismounted. "I shall go with you." She shrugged.

Fu'ad was still chained to the base of the slim flue. He was asleep. Jadira kicked his feet, and he started.

"Marad!" he said. "Well done, my brother! You've taken the she-demon alive."

"No one's taken anyone," Jadira snapped. "The son of Rafik and I have a truce."

"Truce? You can't be serious! Clap her in irons, Marad!"

"Patience, my brother. Much has happened since you were captured. Many things need to be discussed."

The rest of the humans straggled in. Fu'ad counted his men: ten, thirteen, eighteen, twenty-one. Less than half of the Invincibles remained!

"What is the meaning of this?" he demanded.

"Just this, Faziri," said Jadira. "Your men and my friends have survived a murderous battle with a thousand fierce gnoles. Having fought alongside each other, we agreed to talk as comrades in arms, not captives to captors."

"The battle is over and won, sir," said Marad. "The beast-men have been vanquished, and the arms of the Invincibles carried in glory."

"Very good. Now release me," Fu'ad said.

"Not yet," said Jadira.

"This is nonsense! Marad, muster the men and seize the criminals!"

Marad looked at his feet and didn't move. Fu'ad stared at his lieutenant in amazement. "I gave you an order!" he shouted.

"Look around you, Captain," said Jadira. Angrily, he complied. Everywhere he turned, he saw sleeping 'strelli. Most of them still wore their ankle knives.

"Thousands of 'strelli," she said. "Thousands of blades. They cut the gnoles to pieces, Captain, and these same 'strelli are our friends. Marad knows that; that's why he won't act. There's no reason to die needlessly."

Fu'ad pondered this awhile. He said, in a more measured tone, "Will you unchain me?"

Nabul came forward and tossed the key to Fu'ad. The captain unlocked his bonds and rubbed the chafed places on his wrists.

"You have us in a very neat basket," he said. "What do you intend for us? Death?"

Marix, Uramettu, Tamakh, and Nabul all looked at Jadira. Hers was the final word. What would she say?

"No, not death. I am sick of blood and death," she said. "I leave you to face the sultan with your failure. We're going on, my companions and I, and you are returning to Fazir."

"And if I choose not to go?"

"The choice is not yours. Elperex?" The grief-stricken 'strelli appeared. "Your people must escort Captain Fu'ad and his men back through the mountains east. If they deviate from that course, slay them."

"If you wish it, Jadira," he answered listlessly. He roused some sleeping 'strelli warriors and relayed Jadira's request to them.

Fu'ad was provided with a horse. He mounted and joined ranks with his men. "It is not over yet, woman," he said. "As long as I live, I'll hunt you."

"No doubt, Faziri. That is the way of a jackal," she retorted.

Fu'ad waved his men around him, and they all rode off. A canopy of 'strelli followed close overhead, their wings beating slowly in rhythm with the horses' hooves.

* * * * *

The funeral of Elperath was simple. She was carried aloft on a cloth litter to the blazing Joj Xarar. Four 'strelli, each holding a corner of the litter, held Elperath's remains in the flames of the sacred flue. In very little time, her little body was consumed.

Elperex, by custom, was now a non-person. For a specified period of mourning, none of his fellow creatures would acknowledge him, speak to him, or even look at him. He retreated to the caves in the western walls of the crater to grieve, and await the time when a new chief would grant him leave to return to the tribe.

❖ 22 ❖

A Companion Gained

Marix pounded the loose joint with a *keshj* wood mallet. The seam closed. He tested it with a hard tug. The pegs held.

"It's done," he said. Nabul and Uramettu lined up beside him, and together they pushed the two-wheeled cart upright. From wreckage in the gnole camp, they had taken a pair of carts and repaired them. With an ox to draw each one, plus their original complement of donkeys, the companions would not want for carriage.

Marix worried. Oxen were notoriously slow beasts, and High Summer's Day was rushing toward them. Could they still make it to Tantuffa in time?

"Once we leave the crater of the 'strelli, we'll not stop again until we find the seal and deliver it to your Lord Hurgold," Jadira promised. "That's why we need the oxen. They will walk day and night, and we can ride and sleep."

Tamakh developed a fever from his wound. His gentle face whitened and sweat ran off him in streams. Jadira stayed with him, blotting his burning brow with cool cloths and feeding him clear broth. He passed in and out of delirium. Often he mumbled in Zimoran, a language Jadira did not know. Once, when she was changing the bandage on his side, he seized Jadira's arm in a surprisingly hard grip.

"Tamakh, what is it? Did I hurt you?" she asked.

"Why must you leave?" he said.

"I'm not leaving," Jadira replied. "I'm staying right here."

"My life will be over when you are gone." Tears streaked the corners of his clenched eyes.

Marix ducked under the tarp. "How's the holy man?" he asked.

"Is there nothing left for me?" Tamakh exclaimed.

"He's under a delusion," Jadira said. "He thinks I'm someone else." She carefully, but firmly, removed her arm from his grasp.

"Laviya," said the priest, choking. "Laviya."

"Who is that, I wonder?" whispered Marix.

"Someone who hurt him. A lover perhaps. Even priests have lives before their vows." Jadira folded Tamakh's hands across his stomach. His sobbing faded, and he rested silently.

"Nabul's—" began Marix, but Tamakh interrupted him.

"Jadira?" said the holy man.

"Yes, Tamakh?"

"And Marix? Are you there, my boy?"

"I am here, Holy One."

"I have been to the Land of the Dead," he said. "Been there and returned."

"You're going to live, then," Marix declared.

"I shall," said Tamakh. "For many, many years." Jadira could not decide whether he was pleased by the prospect.

* * * * *

Nabul's left eye never regained its sight. For some days, he kept to himself, silent and morose, until Uramettu cornered him in the 'strelli garden.

"Are you going to hide from us forever?" she said.

Nabul spat a cherry pit over his shoulder. "I've lost an eye," he said flatly. "Do you expect me to dance and sing?"

"Are you less a man with one eye?"

He glared. "By the Thirty, no!"

"Then prove it to the rest of us. Come back and try our patience as you used to do." Uramettu held out a hand, fingers closed into a fist.

"What's that?" asked Nabul. She opened her hand, and an oval of bright metal dangled from her fingers.

"It's an eyepatch," she said. "Try it on."

Nabul took it uncertainly. He slipped the thong around his head and positioned the patch over his ruined eye. "What is this made of? Brass?"

"Gold," Uramettu replied. "I hammered out a coin from the purse of Ubrith Zelka."

He touched the patch lightly. "Gold, eh?" Nabul grimaced. "It's cold!"

She slapped him on the back. "What a man you are!"

* * * * *

The 'strelli set about choosing their new chief. By custom, this was done in secrecy by a small assembly of senior females. On the second morning after the battle, a delegation of 'strelli came to the humans' camp. The new chief introduced herself through an interpreter. Her name was Ectoreth.

"For the great service you have rendered to us," she said gravely, "the pip'strelli wish to honor you with a gift. Is there anything of ours we might give you?"

Nabul gave a sharp, sarcastic snort. Marix poked him in the ribs and glared him into silence. "There is, generous Ectoreth," he said.

"What would this be?"

"In the walls of the crater, west of your village, there is a cave. In this cave are many pretty things."

"Yes, *tucca nyth*," said Ectoreth. Marix quizzed the interpreter for an exact translation. The nut-brown male 'strelli struggled for a moment, then said: "Rubbish."

"Rubbish?" asked Marix.

"Rubbish!" said Nabul.

"*Tucca nyth* are the shiny rocks and bits of metal brought in by children after their flight of adulthood," Ectoreth explained. "When our young reach a certain age, they go on a long flight alone. It is a test of endurance, courage, and tracking ability. To prove they have indeed gone far away, the tested 'strelli bring back *tucca nyth*, rubbish from distant lands."

"It has no value to you?" asked Marix carefully.

"Only by what it proves," said the 'strelli chief.

"May we take away some of the *tucca nyth*?"

"As much as you like. It is nothing."

So, later that day, Marix, Nabul, and Uramettu rode one of the ox-carts out to the cave. Nabul nearly fainted when he saw the "rubbish." The shock passed, and he threw himself into the sprawling pool of wealth, rolling and flinging it in all directions.

"We'll be rich as kings! For all this I would gladly lose an eye!" he cried. "Richer! O, you gods, I knew it was right that I come back to aid my friends!"

"Please," said Uramettu. "You're making a fool of yourself."

"I am a fool! A *rich* fool!"

"Not yet, you're not," Marix put in. "Come on, come on; let's fill the cart." He dug deep into the pile with a brass bowl.

With a gnole's helmet, Nabul began scooping up coins and jewels. He and Marix hobbled on their knees to the mouth of the cave. There they flung the treasure into the cart where Uramettu stood. Nabul chortled with every ringing piastre that bounced on the stout wooden planking.

"Would it not be better to fill bags or small boxes?" said Uramettu.

"Why?" said Nabul. "We can carry more this way."

"We have a fair distance to go. It seems rather conspicuous to carry gold and gems loose in a cart like so much winnowed wheat."

"I disagree," said Marix, emptying his helmet for the fourth time. "If we fill the bottom of the cart, we can cover over the treasure with ordinary baggage. Who would ever suspect what lay beneath?"

"Well said, brother!" Nabul added. He grinned at Marix like a drunkard and dumped another bowl full of riches into the cart.

There was a rustle of dry wings. A shadow flickered overhead. Uramettu shaded her eyes and looked up. "Elperex," she said. "I'm sorry. Did we disturb you?"

"No, walking friend. I am pleased at seeing you," he said.

A shower of jingling coins splashed out of the cave. Elperex said, "Why are you taking this trash?"

"Trash to you, my winged friend, but treasure to us,"

said Marix.

"Treasure? Bits of metal and rock?"

"Just so. Have you ever heard of money?"

"That is something humans use. To us it means nothing. You cannot eat money. It does not make flowers bloom or fruit ripen. It cannot bring back the life of one's mate."

Marix paused in his frantic shoveling. He suddenly felt ashamed. Nabul carried on until Uramettu told him to stop.

"But there's so much left!" he complained.

"The cart is groaning now. Would you have us break the axle?" she said. Nabul searched through the mix of treasure one last time. He came up with a fat, uncut emerald in one hand and an ingot of silver in the other. The ingot went in the cart, but the emerald he stuffed in his robe.

Uramettu brought the ox's head around. The cart wheels squeaked violently as it turned. Marix and Nabul jumped down and dusted off their hands.

"Where will you go now?" asked Elperex.

"Beyond the mountains to the sea," said Marix. "Only seven days remain before the conclave in Tantuffa."

"I don't know how many days I shall remain here," said Elperex. "If they choose, the tribe may never call me back."

"Why would they do that?"

"It is hard for a walking one to understand, but pip-'strelli, once proven by flight, must be mated to be a member of the tribe. Mating is for always. If the chosen mate dies, the living one can only return at the choice of the chief."

"You have a new chief," said Uramettu. "She is called

Ectoreth."

Elperex seemed to shrivel at the news. "There was no love between Elperath and Ectoreth. I fear I am doomed to stay in these caves until I die."

Marix said, "Why don't you come with us?"

"Come with you?"

"Certainly. We're an odd band, but you would find us good company."

"Leave the crater?" The poor 'strelli was overwhelmed by the notion.

Nabul came close and tapped a finger on Elperex's chest. "It's a wide, grand world out there, my friend. You'll see great wonders: cities, temples, deserts, seas—"

"Leave the crater!" Elperex repeated.

"You would be welcome," said Uramettu.

Elperex stared into space for a long time. Nabul waved a hand before the 'strelli's eyes and got no response. He shrugged and climbed into the cart driver's seat. "We're off," he said. Marix and Uramettu mounted the sides, and Nabul tapped the ox's broad back with a cane switch. The beast lurched forward.

The laden cart's wheels dug deep furrows in the volcanic dust. The ox plodded on with a loud creaking of traces. When they were a hundred paces from the treasure cave, the three humans heard a sharp whistle.

Elperex fluttered into the back of the cart. His dark, globular eyes were almost pinched shut in the daylight, but he looked at each human in turn.

"I go with you," he said. "*Out of the crater!*"

"Splendid," said Marix, clapping the little creature on the back.

"One boon would I ask of you," said Elperex.

"What's that?"

"May I have the use of your cloak?"

With a look of puzzlement, Marix handed Elperex his Faziri wrap. "Are you chilled?"

The 'strelli hung the cloak like a tent around his high pointed ears. "Hard to see in this brightness," he said.

They trundled slowly to their camp, enriched with both money and a new companion.

* * * * *

"Careful! Careful!"

Tamakh's admonition wavered even as his body was lifted on a stretcher to the rear of the cart. Marix and Uramettu held one end high as Nabul and Jadira struggled to get the other into the boxed-in sides.

"Now, lower together," Jadira said. "Ready! Steady! Go!" Tamakh bumped onto the pile of baggage.

"I always seem to be carrying you, Holy One," said Marix, wiping sweat from his face. Jadira hissed and swatted him lightly on the cheek. "Well, it's true!"

"I regret being such a burden," the priest said.

"Be silent, you two," said Uramettu. "You'll be walking again in a day or so, Holy One."

"And if it would ease your conscience, later you can carry me piggyback to Tantuffa," said Marix. He ducked another buffet from Jadira.

Nabul jumped down from the cart and went to fetch Elperex. They had had to keep the 'strelli under wraps from his fellows, as by custom he was not allowed near the village without the chief's permission. So he stayed cloaked under Jadira's tent until it was time to depart. Nabul picked him up. The sleeping 'strelli was inert, lifeless, and as light as cork. Nabul carried him easily on one arm.

"Is everyone ready?" asked Jadira.

Nabul and Uramettu waved from the second cart, where they sat atop the hidden treasure. Elperex sat nestled behind them. Tamakh, lying behind Marix, waved his readiness.

Marix put one foot on the step and swung onto the bench beside Jadira. "Are the donkeys tied on?" she said.

"Of course."

"And the food and water are—"

"Yes, yes. Let's go," Marix said.

Jadira whacked the ox's rusty brown hide. Ahead lay the highest pass of the Shammat. Beyond that were the plains of Kaipur, the coast, and Tantuffa. There were six and a half days left till the conclave.

PART III:

THE NARSIAN SEAL

The High Pass

The trail led steadily upward, winding and twisting across the face of Mount Bakesh. The oxen proved their worth in the climb, for they never faltered, no matter how steep the angle became. Clouds closed in during the night, with chilling dampness wrapping around them like shrouds.

Elperex contributed his part by going ahead of the carts, using his keen night vision to keep the oxen on the proper track. He learned to ride the lead ox, perching on its neck with a goad. As he peered into the cold murk, he would tap one or the other of the beast's shoulders, guiding the stolid animal away from precipices and rockfalls.

During the second night, snow began to fall. Jadira was dozing against Marix's shoulder when the first cold flakes settled on her face. She stirred.

"Stop it," she murmured.

"Stop what?" Marix replied.

She sat up. Snow drifted through the air in gentle swirls. Jadira held out her hands to catch the white crystals. The delicate tracery of ice vanished as soon as it came to rest on her warm skin.

"What is this?" she said. "Magic?"

He laughed. "No, it's snow. You remember, I mentioned snow to you before."

Jadira lifted her face into the falling flakes. A veil of white clung to her long eyelashes. "This is wonderful," she said. "Do you have snow in your country all the time?"

"Only in winter, maybe four or five months of the year," said Marix. "And you wouldn't find it so wonderful when it's chest-deep to the well."

Jadira wasn't discouraged. She watched flakes accumulate on the dark cloth of the blanket across her lap. With one puff of breath, all of them evaporated without a trace.

Elperex rejoiced in the flurries, too. His blood, like a bird's, was hot and quick. He capered across the ox's back. "I am so happy to be with you," he said. "I feared my life was over!"

"There's so much left to do," said Marix. He threw back his head. "Isn't that right, Nabul?"

In the trailing cart, the thief, not enjoying the cold or the snow, was swathed in all the free blankets. He growled and cracked his switch in the air. "You see, we are a happy band," said Marix.

Elperex skipped back to the ox's neck. He sat there, wings slightly spread, as the snow blew gently over him. Jadira slouched down in the seat again and drifted back into the arms of the god of sleep.

* * * * *

The slant changed. From tilting back, the cart now

tilted forward. Some time in the night, when everyone save Elperex was asleep, they had crossed the highest point of Mount Bakesh and were descending to the plains of Kaipur. Jadira jumped from the cart and waited for the second vehicle to lurch by. She grabbed the bench, stepped on the trace pole, and swung up beside Uramettu.

"Good morning," Uramettu said. "Breakfast?" she added, offering Jadira an orange.

"Thank you." She glanced at Nabul, who was curled up atop his beloved hoard of gold. "Any problems?" she asked.

"Not any worth speaking of. Compared to our early days together, this is a pleasure ride, my sister."

Jadira agreed. She split her orange in two and gave half to Uramettu. "It has been a remarkable journey," she said.

"It is not over yet."

"Oh, perhaps not in terms of time, but all the real obstacles have been overcome. What remains are merely leagues to cover in the allotted time," Jadira said.

"I hope my sister is right." Uramettu bit into her orange.

"You're very thoughtful this morning," Jadira said. "Does something trouble you?"

"I was thinking of the season. In Fedush, this is the time of greening, when the rain stops and everything begins to grow. The impala have calved, the buffalo herds return to the savannah, and Ronta is abroad by night."

"Your panther-god?"

"Yes. It is in this season that we who know Ronta are guided in our selection of a mate."

Jadira began to understand. "Do the panther-folk

mate with each other?" she asked.

"No, not ever. The men choose from the young maidens of the village. Then I am allowed a choice of men, something most women in Fedush do not get."

Jadira said, "I know well what you mean. It is much the same with the Sudiin." She checked herself. "Was; *was* much the same . . . "

The trail flattened out to a small plateau. The mountain fell sharply away, so the view from the plateau was far-ranging. Marix halted the first cart. He and Tamakh got out. Uramettu stopped her ox, and she and Jadira hopped out of their cart.

"There lies the domain of Capzan, lord of the city of Sivan," said Marix, sweeping his arm to the south. "Northward is the territory of Tedwin the Lame, master of Maridanta. In the center, nearer the sea, is the province of Lord Hurgold."

"Will anyone contest our way?" said Tamakh.

Marix shrugged. "It has been so long since I was here, I know little of the local situation. Baron Capzan covets the grazing land owned by Lord Hurgold, just as Count Tedwin wishes to add my lord's watershed to his domain." He surveyed the ridge of mountains glowering above them. "The place where Sir Kannal's party was ambushed is north of here. We will need to enter Tedwin's realm."

Clouds chased across the sky, throwing huge shadows on the plain below. Jadira admired the lush green grassland, but wondered in her heart if it was truly worth the lives of so many men.

The trail down the plateau was even more precipitous than the track down the mountain. The donkeys managed well enough; Marix staked them in a thicket at the foot of the grade. Above, everyone studied the steep path before them.

"The stupid gnoles built carts without brakes," said Nabul. "So how do we get them down there without crashing?"

"Perhaps if we used both oxen to steady each cart?" Tamakh offered.

Uramettu shook her head. "The track is not wide enough for both beasts to go abreast. And placing them one behind the other won't do; the lead ox will drag the second in the dirt."

"If the second doesn't trample the leader first," Jadira added.

"What, then, do we do?" asked Nabul.

Marix appeared at the bottom of the hill. He practically had to go on his hands and knees to get up the incline. By the time he reached the carts, he was panting.

"We'll have to put drag lines on the carts," he said. "Each of us will hold on and steady it on the way down."

"And I?" asked Elperex from under his shading blanket.

"You steer the bullock," Marix said. Uramettu picked up the 'strelli and placed him on the ox's neck. With his bony hands and long switch, Elperex looked like a minion of the demon-king Dutu, ready to steal the ox for his master.

They tied ropes to the axles and traces. Everyone took a place on the ropes, even Tamakh. Jadira eyed him. "Are you well enough for this, Holy One?" she said.

He touched his wounded side gingerly. "I can but try," he replied. "Too long have I lain fallow, letting my friends bear the burden alone." He grasped a length of coarse rope. "I am ready."

"Elperex!" Marix called. "Keep the beast straight!"

"That I will, walking friend." He cooed a soothing

note in the ox's ear. "Good beast; gentle beast. Hold to the center of the path."

"Do you think it understands?" muttered Nabul.

"Pray that it does," replied Uramettu.

"Go!"

"*Chee-ratata!*" The 'strelli's voice chimed like a glass bell. The ox lumbered forward, swaying from side to side on its thick legs. The cart slipped, the leather straps of the harness bumping the ox's hindquarters. The companions leaned against the pull. With each turn of the wheels, their feet skidded in the dirt.

"Someone should make a wagon that moves itself," said Nabul through gritted teeth.

"Absurd," said Uramettu. Tendons stood out in her dark skin and a fierce determination clouded her face. "What would happen to all the draft animals?"

"Eat 'em," grunted the thief.

They wrestled the cart to the foot of the hill. After a short respite, they started back for the second cart. Elperex clung to Jadira's back until she stopped by the second ox's head, where he hopped off. When the ropes were in place, the same struggle began again.

The cart crept forward a bit. The pull was so strong Nabul was snapped off his feet. He dropped the rope and stood up. "Did you feel that?" he said.

"It's the treasure," said Marix. "There must be thrice-a-hundredweight in the bottom of that cart."

"Let's take some out," said Jadira.

"We're not leaving it behind!" objected Nabul.

"No, certainly not; but it will be safer if we take some out before we go," said Marix.

When he heard the word "go," Elperex urged the ox into motion. The cart moved, snatching the restraining ropes from their hands. As one, they cried "*Stop!*" but the momentum was too much for Elperex and the ox. The cart bore down on the plodding animal, shoving it out of the way. The ox turned, the trace poles snapped, and the gold-laden cart somersaulted end over end. Cascades of gold and jewels showered the road, spilling off the edges and ringing down the rocky slope. They watched open-mouthed as the wealth of a great king scattered like chaff. At the end, the tumbling cart rolled off the road and smashed to bits in the ravine below the trail.

"Well," said Jadira at last, "at least it didn't strike the other cart."

Marix's gaping mouth shut with a snap. Beside him, Nabul sagged to his knees. He bowed his face to the dirt and smote the ground with his fists. "Never, never, never!" he said with genuine anguish. "Am I never to have the riches I deserve? Curse you gods, who let me see such wealth but never let me possess it!"

"Don't blaspheme!" said Tamakh, shocked.

"I don't care! Let them strike me dead—it could hardly hurt more than this repeated torment by treasure!"

Elperex herded the ox to them and stopped. He peeked cautiously out from under his hood. "You are angry with Elperex?" he said.

"I'd like to wring your scrawny neck!" Nabul sobbed. The 'strelli closed the blanket over his head.

"Stop it," said Jadira. "Stop crying, Nabul, and get up." The thief rose disconsolately to his feet. "Elperex will pick up as much of the treasure as he can."

"That could take days!" said Marix. She shot a warning glance at him.

"Take one candle-notch," said Jadira. "Then we have to move on."

Elperex hopped down from the ox and began filtering through handfuls of dirt for coins and gems. He dropped any he found in the bottom of his blanket. Nabul watched him wordlessly for a while, then also started searching. Marix joined him. Soon, Uramettu was using her long arms to comb the hillside above the road.

Jadira looked at Tamakh. The priest tightened his sash and lowered himself carefully to his knees. "You, too, Holy One?" asked Jadira.

" 'Even in the dross of the road shall you find treasure.' So said the holy Agopa, in his Fourth Admonition to the Neophytes." The twinkle had returned to his eyes for the first time since his wounding.

"Wise man, this Agopa," said Jadira. She lifted the hem of her robe and knelt, filling her fingers with dirt.

* * * * *

The plain was covered with chest-high grass that bowed and swayed in the lightest breeze. The party followed behind the ox cart, allowing it to break a path through the lush field. Elperex was in his daylight stupor in the back of the cart, so Nabul sat on the bench tending the ox. The beast insisted on stopping every few steps to sample the abundant provender. Nabul whacked its hide repeatedly, but the animal would proceed only when it had swallowed several mouthfuls of fodder.

Jadira slogged along. The turf underfoot was spongy, and the grass roots were thick and clinging. More than once, she, Marix, and Tamakh went sprawling when the earth refused to release their feet.

Uramettu strode ahead. This was her element; the plains of Fedush were oceans of grass. Her pleasure in this new country increased with every step she made. Finally, she raised her spear point high in the air and began to sing.

The others perked up. Uramettu's speaking voice was a warm contralto, but her singing range was higher and lighter. She finished three verses of a Fedushite song. Jadira called out, "That's beautiful. What does it mean?"

Uramettu paused and turned back. "That is the grain-gather song," she said. "The women of my country sing in the fields."

"Your women tend the crops?" asked Marix.

"They do. Men hunt the game, and our women grow barley."

"What do the words mean?" Jadira asked again.

Uramettu translated:

> Go to the fields, sisters,
> Go to the fields.
> Gather the grain, sisters.
> And bring it home.

> Trod down the stalks, sisters,
> Trod down the stalks.
> Gather the grain, sisters,
> And bring it home.

> Take up the heads, sisters,
> Take up the heads.
> Fill up your baskets, sisters,
> And bring them home.

"There are many verses," she said, breaking off. "Clever singers make them up as they work."

Jadira hummed the tune. "It has a good rhythm for working." She imagined the plain worked by women like Uramettu—tall, graceful black women cutting and picking to the steady beat of the grain-gather song.

"Sing some more," said Tamakh.

"Yes, please," said Jadira. "It will ease our task."

Uramettu hummed through one verse, thinking. Then, she cleared her throat and sang

> Follow my steps, comrades,
> Follow my steps.
> We will be free, comrades,
> When we get home.

*   *   *   *   *

The grassland was bordered by a wide, shallow stream running north to south. They decided to water the oxen and donkeys before going on. While the beasts dropped their muzzles in the cold stream, the companions spread out on the bank and the flat boulders that protruded from the water.

"Cheer up, you old city rat," said Marix to Nabul. "We saved quite a lot of treasure, you know."

"Barely half a hundredweight," said Nabul. He threw a stone in the water. "Not enough to live on in the splendor I was dreaming of."

"What do you want, a palace? Slaves to feed you, sycophants to praise you, harem-girls to—?"

"Yes, that's exactly what I want!"

"He wants to be sultan," said Tamakh.

"I can think of worse things to be," said Nabul. "Poor, for one."

Uramettu swirled her bare toe in the water. "I saw Sultan Julmet several times. He would stroll through the Garden of Beasts now and then, trailed by advisors and favor-seekers, attended by concubines, doctors, soldiers, and priests of the official cults. I doubt he ever had a moment to himself, and he looked strained and sick all the time."

"Good," said Jadira. "I wish him boils and a flux to burn his entrails."

Her bad wishes, expressed with such firm conviction, stifled the flow of talk. The sighing grass and effervescent water wrapped around them like soft raiments, comforting each of them as no words could.

Jadira would not be comforted. She jumped to her feet. "Your song was wrong, Uramettu," she said. "I'll never be free, for I have no home to return to."

She skipped from the rock to the sandy bank and slashed off into the high grass. Marix scrambled up the bank after her.

"Let her go," advised Tamakh. "Let her expend her fury on the uncomplaining air."

"No, Holy One," said Marix. "Jadira is mine, as I am hers. If she has bile to vent, let it be on me." He disappeared on the trail she had crushed in the grass.

"Love," snorted Nabul. He threw another pebble in the water.

❖ 24 ❖

The Unseen Hand

"Jadira!" Marix cupped his hands around his mouth and shouted again: "Jadira! Where are you?" He could hear her stomping somewhere ahead. It was easy enough to follow her, but she set such a pace he had to run to catch up. He found her flat on her face, for she had tripped on the soft webbing of roots.

"Let me help you," said Marix, taking her arm.

"Leave me alone!"

"Why should I?"

She shrugged off his helping hand and got up. "Maybe I don't want soothing, from you or anyone else. Did you consider that, my lord?"

He frowned. All sympathy left his face. "Don't call me that," he said.

"You are a noble, aren't you? And I am a nomad, a landless, tribeless woman without a name or place to claim as home."

"Not that again! I love you!"

"Do you? I wonder. If Tamakh were a comely female with milk-white skin, would you care so much for me? If

Uramettu were nearer your height, would I stand so high in your estimation?"

Marix made a fist and raised it to his chest. Jadira watched impassively. He struggled with himself and lost. He struck himself smartly on the forehead.

"I don't understand," he said. "In the crater—I thought you loved me in return."

Her dark eyes searched over him, and her countenance lost its harsh lines. "I do," she said. "That's the curse of it. And the nearer we get to Tantuffa, the more frightened I grow."

He took her in his arms. "What frightens you?"

"The knowledge that you have a place and position to return to, a place that has no room for me."

"I will make room."

"No!" she said, drawing away. "Can't you see? Even among the Sudiin, I was not willing to take what was *given* to me, no matter how much love was in the giving." Jadira clutched the front of her robe. "I can't explain this feeling except to say that I would rather die than be any man's servant."

"Shall I renounce my name, then? Is that what you want?"

Jadira stopped resisting and returned his fervent grip. "I am not to be won, Marix. Join me; be my equal, not my lord or my slave."

"A strange doctrine, this. I'm not sure the world could spin in its proper course if every man and woman were each other's equal."

"Just begin with me," she replied, "and let the world follow its own course."

They walked back to the stream hand in hand. Marix called out to Tamakh and the others, but heard no answer. He and Jadira had been gone half a notch, and when they emerged on the creek bank, there was no sign of their companions. The cart was gone. So were the tethered ox and three donkeys.

"What the—?" Jadira splashed out to the middle of the stream. From there, she could see a long way up and down both banks, yet not another human being was in sight. No gap in the wall of grass betrayed where their friends might have gone. They seemed to have vanished completely.

"Perplexing, isn't it?"

Jadira and Marix whirled. Standing behind them, where no one had been an instant earlier, was a man on horseback. He wore a three-quarter suit of mail and a banded surcoat of black and white. His horse was similarly trapped in quilted cloth. He spoke in lightly accented Faziri.

"Who are you?" demanded Jadira. "What has become of our friends?"

"I am Frolder, son of Narken, captain in the legion of my Lord Tedwin of Maridanta." He mockingly touched his chest and saluted them. "Your friends are on their way to Barrow Vitgis, our military camp in this province."

"But why? We've done nothing wrong," said Marix.

"You entered the domain of Count Tedwin surreptitiously, trampled his valuable grazing land, drank water from his river . . . need I go on? As his lordship's sheriff, it is my responsibility to uphold the law. I can't allow bands of vagabonds to despoil his lordship's property with impunity."

"Vagabonds! Do you know who—" Marix began.

Jadira cut him off. "How may we make restitution to Count Tedwin?" she asked quickly.

"If you will come with me to Barrow Vitgis, I'm sure

we can come to some arrangement," said Frolder. He brought his horse's head around. "Follow the watercourse northward eight *vanzi* and the barrow will be on the west bank."

"Uh, how far is eight *vanzi?*" said Marix.

Frolder considered a moment. "One and a half Faziri leagues."

Jadira saw Marix's hand stray to his sword hilt. No, no, not yet, she thought. Frolder saw his movement, too. He smiled behind his elegant red moustache and reached for the small silver disc that hung from a chain around his neck. He put the disc to his lips and disappeared.

Out came the scimitar. Marix charged forward, kicking up spray. He splashed through the spot where horse and rider had just been.

"Where did he go?" he sputtered.

—and there was Frolder behind him. He lifted his broadsword. Jadira had no time to cry a warning before Frolder brought the flat of the heavy blade down on top of Marix's head. Marix's knees crumpled, and he collapsed backward into the shallow water.

Frolder smiled benignly at Jadira. "Let no one say the son of Narken is not a kindly fellow," he said. He sheathed his weapon. "The Barrow Vitgis; if you care for your companions, you will come."

The magic amulet—for that is what it surely was— went back in Frolder's mouth, and he vanished, this time for good. Jadira rolled the stunned Marix over and picked waterweed from his hair.

"Ow," he groaned. "What hit me?"

"Our friend Frolder. He has an amulet that confers invisibility."

"Is he gone?"

She blotted his face with her sleeve. "How can I tell? I

don't see him, if that means anything."

She found his sword and handed it back to him. "What sort of place would this Barrow Vitgis be?" she asked.

Marix touched the top of his head and winced. "An earthen hill, natural or man-built, topped with a stockade. The provincial sheriff dwells within, with his armed retainers."

"How many retainers?"

"Who knows? Count Tedwin is the richest vassal of Prince Lydon of Narsia. A hundred men-at-arms? Two hundred?" He wrung water from his robe and adjusted his sword belt. "Does it matter?"

She admitted it did not. Jadira and Marix put the afternoon sun on their left and set out for the hilltop fortress where their friends were being held.

* * * * *

Barrow Vitgis was no rude stockade perched on a pile of dirt. It was an entire village, spread out around the base of a conical mound capped by a log-walled citadel. The banner of Maridanta flipped lazily from a mast at the top of the hill. Smoke hung low in the moist evening air.

A soldier in a black brigandine jacket barred Jadira and Marix's way with his halberd. "What do you want here?" he demanded.

"Sheriff Frolder is holding some friends of ours," said Jadira. "We've come to get them out."

The guard smiled unpleasantly. "O' course. Pass," he said, snapping the pole arm to the vertical. As they walked by him, the guard chuckled under his breath.

The long palisade around the village had no gate, only

a baffle to defeat a cavalry charge. Inside, Barrow Vitgis was astir with activity. Pigs and chickens ran free in the muddy lanes; peasant farmers carried bunches of turnips or onions tied to long poles over their shoulders. Here and there were other black-garbed soldiers, men of the army of Count Tedwin.

"I hope this is not some game of deceit," muttered Jadira as they walked.

"So do I." Marix sidestepped a trundle cart bearing a beer barrel. "We're not far from where I buried the seal." She queried him with a sharp look. He nodded to the east. "No more than half a league that way, in a star-shaped olive grove."

At the base of the citadel mound, a spiral road began, leading to the summit. The road was corduroyed with logs to provide a steadier surface for the steep ascent. Marix and Jadira circled the hill four times. At the top they passed through another baffle of rough-dressed logs into the sheriff's military keep. An elderly man in civilian clothes accosted them. He wore a heavy gold chain around his neck, from which hung a miniature human leg wrought in gold.

"Who are you? What is your business here?" said the man haughtily.

"We are travelers, bidden here by your sheriff. He arrested four of our companions and brought them to the barrow," said Jadira.

He looked down his beaky nose at them and sniffed. "You will have to wait until Sir Frolder can see you," he said. "Come with me."

He led them through a wide doorway into the dark interior of the wooden citadel. Skylights relieved the gloom in spots, but the whole aspect of the place was so austere Jadira found it depressing. Bad enough to live inside walls and a roof, but this!

The old man stopped in a large octagonal hall. "You will wait here," he said. To Marix, he held out a hand. "I must ask you to give up your sword—for the time being." Marix slowly reached for the scimitar. "It is the law," the old man insisted.

Marix drew the blade out of its wooden scabbard and handed it pommel-first to their guide. The old man regarded the Faziri weapon with distaste, but carried it away without another word.

"Westerners are strange people," Jadira said when they were alone. "And this Frolder, he's the strangest of them all—appearing and disappearing like my grandsire's ghost! He means us no good, I know it."

"Count Tedwin is a shrewd leader," said Marix. "He's been lame since birth, so he surrounds himself with bold, vigorous lieutenants."

Jadira walked the perimeter of the hall. The walls were decorated with carpets and heraldic shield covers. The floor was covered with fine white river sand. In the center was an octagonal table, finely made from some dark northern wood. Heavy cubic chairs faced the table. As Jadira swung around the last face of the eight-sided room, Frolder blinked into sight in the tallest and grandest of the chairs.

"Good of you to come," he said.

"May we settle accounts and go?" said Marix. "We have duties elsewhere."

"Sit," said Frolder with a regal wave of his hand. When neither Jadira nor Marix moved, he repeated himself with more force: "Sit!"

Marix and Jadira sat side by side. She placed her hands atop his and twined their fingers together.

"I will tell you a story," began Frolder. "A fascinating

story, but one that doesn't have an ending yet. It seems there was this band of travelers. A very select group of men and women. One had the shaven poll of a holy man; another was scraped off a filthy street in Fazir. There was a woman with skin like midnight, tall and handsome to see, who moved silently and watched everything. The next was not a man at all, but a gargoyle with wings, cat's eyes, and pointed ears to boot." Frolder leaned forward and rested his elbows on the table. "Then came the young man. His coloring and carriage were foreign to this region. There's no mistaking noble blood, you know; no ignoring the fellow who's never bent his knee to a higher power save the gods. And the last was a woman, a nomad woman, fierce of eye and strong of will. Who were these travelers, and where did they come from?"

"Are you asking us?" said Jadira.

"No, I'm telling you a story. Don't interrupt; it's not polite." He turned the blood-colored velvet mantle back from his shoulders and stood up. A ruby-hilted dagger gleamed at his waist. The sheriff was enjoying his advantage.

"As I said, not the usual sort of vagabonds one might expect to drift into one's domain now and then. These were people with a purpose, a mission. Now, what might that mission be?" Frolder planted his fists on his hips. "That is the question. What would keep such a disparate band together, do you think?"

"Good comrades need no reason," said Marix. "May we see our friends, Sir Sheriff?"

Jadira expected Frolder to resist and demand answers. Instead, he smiled and relaxed his belligerent stance. "Why not?" he said.

Frolder swept aside one of the wall hangings, revealing an open door. He held the tapestry aside for Jadira and Marix. They ducked through. The corridor beyond was dank and hot. Clumps of lichen grew on the squared-off logs that formed the walls and ceilings.

They preceded Frolder along the hall to a left turn. From there, they emerged outdoors again; in this case, a courtyard surrounded by a high fence. A number of posts were placed around the yard, and Marix and Jadira's friends were tied, one per post. Only Uramettu looked up when they entered.

"As you see, I provided your comrades with accommodations similar to what they were accustomed to," said Frolder. "Warm sun and open air; how healthful! How unlike the grim life of settled habitation!"

Jadira rushed to the nearest post. Tamakh was roped to it. His head hung listlessly. Jadira lifted it and spoke to him. "Holy One, can you hear me?" His eyes were misted, unseeing. Marix went to Nabul and found him likewise befuddled. The two of them converged on Uramettu, as she seemed to be more aware.

"My sister. Friend Marix," she said. Her normally vibrant voice was dull and without feeling.

"What has he done to you?" Jadira whispered.

"Sto-stolen will. Mind can't think . . ."

"Is it magic? Is it a spell?" asked Marix urgently.

"Can't think . . ."

Jadira spied Elperex. The little 'strelli was tied off the ground. His wings were tightly wrapped with a cord and his eyes were open in the full light. She turned angrily to Frolder.

"Cover his face!" she said. "His eyes can't bear bright sunshine. If you don't cover them, he'll go blind."

"Truly? How interesting," said Frolder. Jadira's temper boiled. She quickly unwound her black cotton headdress and made a loose turban from it. This she set over Elperex's head, swathing it completely.

"Charming," said the sheriff.

"Why have you done this?" Marix demanded. "We've done no harm to you."

"Your friends were too clever and too strong for me to keep under simple lock and key. So I had my chief magicker loose their wits for them. Temporarily, until I decide what to do with them—and you."

Jadira sprang for Frolder's throat. She got a good grip before Marix could move to restrain her. The sheriff's white face filled with blood, turning the color of ripe berries.

When he and Marix finally succeeded in breaking her hold, Frolder was halfway choked to death.

"By the god's eyeteeth!" he gasped. "You have hands like a blacksmith! I think perhaps I shall have to send for my wizard to calm you as he did the others."

"No! No, please," Marix said. "Understand, Sir Sheriff, Jadira possesses a quick temper, but is mistress of it almost all the time. She—we—will be docile, I promise."

Frolder rubbed his bruised neck. "Your name is Jadira, eh? Well, Jadira, I owe you some attention. Later, I will—" He paused and smiled his unkind smile again. "But that is for later," he finished.

Frolder went to where a bronze tube hung from a post by a thong. He struck this gong with his dagger blade. Two black-jacketed soldiers entered the courtyard.

"Ah, Dredno. Take these two to the top of the citadel and put them in a guest room. Stay by the door; we don't want them wandering around the barrow with night coming on," Frolder said.

"It shall be done, my lord," said the guard.

The soldiers prodded Jadira and Marix out. When they were gone, Frolder said to the empty air, "Did you hear, Phraxa? He called her by name."

A stout, bearded man of forty years flickered to solidity near the outer wall. He wore an amulet like Frolder's. The silver disc fell from his lips as he materialized. He took a deep breath, coughed, and said, "There can be no doubt now. They are the ones."

"How much do you think we can get for them?"

Phraxa rubbed his many-ringed fingers together. "That depends on who we ransom them to. Hurgold would pay well; Count Fernald would better him. And the sultan—" Phraxa rolled his eyes. "The coffers of Fazir are very deep, my dear Frolder."

"They cannot be too deep for me," said the sheriff. Phraxa laughed. Frolder joined in. The wizard and the sheriff replaced the amulets in their mouths and vanished, Frolder in the wink of an eye. Phraxa seemed to have some trouble with his amulet. He faded out like a waning shadow. Only the echoes of their laughter remained.

❖ 25 ❖

The Curse of Ondrin

In another part of the citadel, two men waited for Frolder's return. Their dusty, stained armor bore witness to the distance they had come and the hardship they had endured. The taller man toyed with a golden trinket. He tapped it on the table, rubbed it with his fingers until it warmed from his touch, and let it dangle from a short loop of chain.

"What's keeping them?" he asked testily. The younger, smaller man could only shrug from ignorance. "I hate treachery," the older man continued. "Even when it serves our master. Betrayers have no compunction about whom they betray; tomorrow, it could be us."

"He would not dare, my brother. His Magnificence knows all that befalls us; if the foreigner breaks faith with us, the wrath of the sultan would descend on his wretched fief."

Fu'ad closed the Eye of the Sultan in his fist. "I hope this Frolder realizes that, Marad," he said.

* * * * *

Jadira paced the tiny room from one wall to the other. "We should have put up a fight," she said.

"What good would it have done?" Marix responded. "Frolder would just have popped that necklace in his mouth, vanished, and spitted us like partridges." His shoulders sagged forward. "We have only three days left. If we don't get out of here by tomorrow, there won't be time to get the seal and make Tantuffa before the conclave dissolves into war."

"There is a chance. You will not like it, but there is one chance."

"What?"

"I will occupy Frolder long enough for you to escape," said Jadira. "Alone."

"I won't leave you here."

"But think, Marix; think of all the lives that will be lost if you don't put the prince's seal in Lord Hurgold's hands."

"Am I to give you up then?" he said in a distant voice.

Jadira stopped pacing and took his hand. "Never give me up," she said. "Just be ready to leave me when the opportunity arises."

Two quick knocks on the door made them spring apart. The thick wooden door swung in, revealing Frolder and a quartet of soldiers.

"Good evening to you," he said with a courtly bow. "I am here to request the pleasure of your company at dinner. As I have other guests of interest to you, I'm sure you will come along without argument. Shall we go?"

Jadira preceded Marix to the door. As she passed closest to Frolder, the sheriff whipped out his dagger. He pressed the flat of the blade to Jadira's neck.

"Your mind is glass to me, lady. I see through you.

Nothing is said or done under this roof that I don't know of instantly," he said.

Jadira put a finger to the tip of the dagger and pushed it away. "Then you know how undeniably hungry I am," she said.

Frolder's red mustache twitched. "Of course. The corporal's escort will show you the way."

When Marix passed by Frolder, the sheriff replaced the magic disc and became invisible. Jadira stiffened. "Keep moving and don't make trouble," Marix whispered.

They returned to the octagonal hall where they had earlier met the sheriff. Now the eight-sided table was set for a meal. A tall chair was placed at each side. A brewer's boy went from place to place, filling large earthenware mugs with foaming beer. Another young boy with close-cut hair lighted candles on the table with a copper taper-holder.

Frolder materialized behind Jadira's chair. "Do be seated, lady," he said. She sat. He pushed the chair forward and went to the place directly opposite. He sat down and rapped on the table. A portly man in a red robe appeared on his left, already seated. Marix sank slowly into his own chair.

"Phraxa," he said, unbelieving.

The fat man looked startled. "Do I know you?"

"I saw you once many years ago. You were on trial for unlawful divination by necromancy."

Phraxa laughed, his jowls quivering like two puddings. "You'll have to be more exact, young fellow. I've been tried many times for necromancy."

"Was it in Dosen?" said Frolder after taking a long drink of beer. It was Marix's turn to look surprised.

"Why do you say Dosen?" he asked.

"Is that not your home? Are you not the third son of Count Fernald?"

"What is for dinner?" Jadira interjected. Marix closed his mouth.

"Not all my guests are here yet," said Frolder. He signaled a guard by the door. The soldier held the door wide as two men walked quickly in. Jadira recognized them immediately.

"Fu'ad!" she said, taking up her table knife. Fu'ad and Marad went around Frolder's chair and took their seats. The officers had forsaken their mail for baggy silk pants and crimson vests, as befitted Faziri gentlemen of position.

"Do be civilized," said Phraxa. "Put down that knife."

"Marix, who is this fat slug?" said Jadira, waving the blunt implement at Phraxa.

"A sorcerer of vile repute, Phraxa of Tel Noa."

"You wound me, sir." Phraxa raised his mug to Jadira. "Lady, as often happens to great men, I am widely defamed because of my skill and success with the black arts."

"You're a grave robber and a poisoner," said Marix. "Even now, our friends languish under the spell of one of your filthy potions!"

"How did you escape the 'strelli escorting you?" Jadira asked Fu'ad.

"Did you really think Invincibles of the empire could be herded like goats by a band of winged lizards?" said Fu'ad. "My brother and I lived to continue the chase."

"Wait, wait!" said Frolder, holding his hands out to all the warring parties. "This is dinner, and you are all my guests. Be civil, if nothing else." A tense silence settled over the table. "Good. Now for our last guest . . ."

Frolder waved at the doorman again. The soldier pushed the portal open and straightened his back against the door frame.

A vague form stirred in the shadowed hall beyond the door. There was a swish and crinkle of stiff cloth. Marix and Jadira leaned forward to see who was coming. Out of the dark stepped a woman.

Every man in the room stood up silently. Jadira, slightly confused by their response, stood up, too.

The woman was clothed entirely in black—a black silk skirt varnished to hold its heavy pleats, a tight-fitting vest of velvet over a raven blouse embroidered with silver. A high collar beaded with pearls rose behind the woman's head, framing a face of rare delicacy and beauty.

"Good men and lady, may I present Her Grace, the Countess Liantha, sister to our lord Count Tedwin of Maridanta," Frolder said.

Countess Liantha approached the empty chair on Jadira's left. Fu'ad beat his comrade Marad to the seat and held it for her. Liantha's only acknowledgement of his gesture was a slight lowering of her brilliant blue eyes. Fu'ad, captain of the dread Invincibles and veteran of many campaigns, blushed behind his freshly trimmed and curled beard.

"Have you found your accommodations at Barrow Vitgis to your liking?" asked Frolder. The countess gave a slow nod of her finely sculpted head. By candlelight, her naturally pale complexion assumed an almost opalescent sheen. Marix found himself staring. Jadira pinched his elbow.

Frolder clapped his hands, and serving boys filed in, carrying the first course—pigeons, stuffed with rice and *gopa* nuts. The platter was taken around the table, starting with the countess, and then the pages brought out bread. Marix was delighted to eat leavened bread again, after so many months on Faziri wheel loaves.

There was no conversation for several minutes as everyone busied themselves with the food. Frolder watched with satisfaction as everyone ate except he and Phraxa. Frolder did empty his mug a few times. He sat back and wiped streaks of foam from his moustache.

"My good friends, Phraxa has arranged for a special entertainment this evening," he said, "one I'm sure you will all find amusing and enlightening."

"I don't like the sound of this," Jadira muttered.

"With due pardon to this gracious lady," said Fu'ad, inclining his head to Countess Liantha, "I have a mission to perform, one that I would like to resolve as soon as possible—namely, the return of the escaped criminals to the lawful custody of His Magnificence the Sultan."

"May he live forever," said Marad.

"Patience, Sir Fu'ad. Did I not promise you would get what you so ardently desire?" said Frolder. He was obviously enjoying himself. The second course—leeks in cream—arrived without being summoned. Again Phraxa and Frolder ate nothing.

"The name of this entertainment is 'Truth.' You, my dear guests, will be called upon to participate," the sheriff said.

"Suppose we don't wish to?" said Marix.

"Oh, your cooperation is assured. Each person seated at this table wants something. Sir Fu'ad and his second want me to deliver the vagabonds into their hands. Equally, young Marix would like to be free to rejoin his father's people in Tantuffa, along with the odd collection of companions he has collected."

"So would I," said Jadira.

"At my request, the countess is here as her brother's representative in our dealings with the gentlemen from Fazir. She is Count Tedwin's ears, you might say." Frolder leaned forward and rested his chin in his hand. "But not his voice, eh?" Liantha's flawless face creased in a deep frown. Her wordless expression was so full of meaning that Frolder leaned back, his composure shaken.

"Ahem," he said. "At any rate, everyone plays. It serves my aims best to have you all together this evening. I cannot afford to have important people like yourselves keeping secrets from me."

"When does this game begin?" asked Fu'ad.

"Oh, any time now."

The entree arrived: a whole carcass of venison, smoked over a slow fire for a day and a night. A nimble lad knelt on the table top and sliced select cutlets for the diners. With this came a pot of rich, red-brown gravy, which a pair of pages bore on a pole across their shoulders.

"You do not eat," Marad said to Phraxa.

"My art allows me only the simplest foodstuffs. This repast is too opulent for me," he said. Jadira wondered how simple his diet could be; he was at least a talent heavier than Tamakh.

When the choice part of the venison had been consumed, Frolder ordered the servants and guards from the room. He pushed himself back from the table and stood up.

"Let the entertainment begin," he said.

Jadira stared at her plate. She looked from Frolder to Phraxa and in a flash understood what was happening. "We're poisoned!" she exclaimed.

Fu'ad and Marad felt it, too. They jumped to their feet, hands to sword hilts. "What did I tell you, my brother?" Fu'ad said. "Treachery lives only for more treachery!"

"Peace, peace. You are not poisoned. Show respect for Her Grace," Frolder said calmly. Reminded of the countess, Fu'ad relaxed. He and Marad sat down. For the beautiful lady's sake, he could play the refined gentleman—for a time.

"The game will be played thus: I will ask questions, and you will answer, but only with the absolute truth."

"How can you know the absolute truth when you hear it?" said Jadira.

"As you suspected, there was something in the food." Alarmed faces ringed the table. "Not poison, no, no; one of Phraxa's efficacious compounds. When taken, it compels the taker to tell only the truth."

The countess struck the table top with her small fist. She rose and made for the door. She found it bolted from the outside.

"Only my word can open it," said Frolder. He laid a hand gently on her velvet-clad arm. "Will you sit, Your Grace?" Liantha returned to her seat with a crush of crinoline.

"Now, who would like to be first? You, my boy?" He clapped Marix on the back. "Why are you here?"

Marix's face contorted as he tried to fight the effect of the potion. "The seal," he blurted. "I must—retrieve—the seal."

"What seal?"

"The seal of Prince Lydon of Narsia." Marix seized his own throat and tried to throttle the truth spilling from his mouth. "It must be taken to Tantuffa before the conclave on High Summer's Day."

Frolder said to Jadira, "What is your part in all this?"

She threw back her head and replied with pride, "I was a prisoner in Omerabad. Marix and I escaped together."

"What stake do you have in the politics of the Five Cities?"

"None, but I love Marix." When she said that, Marix took his hands from his throat.

Frolder had a cruel thought. "And you—does a son of Fernald return love to a nomad woman?" he asked.

"With all my heart."

The sheriff shrugged, his coup spoiled. He went on. "Tell us, Sir Fu'ad, why are you here?"

"You know why!"

"Tell us, gallant Invincible." Fu'ad gripped the edge of the table, but he was not strong enough to resist Phraxa's compound.

"I am afraid of . . . Emir Azrel! He will do terrible things to me if I fail," he blurted. "The emir has a savage temper and knows no mercy."

Marad stared at his captain in astonishment.

"You?" said Frolder. "An officer of the imperial army, afraid?"

"Yes! For my failure, he would pluck out my eyes, strike off my hands, and leave me a crippled beggar in the streets." He shuddered. "That was the fate he inflicted on General Dajal, my first commander, whose failure was less than mine would be. I saw him . . . stinking sores on his knees and flies nesting in his dead eyes! That Azrel had done to a great soldier and a fine commander!"

"So you would do almost anything to get young Marix and his companions back?"

"Not almost anything—anything!"

Smile. "Would you like to add anything, Sir Marad?" Frolder asked.

"Only that I am deeply disappointed that my brother

is so fearful of one man."

Fu'ad gazed at his empty dinner plate and said nothing.

Frolder moved on until he stood behind Countess Liantha. Phraxa licked his lips at the thought of what Frolder would extract from her. The sheriff composed himself a moment, looking with something like fondness at the back of her head. Her smooth black hair was coiffed close to her skull so that every detail, every fine line of her features would show with absolute clarity.

"Your Grace," Frolder began. He paused and said it again: "Your Grace. You are widely considered the most beautiful woman in the Five Cities, are you not?"

She nodded once, sharply.

"You think you're beautiful, don't you?"

Liantha twisted in her chair to see Frolder. Eyes blazing, she nodded again.

"The truth is manifest in your face," the sheriff admitted. "So why don't you speak to us? Tell us how beautiful you know yourself to be."

Liantha split the air with a chopping motion of one hand. Frolder stepped forward and took her by the shoulders. "The truth! You must tell it! Speak the truth to us, Liantha!"

She swallowed, with great difficulty and pain. Faint gurgling sounds issued from her rose-colored lips.

"You must do better. Surely a lady as lovely as you has a voice to make the Mother Goddess jealous. Give us your voice, Countess."

"Leave her alone!" said Marix, sensing her humiliation.

"Be silent, whelp, or I'll ask you worse questions than you can imagine!" Frolder exhaled deeply and let his hands drop to his sides. "Speak, Liantha. Let your voice be heard."

"Ah-ah-op-od—"

"Is she mute?" Fu'ad asked with the brutal candor of the potion.

"No, she can talk. Are you beautiful, Countess?"

"I-I aayam b-byutuffa." Her voice was a deep, horrid croak. Two glass tracks appeared from the corners of the countess's perfect eyes. Frolder went back to his chair. He sat heavily and drank the last of his beer.

"Let me tell you another story, my truthful guests. The story of a great family, a noble house from the western forests. The founder was a shrewd and cunning warrior who seized for himself an estate in the very teeth of the warlords of Dornwald. He made a fortune trading between the wild north and the settled south. But somewhere along the way, this great man committed a sin. Pride, lust, murder—any of these are likely. The exact nature of the deed was shrouded in secrecy by his descendants. It must have been terrible; great men sin on a great scale.

"The gods, in their wisdom, cursed this man and all his family for generations to come. They stole the great man's reason, and made every offspring of his house be born . . . flawed. The great man's name was Ondrin Breakstone, great-great-grandfather of Count Tedwin."

All eyes were on the countess. She was looking straight ahead, still weeping silently. Frolder continued.

"The heirs of Ondrin earned epithets according to their personal defects. There was Sismann the Blind, Thorlic the Toothless, and the countess's own aunt, Jessila the Bald. Other members of the family had even worse deformities . . . strange, ugly specimens without faces, without limbs. Our beloved lord, Count Tedwin, has a clubfoot. He is a rightful descendent of Ondrin Breakstone though, being cleverer than a hundred ordinary men." Frolder extended a hand to Liantha. "And then there was his younger sister. Beautiful Liantha, whose birth was attended by such celebration, as she appeared to be perfect. From babe to toddler, she was coddled and protected as the most precious shoot of the family tree. Then came the time for her to talk—and the curse showed itself. Beautiful Liantha can only croak like a sick frog."

This time, both Fu'ad and Marix leaped up in outrage. Jadira said to Frolder, "Why do you torment her this way? Does it give you pleasure to see her shame exposed to strangers?"

"No. I have pursued Liantha ever since I came to serve Tedwin, six long years ago," he said. His eyebrows rose in surprise at his own candid response.

"You do this out of love?" Jadira said incredulously. Frolder's jaw worked. He clenched and unclenched his fists.

"Yes! I love Liantha more than life!" Frolder finished his declaration and turned to Phraxa. "The potion—I must have swallowed some! But how?"

Phraxa was panic-stricken. "I know not, Sheriff! Perhaps the clumsy kitchen help spilled some in the beer . . ." This idea stayed his tongue. He'd drunk the beer, too.

"Aha!" said Marix. "So now the pike is in the huntsman's belly! Tell me, Sir Frolder, how did you know the Faziris were after us?"

"It was I who arranged the ambush of Sir Kannal's party, four moonturns ago."

"What!"

"I sent a message to Fazir proposing they seize the envoy from Narsia and prevent any alliance between the

Five Cities," said Frolder helplessly.

"Ignorant buffoon! What did you think would happen to Maridanta? What would you do when the Faziris took over the city?" said Jadira.

"I-I would be satrap and rule in Tedwin's place."

The countess covered her face with her hands. Jadira went to her side and pulled them firmly away. "Does your brother know you're here?" she asked. Liantha nodded. "Is he coming to fetch you back to Maridanta?" Another nod. To the sheriff, Jadira snapped, "You plan to murder him, don't you?"

"Yes. Tomorrow, after he arrives."

"And after coercing the countess into marriage, you can claim Maridanta by right as well as treachery," said Marix.

Frolder howled an affirmative. "You clumsy grave robber!" he shouted at Phraxa. "You've ruined everything!"

"My lord! The count knows nothing of the plot! He will still come, and will die as we planned!" the sorcerer babbled.

"That's not why he's angry," said Jadira. "His evil plot has been exposed to the countess. Now she'll never love him."

"Yes!" cried the sheriff. He reached for the fat magician with his large, battle-strengthened hands. Phraxa tried to put his invisibility charm in his mouth, but Frolder snapped the chain holding the silver disc before Phraxa could get it to his lips.

"You want to be unseen? I'll make you unseen, you fat, bloated, corpse stealer!" So saying, he threw himself on the magician. The two rolled off the edge of the table and crashed to the floor. Everyone stood. Before anyone could stop him, Frolder had pried Phraxa's teeth apart and dropped the charm in his gaping mouth. His eyes bulged, his cheeks puffed full to bursting, but the magician couldn't help but swallow. He wavered like a flag on the wind and vanished. The sheriff sank on his knees. "Choke on your own magic!"

"Now!" said Jadira. She and Marix overturned the table. The candles went out and darkness claimed the room. Jadira heard Fu'ad and Marad draw their scimitars. She backed up until she felt the wall behind her. Marix gripped her hand. He found the door latch. It was bolted, but he rattled the handle and shouted for help. The guard outside, alarmed about the disturbance, threw the bolt. In the wink of an eye, Marix had the door open, and he and Jadira were on the guard. Yells and cries from the darkened room alerted the entire citadel. Even as Marix and Jadira fled, they heard the pounding of soldiers' feet converging on the dining room.

A band of soldiers rounded a corner, their naked sword blades gleaming by the light of the wall lanterns. "What are these alarums?" asked a gray-bearded sergeant.

"There!" said Jadira with a wild fling of her arm. "The Faziris attacked Sir Frolder and are trying to seize Countess Liantha for the sultan!"

"Hurry man, save her!" said Marix.

The sergeant waved his men forward. Screams and shrieks rebounded through the wooden halls. The whole citadel was in an uproar, and the pandemonium grew with each new cry. Marix and Jadira came to a crossing of halls. Marix went left, Jadira right. Their arms grew taut, and they snapped back to the intersection again.

"This way!" they said in unison.

"The exit is this way!" said Marix.

"Tamakh and the others are *this* way!" Jadira countered. They went to the right.

The courtyard guards had abandoned their posts to find out what the row was about. Marix and Jadira butted the door with their shoulders. It flew open, and they stumbled into the dark yard.

Clouds obscured the stars, but torches on the log fence lit the scene. Jadira went to Tamakh. The priest had slid down to his knees. His head hung forward limply.

"Tamakh," she said, patting his cheek gently. "Tamakh, can you hear me?" He mumbled a bit and his head lolled, but he couldn't respond coherently.

"He's still bewitched," she said. Marix had examined Nabul, Uramettu, and Elperex and found them also still under the spell.

"What do we do?" Marix said. "What can we do?"

Jadira started to speak, but something touched her face. She recoiled. It was just a brush—like walking into a cobweb—but very definite and inexplicable. "Something's here!" she said. "I can't see it, but it touched me!"

"Frolder!"

"Or the necromancer," she said. Though there was nothing to see, Jadira turned a full circle on her heel. "Who are you?"

Something went thunk in the sand. Marix stooped and found a falchion at his feet. He picked up the short, single-edged sword and saw another object materialize at Jadira's feet. It was a squat clay bottle.

She held the bottle high in the air. "What is this, Phraxa?"

A scraping sound filled the courtyard. Marix plucked a torch from the wall and waved it over the ground. "Here!" he called.

Scratched in the sand was a word: CURE.

"Can we trust him?" said Marix. "It might be poison."

"I don't think so," Jadira replied. "I understand. Phraxa wants to do Frolder an injury." Invisible fingers stroked her cheek. It was a queer, disturbing sensation, but Jadira forced a smile and said, "We understand. Thank you."

Marix cut each of their companions loose. He and Jadira laid them carefully on the ground. Jadira held Uramettu's head and put the neck of the bottle to her slack lips. "I don't know how much to give," she said. Marix shook his head. Jadira poured a small measure in Uramettu's mouth. "Swallow," she said, squeezing the black woman's throat slightly.

The light of reason returned to Uramettu's face. "Keep to my back, little thief, and we'll hold them off—" She sat up suddenly. "Jadira? You're back? It's night! What happened?"

"A very long story. We're in danger."

"Same as it ever was, eh?"

They dosed Tamakh, Elperex, and Nabul with the potion. Each one came to thinking he was still at the exact moment he had lost his wits.

". . . dispel this evil in Agma's name!"

"I can't see them! How can I fight them when I can't see them?"

"I sense the heat of their flesh! There and there—!"

"On your feet everyone!" said Jadira. "It's time we left this place."

Flames gushed from a higher section of the citadel. Someone had set the wooden structure afire. They watched aghast as the flames licked quickly along the shingled gables. The hand of the unseen Phraxa tugged on Jadira's robe. It pulled her toward the opposite wall.

"He wants us to go this way," she said.

A soldier ran in, wielding a short spear. Uramettu grabbed the weapon by the shaft and slung the Maridantan into the wall. His helmet didn't save him, and he collapsed, leaving a deep dent in the wood. Uramettu stripped him of spear, shield, and short sword. The latter she offered to Nabul.

Phraxa jerked impatiently on Jadira's robe. "Come on!" she said.

Smoke was filling the corridors when they entered. Maids and footmen ran pell-mell through the reek, clutching valuables and coughing. The invisible Phraxa led them down the hall, up a twisting set of steps and left them standing before a wide oak door.

"What's this?" said Marix.

"I don't know, but I think we're supposed to go in," said Jadira. She pounded the panels with her fist. "Too solid. We can't break it down with our bare hands."

"Wait!" said Nabul. "This is my specialty." He knelt in front of the door and ran quick fingers over the black iron lock. Taking off his left sandal, he extracted a length of iron wire from the sole.

"So! That's why you insisted on keeping those city sandals," said Tamakh.

Nabul put the pick-lock in the slot under the latch. He worked it round and pulled down the handle. The door swung in.

"Easy as clay," he said.

The room was an armory, with all types of weapons standing in racks and lying on tables. The companions helped themselves. Elperex hopped over a stand of swords. He chirped with delight. Nabul came to see what excited him so.

"The efreet bow," he said. He gave it to Jadira.

Elperex also found something for his own use: a rolled up net of finely stranded hemp, the edges of which were weighted for throwing.

The skylight overhead blossomed red with fire. Ash and hot cinders sprinkled down on them. "Out, out!" yelled Marix.

In the corridor, a group of soldiers blocked the way. Uramettu, Marix, and Nabul moved to the fore, as they were best armed to meet them. Tamakh stood back with Jadira. He tried to cast his glamor over the Maridantans, but the noise was too great for his spell to be heard.

"I see we shall have to do this the old-fashioned way," said Uramettu.

"Hai-yah!" cried Marix, bounding forward with a kick. His blade clashed with a soldier's, rebounded, whirled, and caught up the foe's point. Marix lunged. In the narrow hallway, the Maridantan couldn't avoid his thrust. The keen tip passed through the brigandine. Marix recovered, and the soldier fell, blood pumping from his pierced heart.

Uramettu fought off a pair of men with her longer spear. Nabul made a lot of noise and jumped up and down, but never closed with his opponent. In the end, it wasn't necessary; the fire above burned through the ceiling beams. The upper floor cracked and fell on them.

"Back out! This way!" Jadira said. Separated by flaming beams, the soldiers and companions drew apart. More burning logs joined the heap, and everyone fled for their lives.

Somehow they reached the outer wall of the barrow. The only way down the hill, the baffled gate, was clogged with screaming, desperate people, retainers and soldiers alike. They jammed the narrow gap so tightly no one could escape.

"Can we go over the wall?" asked Nabul.

"We're at the top of a tall hill," said Jadira. "The fall would break our necks."

The uppermost portion of the citadel, flaming logs standing out in the night like burning bones, collapsed to one side and broke apart. An avalanche of hot debris slid into the bailey, sending the packed crowd into new paroxysms.

Uramettu leaned into a section of the palisade. She pushed and rocked the rough-hewn logs. The others fell in beside her and assisted. Soon the section of wall was wobbling in and out.

"Now, together, push!" Uramettu said. The wall went down with a splintering crack. "Get on!"

The five clambered on, with Elperex flying close overhead. On the left Uramettu and Tamakh dug in their feet; on the right, Marix and Jadira did likewise. At a count of three, they shoved off.

The section, six oak logs pegged together with planks and pins, slid down the steep earthen bank. Gouts of dirt flew in their faces, while stones and jagged splinters of wood tore at them with every bump and bound.

"We're going to hit! We're going to hit!" yelled Nabul frantically.

Everyone could see the ditch rushing to meet them. Jadira clutched Marix; Marix grabbed Nabul. Uramettu kept a hand on Nabul and one on Tamakh. Overhead, Elperex screeched wildly.

The wall section hit bottom. The pins gave way, and the whole assembly flew to pieces.

❖ 26 ❖

The Lame Count

It was daylight when Jadira next knew the world. She was on her back in the dirt and bright sunshine was in her eyes. Marix was lying across her waist, unconscious. She moved her right hand and felt wood. A log as wide as her leg had buried its sharpened peak in the dirt and pivoted overhead, finally smashing down a hand-width away from her head. She blessed Mitaali and tried to sit up. Pain lanced through her chest, and she decided it wasn't worth the effort.

"Marix," she cried hoarsely. "Marix, can you hear me?"

He groaned. Shaking his head, he got to his hands and knees. "Are you all right?" asked Jadira.

Marix put a hand to his chest and inhaled. "All is well. I seemed to have landed softly."

"Yes, on top of me."

"Oh! Are you hurt?" He stretched out alongside her.

"My ribs. I may have broken them."

Coughing nearby proved that Nabul lived. Then he said, "Elperex? Where are you, monkey?"

"Nabul, come here," Marix called.

The thief, his clothing hanging in tatters and his eyepatch askew, stumbled into view. His good eye was well blacked. "Have you seen Elperex?" he said vaguely.

"No," Jadira and Marix said in unison.

"Can't find the little monkey. Hope he's not dead. Was going to train him to be a thief . . . what a second-story man he'd make. Small . . . can fly . . ."

"Sit down, Nabul. I think your brain has been scrambled," said Jadira.

At the top of the barrow, smoke poured out of the ruined citadel. Shading her eyes, Jadira could see other segments of the stockade had been thrown down by fleeing inhabitants.

A large figure obscured the sun. Uramettu looked down and said, "My sister, are you hurt?"

"In my ribs. Where's Tamakh?"

"Over there, resting. He broke his arm, but I straightened it and put on a splint."

"Elperex? Elperex?" Nabul called in an odd, off-key voice.

"See to the thief," said Uramettu to Marix. "I will tend Jadira."

Marix took Nabul aside and picked splinters out of his scalp. Nabul had a swelling the size of a goose egg on the crown of his head. Marix sat him down and ordered him keep still, while he shaded him from the sun and fanned him with the tail of his burnoose.

"This will hurt," Uramettu warned. With a hunter's wisdom, she knew the only treatment for cracked ribs was a tight bandage. White-lipped, Jadira nodded that she was ready. Uramettu lifted her just enough to slip a broad band of cloth under her. Jadira clenched her eyes shut and smothered a scream in her throat. Uramettu let her down as gently as possible. She pulled the bandage across and split the ends.

"Inhale as deeply as you can bear," she said. Jadira sucked in her breath carefully. Uramettu quickly tied the bandage ends. Jadira let out her breath, and the cloth strip caught her. "You won't die, my sister. You are too strong to do that."

"Ai," she said. "It hurts too much to be fatal."

Elperex flapped in with a flurry of wings. "Walking friends!" he said shrilly. "Many walking humans in iron approach from the north. Many more go with them on the backs of horses!"

"Faziris?" asked Jadira. Elperex didn't know the difference. "Do they carry any banners or pennants?"

"Yes, a cone of black with stripes of yellow, like the tail of a hornet."

Marix heard and came over. "That's the standard of Maridanta. Count Tedwin is near."

"Is this count friend or foe?" said Uramettu.

"That depends on who survived the fire," said Jadira.

They sent Elperex to keep an eye on the oncoming army. Meanwhile, the other companions extracted themselves from the wreckage at the bottom of the ditch. Tamakh's right arm hung from a crude sling around his neck. Uramettu had bound strips of oak around the broken limb. Nabul was still befuddled, but able to walk. He and Marix carried Jadira between them up the less steep slope of the counterscarp into the wattle-hut village of Vitgis.

The muddy streets were clogged with the dead and injured. Little difference was made between them; often they lay side by side. Helpful villagers washed faces and tended burns of the victims. No one paid the companions any heed.

Elperex returned. "The Hornet People are at the town fence," he reported. "A twisted man in black leads them."

"Tedwin the Lame," said Marix.

"Since we've no time to hide and no strength to flee, there's no point avoiding him," said Jadira. "Shall we go to meet His Lordship?"

The tired, battered companions limped down the main street to the village baffle. Once outside, they saw the host of Maridanta drawn up in battle array. At the front of his troops was Count Tedwin. His cuirass was lacquered in black. A soft velvet hat swept low over his thick, black eyebrows. He rode a black horse with his bad leg draped over a special saddlehorn. A blond giant clad in mirror-bright armor stood by his lord with a drawn six-span sword. The standard of Maridanta whipped in the wind over the giant's head.

Marix moved out in front of his friends. Dirty and smoke-stained, he still managed to convey the attitude of an aristocrat in his stance. He bowed in the shallow western style and said, "Hail, my Lord Tedwin."

"Who are you?" said the lame count. Unlike his sister's, his voice was smooth and powerful.

"Marix, third son of Count Fernald of Dosen."

"Indeed. What has happened here? Where is my sheriff, Frolder, Narken's son?"

Marix explained in barest detail the events of the past day and night. Tedwin took the news of Frolder's treachery without so much as a blink.

"Does he live?" asked Tedwin calmly.

Marix hesitated, feeling the menace from the black-clad lord. He said, "I know not, lord."

"And my sister?"

Marix stared at the ground and shook his head.

Tedwin summoned his general. He ordered his army to surround Barrow Vitgis and allow no one to leave. The count, his personal bodyguard, and fifty men-at-arms would enter to secure the town.

"You will accompany me," he said.

"I?" said Marix.

"And all your companions. Come."

The giant led the way. As Count Tedwin rode by, the villagers prostrated themselves in the filth and ashes. The men-at-arms spread out behind their lord, searching among the fallen for Frolder, Countess Liantha, and the two Faziris.

The street wound through the silent village to the foot of the barrow mound. There the giant raised his hand for a halt. He readied his huge sword.

Out of the swirling smoke strode Fu'ad, straight-backed and commanding even though his beard was singed and his face smeared with soot. In his arms, he carried the still form of Count Tedwin's beautiful sister.

"Are you Count Tedwin?" he said, speaking past the wary giant.

"I am."

"Fu'ad, son of Rafik, captain of the Sultan's Invincible Cavalry. You will forgive me if I do not bow."

Tedwin clucked his tongue, and the blond giant sheathed his sword. He came back to the count's horse, lifted the lame man from the saddle, and set him on his good leg. Tedwin was short, shorter even than Nabul, but his voice and aura of command were greater than any man's present. He limped heavily to Fu'ad.

"My sister is dead," he said. It was not a question.

"She is."

Tedwin touched the wide stain covering the front of the raven silk dress. "How did it happen?"

"When Marix of Dosen and the nomad woman Jadira put out the candles to escape, my comrade Marad and I drew swords and stood back to back to defend ourselves. Sheriff Frolder had a short sword. He called out to the countess to remain seated, but she sought the sheriff and threw herself on his blade."

"Why would she do that?"

"I saw her face, my lord, when the sheriff revealed his cruel plot to kill you and marry her. I suppose the noble lady loved your lordship so much that she died to save you, my lord."

"How do I know you didn't kill her?" Something in the count's voice made Jadira shiver, despite her aching ribs.

"I don't murder women," Fu'ad said loftily. A retort begged for release, but Jadira stifled it.

Tedwin peeled off his black suede gloves and took his sister from Fu'ad. He touched Liantha's fine hair and caressed her cheek. Slowly, painfully, he limped back to his horse. Tedwin made more clicking sounds with his tongue, and the giant stooped to take the countess from his arms.

The count faced Fu'ad. "Where is your comrade, this Marad?"

"Dead. A burning wall fell on him."

"And where are Sir Frolder and his pet magician, Phraxa?"

"Gone—vanished."

Tedwin put his good leg in a stirrup and hoisted himself back on his horse. "Hear me, Captain: because you brought my sister out of the flames, I give you your life. Whatever bargain existed between you and Sheriff Frolder is voided. You have one hour to leave my sight. If I find you in Maridantan territory after that time, I will have your head on a pike."

Fu'ad lifted his chin. "If that be your lordship's will, do it now, for I cannot return to my country dishonored."

"Faziris are so tiresome," complained the count. "Roldof, let it be done." The blond giant handed Liantha down to four waiting soldiers. He drew his great sword and advanced on Fu'ad.

"Stop!"

The group parted and Jadira stepped out. "If anyone is to kill that murdering dog, it should be me," she said.

"By what right?" asked the count.

"This one led the soldiers who massacred my tribe. Their blood cries out for vengeance!"

Tedwin drew a polished, gold-hilted saber from his saddle. He flung it point-first at Jadira. It stuck in the scorched earth at her feet. Without a word, Jadira freed the saber and went to Fu'ad.

"So," he said, "you prevail after all."

"On your knees, butcher."

Fu'ad dropped down and leaned forward on his hands. "I trust the blade is keen?" he said.

"Extremely," Count Tedwin replied.

Up went the shining blade. Tamakh cried, "Jadira, no! Have mercy!"

"Mercy? Did this one have mercy on my husband? My family? My whole tribe?" She gripped the hilt in both hands and brought the saber down. She turned the blade so that the dull side struck Fu'ad on the head. He pitched forward and lay still. Jadira stood hunched over, wheezing from the pain her effort had caused her.

"You missed," said the count.

"No, my lord. I did not." Jadira twisted the chain that held the Eye of the Sultan until it snapped. She threw the gold disc as far as she could. "Have him tied on a horse and whipped back to Fazir. That's the worst punishment for him. The wrath of his vizier will be ten thousand times worse than mere beheading."

The faintest trace of a smile crossed Tedwin's lips. "Let it be done," he ordered.

Jadira returned the saber and rejoined her friends. Tamakh beamed at her. "I knew you would not be so cruel," he said.

"Did you? I was not at all certain what I would do until I did it." She leaned on Marix and sighed. "In my place, Fu'ad would have killed me. All I knew was that he would not be my teacher."

"Thank Tuus for that," said Marix.

* * * * *

The lord of Maridanta had come to Barrow Vitgis on his way to the conclave in Tantuffa. He had weighed the need for unity against his ambition to be sole master of the Five Cities and had come down in favor of unity. After all, no one would be master if the conclave failed. No one but the Sultan of Fazir.

That afternoon, Count Tedwin dispatched Marix with a hundred lancers to retrieve the seal of Prince Lydon. They galloped away, promising to return soon after sundown.

A city of tents sprang up on the plain outside Barrow Vitgis. Tedwin's own chirurgeons looked after Jadira and Tamakh, and gave Nabul a poltice to ease his shaken wits. The count reposed in his great tent, where the body of his sister was laid out for proper funeral rites.

Uramettu shared a tent with Jadira. "What do you think of this Tedwin fellow?" she asked.

"An unhappy man, I'd say, with moods as dark as the clothing he wears," said Jadira. "Yet he has delivered us, fed and housed us, and had our hurts seen to. I find it hard not to like him, all in all."

"That is my feeling too." Uramettu lay down on the soft pallet next to Jadira. "Sleep well, my sister. Tomorrow we ride to Tantuffa."

"Surrounded by friends, for a change."

Though it was not yet sunset, Jadira gladly slept. The learned doctors had given her a soporific, and her pain melted like fresh butter in the desert sun. She drifted away, her mind a mix of images of the dangerous days past.

I ought to cut your throat.

Whose voice was that? Kemmet Serim? Fu'ad? The efreet Kaurous? Ubrith Zelka? The cold line of a knife blade dug into her neck. Jadira squirmed, trying to push the knife away. She struggled enough to revive the tearing pain in her ribs.

Her eyes were open, but her mouth was stopped. A hand seemed to clamp it shut—though no hand could be seen.

Where is Countess Liantha? said a voice in her ear, the voice of an invisible Frolder.

Jadira made weak sounds. The unseen hand lifted a fraction. "In the tent of her brother!" she said in a loud whisper. Her eyes shifted to where Uramettu lay. "Please don't hurt me!"

"Silence! Don't insult an old intriguer with faked pleas for mercy." His voice was quite low but coming from just beside her left ear. "Stand up. Remember, the knife I carry can kill, though it can't be seen."

Jadira started to cough, but the sharp tip of the knife blade dug into her back, and the cough froze in her throat. "If she awakens, I will kill you both," Frolder said. They left the tent, leaving Uramettu undisturbed.

The sun was down. A mild wind from the west blew moist sea air over the tent city. Pairs of Maridantan soldiers patrolled the camp. They nodded politely to Jadira and passed her by. Breath tickled her ear. She resisted an urge to scratch.

Tedwin's tent was easy to find. Taller and finer than the rest, it was lit from within by oil lamps. Jadira walked up to the entrance. Two guards crossed pikes in front of her.

"Who goes there?" said the right-hand guard. A prick in her back warned her.

"Jadira *sed* Ifrimiya, to see Count Tedwin."

"On what matter?"

"I-I have news of his sheriff, Sir Frolder."

"Wait here." The guard on the left ducked under the hanging flap. He soon returned with Roldof, Tedwin's massive bodyguard.

"He will take you to his lordship," said the soldier.

"Thank you," said Jadira.

"He can't talk," said the soldier on the right. "His tongue was cut out years ago."

Roldof stepped back and swept a tree-sized arm ahead for Jadira. She stepped under it and went in.

A flute trilled softly from deeper in the tent. The oily smell of lamps contrasted with a strong scent of roses. Two priestly figures in red, swinging censers, passed them muttering benedictions.

"Are they preparing the countess for her trip to the underworld?" asked Jadira. Roldof nodded his wide head. Up close, Jadira could see his bare arms and lower legs were streaked with dozens of battle scars.

She thought for a moment that Frolder might have

gone until his far-off voice buzzed in her ear again: "Tell the count you must speak to him alone."

"He won't agree to that."

"Do it or—"

Jadira twisted out of his grasp. A searing pain in her chest bent her double, but she saw a deep gash suddenly open in Roldof's neck. As blood spilled from the gaping wound, the giant sank heavily to the ground. He toppled forward on his face, falling through the split gauze curtains.

A phantom hand twisted itself in her long hair and Jadira couldn't smother a gasp as her head was yanked back. Frolder hauled her through the curtains.

Frolder released her. The cloth-walled room was set as a chapel. Jadira saw that Liantha lay on her bier, draped in white. Only her perfect face showed through an oval opening in the shroud. Jadira was stunned by the serenity of that face. What a pity, a sorry wasteful pity!

"What is the meaning of this? Roldof?" said Tedwin. He was bare-headed, and Jadira could better see the resemblance between brother and sister. Had Tedwin been straighter and taller, he would have been as handsome as Liantha was beautiful.

"The sheriff," she blurted. "He is here."

Frolder flashed into sight. The short sword in his hand was red with Roldof's blood.

"Two of my favorite people, together for the last time," said Frolder. Madness darkened his words.

"My humblest apologies, Count," said Jadira. "He forced me here at sword point. He has killed your man."

"What will you do, Frolder?" asked Tedwin.

"You mean, besides kill you? I have come to see Liantha one last time."

"The murderer wishes to admire his victim."

Frolder cut the air with his sword. Jadira flinched, but Tedwin stood unmoved. "I did not murder her! She was my beloved—her life was sacred," Frolder said.

"Yet there she lies dead. Who humiliated her? Whose blade did she fall on? The Faziri said it was yours. Do you deny it?"

The tormented sheriff turned to the bier. "May the gods forgive me. I cannot deny it. After hearing of my plans, she lost her reason. She—she called to me to embrace her, and when I did . . ." He left the tale unfinished.

Jadira was sidling over toward Roldof. The giant carried a dagger in his belt. It was not much smaller than Frolder's sword, and if she could get it—

"You've lost, Frolder, lost everything. Killing me now won't bring Liantha back, or gain you control of Maridanta. The Faziris are gone, and in a few notches of the candle, Marix of Dosen will return with the seal of Narsia. The conclave will take place. The alliance will happen."

Frolder began to laugh. "Do you think I care for cities or empires anymore?" he said. "I hate you, Tedwin. I hate your ugly, twisted leg and black clothes and the cold-blooded wits you live by. To kill you will be the last pleasure in my life."

Jadira snatched the dagger from Roldof's belt. Frolder saw her movement. He didn't try to attack her; he simply replaced the silver charm in his mouth and became invisible.

"My lord, beware! He can slay you though you cannot see him!" Jadira cried.

"Give me the dagger!"

She tossed it to him. "Defend your back!"

So saying, Jadira dashed out. There was only one way

to deal with Frolder, only one weapon that needed no eyes.

At the entrance to the tent, she ran into Uramettu arguing with the guards. The efreet bow was in her hand. "Let her through!" Jadira cried. "Uramettu, the bow!"

The Fedushite woman tossed the efreet's gift over the crossed pikes. As Jadira turned to run, she heard the guards exclaim in terror. A panther's roar resounded through the tent.

Jadira stepped over the fallen Roldof. Tedwin was on the ground, his back to the bier. Long slashes showed through his velvet robe, and the count bled from a dozen minor wounds. Frolder was toying with him, murdering him as slowly as his madness would allow.

Jadira nocked the arrow. Tedwin raised his hand to her. His eyes widened as she took deliberate aim on him.

"Larsa, I know you not, but guide my aim!" she said.

The efreet arrow leaped off the string. Tedwin threw up a hand to ward off the shot, but the arrow veered away. It curved around, farther, farther, until Jadira had to throw herself down to avoid being hit. The arrow circled the tent once before turning in. It stopped suddenly in midair. The arrowhead and a span of the shaft disappeared.

Frolder appeared, blood and the charm falling from his lips. The arrow was in his heart.

"My lord," said Jadira. "Speak if you can!"

"I live," the count gasped, "thanks to you. I thought—in the last you had thrown in with Frolder and—meant to kill me."

"No, lord. This bow has a peculiar way of working. It hits what you don't aim at." Tedwin struggled to his feet. He and Jadira leaned on each other.

Uramettu in panther form bounded into the room. Tedwin's eyes grew large. He raised the dagger, but Jadira stayed his hand. "No, my lord. This one is Uramettu."

"The black woman? Extraordinary." Tedwin straightened. His cool detachment returned. "You know, you really are a remarkable company," he said. "What does the fat priest do?"

Tantuffa by the Sea

The finding of Prince Lydon's seal was the simplest thing Marix had done in a year and a day. "It was right where we put it," he said. "The pile of stones hadn't even been disturbed." He set a moldy leather bag before his friends and Count Tedwin, then backed away, deferring to the count.

"No, you do it. It was your quest, not mine," Tedwin said. Marix peeled back the rotten hide. The heavy seal, twice as big as Marix's fist, gleamed dully. The Narsian coat of arms was intact.

When the moon had shown its face once more, Jadira and her friends were all safely ensconced in the palace of Lord Hurgold, master of Tantuffa. The conclave of the Five Cities took place as planned, and the machinations of the sultan were finally exposed. The five lords exchanged vows of closest cooperation. Treaties were signed, blood bonds made, toasts drunk. And when news of the alliance returned home, great celebrations reigned in the Five Cities for days on end. All the Faziri ambassadors were recalled in disgrace, and the sultan's grand design to dominate the Five Cities was set back. But the corridors of the palace in Omerabad were soon alive with new strategems, new plots.

Wounds healed in flesh and bone but not in the heart. Count Tedwin returned to Maridanta, darker in his soul and harder in his mind. Liantha had been more precious to him than his own life, and with her gone, his joy was gone forever.

Jadira and Marix were joined in marriage. The clerics of the western gods would not sanctify a union between a nobleman and a nomad, so the couple turned to the new word, the way of Agma. Tamakh performed the rites. Uramettu stood by Jadira, and Nabul played the part of Marix's father. ("Fernald always was a thief," Lord Hurgold was heard to quip about the groom's true father). Elperex carried the gilded headbands through the streets and placed them on the couple's heads.

The moon turned twice more. Uramettu took to haunting the docks, seeking a ship south to Tijit. From there overland to Fedush was two hundred leagues, most of it easy travel on the Zanti River.

Tamakh expressed an interest in going with her. Nabul teased him about being in love, but the priest avowed his need to wander and spread the word of Agma. A few days more, and Nabul began to speak of traveling, too. Caravans formed in Tijit daily for the Brazen Ring and Zimora. Nabul said he could be in Fazir picking pockets before the corn was ripe.

"I can't believe this," Jadira said when the six were together on the north portico of the palace. "After all we've done as one, you want to leave us?"

"This country is not mine," Uramettu said. "Though you are my beloved sister, I yearn for the grasslands. The longing grows stronger every day."

"My feet itch also," said Tamakh. "These Tantuffans are pleasant folk; they listen to my teaching, nod and smile. But there's a priest on every corner in the market-place, and no one believes anything they hear."

"How do you know the Fedushites will heed you any better?" asked Marix.

"I don't. The grace comes from the doing."

Jadira spread her hands. "Nabul, you're the sanest man present, as you have oft said. Why don't you stay? There must be rich pickings in Tantuffa."

"So you would think! The merchants here fairly bulge with gold, but I can't get at it. These western barbarians wear these vile *trouser* things, the pockets of which are tightly buttoned! How's a thief supposed to make a living here?"

"I will not leave you," said Elperex. "Tantuffa is a good city. Children give me fruit just to talk to them." Jadira smiled at the 'strelli fondly.

"It's very hard to think of life day to day without you," Jadira said to the others.

"Change is the inevitable course of things," Tamakh observed.

Uramettu brightened. "Why don't you come with us?" she said. "I can show you many wonders betwixt here and Fedush. Strange ruins in Tijit, cities along the Zanti, the wild beasts of the endless savannah—"

"Alas, I cannot go," Jadira said. "Marix's duty requires him to fulfill his pledge of service to Lord Hurgold. And in light of his lordship's many favors to us, it would be ungrateful of us to run away."

Silence. Nabul spoke at last: "How long is this indenture?"

"Three years."

"Ronta would forget me in that time," Uramettu said.

She stood, and the others did likewise. "Though it weighs on my heart, it must be said; we companions must part." Jadira held out her hands. Uramettu clasped them. Tamakh and Nabul embraced Marix, and the thief chucked Elperex under his pointed chin.

"Remember what I taught you, monkey," he said.

Tamakh and Jadira faced each other. "Holy One, if all clerics were as kind and wise as you, the world would be a better place," she said.

"I am simply a humble servant of my god. It is easy to be kind in the company of such good people." He winked at Nabul. "And even easier to be wise."

"Haw!"

"Will you come back some day?" asked Jadira.

"If I have feet to walk on, I'll see you again, daughter of Ifrim." On an impulse, she threw her arms around Tamakh and hugged him fiercely. With a gasp that was only slightly exaggerated, he freed himself and said, "You have the grasp of a wrestler." She had to smile. "Farewell, my dear child."

"Farewell, Tamakh."

Nabul balked at being too heartfelt in his good-byes. He stammered a farewell and hastily retreated. He and Uramettu and Tamakh went to the steps leading off the portico. Jadira watched them gradually disappear behind the white marble wall. When they were gone, she started for the colonnade, to see them once more. Marix held her arm and stopped her.

"It hurts enough," he said. "Let them go."

* * * * *

Night, and the moon rose out of the eastern plains. Jadira, freshly bathed and robed in white linen, stood on

the balcony outside their suite of rooms in Lord
Hurgold's palace. She had taken to wearing Tantuffan-
style clothes, but she still wore a scarf over her hair.

The city and harbor were spread out beneath her. The
view was dotted with yellow lanterns fixed to the bob-
bing masts of ships and the twinkling lights of the city.
Through the tang of the sea air, Jadira felt—or did she
imagine it?—the heat of her homeland. Turning, she
looked for something that could not be seen—the hot,
windswept dunes of the Red Sands.

Marix returned from watch duty with the garrison. He
was weary and dirty, and longed for nothing so much as a
cool drink and quiet sleep. He unbuckled his breastplate
and greaves, letting them clank on the floor. Jadira drew
aside the balcony curtain and beckoned him to join her.

"I did not think to find you awake," he said. "It is
late."

They kissed. "I wanted to see you."

They stood together on the balcony, staring at the harbor. "I know what you're thinking," said Marix.

"Have we been married that long?"

"It hardly requires years of experience to realize you
are thinking of our friends."

"They leave on the evening tide."

"Do you wish you were with them?"

She turned his chin until they were eye to eye. "I
might wish that *we* were with them," she said. "But
where you are is where I shall be."

"You mean your feet aren't aching to tread the Red
Sands again?"

He had her there. Jadira looked away. "I am Sudiin of
Sudiin. Since the day Mitaali formed the nomads from
the sweat of his brow and the dust of his hands, my people have wandered from place to place. A western hus-

band and dresses of fine linen cannot erase the heritage of ages past."

"Nor would I ask you to cease being the one I love," he said. "Three years is not so long. Who knows? There may be expeditions Lord Hurgold will want to send us on, since we are such accomplished travelers."

The brass door knocker boomed hollowly inside the suite. Marix sighed. "That's probably Corporal Golloy, seeking to wear down my resolve. I had to put him on report tonight for taking a bribe from a tavernkeeper." The knocker boomed again.

"All right, I'm coming," Marix called. Jadira followed him inside. When Marix lifted the bolt and opened the door, there stood Nabul.

"I've not seen mouths gape so wide since I stole two carp from the fish market," he said. "May I enter?"

"Enter, enter. Why are you here?"

"Oh, well, it was this way: I was on my way to the quay where our ship was tied, when I passed this Sivonian merchant whose purse jingled so sweetly . . . anyway, I followed him for eight blocks, but he entered a guarded banking house before I could cut his purse string." Nabul pushed a toe into the carpet. "So I missed the boat."

"Poor fellow! Have a draft of wine. It will soothe you," Jadira said.

Marix led Nabul to the sitting room. No sooner were they through the curtains than there came a steady metallic tapping at the door. Jadira opened it, and Tamakh was there, the iron key from the Omerabad dungeon poised in his hand.

"Ah! Jadira! I hope I did not wake you," he said.

"No, not at all. Ah, don't misunderstand me, Holy One, but shouldn't you be at sea right now?" she asked.

"Indeed, that is just where I meant to be, but as I mounted the gangplank onto the ship, this key, in which Agma manifested his divine presence, grew hot in the folds of my garment. I knew this was an omen from the god not to proceed on the voyage."

"So it was Agma who called you back?"

"Just so, just so."

"Then you had better come in and commune with this deity of yours. He must have important work for you here," she said. Tamakh bowed and crossed the threshold. Jadira smilingly directed him to the sitting room.

Elperex flew in and landed on the balcony railing. "Jadira!" he called. "You would never guess who I saw on the western steps of the palace!"

She said, "Uramettu." The 'strelli's excited expression froze in amazement.

"You have the second sight," he said.

"Sometimes. Go to the sitting room and tell Marix." Elperex hopped down and waddled across the polished floor to the curtained archway.

Jadira waited. Before long, three solid raps sounded on the suite door. She counted silently to five and opened the door. "Come in, Uramettu."

The black woman waited sheepishly outside. "You were told I was coming," she said.

"Elperex spied you on the steps."

"The little fellow does see much from on high."

Jadira put out her hand and pulled Uramettu in. "There is a reason why I came back," the black woman said. "A very good reason."

"I'm sure of it," said Jadira.

"It was the hunting life that called me home, and I listened, for it is in my blood. It was not for want of affection that I decided to leave."

"I know."

Uramettu lifted her long arms high. "And there I was on the deck of our ship. Nabul never boarded, and Tamakh begged off before the mooring was cleared. I thought, these men found reasons to stay; cannot I? So I said to the first mate, 'Do you hunt game?' And he answered, 'The brushland around Tantuffa hold many wild boar, aurochs, and lions.' 'Then put me ashore,' I said, 'for if I stay on this ship, I am leaving home, not returning to it.' I rode back to the quay in the pilot's skiff, and here I am."

"I can't tell you how happy I am," said Jadira. "Come to the sitting room and take your ease a while."

They walked in, arm in arm, and found their friends toasting their reunion. "Here's to the strongest bonds of all," said Marix, raising high his cup. "Not chains, not stone walls, nor magic spells, but true and lasting friendship."

Six golden cups rang together as one.

ABOUT THE AUTHORS

PAUL B. THOMPSON remembers clearly the first real book he ever read, a prose translation of the *Iliad*. This was followed by *The Arabian Nights' Entertainment*, and his tastes were set for life. His first novel, *Sundipper*, was published in 1984 by St. Martin's Press. The next year, Thompson began collaborating with Tonya Carter. Though *Red Sands* is the first novel by Thompson and Carter TSR has published, their work has already graced the DRAGONLANCE® anthology *Love and War*, and their second novel, *Darkness and Light*, will be published by TSR in 1989. For recreation, he rides his motorcycle and collects Val Lewton films on videotape.

TONYA R. CARTER attended the University of North Carolina at Chapel Hill, where she met her husband, Greg, and her collaborator, Paul Thompson. After college, she visited England and Ireland. There, in spite of her red hair and Irish ancestry, she was mistaken for an Australian several times. This prompted her to take up Gaelic studies upon her return to the States. In addition to her collaborative work, she has written a number of fantasy, horror, and science-fiction stories, including "To Hear the Sea-Maid's Music." When not writing, she enjoys shopping for books, traveling, and skiing.

AVAILABLE NOW!

Darkwalker on Moonshae
Book One: The Moonshae Trilogy
Douglas Niles

Kazgaroth and blood-drenched minions surround Caer Corwell and the peace-loving Ffolk of the Moonshae Isles. Only Tristan Kendrick, troubled heir to the legacy of the High King, can rally the diverse people of the Isles to halt the spread of darkness.

Black Wizards
Book Two: The Moonshae Trilogy
Douglas Niles

Black Wizards picks up the story of the troubled heir to the legacy of the High Kings, Tristan Kendrick. The prince of Corwell departs on a blood quest, but his journey is interrupted by the vision of a long-dead queen who rises mysteriously from the sea, challenging Tristan with an obscure prophecy. Meanwhile, back on the Moonshae Isles, the Black Wizards plot Tristan's downfall, and once again threaten the peace of the Ffolk. . . .

The Crystal Shard
Book One: The Icewind Dale Trilogy
R.A. Salvatore

The heroic, fated quest of the maverick dwarf Bruenor, the renegade dark elf Drizzt, and the barbarian warrior Wulfgar, to rally the defense of Ten-Towns and defeat the sinister power of the lost artifact, the Crystal Shard.

Spellfire
Ed Greenwood

A young orphan girl hungers for a life of excitement and danger. But when she joins a band of itinerant adventurers, she gets more than she bargained for. She falls in love with a careless young mage, is captured by an evil dragon cult, and finds herself in a spellcasting war that threatens the existence of the entire Forgotten Realms.

Azure Bonds
Kate Novak and Jeff Grubb

Alias, a comely adventuress-for-hire, was having an ordinary day until she woke up with strange sigils inscribed on her arms. Five evil masters are pursuing her, and she doesn't know why. Their hideous agenda is revealed in the dramatic showdown, with Alias and her companions in the region of the Sea of Fallen Stars.

DRAGONLANCE® *Preludes*

Darkness and Light
Paul Thompson and Tonya Carter

Darkness and Light tells of the time
Sturm and Kitiara spent traveling
together before the fated meeting at the
Inn of the Last Home. Accepting a ride
on a gnomish flying vessel, they end up
on Lunitari during a war. Eventually
escaping, the two separate over ethics.

Kendermore
Mary L. Kirchoff

A bounty hunter charges Tasslehoff
Burrfoot with violating the kender
laws of prearranged marriage. To en-
sure his return, Kendermore's council
has Uncle Trapspringer prisoner. Tas
meets the last woolly mammoth and
the alchemist who pickles one of
everything, including kender!

Brothers Majere
Rose Estes

The origins of the brothers' love/hate
relationship. Distraught over his
ailing mother, Caramon reluctantly
allows her to die. Unable to forgive
his brother, or himself for his inability
to help her, Raistlin agrees to pursue
her last wish, an unwitting pawn in
the struggle between good and evil.